Praise for Loree Lough
and her novels

"Loree Lough comes up with a new and interesting twist to this charming baby story."
—*RT Book Reviews* on *Suddenly Mommy*

"Splendidly written, this uplifting romance is head and shoulders above the usual marriage of convenience and definitely not to be missed!"
—*RT Book Reviews* on *Suddenly Married*

"A moving story about love and forgiveness that readers will enjoy."
—*RT Book Reviews* on *Suddenly Reunited*

"Well-defined characters with a believable conflict highlight *His Healing Touch*."
—*RT Book Reviews*

LOREE LOUGH

Suddenly Daddy

&

Suddenly Mommy

Steeple
Hill®

Published by Steeple Hill Books™

STEEPLE HILL BOOKS

Steeple
Hill®

Recycling programs
for this product may
not exist in your area.

ISBN-13: 978-0-373-65139-9

SUDDENLY DADDY AND SUDDENLY MOMMY

SUDDENLY DADDY
Copyright © 1998 by Loree Lough

SUDDENLY MOMMY
Copyright © 1998 by Loree Lough

www.SteepleHill.com

Printed in U.S.A.

CONTENTS

Books by Loree Lough

Love Inspired

*Suddenly Daddy
*Suddenly Mommy
*Suddenly Married
*Suddenly Reunited
*Suddenly Home
His Healing Touch
Out of the Shadows
**An Accidental Hero

*Suddenly!
**Accidental Blessings

LOREE LOUGH

A full-time writer for many years, Loree Lough has produced more than two thousand articles, dozens of short stories and novels for the young (and young at heart), and all have been published here and abroad. The award-winning author of more than thirty-five romances, Loree also writes as Cara McCormack and Aleesha Carter.

A comedic teacher and conference speaker, Loree loves sharing in classroom settings what she's learned the hard way. The mother of two grown daughters, she lives in Maryland with her husband.

SUDDENLY DADDY

I am my beloved and my beloved is mine.
—*Song of Solomon* 2:16

To Carolyn Greene, Cindy Whitesel, Robin Morris,
Mike Sackett and Carla Butler for their faith in
the story, and to Anne Canadeo, whose faith in my
"talents" made this book possible.

Chapter One

Like gunfighters of the Old West, they faced each other in the middle of their living room, intent, it seemed, on making their first fight a humdinger.

"Don't be so naive," Mitch shouted. "Things like this don't happen every day. Besides," he added, jabbing a forefinger into the air, "you *knew* what I did for a living when we met."

Ciara matched his ire, decibel for decibel. "Isn't *this* a fine way to celebrate our one-month anniversary…hollering and yelling and—"

"Well, pardon me all the way to town and back," he retorted sarcastically, "but nobody ever told me I was an idiot for becoming an FBI agent before." He threw his hands into the air. "I sure didn't expect to hear nonsense like that *from my wife!*"

"I never said you were an idiot. I said if anything like what happened to Abe ever happened to you…"

He crossed both arms over his chest. She'd never seen him this way before, so it surprised her that her soft-spoken young husband's eyes darkened when he was angry.

Ciara held her ground. Narrowing her eyes, she said, "Abe died in the line of duty, and you have a bullet wound in your left side…pretty good evidence, wouldn't you say, that *you* could…"

He sighed heavily. "I've told you and told you—I was in the wrong place at the wrong time. It was a flesh wound. And it happened years ago, when I was a dumb kid, straight out of Quantico."

Her eyes widened. "Is that supposed to *comfort* me?"

Shaking his head, Mitch's shoulders slumped. "I don't know Ciara. I honestly don't know."

"It's just that I thought…I hoped once we were married, you wouldn't want to take risks like that anymore."

He plowed his fingers through his hair. "Oh for the luvva Pete. Now you're being downright silly. I don't *want* to take risks, but…"

The tears of frustration and fear she'd been fighting since their argument began, now threatened to fill her eyes. Life had taught her that crying accomplished little more than to make her nose stuffy. If she won this debate, it would be because she had *right* on her side, not because Mitch couldn't stand to see a woman cry. She covered her face with both hands and prayed for control of her emotions.

Mitch's hard stare immediately softened, and he crossed the room in three long strides. "Ciara, sweetie," he said, his voice thick and sweet as syrup, "don't look at me that way." He bracketed her face with both hands. "Aw, honey, I don't want to fight with you."

She looked deep into his brown eyes. *This* was the man she'd fallen in love with…warm, caring, understanding. Ciara was about to tell him she didn't want to fight, either, when he said, "Except for that little mishap, I was always careful—" he wiggled his brows suggestively "—even before I had a beautiful wife waiting for me at home."

He stood a head taller than she, outweighed her by seventy pounds, yet she'd bowled him over with one misplaced pout. *Lord, we both know he's nothing but a big softie. Please don't ever let me take advantage of that.*

She laid her hands atop his. "I *love* you, but I don't know if I can…" Her hands slid to his shoulders, and she shrugged, a helpless little gesture. "I'm not like your mother or your grandmother or your brothers' wives." Unable to meet his penetrating gaze, she glanced at the packing boxes still stacked all around the room. "We haven't even finished unpacking yet, and already we're making plans to attend an FBI funeral."

"I know it's hard, sweetie, but—"

Ciara wagged a finger under his nose. "Don't you *dare* tell me that his wife knew what she was getting into."

He grabbed her finger, kissed it. "Ciara…"

Her voice grew raspy, and she bit her lower lip in an attempt to stanch a sob. "I don't know what I'd do in her place. If anything ever happened to you…"

He held her tighter. "I love you, too. And nothing is going to happen to me, I promise. In a year or two, you'll be so bored with my nine-to-five routine, you'll wonder what all this fuss and bother was about." He kissed the tip of her nose. "In the meantime, you've got to remember that I know how to take care of myself. I don't take unnecessary chances."

She looked directly into his thick-lashed eyes. "I'm asking you not to take *any* chances."

The brown of his eyes went black again as he deciphered her meaning. "You're a cop's daughter, Ciara. You of all people should understand. It isn't just a job—being a special agent is my life."

She jerked free of his embrace. "According to the vows you took four weeks ago, *I'm* supposed to be your life!" Lifting her chin, Ciara added, "You're the center of mine…."

Mitch knuckled his eyes. "Look," he groaned, arms extended beseechingly, "can't we discuss this like grown-ups? Why does it have to be 'either/or'?"

"It doesn't get any more 'grown-up' than this, Mitch. If you keep doing what you're doing, it's just a matter of time until—"

Ciara perched on the arm of the sofa. "If only you could find a safer line of work…"

"Like *what?*"

She ignored his sullen pout. "I don't know. But there must be something…something that doesn't put you in the line of fire quite so often."

His frown intensified. "Well, I could always be a receptionist. Or a secretary, even!"

She ignored his scorn. "Save the sarcasm, Mitch. That's not what I meant and you know it. But at least you're on the right track." Ciara tapped a fingertip against her chin. "My dad left the department," she said thoughtfully, more to herself than to Mitch, "started teaching Law Enforcement at the University of Maryland when—"

"I'd go nuts," he blurted out, "staring at the same four walls all day, every day."

Was he being deliberately mule-headed? Or had this been part of his character all along? Ciara completed her sentence through clenched teeth. "When he realized his job was worrying my mother to death. Dad left the department…because *he cared* about her."

The frown became a scowl. "I care plenty. Why else would I be standing here, trying to justify why I need to bring home a paycheck to support my family!" He paused, looked at her long and hard. "Go ahead, flash those big blue eyes all you want. Getting mad at me doesn't change the facts— your dad quit…because your mom henpecked him into it."

Ciara gasped. "My father is *not* henpecked. And he isn't a quitter, either!"

Mitch clapped his palm over his eyes. "I'm sorry. I shouldn't have said that. But cut me a little slack, will you? I'm still trying to figure out what pushes your buttons."

She had to admit, they *had* gone through the normal courtship process faster than most folks. A *lot* faster. Ciara wondered how many other couples found themselves at the altar three months after their first meeting.

Gently, Mitch gripped her upper arms, gave her a little shake. "I don't know what to say, Ciara, except I love you."

"And I love you. But I want to grow old with you. How can I do that if you end up like Abe?"

He stomped over to the window, leaned both palms on its sill. "You might be just a little slip of a thing, but you've got a stubborn streak wide enough for an NFL linebacker." He faced her, tucked in one corner of his mouth. "I'd never ask you to give up *your* job."

Ciara harrumphed. "I'm not in any danger from my fourth-graders."

He poked his chin out in stubborn defiance. "Give me a break. Those kids are crawling with germs."

She couldn't suppress a giggle. "Nothing that would kill me—" her smile faded "—and make a widower of you."

He pocketed his hands, stared at the toes of his shoes. "Frankly," Mitch said softly, "I'm disappointed. I expected better from you. You seemed so different from other women I'd known. That's why I fell forehead over feet in love. You were more than the most beautiful thing I'd ever laid eyes on, you had a heart as big as your head, and—" Mitch shook his head "—I never expected you to make me choose between the two most important things in my life."

He was a gun-toting, badge-carrying FBI agent, for goodness' sake; couldn't he see the evidence that was right under his nose! *I'm so afraid, Mitch,* Ciara wanted to shout, *I'm terrified of losing you!*

Exasperated, she rolled her eyes. "And here's a 'button' you can avoid in the future, Mahoney—I wouldn't have married a man who could be henpecked. I am not 'making' you do anything."

"Listen, Ciara," he said, massaging his temples, "I can't talk about this right now. I need to find a neutral corner, where I can think, and—"

"Fine," she said, heading for the stairs.

"'Fine' yourself!" he countered at twice the volume. "I'm going to the office for a couple of hours."

Simultaneously the bedroom door and the front door slammed.

It would be the last sound either of them would hear from the other for a very long time.

Ciara ran back down the stairs. He'd locked the bolt from outside, and her hands were shaking so hard it took three tries to get the door opened. "Mitch! Wait!"

But he hadn't heard her, for he was already backing down the drive. He must have been furious, she admitted, to make it that far in so little time. Standing in the open doorway, shivering in the wintry wind, she prayed he would look up and see her there on the porch, pull back into the drive....

Her pleas did not reach God's ear. If they had, the shiny red convertible wouldn't have peeled away from the curb like a speedster in the Indy 500. Probably, when she retrieved the morning edition of the *Baltimore Sun,* she would likely find skid marks from his '66 Mustang stuck to the asphalt, pointing like an accusing finger in the direction he'd gone.

Ciara retreated into the house they'd owned for one whole week and locked the door behind her. Her heart tightened as the bolt slid into position with a metallic *thunk;* it seemed such an ominous, final gesture.

She passed the first half hour pacing back and forth in front of the picture window, elbows cupped in her palms, heart lurching every time a pair of headlights rounded the corner, heart aching when they didn't aim up the drive.

There in the corner, amid to-be-hung pictures and stacks of books, stood their foot-high Christmas tree. Since they hadn't unpacked the ornaments yet, Ciara and Mitch had made do with several pairs of her earrings, a couple of his cuff links, curly ribbon, and a big red bow on top. It had looked adorable when they'd finished it last week—Christmas Eve. It just looked sad now, and Ciara resisted the urge to cry. She should be dry-eyed when he came back, not teary and sniffling, like a spoiled little girl….

It wasn't until she'd chewed a cuticle and drawn blood that Ciara decided to do some more unpacking. The activity, she hoped, would keep her from doing further damage to her fingernails. More important, it would draw her focus from the ever-ticking clock.

She arranged the good dishes and silverware in the glass-doored china closet, stood brass candlesticks on the mahogany sideboard, put a centerpiece of burgundy silk peonies on the table. Ciara had promised that on Sunday she would serve Mitch his favorite meal at this table— lasagna and Caesar salad. Surely things between them would be right by then.

Ciara tossed the empty boxes marked "dining room" into the attached garage, then got started on the family room. On either side of the flagstone fireplace she hung the carved wooden plaques and framed parchment awards he'd earned during his years at the Bureau, stood his guitar and banjo on one side of the hearth, his collection of walking sticks on the other. She filled the bookshelves with hard-bound adventure stories by his favorite authors, Dean Koontz and Jack London, and arranged his assortment of ceramic wolves.

Taking a break, she dropped into his brown leather recliner, which sat in its special place, facing the TV. It was an ancient, cavernous thing that had seen better days, but Mitch loved it, and the deep impressions, permanently hollowed into its cushions, were proof of that. Though it didn't match anything in the room—not the pale oak tables or linen-shaded lamps, not the blue-checked sofa or the white tab-topped draperies—the ugly old chair *belonged*.

She pictured him in it, size eleven feet on the footrest, one hand behind his dark-haired head, the other aiming the remote as channels flicked by at breakneck speed. How many times had she looked at him in this chair, and felt her heart throb with love, her mind reel with amazement that an exciting, adventuresome man like Mitch Mahoney had actually chosen her as his own?

Could she make a man like that happy...for the rest of his life?

Not if tonight was any indicator.

Why did you ask him to choose between you and the agency? she asked herself. *Didn't you learn anything from Mom and Dad's mistakes?*

They'd been three days into the two-week church-sponsored cruise when her mother found out how much time Ciara had been spending with Mitch. "He's a cop," her mother had said. "You want to live the way I have for thirty years? You want to be miserable all the time, worrying every minute that—"

"He's FBI, Mom," Ciara had gently corrected. "And besides, we're just *seeing* one another. It doesn't mean we're going to get mar—"

"He's a flatfoot, just like your father. You want to know how he got that name? By stepping all over *me*, that's how!"

Eyes narrowed by fury, her mother had concluded the tirade through clenched teeth. "Why waste your time, *seeing* him at all…unless you're hoping to end up at the altar?"

Ciara glanced at his big, empty chair. He should be sitting there now, she told herself, rather than in some stuffy office…alone and angry and—

She could only hope that when he came home they could resolve the problem, ensure nothing like it ever happened again. Otherwise, scenes like that would become a habit, as it had with her mom and dad.

She remembered her college roommate, whose parents seemed more in love after twenty-five years of marriage than Ciara's parents had likely ever been. Surely Kelly's mom and dad weren't lovey-dovey *all* the time; in quiet private moments, their *real* feelings for each other surfaced. "They fell head-over-heels in love," Kelly had said dreamily, "just like in the movies." Love at first sight? Ciara had thought. *No way!*

And she'd kept right on thinking that way, until she first caught sight of Mitchell Riley Mahoney….

He'd been in the pool with a half dozen rambunctious youngsters. Judging by his height, his broad shoulders, his muscular arms and legs, she'd decided he must be a professional football player. And when he'd answered "Polo!" to a little boy's "Marco!" Ciara felt certain he was probably a loud, clumsy fellow. "Hey," she'd heard him shout, "play fair. It isn't your turn…it's *mine!*" *Self-centered,* she'd added to her list, and maybe even a bit of a bully.

No one was more surprised than Ciara, when Pastor Boone introduced them at dinner that night. His soft-spokenness, his sense of humor, his intelligence, surprised her as much as the polished manners and thoughtfulness that had him pulling out chairs, opening doors and fetching a refill of punch before she'd emptied her cup.

Like Cinderella, she'd fallen in love before the clock struck twelve.

Smiling, she snuggled deep into his recliner and inhaled its faint leathery scent. Running her fingers over well-worn arms, she closed her eyes and remembered the little boy who'd clung to the pool's ladder that first day. She'd thought it unfair at the time, a bit mean, even, the way he'd ignored the child. But when the game ended and the older kids headed off to catch a movie in the theater, she understood *why* he hadn't interfered…the child was terrified of the water.

Somehow, Mitch convinced him to let go of the ladder. Holding the boy close, he'd walked back and forth in the pool's shallow end, letting the youngster's toes drag the water's surface. The kid hadn't seem to notice, as he giggled in response to whatever Mitch was whispering into his ears, that he was being taken deeper, deeper…

Two hours later the kid was doing an awkward breast stroke…on his own.

Mitch had taught her about lovemaking in that same gentle, patient way. The size of a man, she learned that day, was not a barometer of his capacity for tenderness. Even now she only needed to remember their wedding night, when she had trembled, like a child afraid of the water, for proof.

Ciara had always taken pride in her strength, physical and emotional. What she lacked in height and weight, she believed, she more than made up for with something her grandpa had called *gumption*. But surrounded by Mitch's muscular arms, she had felt precious, treasured, like a piece of priceless porcelain.

Inwardly she gave a halfhearted smile. *It's your own fault, Mitch Mahoney, that I've become the kind of woman I've always despised…weak, whining, clingy….*

Sighing deeply, she rehashed their argument. *If I had it to do over,* she thought, *I would never have brought up the subject of his job.*

Mitch had always been forthright about everything, especially his work. He'd told her how long and hard he'd worked to earn his current status within the Bureau. And she had thought she was being honest with him. "I'm a cop's daughter," she'd told him when he'd pointed out that being married to an FBI guy wouldn't be easy. "If *I* don't know what to expect from marriage to an officer of the law, who does?" She'd gone into the relationship with her eyes wide open, thinking her strength—her gumption— would see her through those trying, worrisome times when he was late and didn't call. She would not whimper and nag, not even in the name of love, as her mother had done....

The trouble was Ciara had not counted on loving him *this* much. Everything changed when she realized that without him life would be empty, meaningless, terrifying. It would be easier now for her to be more understanding of her Mom, she knew.

So what had she done, the very first time she was put to the test? She'd acted like a spoiled brat, that's what. Ashamed—and a little embarrassed—Ciara hid behind her hands. You asked him to give it all up, because—

Because she'd turned on the tiny TV in the kitchen, hoping to catch the evening news as she'd loaded supper dishes into the dishwasher. It hadn't mattered that she'd never heard of Special Agent Abe Carlson before. The story affected her as much as it would have if the stranger had been Mitch's best man, or if he'd lived next door. The live footage of him, young and handsome...and dying in the arms of a fellow agent...had sent a tremor through her that had made her drop the saucepan she'd been holding. "What are those reporters thinking?" she'd asked Mitch. "What if his wife sees this film clip? Or one of his kids? They'd have that picture in their memories, forever...."

Mitch's gaze had been glued to the screen, too, and

she'd watched his expression of horror turn to grief as he put his plate in the sink and silently left the room. She hadn't asked if he'd ever met Abe. Instead, she'd followed him into the living room, and like a pampered little girl, told him to give it all up, just like that.

"You knew what I did for a living when we met," he'd said. And he'd been right. As a good Christian wife, didn't she owe it to him to at least try to be supportive and understanding?

The question gave her new resolve. When he returned—soon she hoped, peeking at the clock—Ciara would show him that she'd married him for better or for worse. You never complained about the "better"—the thoughtful little things he did, the constant praise, the sweet lovemaking—so stop whining about the "worse."

"I've always been careful," he'd told her, "even before I had a beautiful wife to come home to." Being loving and understanding, even when it was tough, couldn't help but improve his chances out there in the mean streets. She would give her handsome young husband plenty of reasons to survive the day-to-day dangers that were a routine part of his job, because underneath it all—beneath the fear that he'd be hurt—or worse—*she loved him.*

Lord, she prayed, *please give me the strength to prove it—help me become the wife he deserves.*

Lieutenant Chet Bradley knew better than to question the Colombian. He'd ordered men killed for slamming doors, for interrupting telephone conversations, for talking out of turn. No one dared cross him; to complain was tantamount to suicide.

He'd been paid well for doctoring files and losing the evidence that would have sent the gangster back to his homeland, not in cash, but in pure, uncut cocaine, whenever and in any amount he requested, no questions asked.

Since the recent deaths of several mules, the Colombian and the U.S. governments had increased the pressure on transport of the white gold. "It's no longer worth the risk," Pericolo explained, ushering Bradley to the door. "Don't be a glutton," he added, handing the agent a small pouch, "for you'll get no more from me."

He'd had to be careful to keep his "fast lane" life in the shadows, so his top-of-the-line stereo equipment, designer clothes, and upscale vacations were things he'd had to hide from fellow agents. If he allowed even one of them to see the way he lived, they'd know in a minute he was on the take, because his life-style was impossible on an agent's salary alone.

No one knew that better than Bradley.

He supposed he could get used to living within his means again, as he had when he'd joined the agency. But he didn't *want* to.

And now, his money supply was dead.

"You look like you just lost your best friend," said Pericolo's next-in-command.

"Not yet," Bradley said, "but it could be terminal...."

"Naw," Chambro said, dropping an arm around Bradley's shoulders. "There are things we can do to, shall we say, save you."

Hope gleamed in Bradley's green eyes. "Yeah? What?"

"Let me walk with you to your automobile, Mr. Agent," the younger Colombian said, "let us talk."

In a hushed voice, Chambro spelled it out: He wanted control of the Pericolo empire, and he could get it...if he got rid of the boss. A few "favors" for Chambro—information leaked, files misplaced, evidence that would get Pericolo out of Chambro's way permanently—and Bradley would be guaranteed a continued supply of ready, untraceable cash. The would-be ruler leaned on Bradley's car door. "I'll leave the details to you, Mr. Agent. I am sure you can come up with a way we can—how do you Americans put it?—kill two birds with one stone." He gave Bradley a jaunty salute, and left him to consider his options.

Three days, Bradley said to himself. You've got three days to figure out how to get rid of Pericolo....

And then he knew.

Something Chambro had said reverberated in his head: "Two birds with one stone," he said, grinning. "Two birds with one stone...."

Mitch never left his office desk lamp on, so the dim light glowing from his cubicle puzzled him.

Lieutenant Chet Bradley hunched over Mitch's desk, riffling through his Rolodex. "Hey," Bradley said, holding up a card that read "Mahoney, Mitch." "I was just about to call you."

Mitch slid his briefcase onto the desktop, glanced at his wristwatch. "Good thing I'm here, then, 'cause it's nearly ten. Kinda late to be calling me at home, isn't it?" he asked, relieving Bradley of the card and returning it to the Rolodex.

He didn't know why, but being around this guy always gave Mitch an uneasy feeling. Maybe it's that weird grin, he told himself; shows every tooth in his head, but it never quite reaches his eyes....

But his mistrust of Bradley went deeper than any grin and farther back than he cared to remember. He'd hoped that once Bradley assumed his role as boss, the resentment would fade.

It had not.

The proof? He'd gone a long way in his years with the Bureau, but since being assigned to Bradley, Mitch had been given only the dullest, most routine cases, instead of the "newsmakers" he'd grown accustomed to working on.

It seemed Bradley was trying to bore him to death…or kill his career.

Bradley made himself comfortable in Mitch's chair and pointed to a thick manila file folder. "Have a seat, Mahoney."

Mitch sat in the chair across from his own desk.

"It's like this," Bradley began, thumb and forefinger an inch apart, "we're this close to nabbing Giovanni Pericolo."

Mitch knew that for years the agency had been trying to put the Colombian away—or, at the very least, have him kicked back to his homeland at the end of a steel-toed boot—but like a greased pig, Pericolo had always managed to slide through the system before they could even issue a warrant that would stick. "What's the charge this time?"

Bradley adjusted the knot of his navy tie. "Tax evasion."

"Like Capone?" Mitch chuckled quietly, despite the fact that his head still ached from having argued with Ciara. "You've gotta be kidding."

"It'll stick, provided we can get copies of certain, ah, financial documents."

Understanding dawned on Mitch. "Ahhh, so that's why you're here. You want me 'inside.'"

Like a rear-window doggy, Bradley nodded. "Philadelphia, to be specific."

If this don't beat all, Mitch grumbled to himself. I'm lookin' down the barrel of the best case he ever offered me, but— But how could he accept it, after what had just happened at home? Ciara had been harping on the dangers of his job ever since their wedding night, when she'd noticed his bullet wound. Maybe if this case wasn't going to be dangerous…

Mitch scrubbed a weary hand over his face. It had all happened so fast. How would he explain to his boss that during his two-week vacation to the islands, he'd seen Ciara onboard ship and gone completely nuts. Except for the hours between midnight and 6:00 a.m., they'd spent every minute of the cruise together, and it had been pretty much the same story once they'd gone home. Two months to the day after he'd met her, he'd put a ring on her finger. One month later they'd been married, quietly, because that's the way they'd wanted it. And what with shopping for a house and packing and moving, he hadn't been able to find the time to tell his boss about it.

"I don't know if you heard, but I just got married…."

He couldn't tell if Bradley was very surprised or very angry. Mitch sensed an imaginary noose hovering over his head.

"I've been meaning to tell you," he added, "but—"

"Is this the little woman?" Bradley asked, picking up the photograph on Mitch's desk.

He nodded, and the loop dropped onto his shoulders.

The lieutenant's wolf whistle pierced the silence. "How'd you get a beauty like that?" he asked, putting the photo back.

Mitch's heart lurched as he glanced at her sweet, smiling face framed in silver. She was everything he'd ever wanted in a woman and more. *I wonder how she'd answer that question, if it was put to her right now?* he asked himself. "Just lucky, I guess," he said, and meant it.

"I guess you know this puts us in a bind, Mahoney. We don't like sending married men under…not for stuff like this."

He swallowed as the rope tightened.

"But you're the best man on my team."

Mitch shot the lieutenant a look that said "What?"

"You were handpicked for this one, Mahoney." He tapped his forefingers together.

Mitch sat up straighter. "To be frank…"

"But I have to warn you, this won't be an easy one."

He'd been around long enough to know what *that* meant; it was FBI code for "high risk." Which was exactly what had bothered Ciara about his job. And, too, he couldn't get Bradley's threat, made years ago on the obstacle course at Quantico, out of his mind: "One of these days, *I'll* have the upper hand, and *you'll* know how it feels to be bested." Mitch had "bested" other guys on the gun range, in footraces, on exams, and *they* hadn't taken it personally....

Now I'm supposed to believe he thinks I'm the "best man" to haul in a guy at the top of the FBI's Most Wanted list? Maybe he isn't trying to kill my *career,* maybe he wants to kill *me....*

Mitch ran a finger around the inside of his collar. "How long would I be, ah, in Philadelphia?"

"You know that's impossible to predict. But if I had to guess, I'd say a week, maybe two."

He couldn't leave Ciara that long. Not after what had just happened between them. Besides, he'd told her he would be back in a couple of hours. "Sorry, boss. No can do," he said emphatically. "Get yourself another man, because—"

"Let me make something perfectly clear, Mahoney— we don't have time to get another man. You're goin' in, and I'm gonna be your point man or else. Get the point?"

Mitch bristled. He wouldn't have trusted Bradley to get a black-coffee order straight, let alone act as his only means of communication with his wife and the people who could pull him out if things got rough. He nodded at the file folder. "How much time will I have to prepare if—"

The lieutenant pulled back the cuff of his left shirt-sleeve and glanced at his watch. "Not *if...when.* And you're already a day late and a dollar short," he growled.

Instinct—and intense curiosity—compelled him to pick up the folder. Paging through its contents, Mitch found himself biting back the urge to wretch. He'd seen plenty of ugly sights in his years with the agency, but *this*…

He scanned the black-and-white pictures, hand-penned notes, fading faxes and speckled photocopies that depicted Giovanni Pericolo's life of crime. He would have a hard time forgetting any of it, particularly the photo he held. Pretty, petite, blond, the young girl reminded him of Ciara.

Mitch's eyes glazed as he stared at the file, unconsciously clicking his thumbnail against his top teeth. The file was full of reasons to put this guy away, but the government didn't have a shred of evidence to connect Pericolo with these heinous crimes. Like a giant squid, the Colombian's tentacles had reached across oceans, sucking the life from thousands of innocents. He seemed to have no particular method by which he chose his victims. Did he throw darts? Toss a coin? The girl who looked like Ciara…what if Pericolo's random selection pattern had zeroed in on *her* instead?

This was no ordinary thug. Pericolo was bad to the bone. If Mitch *did* manage to get in close, he'd have to keep his back to the wall at all times, because Pericolo wouldn't hesitate for a heartbeat when deciding whether or not to kill him. The material in the file was proof of that.

For the second time in as many minutes, he realized he'd named Ciara's greatest fears.

Mitch knew this case was a career maker. Truth was, if he'd been offered this carrot six months earlier, he'd have snapped it up so fast there'd have been an orange streak down the boss's palm.

But a lot could happen in six months. Heck, a lot could happen in half that time—he'd met, fallen in love with and married Ciara in three. Before that he'd been responsible for himself and no one else. Now he had a wife who depended on him, and soon, he hoped, they'd have a family. What better inspiration did an officer of the law need for putting guys like Pericolo away for good?

Mitch turned the question over in his mind. Was protecting his family the reason he wanted this assignment, or merely an excuse to do what he would have done in an instant…if he hadn't let himself be swept off his feet by love for a five-foot, two-inch spitfire?

He wanted to do the right thing, for the Bureau, for Ciara, for himself. But what was the right thing? Mitch drove a hand through his hair. *Lord God in heaven, show me the way….*

"Maybe you could give me a little advice, here. See, my wife—"

"Don't look to me for marital advice," Bradley interrupted, hands up in mock surrender. "My old lady took off for parts unknown years ago."

"Ciara saw the Abe Carlson thing on the evening news."

Bradley snorted his commiseration. "Leave it to the media to make a bad situation worse."

"And she knows I got myself winged back in '90." He shrugged. "She put two and two together, and—"

"—came up with one dead hubby." Bradley shook his head. "It's tough, finding a woman who understands. When my wife left, she said right out that she didn't have the backbone for the undercover stuff."

"Well, let's face it. Hazardous duty isn't an easy thing for a wife to live with."

"Don't get me wrong, Mahoney, I'm really enjoying our little heart-to-heart, but we've got a narrow window of opportunity, here, and we need you in Philly, like, *yesterday.*" Grinning crookedly, he tried to lighten the mood by adding, "You're a CPA, with an impeccable record, and you speak fluent Spanish. You're perfect for the job."

Mitch forced a thin smile. *"Gracias, ser muy mandamas,"* he said guardedly.

"I can't *force* you to take the case, but look at it this way—we both know there's no love lost between us. Go to Philly and consider the hatchet buried."

Mitch shifted uneasily in the chair. He'd faced leather-jacketed thugs in dark alleys. He'd been shot, beaten, kidnapped…had looked Death straight in the eye more times than he cared to remember. But none of it had stressed him as much as the pressure being put to bear on him now.

"You bring Pericolo in, and you're sure to get another medal." Smirking, he added, "And I'll get a feather in *my* cap, too, for being the guy who handpicked you."

He gave his words a moment to sink in. Mitch's mouth had gone dry, and he licked his lips. A big mistake, as it turned out, because the lieutenant read it as hunger to go under.

"First order of business…get rid of those sideburns. No more collarless shirts, no pleated trousers. Wingtips, not Italian loafers. You've got to look the part of a pencil-necked geek." He hesitated. "Let's face it, you're the Clark Kent of accountants. Just do the best you can, stay away from kryptonite, will ya?"

Mitch did not join in Bradley's merry laughter. "The wife and I, we ah, left things in a bit of a muddle tonight. I only came down here to clear my head."

"You had a fight?" Bradley asked. "After just three weeks of marriage?"

"Four," Mitch corrected.

The lieutenant shook his head. "Tough break, pal. You'll be lucky if you even *have* a wife if you get back from this one."

Mitch stared hard at him. *If?* Thanks for the vote of confidence, pal.

Standing, the boss handed Mitch a five-by-seven manila

envelope. "Your new identity," he said, then pointed at Pericolo's file. "You know what to do with that."

It was a copy, of course, and once he'd memorized pertinent information, Mitch would burn it.

Bradley's matter-of-factness did little to blot Ciara's image from Mitch's mind. Every time he blinked, it seemed, he saw the way she'd looked just before she'd rushed up the stairs. He remembered thinking about that as he'd headed for headquarters. Just last week he'd been forced to cock back his arm and punch a thug to get him under control. In those first, tense seconds after fist connected with cheek, the perp's eyes had widened with shock and pain. Ciara had worn the same expression....

He didn't want to leave her, not for a moment, especially not this way. He knew he could get out of going "in." But Bradley had said this case would put a feather in his own cap. He ain't gonna be tickled if you take that feather away, Mitch thought. He'll bump your rank back so far, you'll *never* catch up.

But what if Bradley was right? What if Ciara *wasn't* waiting for him when this was over? What difference did it make if he reached the top if she wasn't there to share it with him?

He needed to be part of this mission, but he needed to know she'd be there, waiting for him, loving him still, when it was all over...because he couldn't afford to be distracted, not this time. And what could be more distracting than wondering whether or not the job might cost him Ciara?

He posed the question lightly, as if it were a mere afterthought. "I won't breach security, of course, but if I could give my wife a quick call, feed her some innocuous details, so she won't worry...."

Laying a hand on Mitch's shoulder, the boss shook his head. "Sorry, Mahoney," he said, almost gently. "You know the rules—the less she knows, the safer you'll both be in the event that…" His mouth and brows formed a "you know what" expression.

Mitch fingered through the contents of the envelope. Passport, driver's license, credit cards, a library card. "It's just…we didn't part on a very pleasant note," he said without looking up.

He gave Mitch's back a brotherly thump. "Now, don't you worry, 'cause ole Uncle Chet is gonna take good care of your little lady."

The thought of it wrapped around him like a cold, wet blanket. Mitch shook off the feeling. He had to keep a clear head.

Every man in his family was or had been a cop. Ciara's father, too. They'd understand. They'd explain it to her, they'd be there for her. She'd be fine….

Still, it was a strange, foreign thing, this feeling of resentment bubbling in the pit of his stomach. He'd never before felt torn between duty and—

"There's a blue Ford Taurus downstairs," he said, grabbing Mitch's wrist, plunking a set of keys into his palm, "and a reservation at the D.C. Sheraton in your, ah, new name." Almost as an afterthought, he asked, "Did you go to church today?"

He nodded.

"Good."

Mitch heard the implication loud and clear. *You'll need all the Divine intervention you can get.*

"Now head on over to your hotel and get a good night's sleep. First thing in the morning get yourself to the nearest mall."

Mitch nodded again. Outfitting himself for undercover assignments had filled his closet to overflowing. Too bad his aliases never had his taste in clothes.

"Pericolo's expecting you, one o'clock sharp," Bradley

added, "so when you get your new laptop, have the sales clerk load it up with all the latest accounting software…general ledger, spreadsheet, the works."

"I'm a CPA," Mitch snarled, "I think I know what I need."

"We're gonna get him this time, Mahoney," he continued, ignoring Mitch's pique. He aimed both thumbs at the ceiling. "I can *feel* it!"

Mitch shuffled woodenly back to his desk, plopped the file and envelope near the phone, picked up the receiver. If Bradley hadn't been standing there, watching and waiting, he might have called Ciara, to explain…or try to, anyway. He took a deep breath, shook his head. It's better this way, he reminded himself. She's safer, and so are you….

He dialed nine for an outside line, then banged the receiver into its cradle. "What am I thinking? I can't call a florist—it's nearly eleven, and they'll all be closed."

"So? Write her a note instead."

Mitch met the man's steely gaze, and despite himself, decided there was truth in his words; a note would be better than a handful of cut flowers and a terse message penned by some unknown saleswoman.

He pulled a yellow legal pad and black felt-tip from his desk. "Dearest Ciara," he wrote, "I'm sorry for upsetting you tonight. First chance I get, I'll explain *everything,* I promise." He underlined *everything* three times, hoping she'd read the message between the lines. "Trust me, sweetie—I need that now. Don't ever forget that I love you more than life itself, and I always will." He signed it "Your grateful husband."

He folded the letter, sealed it in a plain white envelope and wrote her name across its front. With a deep sigh, he handed it to the lieutenant.

A chill coiled around Mitch's spine as Bradley tucked

it into the breast pocket of his suit coat. It was like watching it go down a rat hole. He shook off the disheartening thought as Bradley said, "You're my responsibility, and I take that very seriously. I won't let you down. You have my word."

He wanted to spell out exactly what he thought Bradley's "word" was worth, but thought better of it. *He's not much, but he's all you've got. You can't afford to rile him now….*

He grabbed the file and the envelope containing his new "self," and they rode the elevator down to the lobby. The silence between them continued as they stood on the sidewalk outside headquarters.

Mitch turned up his collar to fend off the wintry December wind. For a moment he stood on the corner of Ninth and Pennsylvania, oblivious to the screaming sirens and honking horns around him. Far in the distance, pin-pricks of light winked from the windows of houses in the D.C. suburbs, reminding him that forty-some miles away, a light glowed in a window in Ellicott City, too. And if he knew Ciara, she was standing in that window right now, watching for him….

Mitch straightened his back. Cleared his throat. Bradley had said two weeks. *Two weeks,* he reminded himself. Maybe less. Not so long, really…. "Well, I'd better get a move on," he said, and headed for the car.

"Two for the price of one…I'm here for ya, pal," Bradley called after him.

Without turning around, he threw a hand into the air, as if to say, "Thanks." But the thought in his head was, *Uh-huh, and the last horse to win the Derby was a mule.*

Mitch believed he understood what Chicken Little must have felt like, and gave a cursory glance toward the sky…just to make sure it wasn't falling….

Chapter Two

A shaft of sunlight, slicing through the bay window, slanted across her face. Ciara came to gradually, and slowly acknowledged every kink and cramp in her joints. She'd fallen asleep in Mitch's chair, cuddling the fluffy pillow he liked to tuck behind his lower back.

She headed for the front door. "Please, God," she prayed as she went, "let his car be out there, where it belongs."

Her sporty white Miata looked smaller and sad, parked alone at the top of the drive, as if it missed the companionship of the little red Mustang.

Ciara didn't know whether to be angry or hurt or terrified. She half ran to the kitchen, grabbed the telephone and dialed his direct line. She didn't know what to say when he answered, but she knew this: it would be a relief to hear his voice. Angry or pouting or tired from spending the night at his desk, at least she'd know he was all right.

She counted ten rings before a man said, "Hullo…"

Once before, another agent had picked up Mitch's phone. But that had been a weekday afternoon, not six o'clock in the morning. "Is Mitch Mahoney there?"

"Hold on, I'll check," said the gruff, unrecognizable voice. And a moment later he said, "I don't see him. Want I should take a message?"

Ciara sighed. "No, thanks. I'll try back later."

"Okey-dokey," he chimed merrily, and hung up.

She showered and dressed and called again. And again an hour after that. "Parker, here," said the agent who answered this time.

Briefly Ciara introduced herself. She didn't want the guys at the office knowing their private business, and so she said, "He left a folder on the table. I just wanted to let him know it's here."

"If I see him," Parker said, "I'll tell him."

"Is there any way I could find out where he is?" Ciara tried not to sound anxious. "I really need to speak with him."

"You could ask his lieutenant. Lemme see if he's in his office."

She put on a pot of coffee while she waited on Hold, made it extrastrong, the way Mitch liked it, in case he came in before she got answers to her questions.

"Lieutenant Bradley doesn't usually get in till nine. I left a message on his desk to call you, Mrs. Mahoney."

A minute later she found herself standing with receiver in hand, staring into space. Ciara hung up, hoping she'd had the presence of mind to thank the man for all his trouble.

"Where could he be?" she whispered.

Chester, who'd been staring out the low-slung bow window in the breakfast nook, trotted over to his mistress. She'd more or less been aware that, as she paced back and forth with the phone pressed to her ear, the dog had been pacing, too…from window to window. He sat back on his haunches and whimpered for some attention.

Distractedly she patted his honey-colored head, then

opened the back door. "No digging under the fence, now," she warned, wagging a finger. Chester sat in the open doorway, cinnamon brows twitching, caramel brown eyes pleading for a moment of affection.

On her knees, Ciara wrapped her arms around his fuzzy neck. "You're worried about him, too, aren't you?" she asked, smoothing back his shaggy ears. He'd taken an immediate liking to Mitch—something not one of her former boyfriends could claim—so much so that she'd felt a pang or two of jealousy as the dog followed him from room to room. "Don't you worry. I'm sure he's fine."

Chester responded with a breathy bark, then bounded out the door.

Ciara stood on the small porch and watched him, scampering after a squirrel. "If only I could stop worrying that quickly," she said to herself.

Something told her it wasn't just the late-December weather that sent a shiver up her back.

"Come in, Mr. Lewis, please, come in." The swarthy man grabbed Mitch's hand, shook it heartily. "My friend and your cousin, Buddy Kovatch, recommends you highly."

Your friend, Mitch thought grimly, is a stooge. But at least he's earning the big bucks the government pays him to be a stooge. Buddy Kovatch had been a trusted Pericolo employee for nearly two decades. His last bust would have sent him up to Jessup for ten-to-fifteen if he hadn't agreed to help put his boss away for good. The government buried the charges against Buddy, and in exchange, he put in a good word for the agency's "plant." And now Mitch, posing as Buddy's cousin Sam, would "keep" Pericolo's books until he gathered enough evidence to arrest him for tax evasion.

Smiling, Mitch bobbed his head good-naturedly. "Please. Call me Sam."

Though he wore a wide, friendly smile, Giovanni
Pericolo's dark eyes glinted with icy warning. "Very well,
then, Sam it is." He gave Mitch's hand a tight squeeze and
added, "I hope for your sake, Sam, that you can live up to
your stellar reputation…."

He took a new deck of cards from his jacket's inside
pocket, unwrapped it, and handed the cellophane to a
white-gloved manservant. "Pick a card, any card,"
Pericolo said. Except for a hint of a South American
accent, he reminded Mitch of every sleight-of-hand
expert he'd seen on "The Ed Sullivan Show." Without
looking at the card he'd chosen, he handed it back to
Pericolo. The Colombian gave it a cursory glance,
replaced it in the deck and, silent smile still frozen on his
face, led Mitch into the dining room, repocketing the
deck as they walked.

"Darling," he crooned, "I'd like you to meet Sam
Lewis, our new accountant. He'll be spending a lot of
time around here from now on." He pulled her to him in
a sideways hug. "Sam, this is Anna, my lovely wife."

The shapely blonde patted her husband's ample belly,
her wide smile barely disturbing her overly made up face.
"It's a pleasure to meet you," she said. "Won't you have
a seat? Dinner will be served momentarily."

Pericolo's chest puffed out like a proud peacock's as
he moved to stand behind a teenaged boy. "My son,
David," he said, gently squeezing his look-alike's shoulders. "He's a big boy for fourteen, don't you think? David,
say hello to Mr. Lewis."

"Hello, Mr. Lewis."

The boy would not meet his eyes, a fact that made
Mitch tense. "Good to meet you, David. You on the
football team at school?"

David shook his head.

"Basketball?"

He glared openly at Mitch. "Don't like team sports," he snapped.

"Don't have the grades to make the team, you mean," said his sister.

David cut her a murderous stare that not only immediately silenced her…it chilled Mitch's blood as well.

"And this," Pericolo interrupted, concluding the introductions, "is my beautiful daughter, Dena."

Mitch guessed her to be sixteen, if that. Her bright red fingernails exactly matched her highly glossed lips, her hair dyed two shades lighter than her mother's. The mini-dress and mascara-thick lashes told Mitch she had not been taught to dress for dinner by a church-going mother.

She tilted her head flirtatiously to say, "Good evening, Mr. Lewis. It's a pleasure to meet you."

"Same here," he said carefully.

Mitch followed Pericolo's move and took a seat, resisting the urge to excuse himself, find a powder room and wash his hands. Pericolo looked like he'd just stepped out of the shower, so why had the brief handshake made Mitch's palm itch, as if he'd smashed a spider barehanded? He reminded himself that Pericolo had a reputation, too. Not just *any* spider, Mitch told himself, wiping his palm on his pants leg, a Black Widower.

Bradley and the director had spelled it all out during the meeting last evening. Tax evasion would be the *charge* they'd hang Pericolo with, but it wasn't the reason he'd made the FBI's Most Wanted list. Mitch didn't know of an instance when anyone had violated the law…man's or God's…the way Pericolo had.

His crimes were far more sinister, more evil than any Mitch had seen to date. And he'd seen some grisly things in his years with the Bureau—drug kingpins, hit men, bank robbers, kidnappers, hijackers—tame as pussycats, in Mitch's opinion, compared to Pericolo. Once he'd heard the details of the Colombian's ghastly crimes, how could he turn his back on the assignment?

Like many young men who dedicate their lives to fighting crime, Mitch, too, had started out with typically high-and-mighty ideals. Maturity, and the things he'd witnessed firsthand, had made him leave most of those lofty sentiments by the wayside. But so far, thankfully, he had managed to hold on to one objective: to do his small part in creating a safer, healthier life for kids. Those he and Ciara would have one day, even Pericolo's kids, deserved that kind of protection.

Rumor had it that Pericolo had no shame about what he did for a living, seeing himself as an "entrepreneur" who provided a certain group of "consumers" with a much desired product. Never mind that Pericolo had become one of the wealthiest men in the world by exploiting the weakest, most pitiful side of human nature.

Mitch had to take this assignment. If he didn't, he wouldn't have been able to live with himself if someday, one of Pericolo's "hollow bodies" turned out to be that of a friend, the child of a friend, one of his own loved ones....

"A toast," Pericolo was saying, "to the newest addition to my business family." Shimmering light, raining down from the Tiffany chandelier like thousands of miniature stars, glinted from the facets of his Waterford goblet and the bold gold-and-diamond rings on his long, thick fingers.

Mitch lifted his glass, glanced at Mrs. Pericolo. Was it a carefully disguised warning...or smug satisfaction...that chilled her smile? How much did she know about Pericolo Enterprises? Did she understand *how* her husband acquired the wealth that put her in this thirty-six-room mansion? He'd seen two Rolls Royces when he parked the rented Ford in the circular drive...was Anna's the silver or the gold one? Surely she suspected *something,* and if so, how had she taught herself to look the other way?

Mitch measured the atmosphere, chatting amiably when he thought it appropriate, nodding somberly when he felt he should. At the conclusion of the long, leisurely dinner in the elegant dining room, Pericolo's wife and children excused themselves, and Giovanni invited Mitch to join him for coffee in his study.

"Please, make yourself comfortable," he said, gesturing expansively toward twin bloodred leather chairs that flanked the massive mahogany desk.

Mitch chose the chair on the right, where he could keep an eye on the door...and keep his back to the wall. Pericolo lifted the lid of a teak humidor. "Cubans," he whispered harshly, tilting the box so Mitch could peek inside.

"Never touch the stuff," Mitch said, holding up a hand, "but thanks."

As Pericolo removed a long, fat cigar, Mitch said, "Mind if I ask you a question?"

Pericolo sat beside him, gold lighter in one hand, hundred-dollar cigar in the other. "You can ask," he said smoothly, his accent a bit thicker now that he'd downed a bottle and a half of Chateau Mouton-Rothschild. Swirling the cigar's mouthpiece between his lips, he ignited the lighter. "But I cannot promise to answer."

Mitch nodded and sipped his coffee. "What was the card game all about, Mr. Pericolo?"

"We needn't stand on ceremony, Sam," he mumbled around a mouthful of cigar. "Starting tomorrow, you will have your nose in the pages of my most personal, ah, shall we say 'affairs'? Please, call me Giovanni." His lips popped as he drew air through the cigar's tip. "Now, back to your question. You were referring to the card I asked you to pick, no?"

Another nod.

He lounged in the chair, broad shoulders nearly

touching each curving wingback, shining black hair matting against the buttery leather. "Ah, yes," came his satisfied sigh. "You're sure you wouldn't like to light one up?"

Smiling thinly, Mitch shook his head.

Pericolo blew a perfect smoke ring, poked the cigar's glowing tip into its floating center. "I have asked many men to choose. Not one has asked me why." His dark gaze bored into Mitch's eyes. And then he laughed, a short staccato burst of snorts and grating snickers. "Perhaps that's because so few *could*."

Crossing his knees, he took another thoughtful drag from the cigar. "You drew a red card. Queen of Hearts, to be exact." Through cold-as-death, narrowed eyes, he studied Mitch's face for a moment. Grinning, he slurred, "You are not satisfied with this answer?"

Mitch shifted carefully in the chair, so as not to spill his coffee. "Ever since I was a boy, I've had this incurable need to know why."

"I understand completely. I have the same…shall we say…affliction." He shrugged. "I have accepted it as a trait of intelligent, ambitious men." He raised one eyebrow as his upper lip curled in a menacing snarl. "Still…it's sometimes smarter…and safer…not to know the answer." The well-practiced smile was gone, and his voice, which had been smoothly polite until now, dropped an octave, growled out as if his throat had been roughened by coarse sandpaper.

To this point Pericolo had been the perfect host, generous, humorous, magnanimous. But this, Mitch knew, was the *real* Giovanni. He felt a bit like he'd walked unarmed into a lion's cage, and found himself face-to-face with a recently captured, seasoned killer that the zookeeper hadn't bothered to feed in a week. To meet the old beast's golden irises meant certain death, for it could read fear in a man's eyes just as certainly as it could smell it emanating from his body. The difference? The lion killed to satisfy his hunger; Pericolo killed *because he enjoyed it*. The similarity? Once their bellies were full, neither gave another thought to their prey.

Mitch pretended to study the delicate rose pattern decorating his Wedgwood teacup. "Perhaps it's because I'm an accountant," Mitch continued, trying to appear nonplussed by Pericolo's not-so-veiled threat, "that I've always believed the devil's in the details. I like to dot all the *i*s and cross all the *t*s." He drained the coffee. "So if you'll indulge me…why ask me to pick a card? And what's the significance of the red queen?" Only then did he meet the beast's eyes.

Pericolo sniffed, gave a nonchalant wave with his cigar hand. "No significance of any importance, really. A man in my position must be careful…I'm sure you understand…."

"I'm afraid I don't."

Another chuckle. "Well," he said, reclaiming his former suave, distinguished persona, "then allow me to explain. One inaccurate assessment of a man could mean—" He drew a finger across his throat. "It has been my experience that people seldom are what they appear to be."

Pericolo, he knew, had taken this roundabout tack to make him nervous. This wasn't the first time he'd been eye to eye with a cold-blooded killer, but it was the first time he believed he might be killed just for sport. Mitch took a slow, quiet breath to ease his fast-beating heart.

"I do as much checking of the backgrounds as I can when bringing a new man aboard," Pericolo continued, shrugging one shoulder. "At best, it's a fifty-fifty proposition. Some will be who they say they are, and others…" He shook his head, hands extended in a pleading gesture. "Despite my Oxford education—or perhaps because of it," he said, laughing softly, "I'm a very superstitious man. The cards, if you'll pardon the pun, are my ace in the hole."

"I'm a thick-headed Irishman, Giovanni," Mitch said, feigning a jolly laugh at his own expense. "I'm afraid I don't have a clue what you're talking about."

Straight-faced, Pericolo reached out slowly, deposited the smoking Cuban into the foot-square ivory ashtray on the corner of his desk. Mitch found it interesting that, despite what this man did for a living, the hand did not tremble, not in the least.

"Allow me to clarify it for you, then," he began. Settling against the chair's tufted backrest, he calmly folded his hands in his lap.

"If you had picked a black card, you would be dead right now."

Pericolo spoke so matter-of-factly, he may as well have been reading yesterday's baseball scores, or repeating the weatherman's prediction. Mitch leaned forward to put his cup and saucer on the desk, more to have a moment to compose himself than because he'd finished the coffee. He had never been fooled—not about men like this. Every last one of them were capable of look-you-in-the-eye, drop-you-where-you-stand murder, but...

"You are a lucky man, Sam."

His best bet, he decided, was to go for broke. "You would have killed me...for picking the wrong color?"

Pericolo's feral stare was all the answer Mitch needed. Yet the man felt inclined to add, "I have nothing more to say, Sam, except that life is fleeting."

Sitting back, Mitch leaned both palms on the chair, careful not to squeeze the armrests too tight, lest this proficient beast of prey sense his fear. "I've never been much of a card player," Mitch said, grinning sardonically, "but

I've suddenly developed a strange fondness for them. Red queens, in particular."

The sound of Pericolo's boisterous laughter echoed in his ears long after Mitch went to bed.

It was 9:05 when Bradley read the pink "While You Were Out" message on his desk. "Call Mitch's wife," Parker had scribbled. Frowning, Bradley wadded the slip of paper into a tight ball, tossed it neatly into the metal wastebasket beside his desk. He'd done the very same thing last night with the letter Mahoney had written to his wife.

If Mahoney hadn't put in for the same promotion, none of this would be necessary. As it was, he'd made himself the unwilling pawn in Bradley's dangerous game against Giovanni Pericolo.

Two for the price of one, he thought, slouching in his chair.

Except for Buddy Kovatch, no one but Bradley knew where Special Agent Mitch Mahoney was right now. And Kovatch wouldn't be doing any talking. Not if he wanted to stay out of prison. He clasped his hands behind his head and smiled. "Sure is nice, bein' boss," he said to himself.

He didn't like admitting that if his uncle hadn't risen through the ranks to a position where he could pull strings, down in personnel, he wouldn't *be* boss.

His uncle's hands had been tied by that very same string—too many promotions would alert the rest of the brass to what was going on downstairs. Mahoney was Bradley's only competition for the upcoming administrative job slot, and there wasn't much doubt in Bradley's mind who'd get the job. Especially if the big dumb guy pulls off this case the way he's pulled off others in the past....

Well, Lady Luck had kissed Mitch Mahoney for the last time, Bradley thought, sneering. And if the fickle gal felt inclined to pucker up for him again, Bradley would be there to see that her lips never made contact.

Bradley had gone undercover once himself, and knew from personal experience that an agent had better not let anything distract him from the task at hand. And nothing, he'd discovered, was more distracting than a rift with a spouse.

His grin grew. Two for the price of one....

He had no intention of being Mahoney's message boy. Or his wife's delivery man, for that matter. He wants to make fast tracks to the top, let him do it without my help!

Mahoney would nab Pericolo, all right. Bradley would be surprised if he lasted three days after bringing in the evidence the U.S. Attorney needed to convict the Colombian. If Pericolo didn't give the order—from his prison cell—to make a door knocker out of Mahoney's head, Bradley had plans of his own for the Irishman....

Two for the price of one....

He snapped the mini-blinds shut, effectively closing himself into his ten-by-ten office. He propped the heels of his wingtips on his desktop and leaned back in his highback chair.

His thin lips curled into a malicious grin.

Two for the price of one....

Chapter Three

When he got the call and heard the agent say he was on his way home, Bradley knew he'd better act fast. As he made the forty-minute drive from D.C. to Ellicott City, he slammed a fist into the steering wheel. *You should have done this weeks ago,* he reprimanded himself. *It isn't like you didn't have plenty of opportunity….*

Grinning crookedly, he recalled the many times he'd visited pretty little Mrs. Mahoney. That first time in particular stood out in his mind. It had been a week to the day after Mahoney went undercover. She'd looked like a high school kid in her faded jeans and oversize Baltimore Orioles T-shirt, long blond hair tied in a ponytail on top of her head. The whites of her big blue eyes were pink from crying, and there had been a box of tissues tucked under her arm when she opened the door. When he flashed his badge, she would have slumped to the floor for sure…if he hadn't reached out to steady her.

"I thought…I thought you were here to tell me he'd been…killed," she'd stammered once she'd regained her balance.

He'd given her a moment to calm down before explaining how things worked. "Mitch has left town, on…well, let's just say…company business."

"Left town? But…but we were just married." Several silent seconds passed before she said, "I suppose you sent Mitch because you had to. I mean, there wasn't anyone else avail—"

"Actually, Mitch volunteered. Seemed quite eager to go, in fact." Shaking his head, he'd added, "I think he's out of his ever-lovin' mind, 'cause *nothing* could have made *me* leave a pretty little thing like you at home."

She had paid absolutely no attention to his blatant flirtation. Ciara's bright eyes had brimmed with tears as she stood wringing her hands, trying hard not to cry.

"Now, just to make sure everybody stays safe," he'd continued, "there can be no direct communication between you two." He had to sound convincing, because one thing Bradley didn't need was a hysterical wife phoning the director, asking when her husband would be home.

She could write letters to her husband, he instructed, as many and as often as she wanted, and Mahoney could answer, when and if his situation permitted. In any case, all messages would be written in Bradley's presence…and immediately destroyed by him once they'd been read.

Her eyes filled with tears again, and she'd looked so much in need of a comforting hug that Bradley gave her one. "I have a feeling you have what it takes to be patient," he'd added, stroking her back.

Even now, seven months later, he remembered how she felt in his arms. She'd trembled, like a baby bird that had fallen from its nest, felt so small, so delicate, that he had to force himself to hold her gently, taking care not to press her too close. Too bad she has to be part of the plan, he'd thought. But the reality of it was that without her, he couldn't pull it off. It was as though she'd read his mind, because no more than a second, perhaps two, ticked by before she'd stiffened, wriggled free of his embrace. The look on her face reminded him of the time when, at sixteen, he'd been caught, red mouthed, kissing Mr. Cunningham's daughter. Hands pressed to her tear-streaked cheeks, Ciara had seemed ashamed to have allowed another man to touch her, even in a gesture of comfort.

Now, as he peered at his reflection in the window beside her front door, Bradley admitted that he'd told one truth that day. "If I had a woman like her waiting for me at home…" The memory of her pretty, sad-smiling face flashed in his mind. If she was *your* wife, he told himself, a lot of things would be different today….

The hostility he'd harbored toward Mahoney intensified as he acknowledged that, yet again, he'd been bested. The grudge went way back, to the days when Mahoney outshot, outran, outscored him at Quantico. These months of watching his wife's devout fidelity only served to sharpen his prickly envy. Would a woman ever love *him* that much? Bradley wondered. Never a woman like Ciara…beautiful, warm, intelligent, endlessly devoted to her man.

He blinked, shook his head. You can't afford to feel anything for her, he admonished. Not admiration, not respect, certainly not concern! It would mean letting down his guard, and to do that around a guy like Pericolo…well, he may as well put a gun to his own head.

Two for the price of one, he reminded himself. Two for the price of one.

Bradley straightened his tie, ran a hand through his reddish blond curls, nervously tugged the cuffs of his sports coat and rang her doorbell. As he waited for Ciara to answer, he rehearsed the plan…one more time.

"Lieutenant Bradley," Ciara said, smiling when she opened the door. "Please, come in." Once he was inside, she asked softly, expectantly, "Is there a letter this time?"

He could have said no and let it go at that. Could have shaken his head sadly, feigning commiseration. "I told you, this is just the way Mitch *is* when he's on assignment." Winking, Bradley lowered his voice. "He says if his babes worry enough, he's guaranteed a memory-making homecoming!"

Sometimes he got the impression that once he'd told her there was no word from Mahoney, she simply tuned out everything else he said. This time, Ciara's silence— and the heat emanating from her blue eyes—told him she'd heard every word.

"I'm sorry. Guess I shouldn't have said that."

As always she shrugged it off. "Then…if there's no news…"

If there's no news, why am I here? he finished, gritting his teeth. I was wondering how long it would take you to get around to saying it this time.

The third or fourth time he'd visited her, Bradley had brought a bouquet of flowers. It had surprised him more than a little to discover that neither his corrupt behavior nor the people he'd been hanging around with lately had snuffed out his conscience. If she hadn't been so doggoned *sweet,* maybe he wouldn't have felt so bad about using her. Guilt had nagged him into popping for two dozen long-stemmed white roses. She'd thanked him. Said he shouldn't have. And stuck the box on the foyer table. May as well have tossed that hundred bucks in the trash, he re-primanded himself, because he had a feeling the prickly green stems would never see water. Not because she was an ungrateful sort. Quite the opposite, in fact. Ciara Mahoney would consider it improper to display flowers given by a man who was not her husband…particularly when that husband had vanished from her life like chimney smoke.

A couple of months back, he'd brought doughnuts and

coffee, hoping this less extravagant, more friendly gift would help her warm to him, even slightly. Ciara had arranged the treats on a blue-flowered plate, poured his coffee from the paper cup into a matching mug and placed a white cloth napkin beside it. Two bites of a cruller and a sip of coffee later, he realized she had no intention of joining him. She sat stiffly across from him, smiling politely, her gaze darting to the kitchen clock every few seconds, as if counting the minutes until he'd leave. She was too polite, too kindhearted to say it straight out, but Ciara Mahoney wanted no part of Chet Bradley.

"Just stopped by to see how you were doing," he said, forcing the bitter memories from his mind. He sighed resignedly as if his message wouldn't be an easy one to deliver. "And to tell you that I saw Mitch again yesterday."

Well, you don't have to look so all-fired pleased about it, he thought when her eyes lit up. You haven't heard a word from that bum in seven months, but *I've* been here every week, like clockwork!

"He looked great," Bradley continued, "happy, healthy, well rested. Seems our boy is having a grand old time on this assignment, so don't you worry your pretty little head about him, you hear?"

He watched a myriad of emotions play across her delicate features before worry lines creased her smooth brow. "When will this nightmare ever end?" she whispered, and he suspected she hadn't intended to ask the question aloud. Her shoulders rose on a deep breath. "Can I get you something? Coffee? Lemonade?"

He plastered a practiced look of concern on his face. "Can't stay. I only came by to make sure you were okay. Is there anything I can do? Something I can get you?"

"No, but thank you, Lieutenant."

Grinning, he took her hand, gave it an affectionate pat. "'Lieutenant?' Ciara, you're breakin' my heart!" He chose his words carefully. "I've spent more time with you than your husband has these past seven long months. It wouldn't be improper for you to call me Chet, would it?"

She gave it a moment's thought. "You're right, of course…Chet."

He placed a mental check mark beside Part One of his plan. And now for Part Two:

"Did you hear something?"

His tense, slightly crouched posture had the desired effect. Ciara hovered near the wall, cringing, hands clasped under her chin, eyes wide with fright. "No, I—"

A forefinger over his lips, he warned her to be quiet. "Now, don't you worry," he whispered. "Chances are practically nil that Mitch has tipped his hand…and that's the *only* way those goons would know how to find you."

Assuming the 'ready, fire' position, he unholstered his weapon, and as though he really believed a gun-toting bad guy had invaded the second floor, Bradley slowly made his way upstairs, darting into doorways, aiming the Glock at imaginary felons skulking along the hall, as if he truly expected an assassin to pop out and draw a bead on him.

The moment he ducked into Ciara's room, he straightened, calmly reholstered his service revolver. Smirking, he reached into his pocket and withdrew a small vial of Homme Jusqu'au Dernier. "Now for Part Three," he said, his voice echoing quietly in the white-tiled master bathroom. "'Man to the Last,'" he translated the cologne's gold foil label. Opening the medicine cabinet, he placed the decanter on a glass shelf and gently closed the door.

Swaggering toward the hall, he pocketed both hands. It was all he could do to keep from whistling a happy tune. Pericolo was safe behind bars. "One down, one to go," he singsonged.

First chance he got, Bradley would pay the newlyweds a little visit. If he knew Mahoney, he wouldn't be in the house five minutes before the subject of the cologne came up. They'd have words over whose fingerprints were all over pretty Mrs. Mahoney.

It wouldn't take much to convince Internal Affairs that the man of the hour had snapped after all those months in Pericolo's headquarters. Bradley's story that he'd killed the enraged husband in self-defense would go uncontested.

"One down, one to go," he repeated, grinning. "One down, one to go…."

Mitch spent the first day and a half of his freedom down at headquarters, typing up the detailed report that outlined the case. He'd turned down the chance to be there when they picked Pericolo up; he'd seen enough of the Colombian to last several lifetimes. He glanced at the clock. They'd have him in custody by now.

He's probably already complaining about the way his orange jumpsuit clashes with his complexion. His Italian mother had been a fashion designer in Milan; maybe that explained why Pericolo was so focused on outward appearances. Ill-fitting prison garb was Giovanni's problem, and Giovanni was the U.S. Attorney's problem from here on out.

Mitch had troubles of his own, starting with the fact that he'd been away from home a long, long time. He'd known from the start that Bradley had underestimated the amount of time he'd be gone. *But seven months?*

The lieutenant had not been in touch once, a fact that had deeply concerned Mitch at first. But he'd been in situations like that before, and knew how to handle himself. It turned out to be a blessing, really, that he hadn't been able to make a single contact with the outside world once arriving in Philly; he may well have picked a red card from the Pericolo's slick deck, but the Queen of Hearts hadn't squelched the man's suspicions….

The phone in Mitch's room had been bugged, and he couldn't drive to McDonald's for a burger and fries without spotting a "tail." Whether brushing his teeth or watching TV or adding up columns in Pericolo's ledger books, he got the sneaking suspicion that he was being watched. Two-way mirrors...or paranoia?

Mitch discounted anxiety when, on a warmer-than-usual January day—the kind that gets folks hoping for an earlier-than-usual spring—he made it to a secure phone. He'd dialed FBI Headquarters in Washington, D.C., but Bradley hadn't been in, so he'd talked to Parker instead. "What's the weather like down there?"

"Same as there, I reckon...ice, snow, freezing...."

Mitch hadn't wanted to break the connection. He'd been in Philly for over a month by then, and the stress of being on Pericolo's payroll was beginning to take its toll. He hadn't been sleeping. Had lost ten pounds. And Ciara was never far from his mind....

He was about to leave a message for Bradley, when he spotted a black Cadillac rounding the corner. He'd seen that car in the rearview mirror nearly every time he'd climbed behind the wheel of his Ford. Mitch banged the phone into its cradle and quickly blended in with the crowd of people milling around the hot dog vender's cart. It had been a close call. Too close. And Giovanni must have agreed, because his men pressed in closer still after that.

Like a babe in the woods, Mitch had no protection in Philadelphia. He had no way to ask for help if he needed it. Didn't even have a weapon. He couldn't risk another phone call...until last week, when he finally got hold of Bradley to say he was in the Philadelphia Metro station. "Had to leave the car, the clothes, the laptop behind," he'd explained, "but I've got photocopies like you wouldn't believe. There's enough in my wallet to get me back to D.C. on the Amtrak. I'll call you when I get in."

Prayer had helped get him that far. Mitch hoped it would be enough to get him through this phone call.

"Hello?"

It felt so good to hear her voice that Mitch found himself swallowing a sob. "Hi, Ciara."

He heard her gasp. "Mitch? Is that…is it really you?"

Thank you, God, he thought, because she sounded genuinely pleased to hear his voice. He hadn't expected that. Not after the way they'd parted. Not after seven whole months apart. You don't deserve a woman this understanding, he admitted.

"I—I thought," she stammered, "it's been…you were…I just—" After a slight pause, her voice tightened. "Where have you been?"

He said it softly, gently, because that's exactly how he felt. "Sweetie, I wrote you…." At least he'd managed to get that one message through before Philadelphia had swallowed him up. Mitch thanked God again.

"Give me credit for having *some* intelligence, Mitch. I admit my behavior that last night was a little out of line, but to punish me this long…"

"Punish you?" He sat forward in his chair. What on earth is she talking about? He took a calming breath. "I know the letter was vague, but I couldn't give you any details. It would have been too dan—"

"What letter, Mitch? I never saw any letter. The only explanation I got about your disappearance was from your father and your brothers. 'All in the line of duty,'" she sing-songed, the quote thick with sarcasm.

"But…" Now he understood why that sense of dread had loomed over him when he'd handed the envelope to Bradley.

"But *nothing*. All I can say is, thank God for Lieutenant Bradley. He stopped by every week to see if I needed anything…and tell me you'd missed another rendezvous.

Which told me one of two things—either you were in too
much danger to keep the appointments, or you didn't *want*
to keep them." There was a long pause before she added,
"He never said it outright, but I got the impression he
believed it was the latter."

"Bradley's a bald-faced liar," he blurted out. "I can't
believe he never gave you that letter!"

Until the pencil he was holding snapped, Mitch hadn't
realized how tense he'd grown. He dropped the pencil
halves and ran his hand through his hair. Bradley had put
him out there alone, and he'd left Ciara the same way.
Burning anger roiled in his gut. He didn't know what
Bradley had to gain by his blatant lies—and he'd obviously told Ciara a pack of them—but he knew this much,
he thought, balling up a fist, he had better not run into him,
because what he would do to him would cost him his
badge.

Mitch gulped down a mouthful of cold black coffee. He
would deal with Bradley later. "I can be home by noon."

Home. The word reverberated in his mind like gentle
rain, defusing his fury.

"Don't hurry on my account," she snapped. "You've
been away from *home*," she said, putting an entirely different emphasis on the word, "for seven long months.
What's another couple of hours?"

He stared at the buzzing receiver for a moment before
hanging up. She had a perfect right to be upset. He only
hoped when the time was ripe, God would feed him the
words that would make things right.

He never would have agreed to take the case if he'd
known he would be gone so long, but once he'd gone in,
one week became two, and before he knew it, months had
passed. There had been no turning back then. Not if he'd
wanted to survive.

An icy sense of dread inched up his spine as he recalled

the last thing Pericolo had said to him. "I'm fairly certain that the last words of men who dared to betray me were 'I'm sorry.'" His near black eyes had glittered when he made his hateful promise. "I have a long memory, Mr. Sam Lewis, and an even longer reach. Don't *you* become one of the 'sorry' ones."

Did the Colombian pack enough power to extend that "reach" beyond the walls of his prison cell? The U.S. Attorney didn't think so. "He's a has-been," the man assured Mitch. "Eduardo Chambro has been chomping at the bit to get control. Kovatch told me he said he owes you a debt of gratitude for getting Pericolo out of his way."

Mitch could only hope the lawyer had been right…and pray that all of Pericolo's soldiers were now loyal Chambro followers.

A moment ago he'd wanted nothing more than to get his hands on Chet Bradley. Now he only wanted to cuddle up with Ciara, close his eyes and let her kiss his worries and fears away, as she'd done on their wedding night, when the horrible dream woke him. Tiny as she was, she'd wrapped him in her arms and made him feel safe and secure and *loved.*

He refused to focus on her angry words, chose instead to remember the relief he'd heard when she'd said, "Mitch? Is that you?" The melody of her voice had been enough to raise goose bumps on his flesh. If it had been that good to *hear* her, Mitch could only imagine how much better would it be to *see* her. And once they were face-to-face, the misunderstanding would fade away.

After rushing through the final paragraphs of his report, he filed it, then drove like a madman around the D.C. beltway toward their home in the Baltimore suburbs. He'd spent a total of four nights in their new Cape Cod-style home on Sweet Hours Way before their argument…before going undercover. It would be good, so *good,* to sleep beside her tonight in their low-ceilinged room at the top of the stairs.

It wasn't quite 10:00 a.m. when he pulled into the drive. She wasn't expecting him till noon. Mitch glanced at the window on the second floor. Their bedroom. Was she up there, getting ready for him, applying mascara, spritzing herself with perfume, brushing her long, lush hair?

He ached to see her, hold her, kiss her sweet lips.

Mitch slid the wallet from his back pocket and withdrew the photograph he'd been carrying for nearly a year now, the one his brother Ian had taken during the church-sponsored cruise. Mitch's big fingertips gently caressed her glossy image—as they'd done thousands of times since he'd left her that cold, bleak night—and smiled tenderly.

There had been other pictures he might have chosen to carry with him—Ciara, looking like a fairy princess in her wedding gown; Ciara in the pink suit she'd worn after the reception; Ciara in sweats and a baseball cap on the day they'd moved into this house. But this, by far, was his favorite.

Weeks after his family and hers had walked away from the cruise ship, long after the film was developed, Ian would look at this picture and remark, "Y'know, you two look good together. You're a perfect fit."

Mitch couldn't deny it then. He couldn't deny it now.

Everything about them was different—size and weight and coloring, and the contrasts were good. She was femininity personified, he, man to the bone, and the balance was right.

He recalled the events leading up to the taking of this picture. They'd been too busy swimming, sight-seeing, playing shuffleboard, to watch the sun set. Once, she'd been sitting in a deck chair, so caught up in her book that she didn't hear the gaggle of kids headed her way. If he

hadn't scooped her up, they'd have run right into her. "My
hero," she'd said, grinning and fluttering those long, dark
lashes of hers.

That night they scheduled a time to watch the sun set.
Arm in arm, they'd positioned themselves at the boat's
bow, waiting to see the blazing fireball slip behind the
horizon and disappear. When it finally disappeared, like
a coin in slow motion, sliding into a slot, she'd faced him,
and in a womanly, wifely way, tucked his windblown
necktie back into his jacket. She hadn't removed her hands
once she'd finished. Instead, Ciara had looked up at him
and smiled. From the dreamy, wide-eyed expression on
her face, he had expected her to say. "It's such a lovely
evening," or "Isn't the view spectacular?" Instead she'd
grinned mischievously. "My stomach's growling like an
angry bear. What say we hunt ourselves up a snack?"

"You're a little nut," he'd said, gently chucking her
chin.

She'd bobbed her head and launched into her own
musical rendition of the once-popular candy bar commer-
cial: "Sometimes I feel like a nut—" her silliness slipped
away, like the sun's fading light "—sometimes I don't...."

That quickly the mood shifted, from lighthearted merriment to something he hadn't been able to identify. He
only knew that his heart was thumping and his pulse was
pounding as she looked into his eyes.

They skipped dinner that night, preferring instead to
stand at the prow until the earth darkened and the black
sky above the cruise ship was haloed by the glow of the
midnight moon. The boat rocked gently as it slogged
through the inky island waves. She'd pointed toward the
horizon. "The water is so bright, so clear blue during the
day. Amazing, isn't it, that now it looks like black velvet."

He'd grasped her shoulders, turned her to face him. It
was as he gazed into her eyes...eyes as bright and clear

blue as the daytime Caribbean, that he knew how to define that look—love. And he'd kissed her, long and hard, as if to seal it between them for all eternity.

He'd walked her to her cabin, kissed her again in the narrow hall outside the door. "Let's do this again tomorrow," he'd whispered.

"Which," she'd asked, wiggling her brows suggestively, "the walk around the deck or the kiss?"

"Both."

And so they had. The very next evening, Mitch missed the sunset altogether, because he hadn't been able to make himself focus on anything but Ciara. After an hour or so of gazing into her eyes, listening as she talked about the kids in her fourth-grade class at Centennial Elementary, as she told him about her golden retriever, Chester, he wrapped her in his arms, pulled her close.

"Oh, my," she'd gasped, fanning her face with a delicate hand when the kiss ended. "You're getting pretty good at that."

Grinning like a love-sick schoolboy, he'd placed a hand upon her cheek, and she'd copied his movement.

That's when Ian snapped the picture.

Looking at this photo of them, outlined by the amber-orange sky, had brought him countless hours of comfort, had given him immeasurable peace in Philly, as he crossed the days, the weeks, the months off the calendar pages.

She was a vision, brighter and more beautiful than any sunset ever photographed. Her hair riffled by the breeze, billowing out behind her like a sunny sail as sun-sparkled waves danced in the background. It was a profile shot, a silhouette almost, with the fire yellow light of evening shimmering around her head like a golden halo.

He'd worn an ordinary summer suit. Nothing ordinary about Ciara's outfit! Even if he didn't have the picture to remind him of it, Mitch knew he'd never forget that dress.

It was pale blue, and made of a flimsy material that floated around her shapely calves on salty air currents. She'd wrapped a matching gauzy shawl around her narrow shoulders, and with every slight draft, it fluttered behind her like angels' wings.

He hadn't seen his bride in seven long months. Their last evening together had been little more than an accumulation of angry words and misunderstanding, and they hadn't communicated, in any way since that night…thanks to Chet Bradley. He wanted their reunion to be so much more…the fulfillment of seven months of yearning and loneliness and dreams.

Would she be his angel still?

Would he be her hero?

When he walked into headquarters, that's exactly what Parker had called him. And so had the TV reporter who'd wanted to interview the man who'd snagged Giovanni Pericolo. Admittedly the case had ended well, with everything falling neatly into place. But Mitch knew he couldn't have done it without Pericolo's help.

Smart as he was, Giovanni had made a stupid mistake: because he'd outwitted the Feds so often, he'd begun to believe himself invincible. Feeling cocky and full of himself, he'd boldly marched down to the Immigration office and applied for U.S. citizenship. And because he'd never been formally charged with any crime, he had as much right to pledge allegiance to the flag as any other immigrant. He greased a few palms, cutting through the usual red tape, and two weeks before Mitch uncovered the final piece of evidence to convict him, Giovanni Pericolo stood among several hundred soon-to-be Americans, raised his right hand and swore to honor his new nation.

The U.S. Attorney's office would have had a long, expensive fight on its hands, had Pericolo still been a full-fledged Colombian when the charges hit the fan. But

Giovanni's dream of becoming a U.S. citizen became his nightmare; he would never enjoy the perks of being a free American from his four-by-eight-foot prison cell.

The praise of Mitch's comrades and a few extra dollars on his paycheck were worthless if he couldn't have Ciara. He needed her steady, sure love now more than ever, to help blot the grotesque images of this case from his mind. He remembered how she'd reacted to the scar on his rib cage, to the news of Abe Carlson's death. It wasn't likely he'd ever tell her any of the details of the Pericolo case. If it messed up a hard-nosed Fed like you this much, he told himself, think what it'll do to a sweet little thing like Ciara.

Mitch tucked the photo back into his wallet and checked the time. Ten-thirty. Too early to knock?

He glanced at the front door. It had been painted black when he'd left home. Ciara had given it a coat of rust-red, and it reminded him of the bright, welcoming doors of Ireland's thatched cottages.

A lot had changed around here in the months he'd been gone, Mitch noticed. Spindly tree branches that had been brown and bare on the cold December night when he'd left now combed the clouds with leaves of every verdant hue. And in flower beds that once sat barren and bleak beneath the many-paned windows, white daisies and pink zinnias bobbed their brightly blossomed heads. She'd planted clumps of hosta along the shaded, curving walkway, yellow tea roses beside the privet hedge.

All by herself she'd transformed what had been an ordinary yard into a warm and welcoming retreat. He could only imagine what magic she'd performed inside, what more she might have been able to accomplish…if he'd been here, at her side.

Mitch got out of the car and slammed the door, wondering what to say when they were face-to-face for the first time in so many months. How are you? You're looking well. Don't shoot…I'm unarmed, he added with a wry grin.

Hands in his pockets, he debated whether to ring the bell or use his key. She had no doubt grown accustomed to her solitary status; he might frighten her if he barged in as he would have done before their fight.

He shook his head, hoping the hundreds of prayers he'd said while undercover had inspired the Lord to soften Ciara's heart. Taking a deep breath, he straightened to his full height and rang the bell.

Ten seconds, twenty ticked by before impatience made him ring it again.

"Don't get your socks in knots," came her voice from the other side of the door, "I'm movin' fast as I can…."

Mitch grinned. At least that hasn't changed, he thought. She's still the same little spitfire.

The light coming through the peephole darkened. His heart hammered with anticipation; maybe she would decide not to open the door when she saw who was standing on her porch.

But the door did open, slowly, and she peeked out from behind it. "Mitch," she whispered, blue eyes wide, "you're early."

He wanted to take her in his arms and hold her close, inhale the fresh clean scent of her soap and shampoo, kiss her as she hadn't been kissed…in seven months. "Didn't take as long as I thought to finish up the report."

Ciara stepped back, smiling a bit as she opened the door wider. "Well, come on in. The electric company already gets enough of my hard-earned money without air-conditioning the front yard, too."

Mitch glanced around the sunny foyer. Last time he'd been in this part of the house, the floor had been piled high with as-yet-unpacked boxes. Now he could almost see his reflection in the highly polished hardwood. "Smells like pine," he remarked, shoving his hands back into his pockets. "Nice…reminds me of my grandma's house."

The way she stood, half hidden by the door, Mitch had barely seen her. He yearned for an eyeful, and faced her now, fully prepared to apologize, eat crow or humble pie, or whatever else it took to get back into her good graces. He wanted to tell her how awful these months without her had been, how sorry he was for having left the way he had, how many thousands of times he'd thought of her. His gaze started at her tiny, white-sneakered feet, climbed to the shapely legs inside the black stretch pants—

And froze on her protruding abdomen.

"What's the matter, haven't you ever seen a pregnant woman before?"

He forced himself to look away from her well-rounded belly. Her eyes seemed bigger, bluer, longer-lashed than he remembered, but there were dark circles beneath them now. And despite her swollen stomach, Ciara appeared to have lost weight. "Well, sure I have. It's just, well…"

"I'm eight months along," she said, answering his unasked question. "You were gone a month when I knew for sure."

He did the math in his head. "So…so you were—"

Ciara nodded. "We didn't know it then, but we were 'in a family way' on the night you left."

To learn that he was going to be a daddy, in this sudden, unexpected way, was by far the biggest shock Mitch had ever experienced. A myriad of emotions flicked through his head. One moment he was overjoyed at the prospect of fatherhood, the next, terror thundered in his heart, because, what did *he* know about being a dad? On the one hand it thrilled him to know that the girl of his dreams was carrying his child, on the other, his stomach churned as it dawned on him that she couldn't have informed him.

She had gone through all this alone.

Mitch didn't know whether to throw his arms around her or get on his knees and beg her forgiveness or continue standing there, gaping with awe at the sight of her.

Ciara headed for the kitchen. "I'm going to have some lemonade. Can I pour you a glass?"

Mitch stood alone in the foyer a moment, staring after her, then followed her down the hall. "Are you all right? Is everything okay? With you and the baby, I mean?" he began, falling into step beside her. "Gee, Ciara, I wish I had known...."

She opened the refrigerator door, wincing as though the slight effort caused her discomfort. "I *tried* to tell you," she said again. Ciara inclined her head and placed a fingertip beside her chin. "Goodness. It seems our devious Lieutenant Bradley has been scheming on *both* sides of the street!"

The sarcasm rang loud, and Mitch knew it was proof she didn't believe he'd written any letter. Mitch clenched his jaw, fully prepared to tell her what he thought of Lieutenant Bradley. But when he noticed her, struggling to lift the half-full pitcher from the fridge, his ire died.

This isn't like her, he told himself. She was always such a sturdy little thing. Instinctively, he relieved her of it. "Sit down, will you, before you fall down," he scolded. Frowning, he added, "You look..."

"Terrible?"

"Yeah." His cheeks reddened as he realized he'd unintentionally insulted her. "No, of course not. Well, gee whiz, Ciara," he fumbled, "haven't you been taking care of yourself at all?"

"Well, golly gee, Mitch," she mocked, hefting her bulk onto a long-legged stool at the snack bar, "you sure are great for a girl's ego."

He grimaced. "I didn't mean to— It's just that you look like you haven't slept in—"

"I *haven't* slept in days."

"In your condition," he continued, "shouldn't you be paying more attention to your health? You know, eating smart, taking vitamins, getting plenty of rest…."

"*You* try sleeping with a watermelon superglued to your body, Mahoney, see how well you rest!"

Ciara pointed to the cabinet above the dishwasher. "Since you're so determined to '*do*' for me," she said, "the glasses are in there. And while you're pouring, give this some thought, Secret Agent Man—you can't just waltz in here after all this time and start bossing me around." She aimed a forefinger at him. "And stop pretending you're so concerned about my well-being. I might have appreciated it…*seven months ago!*"

Anger had put some color back into her pale cheeks, and the flash had returned to her blue eyes. If she didn't look so all-fired beautiful, he might have shouted his response. As it was, Mitch's defense was barely audible. "I'm not pretending anything. I wrote you, the night I left, and I tried—"

She tucked in one corner of her mouth and raised a brow. "Maybe it would have been a good idea to attend a couple of those meetings Chet scheduled, so he could have delivered your concerns." Ciara tucked a wayward lock of hair into her ponytail. "He warned me you'd have a list of lame excuses for not having been in touch."

He'd known the guy more than a decade, and even *he* didn't call him Chet. Mitch rummaged in the freezer for a handful of ice cubes, dropped them noisily into the tumblers. *"Chet?"*

"He asked me to call him by his first name," Ciara explained, "and I agreed because—" she frowned, crossed both arms over her chest "—because at least *he* was here for me, every week of the seven months you were gone."

"Here for you?" he thundered. "If he didn't deliver my

letter to you, and he didn't give you any news at all, exactly what was he here *for,* Ciara?" He glared at her for a moment, then poured the lemonade and shoved a glass toward Ciara. He sat the pitcher down with a thud, splattering the countertop with drops.

"So you're saying you wrote a letter," she said, grabbing a napkin to blot up the mess, "personally handed it to Lieutenant Bradley, and he didn't bother to deliver it."

"That's what I'm saying."

"And you expect me to believe that?"

"Yes, I do."

His words hung in the air like a spiderweb, intricately taut, yet fragile enough to disintegrate with the slightest disturbance. The last time he'd spoken the words, he'd stood in front of the altar at the Church of the Resurrection. "Do you, Mitchell Riley Mahoney, take this woman to be your lawfully wedded wife?" Pastor Rafferty had asked. Heart pounding with anticipation, and love, and joy, Mitch had gazed deep into Ciara's eyes, taken her small hand in his and breathed, "Yes, I do."

Her voice brought him back to the present. "I'm surprised you're having so much trouble with the numbers…considering you have an accounting degree and all. When you left me seven months ago, you said you'd be back in a few hours." She wasn't smiling when she tacked on, "Were you lying to me then, or are you lying to me now?"

"I've never told you a lie, Ciara. And I don't see how you can say I—"

"There's a lot you don't see, Mahoney, because you've got your blinders on again, just like…just like the lieutenant said."

Mitch snorted, knowing she'd hesitated because she'd wanted to say "Chet" instead of "lieutenant." "Your buddy

Chet doesn't know diddly about me, Ciara, but it's beginning to look like even *he* knows me better than you do."

She shrugged. "Can't get to know a man who isn't around."

He planted both palms flat on the counter, leaned forward until they were nearly nose to nose. "Listen, I don't know what he told you—or why—but I know this— I had a tail on me every minute. If I had tried getting in touch with you, we'd both be—"

He clamped his jaws together, knowing he'd just put himself between the proverbial rock and the hard place. By admitting he couldn't contact her, he was supporting her claim that his job was too dangerous.

Just tell her you love her, Mahoney. That's what she needs to hear right now; you can work out the rest of this mess later. He opened his mouth to do just that when the tight, skeptical look on her face stopped him cold. His lips formed a thin straight line. "Seven months ago you asked me to choose. Sounds to me like *you've* chosen to believe that slimeball Bradley over me." He ground his molars together. "Believe whatever you want," he snarled. "Everything I've said is true."

Her eyes misted, and she swallowed. "While you were gone, I saw a movie about an agent who went undercover. *He* managed to call his wife. Even managed to sneak off and *visit* a few times!"

"This isn't Hollywood, Ciara. In the real world we do things by the book…or *die*."

"It was based on fact."

"Did your buddy *Chet* tell you that story, too?"

Ciara only stared at him, eyes blazing and lips trembling. "You know what, Mitch?" she said after a moment. "I was an independent woman before we met, and believe it or not, I managed quite well after you left…once I got used to the idea. I'll admit, those first couple of weeks were pretty rough, but look around you," she added, upturned palms drawing his attention to their surroundings, "I got a lot accomplished, *all by myself.* This house is a home now, thanks to the endless hours I've spent working on it…*alone.*"

Suddenly she was on her feet, pacing back and forth across the black-and-white linoleum tiles, arms swinging, eyes flashing. "What was I to think, when you vanished like something from a magic show…and never came back?" she demanded, coming to a halt in front of him.

"I've given it a lot of thought and prayer since you stormed out of here that night." Hands on her hips, she raised her chin slightly. "I think it would be best if you just packed your things and moved out."

In response to his grim expression, she tossed in, "I can afford the mortgage on this place, thanks to my teacher's salary, so don't you worry about how I'll manage. In fact, every time one of your checks arrived from the Bureau, I put it into *my* bureau, uncashed. I didn't need your help turning the house into a home, and I don't need your money to stay in it. And I *am* staying, because it's a nice, safe neighborhood, with plenty of children, and good schools, and…"

She has every right to be angry, he told himself. She's been alone for a long time, not in the best of health, listening to Bradley's lies. Maybe if he sat quietly and let her vent, the anger and resentment would fade, and she'd look at him the way she had on the cruise ship, as she had at the altar, on their wedding night….

The cruise ship, the marriage, the separation, the pregnancy. All these things had happened in less than a year, yet it seemed like an eternity to him now.

Mitch leaned against his stool's backrest, wondering what she'd do if he just gathered her up in his arms and silenced her with a big kiss. But before he had a chance to put his plan into action, she plunged on, fingers drawing quotation marks in the air, reminding him of something he'd said the night he left:

"So don't feel 'duty-bound' to take care of me. I know your old-fashioned need to meet your responsibilities is supposedly the reason you work as hard…and as *long* as you do, but…"

Was it his imagination, or had her face paled even more in the last few minutes? All this ranting and raving couldn't be good for her *or* the baby. Suddenly it didn't matter who was right and who was wrong. Calming her down, that was all that mattered.

"Ciara, I know I said those things," he began, his voice softly apologetic, "but I never meant it to sound as though taking care of you is a burden. Bottom line—I love you. Have since the day we met, will for the rest of my life. Providing for you will always be an honor, a privilege." He grinned slightly. "Believe me, I've had plenty of time to think about that while…"

Oh, how she *wanted* to believe him! But Ciara had convinced herself that she must focus on the pain his absence had caused in those early days, when she'd been forced to admit the ugly truth: the oath he'd taken for the Bureau meant more to him than the vows he'd made to her. She loved him with everything in her, but if she was going to survive, if her heart was ever to heal, she must stand firm on this issue. She could *not* give in simply because he was standing there, looking at her with those sad brown eyes of his, imploring her to be something she believed she could not be.

She forced a cold, careless tone into her voice that she did not feel. "I'm sure you *did* have lots of time to think while you were away. Well, guess what, James Bond? While you were off living your life of adventure, I had a little time to think, too, and…"

He held up a hand to silence her. "I want to show you something," he said quietly, pulling out his wallet. Slapping her photograph on the counter, he said, "You see that? *That's* what kept me going for seven months. *That's* what gave me the incentive to think smart, to do whatever it took to drag my sorry self home.

"I won't deny that before I met you, I liked the danger and excitement of undercover work, but back then, getting the job done was the only focus." Mitch shrugged, then emphasized his point. "That's why I took unnecessary chances. That's how I accomplished in nine years what it takes most agents twenty. Because who was I, that my passing would make such a difference?"

She picked up the photograph. He must have held it in his big, strong hands hundreds of times, and the proof was that the paper it had been printed on now felt soft and supple as cotton. Her aching heart pounded. *All right, so maybe he loves you a little bit after all,* she thought.

But wait…something he'd said pinged in her memory. He couldn't possibly believe his life had no value, that his existence wasn't important to anyone. He mattered plenty—to his parents, his siblings and their children—to *her.*

Ciara handed back the photograph, tensing when their fingers touched, for she yearned to hold him, to be held by him. "Everyone would miss you if you were—" Ciara hesitated, unable to make herself say "killed in the line of duty." She began again. "A lot of people would be very upset if anything happened to you."

He dismissed her comment with a flick of his fingers.

Ciara straightened her back, reminded herself that she'd decided she couldn't, *wouldn't* go through that agony again. Even if she had the strength to survive the next case—and the next, and the one after that—their children deserved a full-time dad.

"I saved some of the boxes from our move," she began, looking anywhere but into his haunted eyes. "They're in the garage. If you like, I could pack for you. I wouldn't mind…." She was rambling and she knew it, but seemed powerless to stanch the flow of words. "Your brother, Ian, has an extra room, now that Patrick is off at college. Did you know he was accepted at Stanford? Of course you didn't…. Well, I'm sure Ian wouldn't mind if you stayed there until you found a place to—"

"Shut up, Ciara. Just *shut up*."

He'd never spoken to her in such a vulgar, vicious way before, and she felt a sharp pain, deep in the pit of her stomach.

"I realize I've messed things up pretty well," he said, "but I think we can work this out." He took her hand in his. "Give me a chance to make all this up to you." Mitch stroked her fingertips. "Please?"

Hang tough! she reminded herself. Be strong, or these seven months that are behind you now will be a road map of the rest of your life. "Maybe you'd rather do the packing yourself," she continued, as if he hadn't spoken at all. "Or, we could do it together, to make the job go easier and faster."

"I don't believe this!" he bellowed, dropping her hand. "I know we didn't have much time together before—" He stopped. Took a deep breath. And, hands on her shoulders, he started again. "We had something special once. At least, I thought we did. I think it's worth fighting for. Let me prove that to you."

Ciara couldn't believe how much intense physical pain a moment like this could cause. Though she'd rehearsed it and rehearsed it, she'd never imagined it would ache this much.

In response to her strained silence, he walked away from her, stood his empty glass in the sink. "All right. I'll leave, if it's what you want. But…"

She doubled over and gripped her stomach with both hands. "Mitch," she groaned, slumping to the floor, "it hurts. Hurts bad."

Ciara had always been the type who poked fun at people who whined and complained about everyday aches and pains. He knew she must be in considerable agony to have admitted it straight-out like that. Kneeling, he wrapped his arms around her. "It's way too early for the baby, isn't it?"

She nodded. "Call 911."

"No time for that—could take the ambulance an hour to get here." He spoke in a calm, reassuring voice that belied the terror he felt…raw, surging fear like he'd never experienced on the job.

Mitch grabbed the telephone, seeing that she'd jotted her obstetrician's number on the tablet beside it. He dialed, explained that they were on their way to the hospital and hung up. "The nurse says Dr. Peterson will meet us there," he said, gently helping her to her feet. And as if she weighed no more than a baby herself, lifted her in his powerful arms and carried her to the front door.

She melted against him like butter on a hot biscuit. Unconsciously he pressed a kiss to her temple. "Have you been taking childbirth classes?" he asked, kicking the door shut behind them. He wanted to kick *himself*, because he should have been beside her at those classes.

She burrowed her face into the crook of his neck. "Yes," came her hoarse reply.

"Who's your coach?"

"Mom."

"What would she be doing," he asked opening the car door, "if she were here right now?"

Ciara began to sob uncontrollably. "I don't want to lose the baby, Mitch. I love it so," she said, one arm hugging her tummy. "I don't think I've ever been more afraid…."

He'd never seen her cry before. He wanted to hold her this way forever. Comfort her. Tell her whatever she needed to hear. But there wasn't time for that now. Gently he put her into the car. "You're not going to lose the baby, sweetie." He ran a hand through her hair. "The best thing you can do is stay calm. Right?"

Nodding, she wiped her eyes as he pulled the seat belt around her. Ciara grabbed his hand as he clicked the buckle into place. "I don't know how well I'd be handling this if I were alone."

Without even thinking, he placed a quick kiss on her cheek. "You're never gonna be alone again, sweetie, not if I have anything to say about it."

As he ran around to his side of the car, she couldn't help but admit how much she wanted to believe him. *Oh, Mitch, please don't give me false hope, especially not now....*

It was as he shifted into Reverse that Ciara noticed her blood on his hands. He followed the direction of her gaze and gasped involuntarily.

"'It's nothing,'" she rasped, quoting word for word what he'd said when she'd first noticed his bullet wound, "'a flesh wound. No big deal.'"

Mitch turned on the flashers and the headlights, and prayed for all he was worth: *No traffic, no potholes, no red lights,* he begged God as he pealed away from the curb. He glanced over at her, held his breath when he saw how much blood had already soaked the seat. *Get us to the hospital, Lord, and us get there fast!*

Chapter Four

"What do you mean, I can't go with her?" Mitch demanded.

The nurse was nearly his height and likely outweighed him by fifty pounds. She tilted back her red-haired head and held up one hand like a traffic cop. "You'll only be in the way. Now have a seat," she ordered, pointing to the chairs against the wall.

Mitch didn't want a confrontation with this woman. He just wanted to be with his wife. He'd promised never to leave her alone again. He couldn't let her down. Not now.

Ciara had looked so frail and fragile when the orderlies put her on the gurney, so pale and drawn it was hard to tell where she ended and the starched white sheets began. She'd reached out her hand as they wheeled her past, but in the flurry of activity, he couldn't get close enough to take hold of it. The last thing he saw were her teary eyes, wide with fear and pain.

"Listen, lady," he ground out, "that's my *wife* in there, and she needs me. No amount of your self-important hoo-ha can stop me from going in there."

He took a step, and she blocked it. Crossing both arms

over her ample chest and tapping a white-shoed foot on the shining linoleum, her eyes narrowed. "I'm calling Security," she snapped.

"You do what you have to do," he shot back, shrugging, "and I'll do what I have to do." With that he barged into the emergency room. Almost immediately he felt guilty for having behaved like a caveman, but he'd have done whatever it took to be near Ciara.

"Did you see where they took my wife?" he asked the first nurse he saw.

"Little blonde, pregnant out to here?" she asked, making a big circle of her arms.

He nodded.

"Second bed on the right. Now, stop lookin' so worried, hon. Women have babies every day...I've had seven, myself. Trust me," she said with a wave of her hand. "It's a cakewalk."

He didn't bother to point out how elaborate and difficult cakewalks had been for the slaves who'd competed for slices of dessert.... "Thanks," he said, and headed for his wife's cubicle.

"Mitch," she sighed when she saw him. "I heard all the ruckus. I didn't think you'd ever get past her...."

He kissed her cheek, then flexed his bicep to lighten the tense atmosphere. "Hey, it's gonna take more than one coldhearted nurse to keep me away from you, especially now."

She smiled feebly, gave his hand a grateful little squeeze.

"So how're you feelin', sweetie?" he asked, pulling a chair closer to the bed.

"I'm okay," she whispered.

But she wasn't, and he knew it. Smoothing wispy blond bangs from her forehead, he looked into her blue eyes. It was hard to tell the agony from the fear. He felt incredibly powerless, because she was bleeding and in pain, and there wasn't a thing he could to help her. Where were the doctors? And the nurses? Did they intend to let her lie here and bleed to death? Did they…

Well, there was *something* he could do!

Mitch leaped up and stomped toward the pastel-striped curtains. "Hey," he hollered, half of him in the cubicle, the other half leaning into the hall, "can we get some help in here? My wife is—"

A blue-smocked man blew past Mitch. "Mrs. Mahoney?"

Ciara nodded weakly.

"It's about time you got here," Mitch snarled, letting the curtain fall back into place.

Ignoring the husband's grumbling, the doctor stepped up beside Ciara. "First baby?" he asked, a knowing smile on his face.

Another nod, and a small smile, too.

"Well, don't you worry, little lady. We're gonna take real good care of you, I promise." He pulled the blood pressure cuff from a hard plastic pocket on the headboard. "You see, there was a six-car pileup on Route 95 about a half hour ago," he explained, his voice calm and reassuring as he fit it to her upper arm. "The paramedics brought in the last of the injured just minutes before you arrived." A half shrug. "Contusions and abrasions for the most part, but the nurses are hot-footing it, just the same."

He stood silent for a moment, reading the gauge, then put everything back where he'd found it. "You don't mind a lowly resident working on you, do you?" he asked, scribbling a note on the file attached to the clipboard he held.

"It takes a lot of hard work to become a resident," Ciara said, smiling. "There's nothing 'lowly' about your position."

She's lying there getting weaker by the minute, Mitch

thought, and he's making small-talk! Frustration got the better of him. "It's been my experience," Mitch interrupted, "that chitchat can't stop hemorrhaging…."

"Mitch," Ciara protested, a restraining hand on his forearm, "it's all right, I'm—"

"First of all, Mr. Mahoney," the young doctor said, writing another note in Ciara's file, "your wife is losing some blood, but she's not in immediate danger. Secondly, I have a wife, and a kid, myself. If either of them were here now, I'd be breathing fire, just like you are." He clicked off his ballpoint and slid it into his shirt pocket. "Trust me," he said, meeting Mitch's eyes squarely. "We're going to do everything in our power for your wife and baby."

He didn't wait for Mitch's agreement or approval. Instead, he plowed through the curtains and began barking orders, commanding attention, demanding assistance. When he returned a moment later, shoving a tool-laden cart, he looked at Mitch. "How well do you handle the sight of blood?"

"He's an FBI agent," Ciara answered on his behalf. She sent Mitch a crooked little smile. "My husband has seen more than his share of blood."

The doctor snapped a pair of surgical gloves over his hands. One corner of his mouth lifted in a grin. "Stand over there, then, near the wall. If you don't get in the way, maybe I'll let you stay."

Mitch crossed both arms over his chest, fully prepared to follow the doctor's orders to the letter. He'd been away from her long enough. No way he would leave her now, especially not now. He pressed a knuckle against his lower lip, and watched.

He'd been on the scene when emergency medical technicians tended the victims of shootings, stabbings, near drownings. Once, he'd been the only one available to help a woman give birth to twins. Always before though, as his adrenaline had pumped and his heart raced, he'd managed to keep a professional distance from the lifesaving—or life-giving—experiences. Keeping an emotional arm's length from them had been easy, because the people involved had all been strangers.

Admittedly, he hadn't known the beautiful young woman on the gurney very long, but she was his wife, and the great bulge beneath the sheet that covered her was his unborn child. Unconsciously he began to gnaw his thumbnail.

As a small kid his mom was forever admonishing him to keep his fingers out of his mouth. By the age of seven, he'd left the habit behind, along with his nightlight and Peppy, the stuffed bear. And no matter how stress- or pressure-filled the situation, he hadn't chewed his fingernails since, not when he took his SATs, not when he sat for the CPA exam, not before the final test at Quantico.

A tiny stab of pain told him he was back at it again. Mitch searched for a napkin, a paper towel…anything that would blot the bloodstain from his thumb. He spotted some tissues on the small counter against the wall and plucked one from the box. Wrapping it around his thumb, he squeezed.

He tried to see Ciara. She was all but hidden from his sight as doctors, nurses, interns and residents gathered round. He felt like that seven-year-old nail-biter again. He'd been through terrifying situations. He'd faced death at point-blank range. Through it all, he hadn't shed a tear for himself, or anyone else involved. So why was he on the verge of tears now?

Because you could *lose* her, he admitted.

For the first time, Mitch understood how the bad guys must feel once they'd been snagged, frisked and cuffed, because *he* felt caught—smack between his career-focused, solitary life-style and the reality that without Ciara life would be meaningless.

Snap out of it, Mahoney! he berated himself, gritting his teeth. Pull yourself together, for Ciara's sake.

Mitch chanced a glance over his shoulder, caught a glimpse of her between the broad shoulders of the young resident and the shower-capped head of a nurse. He'd seen blood—his own, fellow agents', criminals'—hundreds of times. So why did the sight of Ciara's make him feel as if a tight band had been wrapped round his chest?

Mitch swiped at the sweat that had popped out on his forehead, discovered that his palms were damp, too. His ears started to ring, the room started to spin, and he realized if he didn't get out of there fast, he'd keel over.

He took another look at her: eyes closed, jaw clenched, fists bunched at her sides. She hadn't uttered a word of complaint since he'd cradled her, there on their kitchen floor, when she'd admitted how badly it hurt. You weak-kneed wimp, he chided himself. She's the one going through this, so why are you swooning like an old woman?

Mitch closed his eyes again, took a deep breath and prayed the extra oxygen would clear his head.

It didn't.

Pressing his forehead to the wall, he prayed the dizziness would pass, at least long enough for him to make it into the hall. He turned and headed for the curtain.

"Mitch," came her exhausted voice, "you're pale as a ghost. What's wrong?"

Humiliation washed over him like a tidal wave. Even in her weakened condition, and surrounded by half a dozen medical professionals, her thoughts were of him, not herself. He didn't know what minor miracle had prompted her to say yes when he'd asked her to marry him, but he knew he'd never done a thing in his life to deserve a woman like Ciara.

Too ashamed to meet her eyes, Mitch looked at the young doctor instead. "I, ah, I…"

"Get out of here, Mr. Mahoney," he said, frowning over his round-lensed glasses. "The room's too crowded as it is. I'll come for you when we're finished here, bring you up to speed."

With a nod of gratitude, and another of relief, Mitch hurried out of the cubicle. He slumped into the first chair he came to, a ghastly orange thing of molded plastic, being held up by four aluminum legs. What in God's name is the matter with you? he demanded of himself, an elbow resting on each knee. Mitch hung his head, stuck his face in his hands and prayed for all he was worth.

"Let her be all right," he whispered into the warm dark space between his face and his palms. "Give me a chance to show her how much she means to me…."

"You're doing fine," Dr. Peterson said, patting her hand.

"I'm so glad the hospital was able to get hold of you," she admitted.

"Relax, now. Everything's under control."

But was it?

The baby hadn't moved, not once, since—since right after Mitch had come home. She remembered the exact moment because, when she'd felt the baby stir, she had wanted to interrupt him, in the middle of explaining that he *had* written, to say, "Mitch…our baby is moving…give me your hand…."

Instead she'd stared into the handsome face of the man in her kitchen…her husband, yet a virtual stranger. Had she refrained from sharing that warm "baby" moment with him because he'd left her alone for seven long, lonely months? Or had she kept it to herself…to *punish* him for those months?

A little of both, she admitted, a twinge of guilt knotting in her heart.

"You doin' all right?" Peterson asked.

Ciara nodded.

"Then why the big sigh?"

"Oh, just talking to myself. I do it all the time."

He grinned. "Well, keep it down, will ya? We're tryin' to concentrate here."

His teammates snickered. "Yeah. You're noisier than a gaggle of geese," a nurse said.

"What's the matter," said another, "aren't you gettin' enough attention?"

Ciara smiled weakly. She knew the purpose of their lighthearted banter was to keep her calm, and while she appreciated their attempts to reassure her, she could have saved them the bother. Nothing could calm her as long as she was worried….

She was terrified, right down to the marrow of her bones, that the baby had stopped moving because something terrible had happened.

And what if Mitch didn't want the baby?

Possible, she thought, but not likely. He'd been so sweet and understanding during the drive from the house to the hospital, saying all the right things, patting her hand lovingly, concern flashing in his big brown eyes. But had it all been a joke, like those the doctors and nurses had been telling, to keep her quiet and still? If not, why had he dashed out of the room just now, looking like a deer with a hunter hot on its trail? And why had his usually ruddy complexion gone ashen? Perhaps because the sudden news had overwhelmed him….

She'd known from the moment he'd seen her belly that he would need time to come to grips with the fact that he'd be a father soon. She'd had *months* to get used to the idea—he'd had half an hour before the bleeding started.

Since they'd arrived at the hospital, she'd been lying there telling herself that, in time, Mitch would be as overjoyed and exuberant about the prospect of parenthood as she was.

But what if he wasn't?

Ciara's lower lip began to quiver, and she bit down to still it. Her eyes welled with tears, and she squeezed them to keep new ones from forming. Stay calm, she scolded herself, for the baby's sake.... But the lip continued to tremble, and the tears fell steadily.

"We're almost finished here, Ciara," Dr. Peterson said.

Sniffling, she summoned enough to control to say, "Um...the baby...hasn't moved, not once in all this time...."

"Perfectly normal under the circumstances. You've gotta give the little tyke credit...he's already smart enough to know when to lay low."

He?

Ciara's heart lurched as she pictured a miniature Mitch, running around the house on chubby bare feet. "So...the baby's all right?"

"We've had him monitored the whole time. If there was a problem, I'd have brought in a neo-natal special-ist, stat. Trust me."

His words calmed her, soothed her. She thanked God and all the saints and angels. Thanked God again.

So why on earth are you making a spectacle of yourself, she thought, embarrassed by the tears, the hiccuping sobs. Ciara crooked an arm over her eyes, like the child who thinks because he can't see his mama, mama can't see him, either.

"Get her husband back in here," the resident said to the nurse beside him. "He was lookin' a little green around the gills when I kicked him out. You'll probably find him in the men's room...."

"You know," the nurse said, cocking an eyebrow, "you're gonna be a fine surgeon someday."

He gave her a grateful grin. "You think so?"

"Uh-huh." Smiling, she shoved through the curtain.

"You're a natural…already a master at barking out orders and making nurses feel like peons."

He met Peterson's eyes, then Ciara's. "Nurses," he huffed good-naturedly, "can't live with 'em, can't live without 'em."

Ciara giggled nervously, and she didn't stop until Mitch wrapped his big warm hand around her small, cold one.

Once things were under control, Mitch stayed with Ciara while she slept, and Peterson left to make a few phone calls. When he returned, seeing that Ciara had fallen asleep, Dr. Peterson said, "I have a few questions, but I don't want to wake her." He stood at the foot of her bed, reading her chart. "Tell me, Mr. Mahoney, has she been staying off her feet, like I told her to?" he asked without looking up.

Mitch's heart pounded. She'd been told to stay off her feet? How long ago? And why? If she'd been told to rest, how did he explain the flower gardens, the spotless house, the—

Peterson was looking at him now, a puzzled frown furrowing his brow. Mitch knew it was a simple enough question. Knew, too, that the doctor was probably wondering why Ciara's husband didn't have a ready answer for it.

"It's my understanding that you've been out of town," the doctor said, peering over his half glasses at Mitch. "Maybe she hadn't had a chance to tell you everything…yet."

Mitch swallowed. *The man thinks you're a no-good husband…because that's what you are.*

"We've been carefully monitoring the baby for several weeks now, ever since Ciara started spotting." Narrowing his eyes, he said, "She didn't tell you *any* of this?"

He hung his head. "I'm afraid not." She hadn't told him

anything about the pregnancy, because he hadn't been around. The thought of her going through this alone caused a nagging ache inside him.

"Well, she does tend to be a secretive little thing, doesn't she?"

It was Mitch's turn to frown. "How do you mean?"

"Most young mothers—particularly first-time mothers— love to talk about their plans. You know," he said, shrugging, "the nursery, baby names, whether or not to breast feed...." He looked at Ciara. "Not your wife." After a long pause, Peterson met Mitch's eyes. The doctor cleared his throat. "What happened today is proof she hasn't been taking proper care of herself."

"What *did* happen, exactly?"

"Placenta previa. The baby gets its nourishment and eliminates its waste by way of the placenta, you see," he explained. "In Ciara's case, the placenta began separating a bit. That's what caused the bleeding."

His gaze fused to Mitch's. "She'll have to stay off her feet for the duration of the pregnancy. That means she'll need someone with her at all times." He glanced at his patient again. "From here on out, she cannot be left alone. Not even for short periods of time."

"That's impossible," Ciara said, her voice thick with drowsiness. "My parents are touring Europe. I couldn't get in touch with them, even if I wanted to."

Why can't *you* take care of her, Mr. Mahoney? was the question written on the doctor's face. He turned to Ciara. "Do you have a sister? An aunt? A grandma, maybe?" he asked instead.

"I'm the only child of only children," she stated, "and my only living grandmother is in a nursing home."

"Hmm. Well, that pretty well covers it, doesn't it." He thought for a moment, then said to Mitch, "You could hire a live-in nurse."

Ciara sighed. "They're bound to cost a small fortune." Passing a trembling hand over her worried brow, she added, "I know my teachers' insurance won't cover that. I doubt the agency's will, either."

Mitch was still bristling over the fact that the resident had also zeroed in on what he construed to be a problem between man and wife. Who does that little twerp think he is, sticking his nose in where it doesn't belong? "Doesn't matter if the insurance covers it or not," Mitch all but snarled. "We won't need any live-in nurse. I'm perfectly capable of taking care of my wife."

The doctor removed his glasses and gave Mitch a hard, appraising stare. "Day in, day out…."

What does he expect from me? Mitch asked himself. I come back from seven months undercover—life on the line every day of it—see my wife for the first time, and she's eight months pregnant! And during our first hour together, she collapses. "I have some R and R coming. I'll be there round the clock."

"I'll be back after I finish my rounds," he said, and headed for the door. He left nothing behind but the memory of his smug, know-it-all smirk. Harrumphing under his breath, Mitch remembered his dad's quote: "Give authority to a fool, and create a monster."

But in all fairness, the entire medical team had done a fine job. Mitch couldn't hold any of them accountable for the guilt roiling in his own gut…or for the shame boiling in his head.

You're the fool, he told himself. And if anybody's a monster, it's you. Because, hard as it was to admit, if he hadn't left Ciara alone all those months, she wouldn't have felt obliged to turn their house into a home all by herself. All that work, no doubt, put a terrible strain on her, mentally, physically….

He leaned his forearms over the bed's side rail, clasped

his hands together and watched her sleep. He'd watched her sleep on their wedding night, too. Then, as now, she'd breathed so lightly, he'd had to strain to hear her inhale and exhale, the whisper softness of her sighs, he imagined, were what angels' wings might sound like. What had he ever done in his life to deserve an angel for a wife?

Just before she'd collapsed, Ciara had asked him to pack his things and leave. He hadn't wanted to do anything of the kind at the time, and he certainly had no intention of doing that now.

Well, they'd be spending a lot of time alone together in the few weeks to come. With God's help, Mitch hoped, he could earn Ciara's forgiveness, could make up for the many months he'd left her alone. He would take better care of her than her mother would. Mitch fancied himself a fair-to-middlin' cook, and his stint in the navy had taught him a thing or two about keeping his quarters shipshape.

He tucked the covers under her chin, smoothed the bangs from her forehead. Lord, but she's lovely, he thought. Her gracefully arched brows set off the long, lush lashes that dusted her lightly freckled cheeks, and her perfectly shaped full lips drew back in the barest hint of a smile.

What are you smiling about, pretty lady? he wondered, tucking a tendril of honey-blond hair behind her ear. You married the village idiot, and now you're stuck with him…at least till our baby is born.

Our baby….

Gently, so as not to wake her, he laid a hand on her stomach. "Hey, little fella," he whispered. "How's it goin' in there? You don't know me yet, but I'm your—"

The baby kicked, and Mitch's heartbeat doubled. He'd never experienced anything quite like it in his life…the sudden, insistent motion of his child, squirming beneath his palm. Ducking his head, Mitch leaned in closer and lifted his hand, like a boy who'd captured a butterfly might steal a peek at his prize.

The breath caught in his throat when he saw something—a tiny knee? a little heel?—shift beneath Ciara's pebbly white blanket. The egg-sized lump reminded him of the way Scooter the hamster looked, scurrying beneath Mitch's little-boy bedcovers. Grinning like the Cheshire Cat, his hand covered the mound yet again, following its passage, until the baby finally settled down.

If he knew he had an audience, would he continue to smile? Would he keep his hand pressed to his wife's stomach? Would his gaze remain glued to the stirring of the child—*his* child—alive inside her?

Ciara didn't think so. And so she continued to watch him through the narrow opening between her eyelids. *Thank you, Lord,* she prayed, *for showing me that Mitch does want this baby as much as I do.*

They were going to be spending a lot of time together in the next few weeks. Perhaps in that time, with the Lord's guidance, they could find a way to repair the damage they'd done to their marriage. A girl can hope and pray, she told herself.

Chapter Five

Peterson insisted that Ciara spend the night in the hospital, where she and the baby could be constantly monitored. At midnight, as the floor nurse was busy taking Ciara's vital signs, the doctor ushered Mitch into the hall.

"If you're smart," he said under his breath, "you'll go home, right now, and get a good night's sleep, because starting tomorrow, she's going to need you for everything." There in the dim hallway light, he'd lowered his voice to a near whisper. "I don't want her on her feet *at all.*"

Mitch nodded.

"I know it's none of my business, Mr. Mahoney," the doctor added, "but it's obvious that *something* isn't right between you two." His voice took on a tone that reminded Mitch of his dad, scolding the four Mahoney boys when they allowed anything to interfere with school. The doctor continued, "Whatever your problems are, set them aside. Doesn't matter who's at fault or what it's all about. The only important thing right now is that we keep Ciara healthy so we can to take that baby to term."

Mitch remembered the thirty-six-week explanation:

it's the critical time, the doctor had said, after which the baby's vital organs are mature enough for survival outside the womb without requiring mechanical assistance.

Peterson's voice had come to him as from a long, hollow tube. He shook his head to clear the cobwebs and focused on the man's words. "You realize she's lost a lot of blood...."

Another nod.

"And she may lose more...."

He met Peterson's eyes. Suddenly Mitch understood why, despite the belly, it seemed she'd lost weight. "I thought the bleeding had stopped."

"It has, for now. But placenta previa is a progressive condition," he said matter-of-factly. "She'll have good days and bad days."

"Until the baby's born?"

The doctor nodded somberly. "I'm afraid so."

"Not as much as today...." Four more weeks of that, and she would waste away to nothing....

"I want you to understand the gravity of Ciara's condition, Mr. Mahoney."

As he waited for the doctor to explain it Mitch's stomach twisted into a tight knot. He gritted his teeth so hard, his jaws ached. And deep in his pockets, his nails were digging gouges in his palms.

"If the placenta should tear, even slightly more, Ciara could hemorrhage." He paused, giving Mitch time to wrap his mind around the seriousness of his words. "If it should separate completely, it will mean instant death for your child."

Mitch's head began to pound. "Wouldn't...wouldn't she be better off here, in the hospital, where you guys could keep an eye on her? I mean, if something like that happened at home..." He ran a hand through his hair, scrubbed it over his face. "At least here, she'd have everything she'd need—"

Shaking his head, Peterson said, "I disagree. Placenta previa is a very stressful disorder. The mother is constantly aware that one wrong move could be fatal, for the baby, and possibly for her as well. It's been my experience that mothers-to-be rest and relax far better in their own homes, surrounded by the things—and the people—they love."

Despite the air-conditioning, Mitch began to perspire. He couldn't get his mind off the possibility that, if he hadn't left her alone, none of this would be happening. "What causes plug…ah—"

"Placenta previa," Peterson said, helping him along. Shrugging, the doctor shook his head. "There's no cause or reason for it that we can determine. We only know that it's there, to one degree or another, from the beginning of the pregnancy."

"Should we…should we take precautions so she won't have this problem in the future?"

"Are you asking whether or not the condition will repeat itself in future pregnancies?"

Mitch nodded.

"Despite the way things look now, Ciara is a healthy young woman. There's no reason to believe her next pregnancy will be anything but perfectly normal, with absolutely no complications."

Mitch breathed a sigh of relief. *So if you can pull her through this one, Mahoney…* "I don't mind tellin' you, doc, I'm scared to death. What if I mess up? I mean, there are two lives on the line, here…my wife's and my child's. I can't afford to make a mistake. Not even a small one." He met Peterson's eyes. "You're sure she's better off at home? Because I want to do whatever is best for Ciara."

Peterson smiled for the first time since he'd met the man. "What you said just now is all the assurance I need that she'll be in the best of hands at home."

"But…but what if something goes wrong? What if the spotting turns into something more? What if—"

"I'm going to put in a call right now, so the equipment will be ready for delivery when you get home tomorrow."

"Equipment? What equipment?"

"The home monitor. Hooks up to the telephone and the TV, so we can get a look at what's going on without Ciara having to endure the trauma of driving back and forth for tests. Plus, every other day or so, a visiting nurse will stop by to see how things look, do a blood count. It's costly, but…"

"I don't give a whit about that. I only want what's best for Ciara and the baby." He hesitated. "How reliable is this equipment?"

Peterson's smile widened. "It'll do its job. You do yours, and everything will turn out just fine."

Mitch had undergone years of extensive training to become an FBI agent. Had never felt anything but capable and competent, even in the most dangerous of situations.

So why did he feel totally inept and inadequate now?

For the first half hour, Mitch walked through the house, turning on lights and investigating the contents of every room. Even his staff sergeant would have been hard-pressed to find a speck of dust anywhere. Everything gleamed, from the old-fashioned brass light fixtures hanging in the center of every ceiling to the hardwood and linoleum floors beneath his loafered feet.

He flopped, exhausted, into his recliner—a treat he hadn't enjoyed in seven long months—and put up his feet. From where he sat, he could see every award and citation he'd ever earned, hanging on the flagstone wall surrounding the fireplace. His guitar and banjo stood to one side of the woodstove insert, his collection of canes and walking sticks on the other. The ceramic wolves he'd acquired from yard sales and flea markets held up his hard-cover volumes of Koontz, King, Clancy and London.

The knowledge that, despite the way they'd parted, despite their many months apart, she'd turned this into "his" room swelled his heart with love for her…love and gratitude that she hadn't given up hope…no thanks to Bradley.

He grabbed the chair arms so tightly his fingertips turned white at the thought of his lieutenant's part in their separation. But one glance at their wedding portrait, framed in crystal beside the photo of Mitch taken as he trained at Quantico, cooled his ire. *You can deal with Bradley later,* he thought, grinding his molars together. *Right now, you have to concentrate on Ciara.*

Mitch closed his eyes and pictured her as he'd seen her last.

After thanking Peterson, he'd headed back to her hospital room, to tell her good-night and let her know he was heading home. Her eyes were closed, and thinking she was asleep, he'd started for the door.

"I'm glad to see you have *some* sense in your head," she'd said, her voice whisper-soft and drowsy. "It's about time you went home and got some rest."

He'd pulled the chair beside her bed closer, balanced on the edge of its seat. "How're you doin'? Feeling any better?"

"A little tired, but otherwise I'm fine." With a wave of her hand she had tried to shoo him away. "Go on, now. Get some sleep."

"I will," he'd said, taking her hand, "in a minute." He held her gaze for a long, silent moment. "You had me pretty scared there for a while." He kissed her knuckles. "It's good to see a little color back in your cheeks."

She'd smiled, sighed. "I'm sorry to be such a bother."

He kissed her knuckles again. "You must be delirious, because you're not making a bit of sense."

"I'm just trying to see things from your point of view. You come home from seven months of terrifying, dangerous, undercover work, and what do you find? Your wife, eight months pregnant and grouchy as a grizzly bear. And then—"

Gently, he'd pressed a finger over her lips. "Shhhh. You should be sleeping."

"True. At home. In my own bed. I know it's irrational, but I've always hated hospitals!"

"Dr. Peterson says you can come home tomorrow."

"But I feel fine. Why can't I—"

She'd looked so small, so vulnerable, lying there in that tilted-up hospital bed, that he couldn't help himself. Mitch leaned forward and silenced her with a tender kiss. A quiet little murmur had escaped her lips as she pressed a palm against his cheek. "You could use a shave, mister," she'd said, grinning mischievously as she rubbed his sandpapery whiskers, "unless you're going for that Don-Johnson-Miami-Vice look."

He'd assured her he wasn't, and promised to be clean shaven when he came to pick her up, first thing in the morning. Smiling now, Mitch opened his eyes and glanced at the carriage clock on the mantel. Two-thirty-five. And he still hadn't done anything to prepare for her homecoming….

Mitch dropped the recliner's footrest and got to his feet. Was the linen closet in the upstairs hall? Or was it the extra door in the main bathroom? He didn't have a clue, because they'd spent the first two weeks of their marriage traipsing back and forth between his condo in the city and her apartment in the suburbs as they'd waited for the former owners of the house to move out. And even after settlement, they'd spent alternate nights in his place or hers, too exhausted after putting in a full day at work, then packing all evening, to make the trip to their new home in Ellicott City.

They'd only been in the house, full-time, a few days when Mitch had left on assignment. And what with pictures leaning against every wall waiting to be hung, and stacks of books cluttering the floors, he'd spent most of that time picking his way through the mess.

Taking the stairs two at a time, he went in search of linens for Ciara's daytime bed.

The extra door in the bathroom, as it turned out, was where Ciara stored bathroom linens. Beneath neatly folded towels and washcloths, the shelves had been lined with muted green and blue plaid paper that matched the shower curtain. There had been a hideous black and silver wallpaper in here when they'd bought the place, and a putrid gray rug on the floor. Now, the walls were seafoam green, the door and window frames dusty blue. Like the family room, she'd chosen patterns and colors that were neither overly feminine nor masculine. "A man's home is his castle," she'd said when they'd discussed the changes they would make in the house. "When he comes home from a hard day's work, a man shouldn't be made to feel like he's about to be smothered by ruffles and chintz."

Mitch grinned and headed for the hall. He was beginning to understand why she'd been able to sweep him off his feet…. The things she'd said during their three-month courtship had dazzled him. No woman he'd known had ever talked of being there for him, of doing for him, of taking care of him. As he looked around at square-edged shams that topped off tailored comforters, at fabrics and carpeting and bold-framed prints—each that had been carefully selected and positioned—he realized Ciara had meant every word.

A pang of regret clutched his heart. You could have been enjoying this all these months. And where were you instead? Playing cops and robbers.

He opened the linen closet door, where sheets and

pillowcases, blankets and comforters had been tidily folded and stacked. He'd seen department store displays that didn't look half as orderly. On a high shelf he saw that she'd stowed away a delicate-looking pink-and-lavender-flowered sheet set. Beside it, a set with a bright blue background and big bold sunflowers. She'd put a lot of thought into making this house a home he'd be comfortable in. The least he could do was give equal care to which sheets he'd put on the bed where she'd be spending endless hours. The soft-toned floral pattern reminded him of Ciara…feminine, dainty, utterly womanly. But the sunflowers were like her, too, in that they were spritely, happy, youthful.

You could play it safe…put plain white sheets on the bed…. He bounced the idea around in his mind for a moment. In college, he'd learned a thing or two about the psychology of color. White symbolized purity, cleanliness, and often served as a pallet, an enhancer for other colors. It enlivened, energized, expanded spaces. Shades of purple offered comfort and assurance, while yellow created an atmosphere of energy and cheerfulness….

He grabbed the sunflowers and headed downstairs.

During his three-year stint in the navy, he'd learned a thing or two about making up a bed. Those lessons were for naught, since the sofa bed's mattress was too thin to turn sharp hospital corners, or tuck the ends under, ensuring a snug, smooth fit. But it would do for resting during the day.

During the drive home, he'd worked it all out in his head: at bedtime, he'd carry her upstairs and tuck her into bed, and in the morning, he'd carry her back down to the sofa bed. Because if he'd been the one who'd been confined to quarters for an entire month, he would go stir-crazy, alone in an upstairs room. Besides, she'd spent enough time all by herself already, thanks to him.

Mitch turned back the bedcovers in a triangle, as the maids on the cruise ship had done, smoothed them flat, then stood back to admire his handiwork. Nodding with approval, he headed for the kitchen. As he filled a tumbler with the lemonade she'd made that morning, Mitch noticed a red circle around today's date. It's three-fifteen in the morning; yesterday's date, he corrected, yawning, that's *yesterday's* date.... He squinted, read the reminder she'd printed in the date box. "Pick up Chester at Dr. Kingsley's."

He hadn't given a thought to the dog, and wondered what malady had put the retriever into the vet's office. Fleas? Ingrown toenails? Mange? He'd never been overly fond of canines, and Chester could be a miserable pest, sitting beside the bed at five in the morning, whining until Mitch or Ciara got up to let him out. Just one more of the compromises he'd made in order to get Ciara to agree to marry him.

She hated big-city life, so he'd sold his condo in the singles building near Baltimore's Inner Harbor and agreed to live in the suburbs. He didn't want a dog, but she'd had Chester for five years and couldn't part with him. He'd wanted to honeymoon in a johnboat on the Patapsco River, where he could spend a lazy week casting for trout; she'd wanted to luxuriate in the islands, where they'd met. And so they'd gone to Martha's Vineyard, spent two days fishing and two days walking on the windy beaches. Mitch had a feeling that in the weeks to come, he would experience *compromise* on an entirely new level.

He swallowed the last of his lemonade and headed upstairs, set the alarm for seven. Four hours' sleep would do; he'd gotten by, plenty of times, on less. After a quick shower and shave, he would look up Kingsley's address in Ciara's personal phone book. Wouldn't she be surprised when she got into the car, to find her shaggy pup hanging over the front seat to greet her!

Mitch stepped into the closet with the intention of grabbing the jeans and a short-sleeved pullover to wear the next day. But when he flipped on the light, he could only stare in wonderment at Ciara's handiwork. She'd given him the entire left side of the walk-in, and had hung his suits and sports coats on the rack above his shirts and jeans. Casual and dress shirts had been grouped by color and sleeve length. His neatly folded jeans had been stacked on an eye-level shelf, sweaters on the next, shoes in a precise row on the bottom. Ties and belts had been given their own sliding racks, to make one-at-a-time choosing easier.

How long ago had she organized this? he wondered, moving to the dresser in search of socks and briefs. There, too, her homemaking skills were evidenced by the systematic placement of tennis shorts, T-shirts and pajamas. She couldn't have been serious when she'd said he should pack up and leave. If she *had* been, would she have aligned his possessions in such a creative way?

Mitch didn't think so. She loves you—whether you deserve it or not—and the proof is all over this house! Sighing, he dropped the clothes he'd been wearing into the clothes hamper, pulled back the dark green quilt and maroon blanket and climbed between crisp white sheets. The minute his head hit the pillow, the scent of her—baby-powder light, yet utterly womanly—wafted into his nostrils. He fell asleep, a half grin slanting his mouth, hugging that pillow tight.

"Me and you, and you and me, no matter how they tossed the dice, it had to be," the Turtles crooned, "happy together, so happy together…." Mitch slapped the alarm's Off button and, rolling onto his back, yawned heartily. After a moment of noisy stretching, he climbed out of bed and padded into the bathroom to adjust the spray for his morning shower, humming the melody of the oldies but goodies song that had awakened him. "…and you're the only one for me," he sang off-key. If you've got to have a song stuck in your head, at least this one is appropriate, he told himself, belting it out, then grinning as the sound of his own voice echoed in the master bathroom's tiled stall.

Here, too, Ciara had seen to it there would never be a doubt whose house this was. The walls were white and the trim the same dusty blue she'd used in the hall bath. Like a professional interior designer, she'd carried the color scheme throughout the house, creating a feeling of organized unity that was both warm and welcoming. How'd you get a woman like that? he wondered as he toweled off.

Bradley had paid him a similar compliment that night in his office when Mitch had been given the undercover assignment. The lieutenant had taken one look at the picture of Ciara on his desk and said, "How'd you get a beauty like that?"

Mitch felt his blood boil just thinking about Bradley.

One thing was certain, Mitch knew, as he swiped steam from the mirror, not even nepotism was going to net Bradley the job they'd both been drooling over for over a year. The lieutenant's uncle may have wielded enough power to garner him a grade hike in the past, may have packed enough punch, even, to get him the job that put him in charge of a dozen field agents, but—

"Enjoy it while it lasts, *Chet*," Mitch said, smiling to himself, "'cause when the director hears what you did to me, you'll be history."

It had been Bradley's job…no…his *duty* to act as the go-between for husbands under his command and the wives they'd left behind. He had lied, repeatedly and deliberately, about the letters that should have gone from Mitch to Ciara and back again, and he'd done it to set Mitch up.

At first Mitch blamed the chill snaking up his back on cold air from the floor vent. But he knew better. The creepy "somebody's watching" feeling had nothing to do with air-conditioning. Bradley hated him…enough to see him dead. That's what caused the sensation.

He was hoping that not hearing from Ciara would screw up my head, distract me, make me mess up. Didn't much matter whether those mistakes would cost the government its case…or Mitch his life. Either way, Bradley's competition for that job…and any other down the road…would be forever eliminated.

If he could do it to Mitch, Bradley was just as capable of putting other agents in harm's way…if he saw them as a threat of any kind. Mitch owed it to the agency to see to it Bradley never got the chance to repeat his crime. He was aching to get the old ball rolling…right over Bradley, if possible. But filing reports, verbalizing complaints, setting things in motion would take countless hours down at headquarters. And his place was beside Ciara now, not avenging a wrong.

There'll be plenty of time to see that Bradley pays, Mitch thought, opening the medicine cabinet. "Good gravy," he said aloud, "she's alphabetized this, too." Grinning, he recalled the pantry, where canned goods and cracker boxes had been lined up in *A, B, C* order. Same for the spices. "So my Escada would be…" His forefinger drew a spiral in the air as he tried to guess which of the bottles held his favorite aftershave.

The first, Armando, then Comandante, and beside it, a travel-size flask of Homme Jusqu'au Dernier. "What's this?" he asked aloud. "Hamma Jooo Aw…?" But try as he might, Mitch could not pronounce the fancy French name. "So, Mrs. Mahoney," he said, rearranging the bottles, "you're not perfect after all…*E* comes before *H*…."

Curiosity compelled him to unscrew the foreign bottle's

cap and take a whiff of the cologne she'd added to his regular stock. "Bleh-yuck," he complained, coughing as he peered into the tiny opening.

Half-empty? That's odd....

Even if Ciara had bought it the day after he left, it wouldn't have evaporated this much in seven months. Eyes and lips narrowing, he asked himself why the aroma seemed so familiar. The rage began slowly, then escalated, like an introductory drumroll: It was that no-good Bradley's brand. What's *his* aftershave doing in my—

With trembling hands, Mitch recapped the container and pitched it into the wicker wastebasket beside the vanity. Heart pounding and pulse racing, his mouth went dry, and despite many gulps of water, it stayed that way. He had a hard time swallowing, because his throat and tongue seemed to have swelled to three times their normal size. A vein began throbbing in his temple, and his ears were ringing. His hands became suddenly clumsy, knocking over the toothbrush holder and the soap dish as he attempted to hold a paper cup under running water.

Unable to stand still, he began pacing in the small space, his big feet tangling in the scatter rug on the floor. Mitch steadied himself, one hand on the counter, the other pressed tight to the wall. "What's Bradley's aftershave doing in my medicine cabinet?" he demanded, his hoarse whisper bouncing off all four walls.

Ciara's face came to mind, all sweet and smiling and big-eyed innocence. She'd been a devout Christian girl when he'd left her. Had loneliness and despair driven her into another man's arms? Had she turned to Bradley for comfort, and—

"No!" he bellowed, bringing his fist down hard on the sink. "That's *my* kid she's carrying, *not* Bradley's!" The mere thought of her in another man's arms started his stomach turning. Because she'd asked him to pack his things and leave, even after he explained everything....

But it had been *his* hand she'd reached for in the emergency room, and *his* gaze she'd locked on to for encouragement and support. He thought of their goodbye kiss in her hospital room the night before and the way she'd so tenderly touched his cheek, looking into his eyes as if she believed he'd hung the moon.

She *had* believed that once, before he'd gone to Philadelphia. Did she believe it still? Or had her love for him been strangled by the choking loneliness of endless days and nights without a word from him?

No...she'd genuinely seemed to need him, there at the hospital. But then, she'd been scared to death, for herself *and* the baby. If Bradley had been there instead, would she have clung to *his* hand? Would she have looking lovingly into *his* eyes?

Everything around him, every towel and curtain, every knickknack and picture, every stick of furniture, screamed out that she loved him. What more proof did he need than the way she'd turned this place into a haven for him in his absence?

He ran both hands through his damp hair, held them there. A strange grating sound caught his attention, and he attuned his ears, trying to identify it. He exhaled a great huff of air when he determined that what he'd heard had been the rasps of his own ragged breathing.

He remembered that moment in the foyer, when she'd announced in her calm, matter-of-fact way that she'd been carrying his baby on the night he left. His baby. Of *course* it was his baby! She'd been so proud to be his wife that in those first weeks of their marriage he'd found things all over the house—envelopes, lunch bags, the TV listings—covered with her fanciful script: "Mrs. Mitchell Riley

Mahoney. Ciara Neila Mahoney. Ciara Mahoney. Mrs. Ciara Mahoney."

And what about the way she'd trembled virginally in his arms on their wedding night, when he'd made her his wife in every sense of the word? It had taken time, but his soft-spoken words and gentle touches and tender kisses soothed her fears. "I'll never hurt you," he'd vowed. "Trust me, sweetie…."

Their eyes had met—hers glistening with unshed tears of hope and joy and anticipation, his blazing with intensity—and she'd sent him a trembly little smile.

He'd absorbed the tremors of fear that had pulsed from her, returned them to her as soothing waves of love and comfort. "It's all right, sweetie," he'd crooned, stroking her back. "We'll take our time…."

He'd kissed her eyelids, her cheeks, her throat, his fingers combing through her lovely silken hair. "I love you, Mitch," she'd breathed. "I love you so much!"

And then her touches, her kisses, her words of love rained upon him, as if she sought a way to show him that she'd meant it when she'd said that she trusted him, that she loved him with all her heart.

And for the first time in his life, Mitch understood why God had decreed that marriage was a sacred and blessed thing. The Lord intended this kind of loving warmth as a gift…a physical illustration of His own intense love for His children.

In the morning, he had awakened first, rolled onto his side to watch his sleeping bride. Her cheeks were still rosy from the night's ardor, and he'd reached out to draw a finger lightly down the bridge of her lightly-freckled nose. Her long-lashed eyes had fluttered, opened. "I love you, Mitchell Riley Mahoney," she'd whispered. Then she'd snuggled close.

Later, as she lay cuddled against him, Ciara had said, "Remember what you said last night…?"

He'd met her eyes. "You mean that verse from Eccle-siastes, 'Enjoy life with the wife whom you love.'"

"Yes," she'd whispered. "Marriage to you is going to be very romantic, I think...."

Now, in the distance Mitch heard the dim notes of the carriage clock on the family-room mantel and counted eight chimes. He couldn't have stood there, lost in memories, for nearly an hour! But he hadn't dawdled when the alarm sounded at seven; he'd leaped out of bed and stepped straight into the shower.

Taking a deep breath, he faced the sink. "She loves you. Of *course* she loves you," he told the wild-eyed man in the mirror. Either that, or she's the best actress ever born.

One bottle of aftershave was no proof of any wrong-doing. It might not even be Bradley's...perhaps her father had spent a night or two in the house, to help out, keep an eye on his daughter's failing health. Maybe—

Lord Jesus, he prayed, *I don't want to believe the worst, but*— "You're a special agent with the Federal Bureau of Investigation," he said to himself, squirting an egg-sized dollop of shaving cream into the palm of his left hand. With the right, he painted it over the lower half of his face. "If you can't get to the bottom of this," he added, touching the razor to his cheek, "you don't deserve to carry the badge."

One bright splotch of red bled through the white foam, then another, as his quaking hand dragged the blade over his skin. Mitch barely noticed. The stinging, biting sen-sation of the tiny razor cuts was nothing compared to the ache in his heart.

Chapter Six

The golden-haired retriever scooted back and forth across the linoleum like a pendulum counting the happy seconds until Mitch managed to attach the leash to the dog's collar. "C'mon, fella," he said, ruffling Chester's thick coat, "let's go get Mom."

Chester whimpered.

"I know, I know," Mitch said, unlocking the car door, "I miss her, too."

And he did. He'd decided on the way to the veterinary clinic that it must have been a horrible coincidence that Chet Bradley's brand of aftershave had ended up in his medicine cabinet. Maybe Ciara got a free sample in the mail, he thought. Wrinkling his nose, he thought of its odor, which reminded him of rearview-mirror air freshener and horseradish. He could only hope if the freebie had come with a coupon for a bigger bottle, Ciara hadn't saved it.

By the time he had parked in the hospital parking lot and passed through the main entrance, Mitch believed his head was in the right place. At least he hoped it was. It had better be, he warned himself, or this next month is going to be miserable, for both of you.

As he strolled down the hall toward her room, he heard the melodic notes of Ciara's girlish laughter. The lilting sound of it thrilled him…until the grating tones of a man's chortle joined it, sending waves of heated jealousy coursing through him. "If your husband ever gets bored with you," the young man was saying when Mitch entered the room, "give me a call, 'cause women like you don't grow on trees." He spotted Mitch, leaning on the door frame, one foot crossed over the other, hands in his pockets. "You Mr. Mahoney?"

A tight-lipped grin on his face, Mitch nodded.

The blood technician scribbled Ciara's name on two white labels. "Lucky man," he said. "Where's a woman like this when *I'm* in the market for a relationship?" He stuck the labels to the vials containing her blood samples, lifted his case and walked toward the door. "The lady I'm dating now thinks *man* and *diamonds* are synonymous," he said from the hallway. And with a quick glance back at Ciara, he repeated, "Lucky man," and headed for his next patient.

Not once in the months he'd been gone had Mitch considered the possibility that she'd violate their marriage vows. *One lousy bottle of stinking cologne,* he told himself, *is no cause for mistrust now.* He had no reason to be jealous of Ciara, because she'd given him no reason to be.

The image of that cologne, standing on the glass shelf in the medicine cabinet as if it belonged, flashed in his mind. And right on its heels, the blatantly flirtatious comments of the good-looking young man who'd just left her room. So he told himself: you'd better get used to guys flirting with your wife; it's what you did, first time you saw her. Besides, what did you expect when you married a knockout? Mitch grinned despite himself, and looked at his wife. Yeah, she sure was a knockout.

Despite a night's sleep, Ciara still looked pale and drawn, but she was smiling and seemed happy to see him. "Good morning," she said brightly, her eyes still puffy, her voice early-morning raspy. "Did you sleep well?"

"Like a baby," he answered, the memory of her scent, clinging to the pillowcase, hovering in his mind.

Ciara raised a brow. "Are you aware that babies wake up every two hours?"

Mitch chuckled. "You trying to scare me? 'Cause if you are, you'll have to try harder."

She sent him a knowing grin that was both motherly and wifely. "I'm glad you slept well." The grin became a soft, sweet smile as she leaned back against her pillows. "I remember the way you always prepared for bed. I used to think if it wouldn't mar the woodwork, you'd have cross-barred every opening with two-by-fours and ten-penny nails. It's a wonder you get any sleep at all, worrying the way you do."

Some might call his before-bed ritual eccentric to the point of psychotic. Not Ciara. Even the first time she'd witnessed it, she had treated his fussiness matter-of-factly, as if all the men in America bolted every door, locked each window, pulled the blinds…and checked twice to make sure he hadn't overlooked anything. He'd never explained it, and Ciara had never asked him to. But Mitch had been out there, had seen the vile and vicious things human beings could do to one another. He wasn't about to take any chances. Not with his wife's safety.

She'd viewed it as routine, like showering and shaving. Which amazed him, considering his recurrent nightmare.

It had disturbed his sleep almost hourly those first months after he'd been kidnapped. Gradually it plagued him less often. By the time he met Ciara, the horrid images only came to him when he'd skipped a night's sleep or went to bed more tired than usual.

They'd been married exactly two days, and he'd gone to bed that second night of their honeymoon. The excitement of the wedding, all that dancing at the reception, the long drive to Martha's Vineyard…Mitch should have expected it, should have warned her. But he'd been so happy, so content with his new life that he hadn't even thought to bring it up.

When she'd roused him, he'd almost slugged her, because in that instant between sleeping and waking, he'd mistaken her for the unseen enemy of his nightmare.

He'd felt a deep, burning shame when she'd seen him that way, trembling, breathing like he'd just run a mile, on the verge of tears like a small helpless boy. The man of the family was supposed to protect his wife, he'd chided himself as the tremors racked his perspiration-slicked limbs; the husband was supposed to comfort and reassure the wife after a nightmare, not the other way around.

But her strong yet delicate hand, gently shaking his shoulder, had brought him to, and her soft, sweet voice, had pulled him from the nightmarish haze. Ciara had snuggled close, her cool fingertips smoothing the sweat-dampened hair back from his forehead. "You were having a bad dream," she'd whispered, "but it's all right now. Everything is all right."

Amazingly, it had been. Relieved to be in her arms, he clutched her to him and moaned into the crook of her neck. "Thank God," he'd rasped. "Praise Almighty God."

And she'd rocked him, kissing his tightly-shut eyes. "Shhh. It's all right," she'd crooned. "It's all right."

He remembered thinking at the time that she'd be a terrific mother someday, because she was certainly good at this comforting stuff.

Until she'd begun kissing away his tears, he hadn't been aware he'd started to sob. Her soft touches, her tender kisses, her soothing words of love rained upon him and slowly washed the agony away. The festering sore of his fear healed that night; he hadn't had the dream since. *God in Heaven,* he prayed, *I love her...love her like crazy.*

It had been on the morning after she'd witnessed the aftereffects of his nightmare, as she drew lazy circles in his chest hair, that Ciara had discovered the gunshot wound on his rib cage and he'd told her the story of how it had happened. She'd been shocked, horrified. "It's such a *dangerous* job, Mitch," she'd said, on the verge of tears. Between that and what had happened to Abe Carlson, the idea of his leaving the Bureau was never far from her mind after that.

The sound of her voice reached his ears, bringing him back to the present, and Mitch wondered how long she'd been happily chattering there in the hospital bed, while his mind had been wandering.

"And I don't suppose you got one decent night's sleep the whole time you were gone," she was saying in that affectionate, scolding way that made him feel loved and protected and wanted, all rolled into one. She shrugged, then aimed the finger at him again. "How could you, when the job required that you sleep with one ear perked and one eye open the whole time?"

Mitch chuckled. "You make it sound like I was fighting a war."

She wasn't smiling when she said, "You *were.*"

This was the Ciara he had thought about day and night, the Ciara he'd dreamed of while he'd been away. *This* was the Ciara he'd fallen in love with...caring about his every need, even in her very delicate condition. How could you have even suspected her of being unfaithful? he asked himself.

She's as innocent as that baby she's carrying; either that or she missed her calling as an actress.

The dark thought hovered there in his mind for a moment, blotting out the joy the bright one had given him. Her innocence, her sweetness…could it be nothing but an act?

"I've taken care of the paperwork," he heard her say, "so you wouldn't have to bother when you got here." Ciara sighed, and smiling, a hand on her big tummy.

"Thanks," he said, forcing a grin. "You're too good to me."

"I hate to admit it," she said, her eyes alight with mischief, "but I didn't do it for you." She patted her tummy. "I just can't *wait* to get us home!"

"I have a surprise for you…in the car," Mitch said, and pictured Chester, who was no doubt slathering the rear windows of the Mustang with what Ciara lovingly referred to as "joy juice."

"I don't know if I can handle any more surprises," she said, a half smile on her face.

He sat beside her on the edge of the bed, a hand atop her stomach. "I did this while you were sleeping last night," he said, "and this kid of ours did quite a dance for me. Any chance I'll get a repeat performance?"

She patted his hand. "The little imp wakes me up every morning between five and six. Sorry, but you missed the first show."

Unable to hide his disappointment, Mitch screwed up one corner of his mouth.

"Don't pout, Mahoney. There's usually a matinee right around lunchtime." She tilted her head, studied his face for a quiet moment. "Free admission for dads only," she added, winking.

"I'll be there, front row center," he said, looking into her beautiful, exhausted face. "Now what say we get you dressed and go home?"

Ciara nodded and threw back the covers.

"You were dressed under there?"

"I've been ready since dawn." Then, sending a glance toward the door, she whispered, "They must set the thermostat at ten above freezing. I was shivering in that flimsy T-shirt and stretch pants!"

He tucked a tendril of hair behind her ear. "Then you'll be happy to know it's still a pleasant seventy-five degrees at home," he said. "Now you sit tight, while I scrounge up a wheelchair."

Ciara rolled her eyes and harrumphed. "Wheelchair? I'm going to hate this."

He held up a silencing hand. "I know that lying around for a whole month is going to be tough on a go-get-'em gal like you, but you'll do it…for the baby's sake." He drew her to him in a sideways hug. "Why not look at these 'lady of leisure' weeks as a gift from heaven?"

Ciara leaned her head on his shoulder and nodded. "I suppose you're right. I'll be getting all kinds of exercise once the baby is born, won't I?"

Suddenly she bracketed his face with both hands. "No matter what I say, you stick to your guns, you hear? Keep a tight rein on me, even if I give you a hard time…and I think we both know that's possible."

"Possible!" he said, laughing softly, then kissing her temple. "You may as well say 'It's possible the sun will rise in the east. It's possible spring will follow winter, it's possible—'"

"I'll try to be a good patient, Mitch."

He rested his chin on top of her head. "'Course you will. And I'll be the best doctor stand-in you ever saw." He wagged a finger under her nose. "But I feel it's only fair to warn you…I'm going to be a tough taskmaster where your health is concerned."

She nodded. Sighed. "So go get the wheelchair, Doctor Killjoy," she said, grinning. "I want to go *home*."

* * *

Mitch carried her into the family room and gently deposited her on the sofa bed, got onto his knees and began untying her white sneakers. Their trip home had been swift and Ciara's reunion with Chester had been well worth the trouble of bringing the big guy along.

She grabbed his wrists. "Mitch, you don't have to—"

He sent her a silent warning that silenced her.

Ciara rolled her eyes. "I never thought I'd see the day when I'd be so helpless I couldn't even take off my own shoes," she complained.

"Look at it this way—once they're off, you won't be putting them on again, so you were only 'this helpless' once."

She grinned. "When did you start seeing the silver lining? I thought you were the type who just saw dark clouds?"

Mitch shrugged. "Things aren't always what they seem. You know what happens when you judge a book by its cover?" he smirked good-naturedly. "You bite the hand that feeds you, that's what."

"Please—" she laughed, hands up in surrender "—one more bad cliché, and I'm liable to explode."

He patted her tummy and twisted his face into a pleading frown. "Please, don't. At least not till the equipment arrives."

"Equipment? What equipment?"

"Didn't Peterson tell you? He put in an order for a home monitor. You're gonna be on TV, pretty lady!"

Ciara frowned. "What in the world are you talking about? Dr. Peterson didn't say anything to me about—"

"The machinery will be delivered today. Way I understand it, we're to plug you in to the monitor, then plug the monitor into the phone and the TV, so Peterson can read the printout that'll come out at his office."

"A fetal heart monitor?"

He shrugged. "Guess so. I never thought to ask what kind." He plunged on. "Plus a nurse will be stopping by every other day to do a blood count—" he winked "—make sure you're not melting or anything. You'll get used to it. Maybe you'll even grow to like it."

She'd harrumphed. "'Fetal' attraction, huh?"

"There's more than one way to kill a rabbit." He held up a hand to forestall another cliché warning. "Sorry," he said. "But technically, that was a pun, not a cliché."

Ciara rolled her eyes. "It's going to be a long, long month…."

"No way, honey. Time always flies when you're having fun. And I'm going to see to it you have plenty of fun. Now sit still so I can get your shoes off. You're supposed to keep your feet elevated as much as possible." He tugged at the snow-white shoelace. "First chance I get, I'm gonna write a letter and complain about the condition of the roads in this county. There are more potholes between here and the hospital than a zebra has stripes. That trip home is likely to have—"

She laid a hand alongside his cheek. "No need to waste a stamp on my account. I'm fine. Tired, but fine."

She must have read his mind again, and knowing he was about to say she didn't *look* fine, Ciara glanced around her.

"When did you find time to do all this?" she asked. "You must have been up all night. The bed's made up all nice as you please, and you've moved the end table forward so I can reach it, even while I'm lying flat on my back," she said. "You've thought of everything…tissues, books, magazines, the remote."

She met his eyes, her own wide with surprise. "Wait just a minute, here…you're giving *me* control of the clicker?" Ciara tilted her head and propped a fist on a hip. "Why, Mitchell Riley Mahoney, are you flirting with me?"

The way you flirted with Bradley while I was away?

Mitch shook his head, cleared his throat. Where did *that* come from? he wondered, surprised by the sudden intrusion of the suspicious thought. He forced a smile. "I was hoping you'd be sleeping a lot, and I could slip it out from under your hand now and then."

He pointed at the summer-weight gown and matching robe he'd laid out for her. "Let's get you into your pajamas, and once you're all tucked in, I'll see what I can rustle us up for lunch."

When Ciara glanced at the nightclothes, Mitch noticed the slight flush that pinked her cheeks. They hadn't had much time together as man and wife, but he'd seen her in a nightie before. Surely she wasn't still feeling timid and shy, as she had on their wedding night. I'll bet you weren't this modest with— He stopped himself, wondering where on earth those thoughts were coming from.

"How 'bout I start lunch, let you slip into these…by yourself."

She bit her lower lip. Rolled her eyes. "You must think I'm the silliest thing on two feet." Hiding behind her hands, she mumbled, "It's just— I'm…I'm so *huge,* Mitch. Last time you saw me, I had an hourglass figure, and now I look like a—"

"You've never been more beautiful. Don't you say one negative word about my gorgeous, very pregnant wife," he scolded, "or I'll have to arrest you."

They hadn't been together long, but had managed to develop a private joke or two. Ciara had always known that despite outward appearances—tough-cop sternness, badge and gun, the sometimes violent things he'd been forced to do in the line of duty—Mitch was nothing but a big softie.

Ciara leaned her cheek against his upheld palm, nuzzled against it, like a house cat in search of a good ear scratching. He'd been sitting on his heels and rose to his knees now. "If you don't stop looking at me with those big, blue eyes…" Those big blue *loving* eyes….

"Can't help myself," she sighed. "I'm just so glad to be home." Ciara hesitated, then added, "I'm glad you're back, Mitch."

His arms went around her, as naturally as if he'd been doing it dozens of times daily for the past seven months, and hers slipped around him just as easily. Their lips met, softly at first, and what began as a gentle kiss intensified.

Oh, but it felt good to be with her this way, as man and wife again. He'd missed her while he'd been away, but until this moment—now that her condition had stabilized and she was out of danger—he hadn't realized exactly how much.

She pulled away, inhaled a great draft of air.

Like a man too long in the desert yearns for water, his lips sought hers again.

"Do you still love me?" she murmured against his open mouth.

A palm on each of her cheeks, he sat back to study her face. Surely she wasn't serious.

The raised brows and pouting lower lip told him she was. Did she really think it was possible for him to *stop?* "Ciara, sweetie, I've always loved you. From the minute I first saw you, looking out to sea at the rail of that beat-up old cruise ship, I loved you…."

"Beat-up? I'll have you know that was once *The Love Boat.*"

"Yeah. Right. Like they had such things a century ago. But you can't distract me that easily," he said, an eyebrow cocked. "Every minute that passes, I love you more. I've never stopped. Not for a heartbeat. Couldn't if I tried." Not even if I find out that you and Bradley— Mitch swallowed. His ping-ponging emotions were sure to make him crazy…if they didn't give him a heart attack first.

"Thank you," she said, her voice thick and sweet as syrup.

"Thank you?" he echoed, a wry grin tilting his mouth. "You've been to the movies. You know how it's supposed to be done." He held a finger aloft and began the lesson. "I say 'I love you,' and you say 'I love you, too.' Not 'thank you' but 'I love you.'" Mitch chuckled, tenderly grasped her lips with the fingertips of both hands, and gently manipulated her mouth. "'I love you,'" he said, as if he were the ventriloquist and she his dummy. "Go on, now you try it, all by yourself."

She kissed his playful fingers. "I *am* grateful, Mitch. What's wrong with admitting it?"

She branded him with an alluring, hypnotic gaze. His heart ached and his stomach flipped. There's nothing wrong with admitting that, he wanted to tell her, but it isn't what I need to hear right now.

After a seemingly endless moment, Ciara closed her eyes. "I love you more today than yesterday," she whispered, reciting the old promise with heartfelt feeling, "but not as much as tomorrow."

He held her, and she melted in his arms, her rounded little body feeling warm and reassuring as it pressed tightly against him. "It's good to be home," he admitted, putting aside his worries that she might be carrying another man's child. "I'm sorry I was gone so lo—"

She silenced him with a kiss.

The memory lapse was short-lived.

Did she kiss Bradley? The ugly thought took his breath away, and he ended the intimate moment. Mitch sat on the edge of the sofa bed with his back to her and ran both hands through his hair. What's wrong with you, Mahoney? One minute you're sure as shootin' she couldn't have cheated on you, the next you're just as sure she did. What's it gonna take to make up your mind!

He could ask her, straight-out, for starters. If she was innocent, she'd be shocked, hurt, furious, that he hadn't trusted her. But if she was guilty, didn't he have a right to know?

Mitch shook his head. Asking her was out of the question. At least for now. *If you haven't figured it out by the time the baby's born…* He gulped down the last of the coffee he'd brought her. *Until then, she's to rest and stay calm.*

If the child was his, he wanted to ensure a healthy birth. Even if it wasn't, well, the baby hadn't played a part in the duplicity that led to its conception. It deserved nothing but good things, no matter who its father was.

"Fine waiter you are," she teased, "bringing me fresh-brewed coffee, then drinking it yourself."

He looked over his shoulder at her sweet, smiling face. "I'll get you a refill."

Let it be my kid, he prayed as he headed for the kitchen. *Please let it be my kid….*

Ciara listened to Mitch in the kitchen, clattering pots and pans and utensils, and remembered that kiss. Guilt hammered in her heart. She would never have deliberately hurt him, but she had, and the proof had been the abrupt way he'd ended their brief intimacy.

She'd said a lot to hurt him yesterday. Maybe after lunch they could discuss it a little more quietly than they had the night he'd left, or yesterday morning when he'd phoned from headquarters, or later, before she'd collapsed.

That old spark is still there, strong and bright as ever. Ciara touched her fingertips to her lips, remembering how wonderful it felt to be in his arms again, to be kissing him again. She hadn't realized how much she'd missed him, until the old familiar stirrings of passion erupted within her.

But I need time, she thought, time to forget all those months alone, time to be sure he won't do it again.

Every wifely instinct in her had made Ciara want to reach out and comfort him when he'd ended the kiss, turned away from her and held his head in his hands. But what would she have said? What might she have done? Since nothing had come to mind, she'd chosen instead to make light of it, to behave as if she hadn't noticed at all. "Fine waiter you are," she'd teased when he drained her cup in one gulp.

You're not in this alone, you know, she reminded herself. It's hard for Mitch, too. She sipped the refill of decaf he'd brought her and sighed. Their love had been as deep and wide as the Montana sky, bright with joy, deep with companionship, hot with passion. Will we ever get back to that? Ciara slumped against the cool, pillowy backrest of the sofa bed and closed her eyes. *Please God, help us find our way back.*

Right from the start, she and Mitch, like the boy and girl next door who'd known each other a lifetime, had felt relaxed and at ease in each other's presence. It had been that factor more than any other that told her it would be safe to fall in love so soon after the pastor's cordial introduction.

Ciara missed that serenity, the satisfaction born of the comfort they shared. Not take-you-for-granted comfort, but the old-shoe-dependable kind that she sensed would wrap around them—warming, soothing, nourishing their love—for a lifetime. She'd heard all about the fireworks-and-sparks kind of love, and had never wanted any part of it. I'll take charcoal over flash paper any day, she'd thought, because paper burned hot and quick…and died the same way. Coal might not heat up as fast, but it stayed warm a whole lot longer. She likened Mitch to charcoal— steady, sure, lasting. No one had been more surprised than

Ciara to discover that her calm, dependable guy turned out to be a hot-blooded, passionate man.

You can't judge a book by its cover, he'd said earlier that day. But Ciara had said it first…on their wedding night.

Once they'd passed that initial test, she and Mitch had not needed the traditional "getting to know you" time her married friends had warned her about. It was a miracle, Ciara believed, that they'd *started out* feeling like life-mates. Their time apart had all but destroyed that comfortable, companionable feeling. But the passion was still there; that kiss proved it. Perhaps that was God's way of telling them the rest could be salvaged, if they were willing to work at it.

Ciara prayed for all she was worth. "Lord," she whispered, "I love him, Lord. Help us." She shook her head. "Help us repair the damage, so that our child will never know the loneliness that comes from living with parents who aren't in love."

Her mom and dad had always claimed to love each other deeply, and from time to time, they'd actually put on a pretty good show of it. She suspected things weren't quite right before she was seven. By the time she turned ten, Ciara had seen through their ruse. She didn't want her child wondering the things that she'd wondered as a girl: had their love for *her* been an act, as well?

"I hope you're cooking up an appetite," Mitch called from the kitchen, breaking into her thoughts, "because I'm cooking up one special lunch out here…."

He'd fixed her a meal once, days before he left. Breakfast, as she recalled, chuckling to herself. She'd been in the front hall, trying to decide whether to store their winter hats and gloves on the shelf in the closet or in the sideboard near the front door. "Sweetie," he'd called from the kitchen, "I hate to bother you, but—"

She'd had to jam a knuckle between her teeth and bite down hard to keep from laughing when she walked into the room. Covered by a red-and-white gingham apron, his jeans-covered legs had poked out from the bottom, and the bulky sleeves of his University of Maryland sweatshirt stuck out from its ruffly shoulders. He held a pancake turner in one hand, hot dog tongs in the other. If he'd worn the outfit to a Halloween party, he'd have won the Silliest Costume Prize, hands-down.

"What?" he'd asked, mischievous dark eyes narrowing in response to her appraisal.

"I just missed you," she'd replied, "because you're the most handsome husband a girl ever had."

He'd grinned. "You think?"

"I do." She wiggled her eyebrows flirtatiously, wrapped her arms around his aproned waist. "In fact," she'd said, winking, "I'm giving a lot of thought to kissing you, right here, right now."

The turner and the tongs had clattered to the floor as he pressed her closer. "And they say aggressive women are no fun...."

After their warm embrace, Mitch started digging in a box marked "Kitchen." "Can't make my home fries till we find the big black skillet."

She'd glanced at the counter, where he'd piled enough peeled-and-sliced potatoes and onions to feed the Third Regiment. Ciara opened one box as Mitch popped the lid of another. "I've already looked in that one," he said, poking around inside another. "If you find the vegetable oil, salt and pepper, and Old Bay seasoning, let me know."

"Old Bay?" she'd asked, incredulous. "That's for steamed crabs and shrimp, not potatoes and—" At the startled, almost wounded expression on his face, she'd quickly added, "Isn't it?"

"Just wait till you taste 'em, sweetie," he'd said, licking

his lips and scrubbing his hands together. "They're gonna spoil you for anybody else's potatoes. From now on, you won't be able to settle for anything but Mitch Mahoney's breakfast spuds."

He'd given her dozens of memories like that one…before that awful night. Memories that had lulled her back to sleep when a bad dream awakened her, memories that gave her the energy to unpack every box in their new house within the first week, so he'd have a proper homecoming…*when* he came home.

Night after night as she'd headed for bed, Ciara had stood at the foot of the stairs, one hand on the mahogany rail, the other over her heart, listening for the sound of his key in the lock. Day after day she woke hoping that when she walked into the kitchen, he'd be sitting at the table, reading the morning edition of the *Baltimore Sun,* lips white from his powdered sugar doughnut as he grumbled about the one-sidedness of the newspaper's politics.

When the nights and the days turned into weeks, it got harder and harder to find a reason to hope he might be there waiting when she got home from teaching, a big smile on his handsome face. "Where have you been!" she imagined he'd ask. "I've been dying to see you!"

Every time Lieutenant Bradley's car pulled into the drive, her heartbeat doubled…maybe this time he'd have a letter for her. Ciara played her tough-girl routine to the hilt. She would show the seasoned agent that she knew a thing or two about bravery. She'd prove she knew how to handle being married to the Bureau. Because when Mitch *did* come home, she wanted him to be proud of the way she'd conducted herself.

In truth, her bravado had been almost as much for Bradley as for herself. "I'm so sorry, Ciara," he would say every time, taking her hand, "but Mitch missed another meeting." And every time, she'd pull free of his pressing fingers and focus on the look on his face. It could mean one of two things: Bradley was truly distressed to have delivered unpleasant news…again, or his wingtips were two sizes too small.

She'd never given a thought to the possibility that he'd deliberately kept her and Mitch apart. Why had it been so easy to believe him, instead of her husband? Oh, he was a smooth one, all right, starting out in complete defense of his comrade, slipping in a little doubt here, casting a bit of suspicion there, until he had her thoroughly convinced that the only possible reason Mitch hadn't written was because he hadn't wanted to. But she'd *let* him put those mistrustful thoughts in her head.

Those first unhappy weeks, she'd spent so much time on her knees, hands folded, it was a minor miracle she hadn't developed inch-thick calluses. She had gone over it in her mind a hundred times: from those first, thrilling stirrings of love, she had beseeched the Almighty to show her a sign; if Mitch wasn't the man He intended her to spend the rest of her life with, she would take her mother's advice and stop wasting her time.

And then Mitch had taken her in his arms and kissed her, and it had felt so good so right. How else was she to have interpreted the emotions, except as God's answer to her heartfelt prayer!

She'd waited a long time to meet the right man. Had she jumped into the relationship because she'd been lonely? Had she misread God's response? Maybe it had been nothing but hormones, she'd fretted, dictating her interpretation of the Lord's intent.

The pastor had said, more than once, that prayer alone is not enough to prevent doubt. It takes faith and lots of it, he'd insisted, to forestall suspicion, to keep uncertainty at bay. It was a lesson, Ciara realized, that she'd have to learn the hard way, through time and trial; for try as she might to look for reasons to believe Mitch would contact her—or come home to her—hope faded with each lonely, passing day.

And just about the time she was about ready to give up altogether, Dr. Peterson confirmed what she had suspected for weeks: Ciara was going to have a baby. *Mitch's* baby! The news changed everything. Surely when he heard their baby would be born the following summer, Mitch would do everything in his power to come back. She wrote a long, loving letter, outlining her hopes and dreams for this child growing inside her. When she handed it over to the lieutenant, Ciara had wanted to believe that Mitch would find a way to be with her, to share the joyous news, face-to-face.

But Lieutenant Bradley returned the very next week, wearing that same hang-dog expression she'd come to expect of him, and she set all hope aside. Her mother had been right: he was a cop, first and foremost, and would always put his job ahead of everything—every*one* else— including their unborn baby.

"Mitch missed another meeting," he'd said, hands outstretched, as if imploring her to forgive *him* for her husband's transgressions.

One of the teachers at Ciara's school was married to a divorce attorney, and on the day Dr. Peterson let her hear the baby's heartbeat, she made an appointment to see the lawyer. For the child's sake if not her own, she had to make plans. If Mitch never came back, she had to ensure a stable, secure future for her child. If he did return, it wasn't likely he'd be a dedicated father, and she must protect the baby from such callousness.

She had no one to talk to about the situation. Who would understand such a thing! Certainly not her mother, because from day one, the woman's bitterness against Ciara's father spilled onto Mitch as well.

"He'll never love you as much as he loves his job," she'd said when Ciara showed her the sparkling diamond engagement ring. "The only enjoyment he'll get from life will be related to his work."

Judging by the furrows that lined her father's handsome brow and the way his mouth turned down at the corners when working a case, Ciara found it hard to believe her dad loved his job at all. She'd put the question to him on the night Mitch asked her to marry him.

Her father had answered in his typically soft-spoken way. "All I ever wanted was to see right win out over wrong."

"That doesn't happen very often," she'd countered. "It's in the news all the time…the way criminals get away with murder."

He'd nodded his agreement. "That's true far too often, I'm afraid. But it's so satisfying when the system works as our forefathers intended it to," he'd said, dark-lashed blue eyes gleaming as he plucked an imaginary prize from the air and secured it in a tight fist. "And you forget when the D.A. botched up, or the lab lost evidence, or the arresting officer forgot to read the suspect his rights. You forget that a lot of the time, everything goes wrong, because you're able to focus on what went right."

Her father didn't love his *job,* Ciara understood when the conversation ended, he loved *justice.*

During her first weekend home after finishing up her freshman year in college, Ciara and her mother had been alone in the kitchen, chatting quietly as they'd washed the supper dishes. The contrast had reminded her of the weekend she'd gone home with her roommate, Kelly, to a cozily cluttered house that throbbed with the cheerful sounds of a big family. It hadn't been the first time Ciara had compared other households to her own—somber as a funeral parlor, quiet as a hospital. If her parents were that unhappy, why not get a divorce? she'd often wondered.

She hoped they hadn't spent nineteen miserable years together for her sake, because if *she* was the reason they'd endured all that misery…

Perhaps they'd stuck it out because of the "for better or for worse" line in the marriage vows. But was that what God intended? That two individuals—who made a promise while they were too young and too foolish to understand the gravity or longevity of it—spend the rest of their lives locked in an unhappy union?

Ciara had always seen marriage as a loving gift, hand delivered by the Father. Her parents' marriage had been more a jail sentence than a gift of any kind. When *she* married, Ciara had decided, it wouldn't just be for love. No, she'd consider the future, as her parents obviously had not, because she would not, could not inflict a bitter loveless marriage on any children she might have. Ciara knew only too well what that could be like. If only she had siblings, maybe things wouldn't have seemed so bleak….

She dried the plate her mother had just washed. "Mom, why don't I have any brothers or sisters?"

The answer had come so quickly, Ciara figured out much later, because it was something that was often on her mother's mind. "I didn't think it would be fair to bring more children into this world, children who'd feel neglected and slighted by their own father."

"I've never felt anything but loved by Daddy," Ciara had admitted.

It had been the wrong thing to say to her mother.

Following a disgusted snort, she'd said, "Kids are adaptable. Besides, how would *you* know a good father from a bad one? You have nothing to compare him to."

"My friends' fathers spent as much time at work as Daddy did when he was a cop," she'd said, more than a little riled that her own mother had put her in the position of defending her father, "and they weren't policemen."

"Kids are adaptable," she'd repeated, "and they're good at justifying what's wrong in their lives, too. Well, I'm *not* so good at those things." She'd jammed a handful of silverware into the cup in the corner of the dish drainer. "Now you know why you're an only child."

"Why are you so *angry* with Dad?"

Her mother had stared out the window above the sink for a long moment, as if the answer to Ciara's question hung on a shrub or a tree limb. "I'm angry because I asked him to give it up, to do something safer—for my sake—and he refused."

"But he *did* give it up."

"I asked him to quit long before he was shot, Ciara. You weren't even born yet when I told him how hard it was for me, worrying every minute he was on the job, scared out of my mind if he was five minutes late, imagining all the terrible things that might have happened to keep him from coming home on time." She hesitated. "I found a solution to my worrying."

"What?"

"I taught myself not to care."

Now it all made sense. She'd been eleven when her father had been wounded in the line of duty. The injury to his hip would heal, the doctors had said, but he'd walk with a permanent limp…and because that would put him in harm's way on the job, he was forced to retire.

Strange, Ciara had often thought, that though he worked fewer hours at a far less stressful job, teaching at the university seemed to tire him like police work never had. Stranger still, before the second anniversary of his retirement, his dark hair had gone completely gray and his clear blue eyes had lost their youthful spark. And in addition to the gunshot-induced limp, he began to walk slightly bent at the waist, as though the burden of being unable to make his wife happy was a weight too crushing to bear, even for one with shoulders as broad as his.

One line from a poem she'd read in her English Literature class popped into her mind, "Joy is the ingredient that puts life into a man's soul, just as sadness causes its death." Her father, though the doctors claimed his vital organs were strong and healthy, was dying of unhappiness.

In the kitchen making her lunch, Mitch finished singing one Beatles tune and immediately launched into another, his voice echoing in the cavernous room. From her place on the sofa bed, Ciara smiled. He sounded happy, despite their predicament, and she wanted him to stay happy. The only way she knew to accomplish that goal was to set her own needs aside and let him continue the dangerous undercover work he seemed to love so much.

Could she do that? Should she, now that there was a baby to consider?

"I hope you're hungry," he called to her, "'cause I've made enough food for two Boy Scout troops and their leaders."

She closed her eyes. Oh, how I love him! she admitted silently.

But she couldn't allow love to blind her, not when the baby's future, as well as her own, was at stake. She wouldn't spend decades chained to a loveless marriage, as her mother had done. Had her parents stayed together, simply because of the vows they'd exchanged? Ciara and Mitch had spoken those same words. "What God has joined together, let no man put asunder," the preacher had said.

Ciara closed her eyes. "Lord Jesus," she whispered, "I want to do Your Will, but You'll have to show me the way."

"Ciara, sweetie," Mitch said, poking his head into the family room, "you can finish your nap later." He popped back into the kitchen. "Make a space on your lap for the breakfast tray." His face reappeared in the doorway, a confused frown furrowing his brow. "Ah, do we *have* a breakfast tray?"

"Yes," she answered, giggling softly. "It was a wedding gift from your Aunt Leila, remember?"

"Oh, yeah. Right," he said, nodding before he disappeared for the second time. In seconds he was back again. "Um…where do we keep the breakfast tray?"

She was reminded of an episode of "I Love Lucy," when Ricky insisted on making breakfast so his pregnant wife could sleep in…but continued to call Lucy into the kitchen to find this and that. Grinning, Ciara mimicked Lucille Ball. "Oh, Ricky, it's in the cabinet under the wall oven, standing with the cookie sheets and pizza pans."

"What?"

And after a terrible clatter, she heard him say, "Bingo!"

Yes, Mitch seemed happy. But was she wife enough to keep him that way? Was her faith strong enough to stick with it and to find out?

Chapter Seven

He hadn't been deliberately eavesdropping later that day, but the kitchen and the family room shared a common wall with an open vent. He made a little more noise with the ice cubes and lemonade, hoping to drown out Ciara's mother's nagging voice:

"I just don't understand why you couldn't have married someone like that nice Chet Bradley. He's always so—"

"Mom, please," came Ciara's harsh whisper. "Mitch is right in the next room. You want to hurt his feelings?"

Kathryn laughed. "Feelings? Please. He's a cop, and as we both know, cops don't *have* any feelings."

A moment of silence, then, "He left you alone for seven months, Ciara. Alone and carrying your first child. And a difficult pregnancy to boot!"

"It wasn't his fault," countered his wife. "He was just following orders."

"That's not what Chet said…."

He heard the rustle of sheets. "What are you talking about, Mom?"

"Did you know that Chet is single?"

Ciara had told Mitch that her mother was English,

through and through. There must be a wee bit o' the Irish in 'er, he thought, 'cause she's answerin' a question with a question….

"Not single, divorced," her daughter corrected. "There's a difference…not that it matters. I'm a married woman, and pretty soon now, I'll be a mommy, too."

His mother-in-law's bitter sigh floated to him. "Don't remind me." She clucked her tongue. "I just hope you're happy, young lady, because now you're stuck in the same leaky boat I was in for two solid decades."

Kathryn had never made a secret of her feelings for Mitch, insulting him at every turn, trying to make him feel small and insignificant every chance she got. Obviously, he thought, my little "vacation" hasn't improved her opinion of me.

"If you had listened to me and married a man like Chet, you wouldn't be in this predicament now. At least he has some breeding, unlike certain Gaelic immigrants." She snorted disdainfully. "Chet wouldn't have left you high and dry. He—"

"He's a cop, too, don't forget."

"True. But his job doesn't put him on the front lines. His ego isn't all wrapped up in how much attention the 'big cases' give him."

"Lieutenant Bradley is Mitch's superior officer. He's the guy who made Mitch go away."

"That's not the way he tells it."

"You skirted this question earlier, and if you don't mind, I'd like a straight answer to it now. What do you mean, 'That's not the way he tells it'?"

If he stood just to the right of the stove and crouched slightly, Mitch could see their reflections in the oven window. He saw Kathryn narrow her eyes and incline her head. "Where *was* Mitch all those months, anyway? I distinctly got the impression from Chet that—"

"That doesn't answer my question. And besides, when have you had an opportunity to discuss Mitch with him?" Ciara asked, sitting up straighter.

Kathryn waved a hand in front of her face, as though Ciara's question were a housefly or a pesky mosquito. "Last time I stopped by, he was here when I arrived, remember?" She tucked a flyaway strand of dark blond hair behind one ear, inspected her manicured fingernails. "That was the time he brought you roses, to cheer you up." She smiled brightly. "Such a caring, thoughtful, young man!" She straightened the hem of her skirt and added, "We were in the kitchen, fixing coffee, remember? I didn't see any harm in asking him a few questions. You're my daughter, after all. If I don't have a right to know the details about something that affects you so directly, who does?"

Roses? He brought *roses*…to cheer Ciara up? Mitch ground his molars together. It was understandable that his wife would be down in the dumps, considering the way they'd parted and all, but… How often had good old Chet been in his house, anyway? Often enough to feel comfortable upstairs…in the master bathroom?

Ciara's voice interrupted his self-interrogation. "What did he tell you?"

He knew Ciara well enough to recognize annoyance in her voice when he heard it. She was annoyed now.

Kathryn huffed. "All right, Ciara. I guess a child is never too old to be reminded to mind their manners. I'll thank you to keep a civil tongue in your head when you're talking to me, young lady. You may be a married woman now, but I'm still your mother!"

"I'm sorry if I sounded disrespectful, Mom. Blame it on cabin fever."

She has been in the house an awful lot these past months, Mitch thought. And she always loved to take long walks…must be hard, being cooped up this way….

"You should try your hand at writing mysteries," Ciara added, giggling, "because you're a master at dropping hints and clues. I admit it, you've hooked me. Now *please* tell me what Chet said about Mitch!"

Kathryn joined in on what she believed to be her daughter's merriment. Mitch knew better. Shouldn't a mother be able to recognize when her daughter is getting angry? He'd only known her a few months before leaving for Philly, and even he recognized that Ciara's laughter was rooted in frustration.

"Well," Kathryn said, a hand on Ciara's knee, "it was like this…. It seems Mitch came to Chet late one night with this ego-maniacal idea for capturing a man on the FBI's Most Wanted list. Notorious criminal, Chet said. Mitch had it all worked out, right down to the kind of clothes he would wear. He'd pretend to be a CPA to trick the man."

"Chet didn't want to let him go, once he found out that you two had just been married, but Mitch insisted." Kathryn sighed. "Chet tried and tried to talk him out of it, but in the end, he had no choice but to admit that Mitch *had* come up with a good plan…."

"Interesting," Ciara said.

And Mitch could tell by the way her fingers were steadily tapping against her tummy that she was chomping at the bit to hear the rest of the story. Frankly, I'd like to hear it, too, he admitted.

"Chet didn't hear from Mitch the whole time he was undercover. Did you know that? It's his duty to report to his commanding officer, and he didn't phone in once! If he's that irresponsible about his job, think what a wonderful father he'll be."

Her voice dripped with sarcasm and bitterness. I love you, too, Kathryn, was his snide thought.

"I've told you and told you," Ciara said, "Mitch

couldn't call. They were watching him night and day. One false move, and he might have been—"

Kathryn patted her daughter's hand, turned to face the kitchen. "Mitch! What's keeping you?" she called. She leaned forward and lowered her voice. "Send him to the kitchen for lemonade, and he's gone a half hour. Send him on a week-long assignment, and he's gone seven months."

That low-down lout, Mitch thought. What was he doing telling her the details of a case that hadn't even gone to court yet?

Kathryn snickered behind her hand. "Being elusive must be part of his nature. Now, if you had married a man like Chet…"

He'd heard about all of that he could handle. Straightening from his position in front of the oven window, Mitch left the glasses of lemonade on the kitchen counter and barged into the family room. "I don't mean to be rude, Kathryn, but Ciara looks awfully tired."

Ciara shot him a grateful look.

"I promised her doctor that at the first signs of fatigue, I'd make her take a nap." Gently he grabbed Kathryn's elbow and helped her up. "Why don't you come back in a day or so and bring Joe next time. I haven't seen him in—"

"In over *seven months!*" his mother-in-law finished, jerking free of his grasp.

Mitch handed her her purse and walked toward the front door. One hand on the knob, he smiled politely. "Why don't we make it Sunday afternoon. I'll fix a nice dinner. I'm sure Ciara will be rested up by then. Won't you, sweetie?"

Her blue eyes were twinkling when their eyes met, but when her mother faced her, she slumped weakly against her pillow. "I don't know…maybe you'd better call first, Mom, just to make sure I'm up to having company…."

Kathryn laid a hand on her chest, eyes wide and mouth agape. "Company! Your father and I aren't 'company,' we're *family!*"

"Thanks for stopping by," Mitch said, opening the door. "As always, it's been…an experience."

"'Here's your hat, what's your hurry?'" Kathryn quoted, snatching her purse from his hands. "You'd better not let anything happen to my daughter," she snapped, shaking a finger under his nose. "I intend to hold you personally responsible for—"

"Kathryn," he said, calmly, quietly, "you have my word that I won't let anything happen to your daughter. She happens to be the most important person in my life."

She huffed her disapproval. "You sure have a funny way of showing how you feel."

Smiling thinly, Mitch said, "You know, you're right about that." He opened the door and with a great sweep of his arm, invited her to step through it. "See you Sunday?" he asked once she was on the porch. "How does two o'clock sound?"

"I'll…"

"Drive safely now," he added as the door swung shut, "and be sure to give Joe my best."

Whatever Kathryn said in response was muffled by the closed door.

"Is she gone?" Ciara whispered when he came back into the family room.

Nodding, he sat on the edge of the sofa bed.

"Thank goodness. I love her, but she doesn't make it easy sometimes."

Mitch flexed a thick-muscled biceps. "You want her to stay out, it'll be my pleasure. *Trust me.*"

Ciara giggled. "I couldn't keep her away. She means well, it's just that she has—"

"The personality of vinegar?"

She pursed her lips. "Well, lemons, maybe…."

He stood, picked up the empty cookie plate he'd brought out when her mother had arrived. "I'm going to throw a load of sheets into the washer," he said, bending down to kiss her forehead. "How 'bout catching a catnap while I'm gone. You look like you could use it."

Yawning and stretching, she smiled. "I might just do that."

He started to walk away.

"Mitch?"

He stopped.

"What are we going to do? After the baby is born, I mean?"

Mitch held his breath. His heartbeat doubled, and his pulse pounded in his ears. She'd turned onto her side, making it impossible for him to read her expression. Was the question a throwback to her suggestion that he pack up and leave?

"You're taking such good care of me…of everything…that I'm going to be spoiled rotten by the time this baby gets here."

Relieved, he exhaled. "You've done more than your share, turning this house into a home all by yourself. You deserve to be spoiled rotten."

She lifted her head and grinned.

"At least until the baby is born," he finished, winking.

She snuggled into her pillow and in moments was fast asleep.

I didn't tell you the whole truth, he admitted to his peacefully sleeping wife. *I have no intention of spoiling you rotten just till the baby comes. I'm going to treat you like a queen for the rest of your life.*

The next few days passed quietly and without incident. The lines of communication between them were beginning to open, as he took her temperature, brought her her vitamins, saw to it she drank plenty of water….

Ciara admired him, for although he had a different way of doing things, he accomplished every task with productive efficiency.

He had a plan for everything—usually written out on a five-by-seven tablet—and made so many checklists, Ciara believed all the ballpoint pens in the house would run out of ink before he had accomplished every task.

Mitch had written up his first list the night before he brought her home from the hospital. Once he helped her get settled the next morning, he whipped out a little notebook and sat on the edge of the sofa bed. "Breakfast at nine, lunch at one, supper at seven, a light snack at ten, lights out by eleven. You can read or watch TV in between, but I want all the power off a couple of hours in the morning, again in the afternoon, so you can catch some shut-eye. What do you think?"

The dog sidled up to him and nudged Mitch's hand with his nose, as if to say Where do I fit into the plan?

"Don't worry, boy, I won't neglect you." Mitch flipped to the second page in his tablet. "See," he said, as if Chester could read what he'd printed in bold black letters, "you'll get yard time while your mommy, here, takes her naps." Patting the top of the dog's head, he'd added, "I'm afraid long walks around the block are going to have to wait till she's up and at 'em, 'cause we can't leave her alone."

Chester's silent bark seemed all the approval Mitch needed. "It's settled, then." To Ciara he added, "I've already put clean sheets on our bed, so…"

"I don't really have to go to bed at eleven," she said, hoping he'd agree because she'd said it so matter-of-factly.

His stern expression told her that she did have to retire at eleven.

"But…but I like to watch the eleven o'clock report on Channel Two before I turn in," she protested. "Besides, it isn't like I'll be doing anything to wear me out. Staying up late won't hurt me."

Unconsciously he ruffled Chester's thick coat, frowning as he turned her words over in his mind. "I hate TV news—nothing but a serving of pap for the feel-good generation, if you ask me. So…"

"I didn't ask you," she interrupted, grinning.

He held up a hand, and she'd giggled.

"How 'bout we make it an every-other-night thing," he had continued. "Tonight, the news. Tomorrow, bed at eleven."

She hadn't heard anything but *bed.* The word echoed in her mind. She hadn't shared anything with him—not conversation or a meal, their home, *certainly* not a bed—in seven long months. Did he really expect her to pick right up where they'd left off, as if he'd been away on some fun-filled, weekend fishing trip with the guys? Didn't he understand that during nearly every moment of their separation, she had reviewed thousands of scenarios that would explain his lengthy absence— shootings, stabbings, beatings, kidnappings—horrible, torturous images.

She blinked those images away. "There's no reason for you to cart me upstairs every night, then back down in the morning." Consciously, deliberately, she phrased it as a statement of fact.

"You can't get a decent night's sleep with a metal bar diggin' into the small of your back," Mitch pointed out. "You'll sleep upstairs on a real mattress or—"

"I'll be fine, right here on the couch."

He crossed his arms over his chest, lifted his chin a notch. Mitch was not smiling when he said, "We can compromise on TV or not TV, but this subject isn't open for negotiation." He paused thoughtfully. "Well, I suppose I ought to give you *some* say in the matter...."

She should have waited a tick in time to display her victorious smile.

"You have two choices—sleep upstairs or stay upstairs. It's entirely up to you."

His stern expression, his cross-armed stance, his no-nonsense voice made it clear she would not win this battle, and yet Ciara couldn't help thinking what a wonderful father he'd be if he disciplined their children with the same gentle-yet-firm attitude. She got so wrapped up in the concept that she didn't give a thought to the fact that if she gave in on this point, they'd be sleeping together every night, like any other married couple.

And they were nothing like other married couples....

Chester looked back and forth between them and whimpered, reminding her of how helpless and afraid she'd felt when her parents argued.

"You'd really leave me up there," she asked breathily, "all alone, all day?"

"I'd much rather have you down here, where you can keep me company, but we'll do it that way if we have to."

And so the deal was struck.

Ciara snuggled beneath the crisp top sheet, remembering the way he'd carried her up the stairs that first night. Her heart had drummed and her stomach had clenched. After all those nights alone, clutching her pillow...and pretending it was him...what would it be like, she'd wondered, lying beside the real thing?

Chester, who had become Mitch's four-legged, shaggy shadow, had tagged along and flopped in a graceless heap on Ciara's side of the bed. Almost immediately he'd rested his chin on his paws and fell asleep.

If only *I* could get comfortable that easily! she'd

thought as Mitch tucked her in and turned out the light. It had been a dark night, without so much as a moon sliver to brighten the room, and for those first few seconds, Ciara blinked into the blackness, listening....

Silence.

Had he decided to sleep downstairs? Had he made up the guest bedroom for himself?

By then her eyes had adjusted to the darkness, and she'd seen his shadow pass in front of the window. Almost immediately, he'd been swallowed up by the blackness, and she'd strained her ears. First, the sound of heavy footfalls, padding across the carpeted floor, then a muffled *clunk* as his belted trousers had landed on the upholstered bedside chair. The mattress dipped under his weight, the sheet billowed upward, like a plaid parachute and settled slowly over them.

Then he'd rolled onto his side and slid his arms around her. "G'night," Mitch had whispered, kissing her temple. "Sweet dreams." He'd tucked a hand under his cheek, rested the other on her tummy. "G'night, li'l sweetie," he'd added.

More silence.

Then the unmistakable, comforting sound of his soft snores.

Ciara didn't know how long she'd lain there, snuggled against him, but listening to his steady, deep breaths had relaxed her, lulled her. Before she'd known it, the bright light of morning had beckoned her.

The morning after his return, Ciara had at first thought she'd been dreaming again, that he wouldn't be there when she opened her eyes, and then she'd seen him there, flat on his back, gentle breaths counting the seconds. One hand had rested on his slowly heaving chest, big fingers splayed like a pianist's. The other, he'd tucked under his neck. A lock of dark hair had fallen across his forehead, and the shadow of a night's growth of whiskers dusted his cheeks and chin. She had needed to use the bathroom, but he'd looked so peaceful—like an innocent boy, without a care in the world—that she hadn't wanted to wake him.

Instead, she'd tucked the misplaced curl into place. His thick black lashes had fluttered in response to her touch. He'd focused on the ceiling and frowned, as though trying to remember where he was. A tiny smile lifted the corners of his mouth, and he'd slowly turned to face her.

"G'mornin'," he'd said, the bass of his sleepy voice guttural and growly. He'd worked his arms around her. "Sleep well?"

Ciara had tucked her face into the crook of his neck. "Like a log," she'd answered. "And you?"

"Terrific." And as if to prove it, Mitch had yawned deeply. He climbed out of bed and thumped groggily around to her side, and carried her into the bathroom. "I'm going to go down and start the coffee," he'd explained. "I'll only be a minute, so don't you move from there, you hear?"

"I hear," she'd agreed as he closed the door.

Almost immediately, she'd noticed the milky white bottle in the wicker waste basket. "Homme Jusqu'au Dernier," she said, reading the label aloud. Mitch had never worn that brand before he'd left…. Ciara couldn't reach it without getting up, so she didn't know if she liked his new cologne. She would ask him about it when he came back for her.

The clatter of cabinet doors and canister lids, and the sound of running water had blotted the question from her mind. And true to his word, he was in their room in minutes, opening and closing drawers and doors, his big bare feet thudding as he crossed from closet to dresser and back again.

One sleeve of his white T-shirt had rolled up, and the legs of his boxers had wrinkled during the night; his dark waves were tousled, his cheeks sheet wrinkled when he burst into the bathroom. "Finished?"

The little-boy, rumpled look had been so appealing that Ciara had been forced to look away to diminish the passion stirring deep inside her. She mumbled a polite "Yes, thanks," and just like that, he'd lifted her into his arms and sat her on the edge of the bed.

On his knees, he'd gently gripped her wrists, held them above her head and slid her nightgown off. The nothing-but-business expression warmed as he focused on her naked stomach. Lifting his gaze to hers, he'd smiled tenderly, blinking and shaking his head slightly. He'd broken the intense eye contact, looked at her broadened waistline again and stroked its roundness.

The heat of his hands, pressing against her taut skin, sent eddies of desire coursing through her. "You're beautiful," he'd rasped, kissing every inch of her stomach, "so very beautiful."

And then his eyes—dusky chocolaty eyes that blazed with need and yearning—had met hers. It seemed to Ciara that he hadn't wanted her to read his mind and discover the longing there; why else would he have slowly, slowly dropped the densely lashed lids?

No, she'd thought, almost sadly, don't shut me out. She'd placed a palm on each whiskered cheek, thumbs massaging the tight muscles of his jaw. She'd been stunned when he opened his eyes again, to see the thin sheen of tears glistening there. "I'm so sorry, Ciara," he'd husked. "I should have been here, right from the beginning."

His arms had slid around her, his ear cleaving to her midsection. "Can you ever forgive me?"

There had been moments, while he'd been gone, when

Ciara had said she despised him. It would have been easier, accepting his absence, if only she could hate him. But try as she might, the words had never rung true. On the day they'd met, she'd fallen in love with his silly jokes and his opinionated politics and his bighearted nature. Standing at the altar of God, she'd vowed to love him for better or for worse, and no matter how many miles and months separated them, her last words on this earth would likely be "Oh, how I loved him!"

She had felt the dampness between his skin and hers that morning, as Mitch had nestled his face against their unborn child. Any anger she had felt for him was swallowed up by his heartfelt tears. Every maternal instinct inside her had risen up, and she'd held him near, fingers gently raking through his plush chestnut curls.

One day soon, she would ask him about the assignment that had put time and space between them. But for those few moments, it hadn't mattered where he'd gone, or why. He had come home, had come back to her.

He had sniffed, and shaken his head, then sat back on his heels to gather up the clothes he'd set out for her. He'd given the big white T-shirt—one of his own—two hearty flaps, and slipped it carefully over her head. She picked up the brush that had been hidden under the shirt. Mitch had held out his hand, and she'd handed it to him and, standing, he'd run the boar bristles through her hair, one hundred strokes; she'd counted them. "Shines like the sun," he'd said, then he'd lifted her in his arms and carried her downstairs.

Though he'd daubed a light kiss upon her cheek each time he brought a cup of coffee, a plate of cookies, Mitch had not repeated any part of that lovely scene since…despite the countless hours she'd spent wishing and hoping that he would. Was it something hormonal, induced by her condition, she'd wondered, that made her ache for the intimacy of his touch? And why had he stoically withheld it?

They'd been back together for four days now, and Ciara decided the best way to divert her attention was to focus on the burning questions—where he'd been, what he'd been doing—that had plagued her while he'd been gone. When the time was right—and she'd have to trust God to tell her when that moment arrived—she would ask Mitch about the assignment. Had he wanted to take it, or had it been foisted upon him? The answer would make all the difference in the world....

Now as Ciara watched him folding towels as he sat on the foot of the sofa bed, grinning as Chester wrestled with a Lambchops doll, she said, "Mitch, let me help. Folding clothes is hardly strenuous activity, and I feel so useless."

He looked at her and said, "Since I'm the one sitting here doing it, I know for a fact that the job requires the use of stomach muscles. You're not doing anything that puts any strain on that baby." Smoothing the washcloth he'd just doubled, he added it to the neat, colorful stack. "Got it?"

She flopped back against the pillows he'd stuffed behind her. "Got it," she droned.

He reached for the laundry basket. "When I'm finished putting this stuff away, I'll—"

Changing positions, Ciara winced slightly.

"What...?" He leaped up so fast, he nearly toppled his tower of towels. "What's wrong?" His big hands gripped her upper arms. "Are you in pain?"

"Goodness gracious sakes alive, Mitch," she said, frowning slightly, "my back is a little stiff from all this inactivity. It was a muscle cramp, that's all." Shaking her head, Ciara rolled her eyes and punched the mattress. "I *hate* being completely helpless. It makes me feel so...so."

He stood for a moment, pinching the bridge of his nose

between thumb and forefinger, then heaved a deep sigh. "You scared me half to death." He stuffed the linens into a wicker laundry basket and grinned. "Mrs. Mahoney," Mitch said, rubbing his palms together, "get ready for the best back rub of your life."

She grinned. "I've never had a back rub, 'best' or otherwise."

Mitch's brows rose. "Never?"

Ciara shook her head. "Never."

"Never say never. Now, roll over, Beethoven."

She wouldn't have admitted it—not until she knew he loved her as much as she loved him—but having him near was like a dream come true. Ciara did as she was told. Hiding her face in the pillow, she closed her eyes and bit her bottom lip to gird herself. Those moments in their room, when he'd so lovingly held their unborn child, haunted her. He hadn't left her side, had taken such good care of her, all without a word of complaint. She had worried in the hospital that he might not want this child; what had motivated his loving ministrations…love for the baby, love for her, or both? Until she knew, Ciara could not admit how much his physical presence meant to her.

He lay down behind her, hiked up the oversize T-shirt and ran his palms over her skin, paying particular attention to the small of her back. His fingers slid up, kneaded her neck and shoulders, then moved down to rub her biceps.

Ciara relaxed her grip on the pillow, as unconscious sighs slipped from her lips. Her mind was wandering in a half awake, half asleep state, floating, soaring, surrounded by yards of satin under a sky full of puffy clouds when Mitch leaned forward and brushed her ear with his lips. "I love you," he whispered. And lowering his dark head to hers, he kissed her cheek, softly, then more urgently as moved down the side of her neck.

He pressed so close, that not even the barest wisp of a breeze could have passed between their bodies. She was his, and he was hers, and at the moment nothing mattered except her fierce love for him. She trembled as his fingers played in her hair, shivered as his palms skimmed the bared flesh of her back, tingled as his lips nibbled at her earlobe.

He climbed over her then, putting them face-to-face, and placed his palms upon her cheeks. Raw need glittered in his eyes as he held her gaze, analyzing her expression, studying her reaction. She blinked, feeling light-headed, and hoped he wouldn't read the passion smoldering inside her.

"I love you," he said again, a tinge of wonder in his voice.

She looked away, shifted restlessly, but the look of helpless uncertainty on his face wasn't that easily forgotten. He loved her. He loved *her!* Ciara ignored the voice inside her that warned her to be still, to be silent. It was surprisingly easy to admit the truth, once the words started tumbling out: "Oh, Mitch, I've missed you so." She wrapped her arms around his neck, drove her fingers through his thick curls. She kissed his cheeks, his chin, his eyelids, punctuated each with a heartfelt "I love you."

He cupped her chin in his large palm, his eyes scanning her face, as if to read her thoughts. "Do you?" he asked. "Do you really?"

She didn't understand the pensive darkness in his eyes. Ciara held his face in her hands. "You know I do."

"Just me? *Only* me?" he asked through clenched teeth.

He'd been so confident in her love before he'd gone away. What had he seen or heard or experienced to shake his trust in that love? Till now, she'd been struggling with her own emotions, trying to hold on to some semblance of pride. None of that mattered now. Ciara wanted nothing but to comfort and assure him, to restore his faith in her. She put everything she had into it, every happy memory, every heartache, every nightmare, every dream she'd had while he was gone. Would she have gone through all that if she *hadn't* loved him? "I love *you,* Mitch Mahoney. Only you, and no one *but* you."

He closed his eyes and heaved a great sigh. She hadn't thought it possible for him to gather her closer, but he did. The rhythmic thumping of his heart lulled her, soothed her and quieted the child within her.

He was smiling slightly when she tilted her face up to his. His dark eyes burned fervently into hers for a silent moment. His kiss caused a small gasp of pleasure to escape her lips. Her blood surged, her pulse pounded. "Mitch," she rasped. "Oh, Mitch…" She loved him hopelessly, helplessly, blindly; the most powerful emotion she'd ever experienced. Heart and mind and soul throbbed with devotion as she pressed her pregnant body against his. He belonged to her and she to him, and this baby was theirs. "Mitch," she sighed, "I wish…"

"Shhh," he said, a fabric softener-scented finger over her lips. His fingers combed the hair back from her face, and he looked deeply into her eyes. What *was* that expression on his beautiful face? Fear? Regret?

And then she knew: Guilt.

Mitch felt guilty for having left her alone. No doubt he blamed himself for the complications of her pregnancy, as well. Hadn't Dr. Peterson explained it to him? Hadn't he told Mitch that her condition had been there, right from the moment of conception?

Something told her this was a situation she must handle carefully, delicately, or his ego could be forever damaged. Ciara would not do to Mitch what her mother had done to her father. She would not subject him to a lifetime of misery for not having done everything her way. Somehow she had to find a way to let him know there were no hard feelings, nothing to forgive, everything to forget.

Ciara snuggled close, closer, until his lightly whiskered cheek bristled against her throat. They lay that way for a long time, Mitch stroking her back, Ciara running her fingers through his dark waves as his warm breaths fanned her. Finally she felt him relax. *There's no time like the present to tell him he has nothing to feel guilty about, not now, not ever again.* Ciara wriggled slightly, shifting her position so that she could meet his eyes.

She had to hold her breath in order to stifle the giggle…because she didn't want to wake him.

It wasn't until something cold and wet pressed against her cheek that she realized she'd fallen asleep, too…had been out quite a while, from the looks of things.

Chester's fur was still damp. "So you've had yourself a bath, have you?" she asked, rumpling his shining coat. *I must have done something mighty good in my childhood,* she thought, *to have earned a husband like this.*

Mitch bent over to pick a speck of lint from the carpet, noticed her staring. "What…? Do I have spinach on my teeth or something?"

"No. I'm just trying to decide if you're real, or a very pleasant mirage."

Grinning, he walked over to her, leaned down and kissed the tip of her nose. Her cheeks. Her lips. The kiss lasted a long, delirious moment. "Could a mirage do that?"

Sinking back into the pillows, she sighed, a dreamy smile playing on her freshly kissed mouth. "If it can, I don't know why folks are so all-fired disappointed when they discover they've seen one."

"I'm making your favorite for supper," he said, changing the subject.

Unconsciously she licked her lips. "Gnocchi?"

Mitch frowned slightly. "I thought breaded cubed steaks were your favorite."

"They're great," she replied with a wide smile. Maybe too wide, she quickly realized. You are an insensitive boob, Ciara Mahoney. Now you've gone and hurt his feelings. "Oh, *that* favorite," she quickly added.

"I don't even know what a naw…a no…what is it, anyway?"

"Nyaw-kee," she pronounced the Italian pasta. "And it's plural, because just one wouldn't be the least bit satisfying. They're fluffy little potato dumplings that melt in your mouth. They sell them, frozen, at the grocery store. They're not nearly as tasty as the ones they make at Chiaparelli's, down in Little Italy, but they'll do when a craving strikes."

He jammed the handle of his feather duster into a back pocket, leaned over to clean up her snack plates. "So, you're having cravings, are you?"

She shrugged, thinking of their massage session. "Maybe one or two…." Then, giggling, she added, "You look like a rooster, with that thing sticking out of your pocket."

He shook his bottom and cock-a-doodle-doo'd for all he was worth, sending Chester into a feather-chasing frenzy. Mitch and the dog rolled on the floor for a moment, playfully wrestling over the cleaning tool. "You two are going to make a terrible mess," she warned, laughing. "You'll be cleaning up feathers for a week."

"But," Mitch groaned, chuckling as he tugged on the plastic handle, "he won't let go."

"Chester," Ciara ordered, "sit."

Immediately the dog obeyed.

"And only one feather out of place," she boasted, buffing her nails against her chest.

He plucked the peacock blue feather from the carpet,

tucked it behind her ear. "Did I ever tell you how beautiful you are while you're sleeping?"

"You're pretty cute with your eyes closed, yourself," she said.

Mitch smiled. "I've got to get back in there before the meat burns. Can I get you anything? Your wish is my command."

She couldn't think when he looked at her with that dark, smoldering gaze. "I can have any wish I want?"

"Any wish you want."

I wish we could make love, she thought, remembering their recent intimacies, the way we did before you left me. "Is it too late to whip up some of those fantastic home fries of yours to go with the steaks?" she asked instead.

Chapter Eight

"Don't pull the plug till I get back, 'cause we don't want you going down the drain...."

Ciara grinned with disbelief. "Six months ago, maybe, but now? Down the drain? I can barely fit in the tub, so you've got to be kidding." She adjusted her headset and snapped an Amy Grant tape into place, then waved him away. "Go on, read your morning paper and leave me to my bubbles."

"Back in ten," he said, smiling as he pulled the door shut behind him.

From the semicircular window in the landing, he could see all the way to the end of their driveway, where the mailbox stood. Earlier, Ciara had sent him outside to put a card in the box and flip the flag up. "Can't forget Ian's birthday," she'd said, grinning, "not this year. It's the big four-oh, y'know."

Mitch craned his neck; if the flag was down, it would mean the....

Instead of the red flag, Mitch spotted a sleek black Ferrari, parked behind Ciara's Miata. One of Pericolo's goons drove a car like that.... Every muscle in him tensed

as he took off down the stairs. In the foyer he breathed a
sigh of relief. *All's secure here*, he thought, jiggling the
bolted knob. *Now for the back door....* He headed for the
kitchen by way of the family room and stopped dead in his
tracks.

The man in Mitch's recliner wore a black suit, maroon
tie, and peered over the pages of the newspaper he held in
one hand. "Well, now," he said, assessing Mitch's
summery attire, "aren't you the picture of suburban
life...deck shoes, Bermuda shorts, madras shirt." With a
jerk of his head, he indicated the side yard. "Don't tell
me...there's a cabin cruiser out there with 'Mahoney's
Bah-lo-nee' painted across its back end, right?"

Mitch's fingers balled into fists. "What're you doin'
here?" he demanded, planting himself in front of the chair.

"Just paying my weekly visit to the little woman." He
shrugged. "You don't expect us to go cold turkey, just
'cause you're home, do you?"

Mitch leaned both palms on the arms of the recliner. "I
don't know what you're up to, Bradley, but it ain't gonna
work. Now beat it." He straightened. "Way I'm feeling
'bout you, this is a dangerous place for you to be...."

Bradley shifted uneasily in the chair. "Hey," he said,
grinning nervously, "is that any way to talk to your boss?"

"*Ex*-boss. I made a couple of phone calls, and—"

The grin became a scowl. "You tryin' to scare me,
Mahoney? 'Cause if you are..."

Mitch's upper lip curled in contempt, his arm shot out
as if it were spring loaded, and he grabbed a handful of
Bradley's collar. "*If* I was tryin' to scare you," he snarled,
twisting the shirt tight against Bradley's throat, "I
wouldn't need a telephone."

Bradley shrank deeper into the chair cushions, eyes
wide with fright as frothy spittle formed in the corners of
his mouth. The hand that had been holding the newspa-

per went limp, and the sports section of the *Baltimore Sun* fluttered to the floor like a wounded gull.

Through the thin material of his T-shirt, Mitch felt something cold and hard pressing against his ribs. Looking down, he saw that Bradley's other hand, sheathed in a surgeon's glove, held a chrome-plated, pearl-handled .35 mm handgun.

The face-off lasted a terrifying moment, Mitch increasing the tension on Bradley's collar, Bradley stepping up the pressure of the gun. "Like I said," Bradley husked, his face reddening further from lack of oxygen, "just stopped by to see how the missus was doing."

In response to the unmistakable *tick-tick-tick* of the hammer being pulled back, Mitch unhanded Bradley's shirt and slowly straightened, held his hands in the air. The man had a loaded weapon trained on him, and he could see by the wild glint in his eyes that he was fully prepared to use it. "Nice piece," he spat. "New?"

"Yes and no." He smirked. "It shoulda been tagged as evidence, when our boys busted Pericolo last week." Shrugging, he added, "It got kind of, ah, misplaced."

Mitch's brow furrowed. "You stole it from the evidence room?"

"You're not as smart as everybody thinks, are ya, Mahoney? It never—"

"Never made it to the evidence room?"

Using the gun as a pointer, he answered, "Have a seat, Mr. High and Mighty, and keep your hands where I can see 'em."

Ciara was upstairs in the tub, alone, naked, vulnerable. Stress was as potentially deadly for her and the baby as that gun in Bradley's hand. *You've got to get that weapon,* Mitch commanded himself. *Somehow you've got to disarm this son of a—*

Still standing, he said, "They're on to you down at

headquarters. Anything happens to me, or to Ciara, they'll know exactly who to—"

"A bluff like that might be useful in poker…" A sinister smile cracked his face. "Speakin' of cards…" He slid a pack of Bicycles from his jacket pocket, slammed it onto the coffee table. "Pick a card, any card."

Mitch's lips formed a thin, stubborn line.

"Do it," Bradley demanded, leaning forward in the chair, tapping the deck with the .35 mm.

He wouldn't know about Pericolo's trick unless—

Stay calm, he warned himself. You lose your cool and you're a dead man. And Ciara… Mitch didn't want to think what Bradley might do to her in his present state of mind. He took a breath to steady his nerves, reached out and grabbed a card.

The ace of spades.

"You know what old Giovanni says about black cards…."

Mitch knew, only too well. He'd passed the sociopath's test that first night, but during his months in Philly, he'd seen two men fail it. Something told him he'd hear their screams of anguish and terror till he drew his last breath.

Bradley reached out, flipped the deck over. Skimming a hand over them, he spread the cards in a neat arc, displaying the ace of spades…times fifty-two.

Then he laughed, a sound that chilled Mitch's blood. "So where's your pretty little bride?" Bradley asked, interrupting Mitch's worrisome thoughts.

He stood taller, squared his shoulders, pretended not to have heard the question. He'd do whatever it took to keep Bradley's focus off Ciara, even if it meant stepping in front of a—

"Don't look so worried, Mahoney. I'd never do anything to hurt her." He snorted. "Won't have to. Once you're out of the way, she'll come with me willingly…she and that…baby she's carrying." He smirked. "Who do you think the little guy'll look like?"

His blood turned to ice, freezing in his veins. It isn't true, *can't* be true, Mitch told himself. Because if it was, everything he believed, everything he held dear about their relationship had been a lie.

And there sat the one man in the world who knew the ugliest fact about him. Mitch was filled with such fury that he wanted to teach him a lesson he wouldn't ever forget.

But Mitch had no proof of her sin. None…except the word of this…to call him a cur or a swine would be to insult all pigs and dogs! Mitch thought. He wanted to punish the smooth-talking, low-life predator. But having no weapon at the ready, he settled for a mild insult. "Come with *you?* Have you taken a good look at yourself lately? You're nothin' but a good-for-nothing hunk of garbage."

"Shut up," Bradley snarled.

"So when did you turn, Bradley? Or have you always been like this, even as a rookie?"

"Careful what you say," Bradley interrupted, waving the gun in the air, "or I'll…"

He was beyond reason now. Nothing scared him as much as the thought of this animal touching his wife. "Or you'll *what?* Take me out? How're you gonna explain *that?*"

Bradley licked his lips, wiped perspiration from his forehead with the back of his gun hand.

Mitch's fingers splayed, and he tensed, ready to grab it.

"I wouldn't if I were you," came Bradley's gravelly warning. His green eyes glittered, like a panther ready to pounce. Then he rested an ankle on a knee, balanced the gun there.

"I could always say I stopped over to see how you were doin'," he said, answering Mitch's question. He laughed softly. "Does this have post-traumatic shock written all over it, or what? I mean, think about it from the point of view of those knuckleheads down in Internal Affairs…guy like you, undercover all those months with a maniac like Pericolo…." He shrugged nonchalantly. Chuckling, he added, "Here's the cherry on the sundae—I could plug you, call it self-defense, and you'd still get a hero's burial. Wouldn't be *your* fault you went nuts."

The way Bradley was quivering, Mitch believed he could wrest the gun from his hand, if he could just get in closer….

"Naw, that's way too complicated. There'd be a hearing, I'd be on administrative leave while IA investigated. Truth is, you ain't worth all that bother."

He tilted the weapon left and right. "For your information, this little number here has Pericolo's prints all over it." He grinned proudly. "I've got this one all tied up with a pretty red bow, eh, Mahoney?" He stared hard, as if debating whether to answer his own question or pull the trigger.

"The weapon may have Pericolo's prints on it, but the guards on his cell block will give him an airtight alibi—or did you forget that small detail, Bradley?"

Bradley got to his feet. "Enough conversation, wise guy. Turn around."

Mitch lifted his chin defiantly and, crossing both arms over his chest, planted his feet shoulder width apart.

"You never did like taking the easy way, did you, Mahoney?" Bradley took a step closer, prepared to forcibly turn Mitch around.

It's now or never…. He grabbed the deck of cards. "Mind if I shuffle and draw again? Might improve my odds."

Bradley chortled. "What's the point? You know they're all—"

Mitch flicked the deck in Bradley's face, and as his hands instinctively went up to protect his eyes, Mitch's left hand shot out, grabbed the gun barrel and pointed it at the ceiling. In a heartbeat, he elbowed Bradley in the Adam's apple, socked him in the stomach, stomped on his instep, rammed a hard shoulder into his nose.

Bradley doubled over, wheezing and moaning. Mitch had the gun now, and he knew it. Holding up the gloved hand, he choked out, "Don't…don't shoot…."

Mitch snorted with disgust. "You're not worth the mess," he ground out. "Now assume the position, while I—"

He heard a thump overhead, and Ciara's muffled voice: "Mitch…what's going on down there?" Mitch cut a quick glance toward the ceiling, and Bradley used that tick in time. Hot on his heels, Mitch ran for the back door and saw the lieutenant leap the fence and duck into the yard next door, where the neighbor's toddlers were splashing contentedly in their blue plastic wading pool.

Mitch drew a bead on Bradley's left shoulder, squeezed back on the trigger, slowly, slowly…

Just then, one of the twins jumped up, putting herself directly in the line of fire. "Mine!" she squealed, grabbing an inflatable horse from her towheaded brother.

Mitch eased up on the trigger as the little boy pulled her back into the water. "No," he insisted, "mine!"

Squinting one eye, he zeroed in on Bradley's shoulder once more, every muscle tense and taut as he held his breath. And then the kids were up again, right in his sights, hollering for their mommy.

From the other side of the forsythia hedge, Bradley saluted and disappeared.

The car…he's gonna circle 'round to get the Ferrari.

Slamming the back door, then bolting it, he blasted through the house. Cursing the knob lock and the dead bolt, he struggled to yank open the front door.

Somebody was out there, all right, standing behind the Ferrari's back bumper. "Good morning, Mitch," said Mrs. Thompson. "How's Ciara this morning?"

Heart hammering, Mitch ran a hand through his hair, jammed the gun into the belt at the small of his back. "Fine…you?"

"Oh, my arthritis is acting up, but in this humidity, what can a seventy-two-year-old expect?" She nodded at the Ferrari. "Fancy car…."

"Belongs to a—" He couldn't make himself say *friend.* "One of my co-workers left it here." The .35 mm wasn't Bradley's, and neither was the car. The lieutenant couldn't afford to come back for either. Mitch knew that now, like he knew his own name. "I think I hear my wife calling," he said, closing the door. "You have a nice day."

Mrs. Thompson smiled, waved. "Tell Ciara I said hi."

Mitch's shoulders slumped and he walked back to the kitchen. He hid the gun in the cookie jar on top of the fridge and grabbed the phone, dialed Parker's extension down at Headquarters. The guy didn't seem the least bit surprised when Mitch filled him in on what had just happened.

"He's never been wrapped too tight," Parker admitted, "but lately…." He whistled the "Twilight Zone" theme.

"You've gotta find him," Mitch interrupted. "My wife's—"

"I know, I know…Bradley told us all about her condition."

"Listen, Parker, he's still out there. I've got his weapon, but he won't have any trouble getting another."

"Okay, okay, Mahoney. Settle down."

"Don't tell me to settle down! If my guess is right, now that I know he's been on the 'take,' and his reputation is ruined, he's got nothin' to lose. I don't have time for your patronizing—"

"Sorry, Mitch. I didn't mean to." He paused. "Look, I know it won't be easy, but you have to settle down, for your wife's sake."

Mitch took a deep breath. "When you call in the APB, get a tow truck out here to pick up this Ferrari in my—"

"Ferrari?" Parker snickered lightly. "Did you get a raise for this last caper, buddy?"

"It's Bradley's…or else it belongs to whoever he's workin' for. You've got to get it out of here. If Ciara sees it, how am I gonna explain…?"

"I'm on it, Buddy."

"Keep me posted, will ya?"

"You bet."

"And send somebody to—"

"I'll get a surveillance guy out there, pronto."

"'A guy'? I put my neck on the chopping block to nab Pericolo. You'll send more than 'a guy'! Who knows what kind of backup Bradley's got…or where he got it. I'm a sittin' duck out here, and—"

"Sit tight, Mitch. I'll see what I can do."

He exhaled loudly, ran a trembling hand through his hair. "Keep me posted, will ya?"

"You bet," Parker said, and hung up.

Mitch glanced at the wall clock. When he came downstairs earlier, he had promised to get Ciara out of the tub in ten minutes. Amazingly, he had three whole minutes to spare. Three minutes to calm down and get up there and pretend everything was hunky-dory.

"Sweet Jesus," he prayed aloud, "give me strength."

Chet Bradley was a bald-faced liar. A turncoat, possibly a burglar—since he'd picked the back lock to get into the house—and a killer. The pampered little rich boy had never wanted for anything in his life—the fact that he was Mitch's boss without having had to pass the customary tests, was proof of that—so, was it any surprise that faced with temptation, he'd shown no self-control, snatching up bribe money with both hands? His whole life was a story of instant gratification…why should that change now?

In Mitch's mind, men like Bradley were worse than the Pericolos of the world; at least folks knew where they stood with a guy like Giovanni. Bradley was repugnant, foul, lower than a gutter rat. He'd come to the house for the express purpose of murdering Mitch, to keep him from testifying against him at an interdepartmental hearing…or in a courtroom. If he'd had to take Ciara down first to get to Mitch, he'd have done it in a whipstitch.

He raised the book he'd been pretending to read, glanced over its pages at Ciara, who absentmindedly twirled a length of flaxen hair around her forefinger as, word by word, she filled in the blocks of her crossword. Suddenly she exhaled a sigh of vexation, pencil eraser bouncing on the puzzle. The feminine arch of her left brow increased, the gentle bow of her lips smoothed, dark lashes dusted her lightly freckled cheeks as she slid a dainty fingertip down a column of definitions in the dictionary.

She was, in his opinion, the loveliest woman on two feet. Pregnancy had only enhanced her beauty, filling out the sharp angles and planes of her girlish face in a womanly, sensual way.

Sensual enough to reach out to Bradley for physical comfort in her husband's absence?

He remembered the things her mother had said, things that made it clear Bradley had spent countless hours in this house, alone with his wife. Mitch felt the heat of jealous fury rise in his cheeks, took a sip from the glass of the ice water, standing on a soapstone coaster beside him, hoping to cool his temper.

Is she the innocent young thing you married, or a passionate woman? She's both, he admitted, the edge of his uncertainty sharpening.

Mitch now pressed a thumb to one temple, his fingertips to the other, effectively blocking her from view, and remembered their wedding night, how she'd stared up at him, willing him to hold her close with nothing more than the silent draw of her long-lashed crystalline eyes.

The moment he'd slipped his arms around her, he knew…knew he'd be with her till the end of his life. Mitch knew it now, too, even if he discovered that every one of his ugly suspicions were true.

He'd lived a rough, rugged life, and his women had been a reflection of that, because he'd had neither the time nor the inclination for love. Life was mean, and so he lived it that way. Tenderness? Compassion? A lot of romantic nonsense, in his opinion. Besides, what did a man like him, who had committed himself to spending his days dogging bad guys and dodging bullets, need with love? He couldn't afford to fritter away even one precious moment, seeking something he believed he should not have.

And so he'd guarded his heart with extreme caution. Built a sturdy wall to protect himself. If he couldn't accept love, why bother to give it? But Ciara had burrowed under that wall. Yes, life was mean…past tense. She had changed all that. He'd built a wall around his heart, all right, but he hadn't built it nearly tall enough or strong enough, because he hadn't counted on meeting a woman like Ciara….

When she laughed, her whole body got involved. And if something saddened those close to her, it was apparent to anyone with eyes that she felt the pain, too, all the way down to her size-five feet.

That night on the cruise ship, when she'd looked into

his eyes, he realized that she saw him as the man he'd always wanted to be. No need for a fancy suit or a Boston education. No need for pretense or pretty words, not with Ciara!

She could read his moods by something as insignificant as a quirk of an eyebrow or the slant of his smile. Mitch strongly suspected she could read his mind, too, for on more than one occasion she'd spoken aloud the thoughts pinging around in his head.

She seemed to sense how alone he felt, despite the fact that he had three burly brothers and two sisters, parents, grandparents, aunts and uncles and cousins. She had taken one look at his college graduation picture, crinkled her face with compassion and said, "Oh, Mitch, why do you look so *sad?*"

When his mother had seen the photo, she'd said, "Such a handsome boy, that youngest son of mine!" And his dad had agreed. "He's got the Mahoney jaw, all right." Why hadn't the people he'd known all his life been able to see the quiet fear, the desperation burning in his eyes, yet Ciara, who'd known him mere weeks the first time she'd viewed the portrait, had spotted it right off?

Mitch had marveled at that, because until she'd pointed it out and followed it up by dispensing her unique brand of all-out love like warm soothing salve, *he* hadn't admitted it!

Starting on their wedding night, without regard for her own needs and desires and fears, she gave what *he* needed. And in her tender, feminine embrace, he felt at once sheltered and exposed, strong and weak, manly and boylike.

And more alive than he'd ever felt in his life.

Doggone if she isn't some kind of woman! he thought. Li'l thing whose head barely reaches your shoulders, becoming the biggest thing in your life....

Mitch had never felt any regret about leaving places or

people when his cases ended, and it was time to move on. But Mitch knew if he ever had to leave Ciara, he'd miss her more than he would miss water.

The breath caught in his throat as he recalled the sensation of her slender fingers, weaving through his hair on the night the preacher made them man and wife. Her whisper-soft sighs had floated into his ears as she responded to his touch, and her heart—the same heart that had beat hard and angry when faced with life's injustices—thumped wildly against his chest as he held her close.

The first time he'd said those three words on the cruise ship deck, he'd asked himself, Are you crazy? Shut up, man! Say whatever she wants to hear, but don't say that! And he'd shrugged, thinking that when a man thought a thing a thousand times or more, wasn't it just natural to say it out loud? He'd spent his whole adult life avoiding that phrase, words that, until Ciara, had been fearsome. Yet they'd linked together and rolled off his tongue so easily and naturally, all he could do was hope they'd spilled out quietly enough that she hadn't heard them.

"What did you say?" she'd asked, her voice husky.

He couldn't very well repeat it, now could he? It wouldn't have been fair to either of them, since he knew full well he wouldn't be seeing her once the trip ended, no matter how much he'd meant what he said.

Oh, how she'd *moved* him! She'd reached places in his heart and soul and mind that he would have bet his last dollar were impossible to reach…if they existed at all.

"What did you say?" was her quiet, honest question.

Mitch wouldn't have hurt her for all the world. He'd rather die than cause her a moment's pain. So he'd stood there, trying to conjure up a similar-sounding phrase that would answer her…painlessly. No matter what he said, *he'd* be hurt….

If she hadn't branded him with that loving, longing look as she traced his lips with her fingertips right then, Mitch might have summoned the strength to pull it off. But that intimate, yet innocent, gesture was the final hammer stroke to the already crumbling wall he'd built around his heart.

He'd watched her with his nieces and nephews, doling out instructions and admonitions and compliments with equal care. He'd seen her minister to her elderly aunt, and to her parents, with a compassion he'd once believed reserved only for God's angels.

He had never let anyone see him cry. Not even the threat of dying in the trunk of a car had pushed him that far. But gazing into her eyes, seeing the purity of her love looking back at him, woke emotions long asleep. And once awakened, those feelings bubbled up and boiled over like a too-hot stew pot. He'd never wanted anything in his life more than he wanted her and her pure, unconditional love.

So he'd gathered her close, closer, whether to hide his tears from her or hide her from his tears, Mitch didn't know, and rested his chin amid her mass of soft, pale curls. "I'd better get to my cabin," he'd said, his voice gruff and hard from biting back a sob. And he'd walked away, just like that, without a backward glance or a by-your-leave.

And the night stretched on endlessly.

He'd exposed his most vulnerable self to her. How could he face her again, knowing she'd seen his weakness? Mitch fretted about it all through the night. Yearning, he understood, was an emotion born of experiencing perfection, and he wished he'd never begun this dangerous game of flirtation-turned-fondness-turned-love. Because he didn't believe he deserved the devotion of one so fine, so pure, so innocent. Didn't believe he'd earned the loyalty of a woman that fine.

He'd been like an animal these past years, like a mole, always seeking shadows as he moved from place to place in search of safety, in search of peace. Survival of the fittest, he'd heard, was the law of the land. Well, he'd survived top-secret cases, but to what end? To find safety and peace in Ciara's arms, only to discover he didn't deserve it? Far better never to have tasted fine wine at all than to have it snatched away, forcing him to live forever-more without even the smallest sip.

He had learned to accept the fact that, because of his career choice, he'd never have a family. A home. The love of a good woman. But could he learn to live without Ciara's love, now that he'd tasted the sweetness of it?

A sob ached in his throat, and Mitch buried his face in the pages of his book. If she shared herself with *him,* he thought, gritting his teeth, even if it *was* because she was lonesome, and scared, I'll—

"Mitch? What's wrong?"

Like the angel she was, Ciara had read his heart. "Nothing," he said, holding the book high, to hide his teary eyes.

"I'm cold," she said, patting the mattress. "Would you hold me…get me warm?"

He put down his book, crossed the room in two strides and settled beside her. He buried his face in her neck and wrapped both arms around her, holding this fragile flower who had planted the seed of her love deep in his heart, as the wild rose vine plants its seed even in the craggiest out-cropping of a snow-covered mountaintop. He would hold tight to perfection for as long as he could, so at least he'd have these moments to remember, in case she'd meant it when she told him to pack up and leave.

Placing a tiny hand on either side of his face, she brought him out of hiding. Tears shimmered in her eyes and glistened on her long, lush lashes when she said, "I love you, Mitch."

She pressed her lips to his, softly at first as she combed delicate fingers through his hair, more urgently then, as those dainty fingers clutched at his shoulders, his back, his neck, with a strength that belied her size and condition.

Oh, how he wanted her! Wanted her with every echo of his soul, with every beat of his heart. But he dared not want….

He'd seen film footage of the floods in the midwest the summer before, when the rivers rose and threatened to devour every building and barn, every mortal man or mammal for miles. The surging water's awesome power humbled him as he watched it sluice through the streets, hissing like a giant turbid snake.

What emanated from Ciara, who felt so small and helpless in his arms, was far more powerful than the river's rage. And though she didn't know it—and certainly wouldn't have intended it—she stirred more fear and apprehension in him than the roiling waterway.

Mitch had survived numerous near fatal experiences, but with nothing to live for or look forward to, death had no authority over him. Even Bradley, brandishing his loaded gun, hadn't terrified him as much as this tiny woman in his arms. She loved him. He could see it in her eyes, in her smile. Could feel it in her touch, taste it in her kiss. And he loved her more than life itself. If she *had* succumbed to temptation, it had only been because he'd left her alone for so long….

He looked inside himself for the strength to turn away from the love so evident on her face, and rested his hands on her thickened waist.

They were strong hands. Hands that had not wavered, no matter how strenuous the task. And yet, when he put those work-hardened hands on this woman, they trembled, the way a crisp autumn leaf shivers at winter's first icy blast.

He looked into her eyes, read the love there. Hesitantly he ran a hand down her back, and when he did, a rough callus caught on the finely woven fabric of her nightgown. He stopped, pulling abruptly away, embarrassed that his big clumsy hand had damaged the pretty gown.

Yet again she read his heart. "It's all right," she whispered.

But it wasn't all right. Nothing would ever be all right, until he knew for certain whether she had betrayed her vows. Because he loved her like he'd never loved anyone, like he'd never known it was *possible* to love, and the moment he admitted it, Mitch was doomed.

She pressed his "offending" hand to her chest. "See? I'm nervous, too…."

He felt the wild thrumming of her heart, felt it vibrate through his palm, past his wrist and elbow, straight to the core of him. They were connected, for the moment, by hard-beating hearts, by desire that coursed from her into him.

In a move that stunned and surprised him, she boldly reached out and grabbed his shirt collar, drawing him near, her soft yet insistent kisses imprinting on his heart as surely as a cowboy's branding iron sears the rancher's brand to his cattle.

His mind whirled as a sweet, soft moan sang from deep within her, its music moving over him like wind ripples on a still pond, and he returned her kiss with equal ardor.

"Easy," she sighed. "Easy…."

Misunderstanding her intent, Mitch immediately withdrew. Ciara read the hurt and humiliation burning in his eyes. "I said *easy,*" she smiled mischievously, "not *stop.*"

His left brow quirked and his lips slanted in a grin.

"You weren't really cold, were you?"

Ciara shrugged. "Would I have said I was if I wasn't?"

He nodded. "I think you would."

Her fingertip traced his eyebrows, his cheekbones, his jaw. "Are you saying you think I'm dishonest?"

"Never intentionally," he said.

Frowning, she gave him a crooked grin. "What does *that* mean?"

You're a passionate woman, he told her mentally. You're not the kind who can be left alone, to wilt and die without—

"Mitch," she said, interrupting his reverie, "what's going on in that head of yours? You've been acting strange all day. Is there something you're not telling me?"

I could ask you the same question, he thought. And then Bradley, the gun, the knowledge that the fool was out there somewhere, carrying a heated vengeance around in that sick, twisted mind of his, blotted out Mitch's response.

She backed away to arm's length, gave him a stern look. "I'm not a child, Mitch. If there's something I should know…"

Mitch wasn't about to upset the apple cart. Her blood count, the readouts Peterson had been getting by way of the monitor, everything had been going fine, up till now, and he intended to keep it that way. "I'm just worried about you," he said truthfully, pulling her closer, resting his chin atop her head.

Worried that this baby is going to die, or kill you, and wouldn't that be ironic if it isn't even mine….

"Mitch?"

"Hmm?"

"I love you…."

He closed his eyes tight. *Dear God in Heaven, give me strength….* "I love you, too, sweetie. I love you, too."

Chapter Nine

*T*he bright blue sky warmed the mourners who stood in
a tight semicircle, heads bowed and hands folded, as
sunlight glinted off the polished brass handles, pointing
toward heaven like luminescent arrows. And Ciara, dry-
eyed and tight-lipped, stared at the white enamel casket,
trying to focus on the preacher's powerful voice.

"And our time comes to an end like a sigh...." He
closed his eyes, smiled serenely and began reciting from
the Book of Job: "'Thine hands have made me and fash-
ioned me together roundabout; yet thou dost destroy me.
Remember, I beseech thee, that thou hast made me as the
clay; wilt thou bring me into dust again?'" Closing the
Holy Book, he bent down, scooped up a handful of freshly-
dug dirt and sprinkled it into the hole. "'You shall return
to the ground,'" he quoted Genesis, "'for out of it you were
taken; you are dust, and to dust you shall return.'"

Ciara wanted to shake a fist at the sky. *Why, God? she
wanted to shout.* Don't You have enough cherubim and
seraphim? Did You have to take *my* baby boy...?

*She had not cried over the death of her child, had not
shed a single tear. Would tears bring him back to life?*

Would sobs revive him? Would the ache in her heart matter at all to the One Who had taken him?

Absentmindedly she kneaded her stomach, where so recently the infant had nestled in her nurturing womb, taking quiet comfort from her steadfast love. He had moved inside her, each strong jab and kick proof of his vitality and vigor.

In a flash, the bright blue sky turned blinding white, and Ciara was in the delivery room, perspiring and panting as the contractions contorted her face.

It's all right, *she told herself.* The pain is only temporary. When this is over, you'll have a beautiful baby boy....

She didn't know how she knew it was a boy, but she knew. She knew....

Soon, the doctor would lay him on her chest, kicking, crying, arms akimbo. She'd smooth back his wet hair, count teensy fingers and toes, inspect every tiny joint, every minuscule crevice, each contour and curve and line of his warm little body. She'd soothe and comfort him, and his small, hungry lips would seek nourishment from her milk-laden breast.

"Just a few more minutes," the doctor said. "Just a few more minutes."

Pride and joy and thankfulness filled her eyes with tears, put a sob in her throat. Just a few more minutes, she repeated, smiling. In a few minutes, I'll be a mommy.

She made herself focus on the bustle of activity in the blindingly bright delivery room—shuffle of paper-shoed feet, the rustle of surgical gowns, banter of the staff, clank of tools against stainless steel trays—instead of the pain, the gripping, never-ending, powerful pain....

Then, for a half second, maybe less, silence—deep and still and falsely calm. No one moved or spoke or breathed, as if the world had stopped spinning and everything, everyone in it had ceased to exist.

In the next eyeblink, life!

Ciara knew—though she didn't understand how she knew—that during the instant of deadly quiet, her baby boy had died. She knew because the pain of childbirth had ceased, and in its place, heartache like none she'd experienced.

The doctor gave her knee an obligatory pat, pat, pat. "I'm so sorry, Mrs. Mahoney, but…"

Her heartbeat doubled, tripled.

"We did everything we could, but," he said softly, so very softly that Ciara thought perhaps she'd imagined it; perhaps it had been part of a pain-induced hallucination. "There's no easy way to say this, I'm afraid… but your baby is dead."

With every beat of her heart, every pound of her pulse, the word echoed in her head. Dead. Your baby is dead…dead…dead.

The eye-blinding white light warmed to a golden glow, and she found herself in the cemetery again, eyes locked on an ivory coffin hardly bigger than a breadbox. Any minute now it would be lowered into the rectangular hole carved into the earth by shovel and pickax. The hole was hardly bigger than the casket, yet it seemed to gape and yawn like a ravenous, savage beast, hungering to swallow up her newborn son, forever.

Ciara forced her gaze away from her boy's eternal bed, focused on the faces of the people who had gathered around: her mother, daubing her face with a lace-trimmed hanky; her father, staring stoically straight ahead; sniffling in-laws; sad-eyed neighbors and co-workers; a few of her students, looking bewildered by this thing called Death; and their parents, whose expressions said, I'm sorry, but better you than me…. Everyone had shed at least one tear for the infant whose birth caused his death.

So why not Ciara? People will think you didn't love

him; people will think you don't care. And that was a lie, the biggest lie ever told.

Ciara had never held him to her breast. Had never looked into the miracle that was his face. Had never inhaled the sweet scent of his satiny skin. Would not hear his soft coos or his demanding cries. Could never feel the miraculous strength of his tiny fingers, wrapping around her own. But she loved him, and oh, how she missed him!

It began as nothing more than a solitary thought in her head:

No....

And became a soft whisper that no one, not even those right beside her could hear: "*No....*"

Then heads turned, and the monotonous din of voices, joined in prayer, quieted when she said more loudly, more firmly, "No."

"No!" she screamed, falling across the coffin. "No, no, no, no, no...."

A man's voice, deep, powerful—her father's?—floated into her ears. "Ciara, sweetie, don't—"

Don't what? Don't grieve for my baby? Don't make a scene? Don't make the rest of you uncomfortable?

She gripped the little casket tighter. "You can't have him, Lord!" she yelled. "You can't take him, because he's mine!"

Then, utter silence.

Ciara looked around her, surprised that the other mourners were gone, all of them.

Car doors slammed.

Engines revved.

The grounds crew stepped forward. Where had they come from? And a beer-bellied man in a grimy baseball cap stuck out one gloved finger, pressed the red button and started up the machine that would carry the casket down, down into the dark, damp dirt.

Rage roiled inside her. Don't! *she ordered.* Stop that, right now! *But the motor continued grinding.*

Ciara wanted to grab his fat wrist, crush every bone in the hand responsible for beginning her son's slow, steady descent into the cold, unwelcoming earth.

The mournful moan started softly at first, then esca-lated in pitch and volume, like the first piercing strains of a fire engine's wail. She couldn't pinpoint the source of the grief-stricken groan, and, frightened by it, Ciara clapped her hands over her ears. The keening call echoed all around her, bounced from marble headstones, granite angels, trellised tombstones and returned, like a self-willed boomerang to its genesis.

"No-o-o-o-o-o-o…"

Then, big hands, strong, sure hands gripped her shoul-ders.

"Ciara? Ciara…"

"Where's Mitch?" she sobbed. "Where is my husband? Why isn't he here? Why!"

"I'm here, Ciara, I'm here, right here, right—"

"That was some dream," Mitch said when her eyes fluttered open. He slipped an arm under her neck, pulled her near. "Aw, sweetie," he sighed, kissing her temple, "you're trembling." He tugged the sheet over her shoulder, tucked it under her chin. "How 'bout a cup of warm milk?" he asked, holding her closer. "Maybe that'll relax you, help you get back to sleep…"

"I hate milk," she mumbled, her voice sleep drowsy.

Something you should know after eight months of marriage, he scolded himself. Holding her at arm's length, Mitch cupped her chin in a palm. "You want to talk about it?"

Ciara shook her head, then buried her face in his shoulder. "You weren't there," she whispered brokenly. "You…weren't…*there.*"

She sounded so forlorn, so frightened, like a child lost in the woods. His heart ached, because once again, he felt powerless to comfort her. "I wasn't *where,* sweetie?" he asked, brushing the bangs from her forehead.

Ciara shook her head. "Nothing…just, just a dream…"

Nearly every inch of her was pressed against him, yet Mitch felt as though someone had built a brick wall between them. Her taut muscles, her refusal to tell him about the nightmare, the way her voice trembled when she'd said, "You weren't there…"

He held her a long while, not talking, not asking her to. A shaft of moonlight had slipped under the window shade, cutting an inch-wide slice of light through the blackness. It lit the room just enough for him to see her sad, still-sleepy eyes.

"I know I wasn't here," he said at last, a tremor in his own voice. "I can't tell you anything that'll undo what's already done, but I can tell you this—I'll be here for you from now on. I promise."

He waited for a reaction of some kind: a nod, a sigh, *something.*

Either she's asleep, he told himself, or she doesn't believe you.

Tears stung his eyes, and he held his breath to keep them at bay. He had done this to her—he, and the Bureau—and if she *had* strayed during his absence…

He held her a little tighter, kissed the top of her head.

"What're we going to do, once this baby is born?" she'd asked earlier, worried he might spoil her, waiting on her constantly.

The question became a chant in his wide-awake mind: What're we going to do? What're we going to do?

Her health was precarious, at best.

The baby, if it survived, might not even be his.

And Bradley was out there somewhere, fully convinced

that the only way to stay out of prison was to silence Mitch…permanently.

Mitch shivered involuntarily. He certainly didn't want to die, especially now that he and Ciara were so close to getting back what they'd once had. If something happened to him now, who would look after her?

Lord Jesus, he prayed, *what am I going to do?*

She couldn't get that dream out of her mind until the baby moved inside her. Even then, the eerie aftereffects flashed in her mind.

Ciara put her full attention on the cross-stitch she'd been working on. Better that than try and make small talk with Mitch, she thought. "I'm just tired, that's all," she'd fibbed, when he'd asked if she was feeling okay. "It's nothing," she'd answered, when he'd wanted to know if something was wrong. "Thanks, but I'm fine," she'd said, when he'd offered to bring her a snack. What else *could* she do…admit she was furious at him for something he'd done or hadn't done…in a *dream?*

Mitch made a few calls on the kitchen phone, pacing as far as the twelve-foot cord would allow, talking in low, steady tones, rousing her curiosity and more than just a little of her suspicion. Who was he talking to, and what topic demanded such privacy?

Had he met a woman while he'd been undercover? Someone who had made his lonely days more bearable; someone who hadn't been so easy to say goodbye to?

Or were there loose ends, still unraveled, ends that could choke him if he didn't tie them up?

This job of his is going to be the death of me, she fumed.

The thought distracted her from the needlework, and she pricked her finger. "Ouch!" she said, popping it into her mouth.

Holding the phone against his chest, Mitch stuck his head into the doorway. "You okay in there?"

She held her finger up, as if testing the direction of the wind. "Stuck myself," she said, rolling her eyes. "No big deal."

Nodding, he smiled. "Whistle if you need me," he said, and popped out of sight again.

She could have picked up the portable, pretended she'd forgotten he was using the extension. Perhaps a snippet of conversation would answer her questions. Maybe a word, a phrase, overheard before he realized she'd joined him on the line, would ease her fears.

Or you could act like a grown-up, and ask him straight-out, she told herself. No…just because he's your husband doesn't mean you have a right to know *every* intimate detail of his life.

Intimate?

Could a man like that have sought comfort in the arms of another woman? Ciara shuddered, shook her head. Not Mitch. Anyone but Mitch. She had never met a more fiercely loyal man. He was devoted to his family. Dedicated to his job. Unwavering in his reasons for choosing a career in law enforcement.

"What are you making, there?" Mitch asked.

Gasping, Ciara lurched with fright.

He was beside her on the sofa bed in an instant. "Are you all right? Geez, I'm sorry, sweetie. I didn't mean to scare you."

"It's okay," she said, patting her chest, as if the action could slow the rapid beating of her heart. "It wasn't your fault." She had always liked working in complete silence, without radio or stereo or TV to interfere with her private thoughts. And at the moment when his voice had cracked the stillness of the afternoon, her thoughts had been very private, indeed.

He turned his head slightly, regarding her from the corner of his eyes. "You sure you're okay?"

She nodded.

"And you don't want anything? More tea? A cookie? Some—"

"I'm fine, honest," she interrupted.

Mitch continued to study her face for a moment more. "All right, if you say so."

The glint in his dark eyes told her he didn't believe a word of it. "You want the truth? Really?"

His brows rose in response to her terse tone. Blinking innocently he said, "Well, I asked, didn't I?"

Ciara narrowed her eyes, set her needlepoint aside, crossed both arms over her chest. "You asked for it…."

He lay on his side facing her, drove his elbow into the extra pillow, and propped his head on a palm. "Go on. Start talkin'. I'm all ears."

You weren't there for me in the dream, and you weren't there for me in real life, she thought, the stirrings of anger niggling at her. Ciara remembered the day she discovered she was going to have a baby. The first person she had wanted to tell, naturally, had been Mitch. And where were you? she demanded mentally. You were off somewhere making like James Bond.

And when the doctor had diagnosed her condition, warned her to stay off her feet. Where were you then? Where *were* you!

He had been so gentle and affectionate, so tender and loving when the nightmare had awakened her. He had been that way, practically from the moment they'd met, and those very qualities had made being without him all those months so much harder to bear. Ciara seemed to remember muttering and mumbling noncommittal responses to his quiet questions. But what would he have done if you'd told him the truth? she wondered. How affectionate would he have been then?

"What are you trying to do," he asked, grinning, "win the Alfred Hitchcock 'Keep 'em in Suspense' award?"

Their gazes fused on an invisible thread of tension…his the result of confusion, hers caused by steadily mounting anger.

Mitch reached out slowly, gently laying a palm against her cheek. "You look so tired, sweetie," he said. "Let me hold you so you can take a little nap, right here on my shoulder."

She planted both palms on his chest, locked her elbows and managed to keep him at arm's length. "Do I smell beer on your breath?" she asked, narrowing one eye suspiciously.

He held up two fingers. "I had two. That's all. While I was cleaning up your lunch dishes." He snickered. "Just two…on an empty stomach."

Ciara looked into his eyes. He was right…he hadn't had a bite to eat all day. He looked so cute, so helpless; how could she lambaste him in this condition!

"So, what do you say? You want to take a little nap?"

"I'm not sleepy, Mitch. I'm…I'm bored, and I'm tired, and I'm achy from lying around like a hundred-year-old house cat all day. I'm sick of looking at these four walls, and I'm—"

"Tomorrow is the Fourth of July, you know."

She gave her head a little shake, drew her brows together in a frown. "What?"

"Oh, sweetie, I've got it all worked out! First, we'll have a big country breakfast…pancakes, home fries, eggs over easy. After your bath, we'll get you into some real clothes for a change, watch the parade on TV. This evening we'll have a cookout—steaks, potato salad, baked beans— the works! And after that, we'll lounge around in the deck chairs, watching the sky get dark…." Mitch wiggled his eyebrows. "Did you know that we can see the fireworks from the mall in Columbia from our backyard?"

Smiling, Ciara shook her head, so caught up in his excited recitation that she almost forgot why she'd been mad in the first place. "You're a grown man, Mitch Mahoney. How can you get so caught up in a light show?" she asked affectionately. "Besides, how do you know that?"

"I don't see anything wrong with looking forward to some stars and spangles," he said defensively. And just as quickly he added, "Old Mrs. Thompson told me the other morning. She's comin' over for the barbecue and bringing her grandson. He's four." Squinting one eye, he looked toward the ceiling. "His name is Nicky or Ricky or something like that. Your folks are coming, too, and so is the entire Mahoney clan."

Ciara's eyes lit up. "You're kidding. When did you plan—"

"This morning. I made about a dozen phone calls while you were working on…" He leaned forward. "What *is* that thing, anyway?"

She clutched the fabric to her chest. "I don't like people looking at my needlework until it's finished."

He went back to resting on his palm. "You've been working on it for days," he grumbled good-naturedly. "When is it going to be finished, anyway?"

He looked like a little boy, Ciara thought, when he pouted that way. Grinning maternally, she answered him as if he were one of her fourth-graders. "It'll be finished when it's finished, young man."

Mitch grabbed the finger she was shaking under his nose. "Didn't your mother teach you it isn't polite to point?" he asked, kissing it.

"She did. But I wasn't pointing. I was scolding. There's a difference."

"Not when you're on the receiving end, there isn't." He kissed her palm. "Besides, 'When you point a finger at me, you're pointing three more right back at you.'" Pressing his lips to her wrist, he added, "I learned that in the second grade, when I accused Carrie Butler of putting a valentine card in my tote tray."

"Carrie Butler, eh?" Ciara asked, one brow up in mock jealousy. "You sure pulled that name out of the air pretty quick, considering how long ago you were in second grade."

"Hey," he mumbled into the crook of her elbow, "watch it. It wasn't *that* long ago."

"I'd say a quarter of a century ago is a long time." She giggled. "Mitch. Stop that. It tickles."

"What…this?" he teased, kissing the spot again.

"Yes, that. Now cut it out," she insisted, laughing harder. "I mean it now…."

"Okay. Sorry. I was just trying to distract you, is all."

She looked into his handsome face. "Distract me? Distract me from what?"

"From asking any more questions about Carrie." He winked, then sent her a mischievous smirk. "I asked her to marry me, you know."

Grinning now, Ciara gasped, pressed a palm to her chest. "But…but you said *I* was the first woman you proposed to…."

"You were the first *woman.* Carrie was the first *girl.*" He rolled onto his back, tucked both hands under his neck and exhaled a dreamy sigh. "I met her in kindergarten, in the sand pit. She beaned me with a red plastic shovel. It was love at first strike."

Another gasp. "You said she was the *first* girl…there were others?"

He shrugged. "Oh," he said lightly, inspecting his fingernails, "one or two."

She grabbed a handful of his shirt. "How many others? I want names and addresses, mister, 'cause I aim to hunt them down, every last one of them, and—"

"Whoa," he interrupted, hands up in mock surrender. "I've never seen this side of you before."

"What side?"

"The jealous, vindictive side."

She blew a puff of air through her lips. "Jealous? I'm not jealous. I'll have you know I don't have a jealous bone in my body."

He looked almost wounded. "You don't?"

Shaking her head, she announced emphatically, "Not a one."

"So it doesn't bother you that Carrie was my first?"

She giggled. "Not in the least!" After a moment she added, "Your first what?"

"My first love, of course."

Grinning, Ciara rolled her eyes. "You weren't in love. You were *seven*."

"I wasn't seven."

"Everybody is seven in the second grade. Didn't you just say you asked her to marry you in the second…."

"Yes, but I asked her again when we were in high school."

This wasn't funny anymore. He'd known this Carrie person since kindergarten, had asked her to marry him in high school. "So what did she say?"

Mitch blinked. "What did who say?"

Ciara gave his shoulder a playful slap. "Carrie, silly. When you asked her to marry you…the second time… what did she say?"

"She told me to take a flying leap." He did a perfect Stan Laurel nod of his head.

"But…but you must have been sweet and handsome even then. *Why* did she say no?"

"Did I say she said no?"

"You said she told you to—"

"Take a flying leap. That's right."

Ciara exhaled a frustrated sigh. "If that isn't a rejection, I don't know what is."

"We were both on the gymnastics team. I was on the parallel bars. She kept pesterin' me to get off, give her a turn. And I said, 'Gosh, Carrie, you sound just like a wife. Maybe we should get married.' And she said, 'Mitch Mahoney, why don't you—'"

"'Take a flying leap?'" they finished together, laughing.

They lay there cuddling in silence for a moment before Ciara said, "What did this Carrie girl look like?"

"Mmmm," he growled, "she was hot stuff. Blonde, blue-eyed, with the cutest nose I ever—"

"Sounds like you're describing me!"

"Hmmm." He rubbed his chin thoughtfully. "I hadn't noticed…."

She quirked a brow. "Did you ever ask her to marry you again? After the uneven bars incident, I mean?"

"As a matter of fact, I didn't."

"Why not?"

"Hey, I wasn't the brightest bulb on the tree, but nobody coulda called me dim-watted, either."

"Dim-witted," she corrected with a twinkle in her eye.

Mitch sighed. Clapped a hand over his forehead. "*Carrie* always got my puns." He peeked between two fingers. "She thought they were funny, too."

Ciara sniffed indignantly. "Well, she must have had a very strange sense of what's funny." She paused. "Did you *want* her to say yes?"

"Maybe, but only a little."

She clucked her tongue, then said, "Say, our names are awfully similar…Carrie, Ciara…why you can barely tell them apart!"

"Hmmm." He went back to massaging his chin. "What do you suppose it means?"

"That you were searching for a Carrie replacement…for *years*…and you found it in *me!*"

He wrinkled his brow. "You think so?" He gave it a moment of consideration. "Naw. I don't think so."

"I wonder what Sigmund Freud would say about it?"

"He'd say, 'Mitch, if you have a lick of sense, you'll get your high school yearbook and show your pretty little wife what Carrie *really* looked like, before she boxes your ears.'"

"What are you talking about?" she asked, when he climbed off the sofa bed.

Mitch rummaged on the bookshelf, slid the black volume from between three other yearbooks. He flipped to the back, skimmed the glossary, chanting, "Butler, Butler, Butler…ah, there she is. Page two-sixteen."

He opened the book to the right page, handed it to Ciara.

She slid a finger over the glossy paper, stopping beside the postage-stamp-size black-and-white photo of Carrie Butler. The girl had short dark hair, a monobrow, and a slightly hairy upper lip. "'French Club president, Math Club, Chess Club,'" Ciara read. She eyed him warily. "You really asked her to marry you?"

"What can I say? The guys were always pickin' on her."

Her heart thumped with love for him. "You mean, you risked being teased by the other kids, because you felt sorry for her?"

He shook his head. "Shoulda let you go on thinking Carrie was your twin, 'cause this is embarrassing."

His reddened cheeks told her he hadn't been kidding. "Mitch, I don't think I ever loved you more than I do at this minute."

He tucked in his chin. "Why?"

"Because," she said softly, "you have a heart as big as your head, that's why."

And a man with a heart like that, she told herself, smiling happily, couldn't cheat on his wife.

Chapter Ten

Ciara looked around her at friends and family who had gathered in response to Mitch's invitation. On blankets spread on the lawn, in deck chairs, at the umbrella-shaded patio table, they sat, sipping iced tea and munching hot dogs.

"How's my girl?" Joe Dorsey asked.

She held out her hand to the tall, gray-haired man who sat in the chaise lounge beside her. "Better than I've been in a long time, Dad."

He squeezed, then patted her hand affectionately, his blue eyes glittering. "I have to admit, you look good. You look happy."

"I am happy." Ciara turned slightly in the chair to face him more directly. "Am I crazy, Dad? Am I out of my ever-lovin' mind to feel this way?"

He frowned slightly. "Of course not. You're young and beautiful and a wonderful human being. You have every right to be happy."

Sighing, she glanced across the yard, where Mitch stood, tossing a softball back and forth with his nephew. The gentle July breeze riffled his dark curls, giving a boyish quality to the masculine angles and planes of his handsome face. Sunlight, dappling through the leafy trees overhead, sparkled in his dark eyes. His smile reminded her of the way she felt whenever, after days and days of gray skies and rain, the clouds lifted and the sun would come out. *Lord, how I love him,* she prayed silently.

But he'd left her, with no word or warning. Had put himself in harm's way to apprehend an unknown criminal who'd committed some heinous crime.... Would he ever tell her where he'd been? What he'd been doing? Why he'd left the way he had?

Ciara sighed. "I love him," she said softly, squeezing her father's hand. "Maybe I *am* crazy, because I don't know if I have what it takes—"

"To love him? Of course you have what it takes. Look at you," he said with a nod of his chin, "sitting there. You've been sitting around, doing nothing, for two solid weeks now." One graying brow rose as he added, "I know that must be tough, real tough, for a bundle of energy like you. But you're doing it, because..." He waved a hand, inviting her to complete his sentence.

Smiling, she said, "Because I love this baby, that's why."

"And no sacrifice is too great for one you truly love."

She gazed into his blue eyes. When she was a girl, they'd often played the "whose eyes are bluest" game. "Your eyes are so blue, the cornflowers will be jealous," she'd say. "And yours are so blue, the sky wants to duel at dawn." Shaking her head fiercely, Ciara would respond, "Mother robins could mistake your eyes for baby eggs." "And the miners in the sapphire mines come home depressed," he'd counter, "because they can't find any stones as blue as your eyes."

"Was it hard, Dad? Leaving the department, I mean."

He nodded so slowly it was scarcely noticeable. "I've done easier things, I suppose."

Ciara watched him glance around, saw that when he focused on his wife, his jaw automatically tensed and his lips tightened.

"She was miserable," he said in a barely audible voice. "You were too small to remember, I suppose, but there were times when I thought she might have a nervous breakdown." He met Ciara's eyes. "I couldn't let it go on. I had hurt her for so long already. I had to do something to stop her pain."

"You loved her a lot, didn't you?"

His eyes crinkled a bit when he smiled. "You say it in the past tense. What makes you think I don't love her still?"

"Oh," Ciara sighed, "I'm sure you love her…the way Mitch loves Ian, the way I love you." Slowly she shook her head. "But you don't love her in a romantic way."

For a moment—such a fleeting tick in time that Ciara would have missed it had she blinked—she read the gut-wrenching pain he'd buried in his heart for so many years. Her father tore his gaze from hers, stared at the dark green clover leaves between his sneakered feet. She had done more than strike a nerve with her observation. For the first time in her twenty-eight years, Ciara saw him not merely as her father, but as a flesh-and-bone man, with needs and dreams and yearnings like any other man had.

"You never did love her that way, did you, Dad?"

The corners of his mouth twitched as he struggled to retain his composure and control. "Ciara," came his raspy whisper, "she's your mother. You haven't the right to say things like that."

"I'm sorry, Dad. I just want to hear the truth…from you."

"Well, *I'm* sorry, because I will never say anything disrespectful about her. She did a spectacular job raising you, and—"

"And you're grateful for that. You even *love* her for that." Ciara paused. "It's all right, Dad. I'm not a little girl anymore. Lately," she said, looking over at Mitch again, "it's hard to believe I ever *was* a little girl."

She sighed, returned her attention to her father. "I saw more than you realized. I know you both tried to hide it from me, but I knew, I always knew, that whatever you had wasn't what some other kids' parents had."

He faced her, his eyes boring deep into hers. "What are you saying, Ciara?"

"That I love you both for what you did. You mentioned sacrifice a little bit ago. 'No sacrifice is too great for one you truly love.' You didn't leave the department because you were worried about Mom. You left because you loved *me,* and since Mom was mostly in charge of me…"

His broad shoulders slumped, and Ciara wanted to climb into his lap as she had when she was tiny, snuggle into the crook of his neck and hug him tight until everything was all right again. But she couldn't do that now, because she'd grown up and married, and soon she'd be a parent herself. If you didn't learn anything else in these seven months alone, she thought, eyes on Mitch again, it's that it takes a lot more than a hug to make everything all right again.

"If I'm even *half* the parent you've been," she said, patting her tummy, "this little tyke will be the luckiest baby ever born."

He swallowed. Blinked. Took a deep breath. "We were so young when we met, Ciara." Shrugging, he said, "I had no idea what love was at sixteen. Never had another girl-friend. Never had a chance to…" He cleared his throat. "And I was too stupid to get down on my knees, ask the Good Lord if she was the woman He intended for me." He shook his head again. "I don't mind telling you, I did a lot of praying since you met Mitch."

"Praying? Whatever for?"

A mist of tears shimmered in his eyes when he looked at her. "I prayed that you weren't making the same mistake…handing your entire future over to someone who might have ulterior motives, to someone who saw what they could get and—"

He was angry now. Very angry. Ciara knew, because it was the only time he made that tiny pucker with his lips. Almost immediately he reined in his emotions. Taking a deep, cleansing breath, he cleared his throat.

"Ulterior motives? What ulterior motives would Mitch have had?"

"By taking all you had to give and giving nothing in return," her father continued. "By choosing their needs over yours, without another thought—" He clamped his jaws together suddenly. "I've said enough." He held one hand up as if to silence himself. "Said too much." He sandwiched her hands between his own. "I'm sorry, sweetie. I shouldn't have burdened you with—"

"You haven't told me anything I didn't already know."

His brows rose at that. "But how could— I worked so hard to hide it from you. And to give her her due, I think your mother did, too."

Ciara shook her head. "Don't get me wrong, because I love Mom, but contrary to the old cliché, love isn't blind."

The furrow between his brows deepened.

"I know what she is. I know what she's done. I know, because she told me, Dad. A long, long time ago."

"What are you saying, Ciara?"

He already looked so miserable, how could she tell him that she knew *why* he had so quickly agreed to leave the department. He'd been wounded in the line of duty, and the injury would have prevented him from front-line work, but it wouldn't have forced him into early retirement. He'd given it up because her mother had found out about his one marital misstep….

Ciara, still in elementary school at the time, had come home to find her mother crying at the kitchen table. Kathryn had wrapped her arms around her little girl and the words tumbled out in a puzzling, dizzying swirl. Words like *betrayal* and *affair,* and phrases like *stabbed in the back* and *best years of my life.* She'd been too young to understand fully…and just old enough to be afraid, more afraid than she'd been to date.

That night, through the wall that separated her room from her parents', she heard their muffled voices in heated debate. And heard more confusing, scary words, like *ultimatum* and *divorce,* and one phrase that would echo in Ciara's mind for a lifetime: "We'll disappear, and you'll *never* see her again."

A week later her father had handed in his badge and gun.

A week after that, he'd begun teaching at the university.

She remembered those months just prior to the confrontation. It was the only period in her memory when her father had seemed truly happy. Had the "other woman" put that joy into his eyes? Had she opened up the part of him that had been sealed off by loyalty and vows spoken, and shown him what a good and lovable man he was? Ciara knew she should hate this woman who had come between her mother and her father. But how could she hate the one person who had made him realize his self-worth, who had made him smile…*with his eyes?*

She had overheard him once, sitting at that same kitchen table with his brother. They'd tipped a few bottles of beer, loosening their lips, and her father had poured out his soul.

It didn't matter that Kathryn belittled and criticized him at every opportunity. Or that in place of the big family she'd promised, Kathryn coldly announced she would never have children. Years later, seeing the 'I'm leaving' handwriting on the wall, she appeased him by consenting to give him one child.

And it didn't matter that she'd always put her own needs ahead of his, spending money faster than he could earn it, stuffing their house full of ancient, ugly things despite the fact that he'd made it clear he preferred a simpler, sparser life.

What did any of it matter, her father had asked his brother. *Kathryn* had committed no "sin," and there was no getting around the fact that *he* had committed one of life's most grievous transgressions. Little-girl Ciara, still hiding behind the pantry door, had whispered to herself. But being mean is a sin, and pretending is the same as lying, and lying is a sin....

She had replayed that conversation in her mind, many times, and in Ciara's opinion, her mother's icy anger was also a sin, a sin all its own. For decades, Kathryn's acrimonious, acerbic feelings for her husband throbbed and seethed just beneath the surface, visible to friends, relatives, neighbors. Hadn't Kathryn gotten the meaning of Matthew, Chapter Seven, Verse One: "Judge not, that you not be judged"? Didn't she believe, as Ciara did, that God was all merciful, all-loving...no matter how great a man's sin? If a small child could understand this, and the Almighty could extend the hand of forgiveness, *why couldn't Kathryn?* Her father had admitted his sin, had atoned for it tenfold. The moment he acknowledged his wrongdoing, God had cleansed him of it, freeing him from further punishment. How long did his wife intend to penalize him!

"What are you saying?" her father repeated.

Ciara would not add to the burden that had bent him over, a little more each year, by telling him she knew what he had done as a younger man.

Ian stepped up just then. "You two must be discussing the stock market," he said. "I don't know any other subject that would put scowls on such handsome faces."

Admittedly, the conversation had forced Ciara to take stock….

"Are you staying to watch the fireworks with us?" she asked her brother-in-law.

"Wish we could, but I promised the kids we'd go down to the Inner Harbor this year." He rolled his eyes. "If it were up to me, we'd watch the fireworks in air-conditioned comfort on TV, but they've got their hearts set on it, and—"

"And as I've been telling him for years," his wife interrupted, wrapping her arms around him from behind, "our kids are nearly grown. This could be the last time we see the fireworks with them."

They're so much in love, she told herself, after all these years together, they're still crazy about each other, and it shows. Mitch had told her that Ian, the oldest of the Mahoney boys, had married at twenty; Gina had just turned nineteen. Theirs, too, had been a whirlwind courtship, speeding from a chance meeting to a date at the altar in less than a year. Isn't it ironic, Ciara thought, that Mom and Dad went steady for three years, were engaged for two more before they said I do. If anyone should have been sure of themselves, it should have been the two of them….

She remembered something her father had said earlier: he'd been too young to know, too foolish to ask for God's guidance. All the time in the world, she acknowledged, can't give us the peace and assurance that comes from a moment of heartfelt prayer.

Gina directed her attention to Ciara's father. "You're looking good, Joe. What have you been doing…taking vitamins or something?"

He shook his head. "I guess the prospect of becoming

a grandpa agrees with me. You know, seeing a part of me living on in a new generation."

"Well," Gina huffed, "you don't look old enough to be a grandpa, if you ask me." Playfully she elbowed Ian. "I say that because Patrick has a steady girl now, and things seem to be heating up. *We* could be in your shoes in a year."

Ian chuckled. "Who, me? A grandpa?" Smiling serenely, he added, "Maybe I'd better reread *Grimm's Fairy Tales*. It's been a while since I told a good story."

"Oh, give me a break," Gina teased. "You tell a story every morning of your life, when you say I'm the loveliest thing you've ever seen."

Opening his eyes wide, he tucked a finger under her chin. "Sweetheart," he said, doing his best Jack Nicholson impression, "you can't handle the truth." He punctuated his comment with a kiss to the tip of her nose.

"Ian, really," Gina scolded, smiling and blushing like a young girl, "you know how I feel about—"

"'Public displays of affection.' Yes, I do. And you know I don't give a whit who sees how I feel about you." As proof, he kissed her again, on the lips this time.

Giggling, she shoved him away. "So tell me, Ciara," she said breathily, "how're you feeling?"

Ciara grinned. Like I'm watching an X-rated movie, she thought. "Well, let me put it this way," she said instead. "If this baby doesn't get here soon, Mitch is going to have to hog-tie me, 'cause all this lying around is driving me nuts!"

"Hey," Gina advised, "enjoy it while it lasts." She winked at Ian. "Trust me, when that baby has you up every couple of hours, you'll be asking yourself why you were complaining!"

"Complaining?" Mitch knelt beside Ciara's chair and slipped an arm around her shoulders. "I'll have you know this girl hasn't uttered a word of complaint, not once in the two weeks I've been home." He kissed her cheek. "She's a real trouper," he boasted.

"Well, all I can say is you're lucky you didn't marry *me*," Gina admitted. "I'd be whimpering and whining every five minutes if I had to stay off my feet for four solid weeks." She wriggled into her husband's arms. "Isn't that right, honey?"

"Oh, I don't know. Hard as it is to get you out of bed on a Sunday morning…"

"Much as I hate to admit it," Gina said, bobbing her head, "he's right."

"Say, Joe," she put in, "tell your motorcycle story. I tried to tell it the other day, but I couldn't remember the punchline…."

Ciara's father rubbed his palms together and grinned, blue eyes twinkling merrily. "Okay, you asked for it…" Standing, Joe held a finger aloft, and began:

"There were two Irishmen," he said with an exaggerated brogue, "travelin' the A-1 on a motorbike. 'Tis mighty cold, McAfferty,' said the one on the back. 'Well, no wonder, Casey, ye've got yer coat on backward.' McAfferty parked, turned Casey's jacket 'round, and zipped it up the back. 'There, now,' he said, tucking the fur collar under Casey's chin, 'that'll keep ye warm.' They took off again, and after a bit, McAfferty noticed Casey wasn't there, and headed back the way they'd come. He spied a couple of farmers, starin' at somethin' in the middle of the road. 'Why, it's me friend, Casey,' McAfferty said. 'Is he all right?' 'He were fine when we got here,' one farmer said, 'but since we turned his head 'round the right way,' said the other, 'he ain't said a word….'"

Their laughter acted like a magnet, attracting Kathryn. "There you are, Joseph, I've been looking everywhere for you." The words, if printed on a page, might have convinced bystanders his wife felt something akin to affection for her husband. But Ciara had heard that "why do you torture me so?" tone in her mother's voice before, too many times to count. Had seen that look, too, hundreds of times…one brow up, lips pursed, shoulders slumped in long-suffering exhaustion. "Has he been telling that awful motorcycle story *again?*" she asked. Rolling her eyes, she sighed heavily. "Thank goodness I walked up when I did! If you only knew how many times I've heard that stale old story."

Gina, Ian and Mitch smiled stiffly in response to her obvious insult. Ciara had seen *those* looks before, too…looks that blended pity for Joe with disapproval for Kathryn. How long will she make him pay for his mistake? Ciara wondered.

She couldn't have known that her mother's contemptuous treatment of her father had started long before she'd learned of his affair, but evidence to support that fact was there, etched in the tired lines and weary smile on his sad-eyed face.

I won't live that way, she told herself. Better to let Mitch go…better to *send* him away than to condemn him to a life of arm's-length neglect and open disdain.

Mitch was looking at her when she tore her gaze from her mother's hostile expression, from her father's lethargic acceptance of it. He shook his head, a small smile lifting one corner of his mouth as he winked. "Don't worry," was the message emanating from his brown eyes, "we won't let that happen to us."

Her heart fluttered in answer to his promise. Ciara wanted to believe him, wanted to grasp it as truth.

Still…

So far, they had all but walked in her parents' marital footsteps. Dread and fear hammered in her heart. Is there any way to avoid other stumbling blocks along the way?

She loved him with every cell in her body, with every pulse of her heart. But like her father, she had not been wise enough to seek Divine Guidance in choosing a mate. What price would she pay for that foolishness? Was it too late to right that wrong, or could their marriage yet become what it might have been…if she'd had the foresight and the insight to ask the Lord what *He* intended for her future?

She looked at her parents, read the indifferent compliance that yoked them to each other, then looked at her in-laws, and saw the esteem, the friendship, the respect and admiration they felt for one another. *That* is what she wanted to see in Mitch's eyes, twenty, thirty, *fifty* years from now.

"What God has joined together, let no man put asunder," the preacher had said, sealing the vow that made Ciara and Mitch husband and wife. Surely, now that they were married in the eyes of God and man, He would show them how to make theirs a strong union, rooted in faith, nourished by steadfast devotion. If they could accomplish that, how could their love do anything but grow, like Ian and Gina's, as the years went by?

The words of a hymn hummed in her head: "Let there be peace on earth, and let it begin with me."

Mitch grasped her hand, gave it a hearty squeeze as Ian said, "Well, thanks for the eats, but we've got to make tracks."

"We ought to hit the road, too," her father said. "I have lesson plans to write."

She watched the two couples leave, walking side by side through the gate and out of the yard. How similar, yet how different, Ciara thought, biting her lower lip. Unconsciously, she gave Mitch's hand a little tweak. She thought she knew the secret that had given Ian and Gina years of happiness…and her parents decades of misery.

Teach us to love selflessly, Lord, she repeated, echoing the words of the song, *and let it begin with me....*

"What time is it?" she asked, her voice whisper soft.

"Don't know," Mitch answered. "Can't read my watch."

"Shouldn't the fireworks have started by now? It's been dark for an hour."

"You're a grown woman, Ciara Mahoney," he teased, quoting what she'd said the day before. "'How can you get so caught up in a light show?'"

There was just enough moonlight to allow him to see her playful sneer. He rolled onto his side, propped his head on a palm. "Yeeesh," he said, grimacing, "if looks could kill, I'd be worm food."

Ciara rolled over, as well. "Don't say things like that, not even as a joke," she scolded.

He drew her to him. "I'm sorry, sweetie. I keep forgetting…"

She laid a finger over his lips to silence him. "Shhh." She raised the same finger into the air. "Listen…I thought I heard one."

"Heard one what?"

"A firework, silly."

"'Firework?'" he quoted. "*Now* who sounds silly?"

"Well, if all of them are fireworks," she said, accenting the *s,* "doesn't it make sense that one is a—"

Chuckling, he nodded. "Okay. All right. 'Firework.' You're the teacher, after all."

"And don't you forget it," she said, smiling as her forefinger drew lazy circles in the chest hair poking from the vee of his shirt.

They lay on a makeshift bed he'd created from two thick quilts, a crisp bedsheet and three overstuffed pillows for each of their heads. Beside her, a foot-high table was laden with decaffeinated sodas, a bowl of strawberries, a plate of cheese and crackers. Beside him, nothing but a fly swatter. All the stars in the universe winked at them from the inky sky above. And all around them, crickets and tree frogs chirped.

"This is nice," Ciara told him. "I'm glad you thought of it."

He pulled her closer. "Me, too."

"I thought Mrs. Thompson was going to watch the show with us and bring Nicky."

Mitch shrugged. "Guess she changed her mind…or Nicky changed it for her."

"She's something, isn't she? Seventy-two and doesn't look a day over fifty. I hope I age that gracefully."

"Are you kiddin'? You'll be the envy of every old woman in the retirement home."

"Only because every old woman will be wishing they had *you*."

He grinned. "*You* think?"

She nodded. "*I know.*" Ciara yawned, stretched. "If the fireworks don't start soon," she said, "I'm liable to sleep right through them."

"If you doze off, I'll set off a firecracker near your ear."

"You just try it, Mister Big Shot, and I'll…I'll…I'll fire *your* cracker!"

"What in the world does that mean?"

"I have no idea…."

Their laughter blended in sweet harmony, as Ciara snuggled closer, closed her eyes. "This is nice," she said again.

And he nodded. "Yep, nice." Two minutes, perhaps three, passed before her breathing slowed and shallowed, telling him she'd fallen asleep. He leaned back a bit, so he could see her face. The soft breeze combed through her hair, fluttered the ruffle at the collar of her blouse. Long lashes curved up from her pale cheeks, and soft breaths passed her slightly parted lips. He knew it might wake her, if he touched her, but Mitch couldn't help himself. Gently he pressed a palm to her cheek and marveled at the miracle in his arms.

Miracle, because she was lovely and sweet, and good to the marrow of her bones. The baby kicked, and he felt the powerful little jab against his own stomach...a subtle reminder that soon, he might be forced to call another man's child "son."

Mitch held his breath, ground his molars together. Why, he asked himself, when you've been praying like crazy for weeks, can't you get that thought out of your head?

Because of what Bradley had said, that's why: "She'll go with me willingly." And "Who do you think the baby will look like?"

Headlights panned the yard, distracting him, and Mitch squinted into the brightness. They'd considered themselves fortunate to have found a corner lot...the appearance of twice the land, with only one neighbor to contend with, but it had its negative aspects, as evidenced by the beams of every passing car.

Hey...that's the same car that went by not ten minutes ago, he told himself, staring harder at the four-doored black sedan. It's just someone looking for an address, he told himself, someone lost in the maze of streets that comprised the neighborhood.

Ciara sighed quietly as the car slipped out of sight. He rested his chin upon her head and relaxed a bit—but only a bit. A quiet *pop,* followed by several more, told him the fireworks had begun. "Sweetie," he whispered, kissing her cheek, "they're starting...."

Wriggling, she blinked. "Hmmm?"

"The fireworks," he repeated, gently shaking her shoulder, "hear 'em?"

She rolled onto her back, smiling as the sky brightened with starbursts of red and blue and white. "It's beautiful," she said. "Isn't it just beautiful?"

He hadn't noticed. He was too busy watching her face, painted in shades of pink and gold and green by the reflected light. "It's beautiful, all right," he agreed. "Most beautiful thing I've ever seen."

If not for the darkness, he'd have seen a blush, Mitch knew, for her big eyes fluttered in response to his scrutiny. "Pay attention," she scolded sweetly, "you're missing all the good stuff."

"That's a matter of opin—" The black car crept by, choking off the rest of his words.

"What's wrong?" she asked, eyes on the sky.

"Nothing," he lied, levering himself up on one elbow as the car inched past. "I'm having the time of my life. How 'bout you?" He could almost feel the intense gaze of a back-seat passenger boring into him through the blackened windows. Had Bradley rounded up the troops? What better night to pull a stunt than the Fourth of July, when explosions in the sky competed with Roman Candles and other assorted firecrackers on the ground? Who'd notice a gunshot amid all the rest of the noise?

"This is the most fun I've had in—" She gasped. "Mitch, what is it?"

He was torn between keeping his eyes on that car and looking into Ciara's face to reassure her. The hammering of her heart against his rib cage decided it. "Just a little headache," he fibbed, wanting to calm her, soothe her, because a rise in blood pressure could be deadly.

"Are you sure? Because you look like you've just seen a ghost."

He kissed her cheek, gently turned her face toward the sky show. "It's no big deal. I'll get an aspirin when the fireworks are over."

He felt her relax in his arms. "Well, if you're sure…."

"I'm sure." And with the tip of his forefinger, he gently pushed her chin, until she was looking up into the sky again. "Wow," he said, "I felt that one all the way to my toes!"

Ciara giggled. "The rib-rackers are my favorites. Those, and the ones with the squeaky little squiggles…."

The night had swallowed up the car again; either its driver had found the address he'd been looking for…or had found a place to park, where he could watch the Mahoney house, undetected.

Except for the half-dozen or so strange phone calls he'd intercepted, Mitch had no reason to believe he was in any danger. The U.S. Attorney had pretty much assured him Pericolo's men, relieved to have gotten rid of the boss with the hair-trigger temper, had lined up behind Chambro. And it wouldn't be very smart for Bradley to show his hand, not with everybody from the dog catcher to the CIA looking for him.

Mitch remembered that old saying: "Just because you're paranoid, doesn't mean they're not out to get you."

But who was *they,* and what would they get him *for?*

Ciara had been right; his job was dangerous. In the past he'd been the only one in harm's way. Now, simply because she'd chosen to stand beside him through life, she stood in the line of fire with him.

If anything happens to her because of my job…

Mitch clutched her a little tighter to him, pressed a kiss to her temple as she oooh'd and ahhh'd at the skylights. *Lord Jesus,* Mitch prayed, *thanks for protecting her from reading my fears. I'm counting on you to keep her safe and sound.*

Clenching and unclenching his fists, David Pericolo sat in the blackness, counting to ten, taking deep breaths. It was natural to be a little nervous, even though he'd taken every precaution. He recalled his last visit with his father at the penitentiary, how his father had laughed at his plan. Well, he'd prove himself worthy of respect yet. He'd make his father proud. For weeks, he'd been watching Mahoney from his hiding place across the street.

It was time to make his move. And this time, there would be no slip-ups, as there had been a week ago…

You got too sure of yourself, and it made you lazy, he told himself. You overlooked something, all wrapped up in memories the way you were….

He'd been thinking of his grandfather, who'd been a demolitions expert during World War II. If the old man could see you now, he'd thought.

What was the expression his grandfather had used? "A rude awakening," that's it! He'd lifted the black lid of the boot box on the dresser, wiggled a red wire, jiggled a black one. Agent Mitch Mahoney, he thought, smirking, is in for a rude awakening.

He had waited until the letter carrier filled Mahoney's box with a handful of mail, slipped the bomb inside, carefully attaching the wires to the hinged door. Then he'd climbed back into the car, wondering as he waited if, like himself, Mahoney had ever wanted to be an astronaut. The minute you open that door, kaboom! you're gonna experience space flight, first hand.

Then some kid in baggy jeans shorts and a backward baseball cap had sauntered up, and slipping the top flyer off the pile of bright blue papers tucked under his arm, and opened the Mahoney mailbox. It had taken every bit of control he could muster to keep from hollering "Get away from there, you little jerk!" He rolled the window down an inch, intending to distract the boy, offer him a couple bucks for his bundle, and send him safely on his way.

But he hadn't been quick enough. "Cool," he'd heard

the boy say, grabbing the bomb. "Hey, Gordie," he called to his buddy, who was delivering flyers on the other side of the street, "check this out." The boys stood, cap brim to cap brim, muttering under their breaths for a minute before the taller one said, "It ain't nothin' but a hunk of junk." The first kid shrugged, then tossed the bomb into a nearby trash can.

Junk!

He had rolled the car window back up. It took me three hours to build that "hunk of junk"!

Now, in the steamy darkness of this July night, he stared at the Mahoney house and grinned. This bomb was no hunk of junk.

He had never missed the fireworks before…but then, if everything worked as he expected it would, he wouldn't miss them this year, either.

Any day now, Mahoney would open his front door, reach for his morning paper, and get the worst news of his life.

Chapter Eleven

Ciara looked up from her needlework when the doorbell rang. "Who could that be? It's nearly supper time."

Mitch shrugged. "I didn't feel much like cooking tonight, so I ordered us a little something special."

"Pizza?" she asked expectantly. "I haven't had pizza in weeks. I hope you got two large ones, with the works, 'cause I'm famished."

Grinning, he fished his wallet out of his pocket and headed for the door. After a moment of front-porch small-talk, she heard the door close, bolts click into place, Mitch's bare feet padding up the hall and into the kitchen. The clatter of dishes and the clank of silverware inspired her to call out, "No need to get fancy, Mitch. Paper plates will be—"

He was back before she could complete the suggestion, positioning a tray table over her lap, putting a neatly folded napkin on the left side of her plate, arranging a knife and fork on the right. "I made lemonade and decaffeinated iced tea. Which would you prefer?" he asked, bowing low at the waist.

"Lemonade, with—"

"Lots of ice," he finished. "I know."

When he returned this time, he balanced a crockery bowl and a basket of bread on the tray carrying the drinks. "This," he said, removing the towel that hid the bowl's contents, "is to calm a craving."

Her eyes widened with surprise and delight. "Mitch! Where did you—"

And then she read the label on the napkin that lined the bread basket. "Chiaparelli's? You ordered gnocchi from Chiaparelli's?"

"None other," he said, spooning a huge portion onto her plate.

She waved a hand over the steaming dumplings to coax the tempting aroma into her nostrils. Closing her eyes, she sighed. "How did you know?" she asked, looking at him. "Surely not from that little slip of the tongue the other day...."

"That," he admitted, "plus you talk in your sleep."

"I do not." She speared a gnocchi.

Nodding, Mitch sat in his recliner and balanced his plate on his knees. "Oh, yes you do. It's just a good thing we have air-conditioning, because I don't know what Mrs. Thompson would think if she heard you moaning through the open windows, 'gnocchi, gnocchi, *gnocchi!*'" he said, pronouncing each louder than the first.

"She'd think you have a very strange appetite," Ciara explained, wiggling her brows suggestively. Then she popped a pasta into her mouth, and uttered a satisfied "Mmmmmm."

"Is it good?" he asked, taking a stab at one.

"Better than good," she breathed. The fingers of her left hand formed a small tulip. *"Delicioso!"*

He bit into one, chewed for a moment, nodded thoughtfully. "Not bad," he affirmed, eating the other half. "Not bad at all."

She gobbled up a dozen more dumplings before saying, "I have a feeling when Donna comes to weigh me tomorrow, I'm going to tip the scales!"

"Gimme a break. If you come in at a hundred and twenty, even in your condition, I'll be surprised."

"I was a hundred and thirty-five day before yesterday, I'll have you know."

"A hundred and thirty-five? You don't say!" He chuckled. "There's probably not a woman within a one-hundred-mile radius of this house who'd say a thing like that with such pride in her voice." He smirked, patted her tummy. "Come to think of it, *you're* almost a hundred-mile radius…."

"Stop it," she said, giggling, "and let me enjoy this. It's the most I've weighed, ever."

"Well, since you seem to like it so well," he said, pinching her big toe, "maybe I oughta just keep you barefoot and pregnant *all* the time."

Her smile waned, her eyes filled with tears, and she hid behind her hands.

He leaped out of the chair, nearly overturning his plate when he deposited it on the cushion. "Sweetie, what's wrong? Did I say something? I'm sorry if…"

"Stop it," she sniffled. "It isn't your fault my hormones are raging out of control."

"But you were fine till I…"

She blotted her eyes with a corner of the napkin. "You didn't do anything wrong, I'm telling you! It's me. All me." Ciara thumped a fist onto the mattress. "It's because I've been cooped up inside so long, getting no exercise. I'm trying to stay current…reading the paper, watching the news…but my mind is turning to mush. I'm becoming the kind of woman I've always despised, Mitch, weak and wimpy and whiny and—"

"Aw, sweetie," he said, taking her in his arms. "You're

the strongest woman I know, and the proof is the way you're handling this situation. You're a hundred months pregnant, for goodness sake. Cut yourself a little slack, why don't you?"

She mulled that over for a moment, then started to giggle. "A hundred months?" she repeated, her voice muffled by his shirt. "Even elephants have babies in less time than that." She shook her head. "Sometimes I think I'm doomed to stay this way for the rest of my life."

Ciara leaned back slightly to meet his eyes. "Oh, Mitch," she whimpered, "do you think your baby will *ever* be born?"

His eyes widened slightly. *My baby?* Would she have said it that way if she suspected Bradley might be the father? Mitch didn't think so. She'd blurted it out without even thinking, so it must be true. *My baby,* he repeated, kissing her tears away, struggling to hold back tears of his own. *My baby!*

"Shhh," he soothed. "Your gnocchi is getting cold."

"Do you really want to have more children with me?" she asked, her voice small and timid, like a child's. "What if I'm like this every time I get—"

"Ciara, listen to me now," he said, tapping a finger against her nose. "I mean, think about it…a lifetime with whoever that is in there," he added, patting her tummy, "for a few weeks of inconvenience."

"Easy for you to say," she teased, "I have to lie here like a lump while you get to empty the trash and do the dishes and—"

"I'll be more than happy to turn all the fun stuff over to you after the blessed event," he said, laughing. "Promise."

"So you really wouldn't mind going through this all over again?"

"Peterson assured me the chances of this happening a

second time are practically nil, but no, even if the whole thing repeated itself exactly, I wouldn't mind. Not a bit." He pushed a pink satin nightgown strap aside to kiss her shoulder. "Look at it from my point of view—how many other husbands get to see their wives in gorgeous lingerie all day, every day, for weeks on end?"

Another soft giggle, then, "How many times?"

"How many times would I do this?"

She nodded.

He kissed her shoulder again. "Until my lips wear out."

"No, silly, I mean…"

"Six," he said without hesitation, "just like we discussed before we got married."

"Half a dozen," she sighed. "We'll have to add a whole wing onto the house."

"Or buy a bigger one."

"In the country, maybe," she said dreamily, "where we can have cats and dogs and—" Ciara looked around. "Speaking of dogs, I haven't seen Chester all afternoon. Is he out back?"

Mitch nodded. "He treed a cat out there, and I couldn't get him to come in, not even for a rawhide bone."

Ciara frowned a bit. "I wonder what he'll think of the baby."

Snickering, he said, "Are you kiddin' me? He's gonna make that big-hearted old nanny mutt in Peter Pan look like Cujo. Now eat your gnocchi, before I do."

Ciara stuck her fork into a dumpling. "I don't suppose there's dessert…."

"As a matter of fact," he said, picking up his plate, "there is."

"Cheesecake?"

He sat in the recliner. "With cherries on top."

"How big a piece?"

"I went for broke. We've got a whole cake to ourselves."

She licked her lips. "If I break the visiting nurse's scale," she asked, grinning mischievously, "will our insurance pay for a new one?"

"Blood presh-ah and pulse rate are fine," Donna said, her Boston accent making the details of the routine exam sound far more interesting than it was. "Your blood count is a little low, but nothin' to worry about." She strapped the monitor into place. "Now, let's see how the little one is doing...."

The machine clicked and beeped quietly for a few minutes as the nurse squinted at the screen. A thin green line of phosphorescent light blipped, counting the baby's heartbeats. "Lookin' good. Lookin' real good...." The diminutive woman had small, deceptively powerful hands. With firm gentleness, she palpated Ciara's stomach. "Hmmm. He's dropped some since I was here day before yesta-day. If I had to guess, I'd say you have a week till you join the ranks of mothahood. Maybe less." Propping a fist on a hip, she narrowed one blue eye. "You experiencin' any cramping?"

Rolling her eyes, Ciara shook her head. "Not unless you count the ones in my rear end, from sitting on it hour after endless hour."

"Well, don't you fret. It won't be much longah now."

"You're not sugarcoating things to keep me calm, are you?"

"Oh, right...I've stayed in this line of work all these years 'cause I enjoy fibbin' to my patients." Then she got serious. "Stretchin' the truth makes everything seem scarier, no mattah how good or bad the situation really is." The perky blonde winked at Mitch. "I'll leave the shugah-coatin' to your hubby, here. He looks like a man who knows how to lay it on thick...."

"Now, wait just a minute here," he said, grinning in

mock self-defense. "I believe in telling it like it is." Then, in a more serious tone, "You'd tell us if something wasn't quite right…even slightly?"

"I would indeed. You two have got to stop all this fussin', now, 'cause everything is fine. And do you know why?"

Like obedient students, husband and wife shook their heads simultaneously.

"Because *you,* Mistah Mahoney, have been doin' a bang-up job takin' care of the missus. There oughta be a medal for husbands like you. I've seen plenty of men go through this, but not one of 'em handled things like you have." She gave an approving nod. "No mattah what time of day I drop by, this house is squeaky clean from top to bottom, Ciara's sheets are always fresh and crisp, and by the looks of those roses in her cheeks, you must be a dandy cook, too."

"It'll probably take me two years to get my girlish figure back!" Ciara agreed.

"Well, don't let this one out of your sight, missy," was Donna's advice. "He's a prize, and I know a dozen gals who'd snap him up in a heartbeat!"

"They might *think* they want to snap me up," he said, slipping an arm around his wife, "but none of 'em would have the *stomach* for me." He patted her tummy. "Would they, sweetie?"

"Yeah, well, if they try, they'll have to go through me first!"

"Might be a bit difficult, in your condition," Donna pointed out. "Aren't you glad he's the trustworthy sort?"

She nodded, met his eyes. "Yes. I'm glad," she said in all seriousness. "And thankful, too. He hasn't left my side for a minute, not once in sixteen days."

"Cut it out, you two," Mitch said, smiling sheepishly, "or I'm going to have to make all the doorways keyhole shaped, so I can fit my swelled head through 'em."

"Joke if you want to," Donna said matter-of-factly, "but men like you are one in a million. I've seen my share…personally and professionally…I know what I'm talkin' about." Hefting her nurse's bag, she headed for the door, waving to Ciara. "See you day after tomorrow." As she passed him, she whispered to Mitch from the corner of her mouth, "Stick close by from here on out. She could blow any day now!"

Blinking, he stood gap-jawed in her wake. Any day now? he repeated. Yup, any day now, you'll know for sure who that baby's daddy is….

He had tossed and turned so much through the night that Ciara didn't think either of them could have slept more than two hours. What had he been dreaming about as he'd writhed so fitfully, moaning and groaning under his breath? Was he reenacting scenes from his undercover days? Reliving the day he brought the bad guy in? Experiencing a near-death experience, like the time he'd been locked in the trunk of a car?

Today is the day, she decided, that you'll ask him to tell you about the case. Good or bad, his answers would be a blessed relief, because anything was better than not knowing at all!

Mitch was sleeping peacefully now, and she turned on her side to get a better look at him. Once, before he'd left her, she told him he had the most amazing profile she'd ever seen. Totally masculine, it was Michaelangelo's *David* and Rodin's *The Thinker* all rolled into one. She had traced it with a fingertip, saying, "I wish I were an artist, so I could sculpt it from clay, or carve it from wood. That way, I'd have it to look at, even when you were at work…."

She looked at his profile now, the strong forehead, the patrician nose, the powerful jaw that was boldly, wholly *man*. Long, thick lashes fringed his eyes, giving him a boyish quality that softened the look, kept him from appearing too severe, too stern. And his lips, those full, well-rounded lips, only added to his very male appeal. Lightly, lovingly, she skimmed the backs of her fingers over his whiskered cheek. "I hope our baby looks exactly like you," she said in a voice so soft, even she barely heard it.

Ciara rested her hand on his chest and, assured by the steady *thump, thump, thump* of his heart, drifted into peaceful slumber and dreamed of a chubby-cheeked infant with dark curly hair and enormous brown eyes, and a smile that could charm the birds from the trees….

He'd been dreaming he was walking through their house, pointing out things of interest to the baby boy in his arms. "Now son, this is your mom's favorite afghan," he said. "Her grandma brought it over from Italy, so whatever you do, don't spit up on it. And this," he added, plucking the strings of his guitar, "is your dad's git-fiddle. Maybe when you're older, I'll teach you to play…."

He hadn't known know what woke him…Ciara's feathery touch, tickling over his stubbled cheek or her rustling sigh: "I hope our baby looks exactly like you." All he knew was that her touch, her words washed over him like warm Caribbean waves.

I love her, and I love that kid because it's part of her. If she'd transgressed—and it was beginning to look less and less like she had—it had only been for want of him; could he begrudge her a stolen moment of comfort? Would it have mattered, really, whether he or Bradley had fathered her child? In truth, it would have mattered a great deal. But he thought he knew the truth now. "And the truth shall set you free."

Smiling, he pressed a palm to her roundness, hoping to feel forceful little feet or the powerful punch of a tiny elbow. After a moment of absolute stillness, Mitch admitted, regretfully, that the child, like its mother, was at complete rest.

When he was a little boy, his mother would listen to his prayers, tuck the covers under his chin and sing a verse from a song she'd learned as a child: "May the Good Lord grant you beautiful dreams and send a legion of angels to watch over you," she'd croon, brushing back his wild, wayward curls. He sent the same prayer heavenward on Ciara's behalf, then succumbed to drowsiness himself.

But not before this soughed from his lips:

"I love you, Ciara Mahoney, and I always will."

They woke slowly, gently, to the distant trilling of the phone. "Who can be calling at this hour?" he grumbled, reaching for it.

"Mitch, it's after ten o'clock! How could we have slept so late?"

Stretching, he said around a yawn, "Must have needed it, that's all I can say." And then, into the telephone's mouthpiece, he muttered a groggy "Hullo?"

Silence.

He cleared his voice and said more firmly, "Hello."

Nothing.

"Who is it?" Ciara asked.

He banged the receiver into the cradle. "Wrong number, I guess."

But he knew better. This hadn't been the first such call they'd received; it was the eleventh or twelfth, by his count. At first, he'd dismissed it. Could be some kind of computer error down at the phone company, he'd told himself, or maybe one of Ciara's students has a crush on his pretty teacher and he's calling just to hear the sound of her voice.

He had learned to trust his gut instinct, and his gut was telling him not to blame coincidence or accident or happenstance.

But who had been calling…and why?

Could be Bradley.

One of Pericolo's men.

Some other felon he'd arrested….

Truth was, he could think of a hundred possible explanations for the silence on the other end of the phone; *trouble* was, the more explanations he came up with, the more nervous Mitch became.

A week or so ago, while Ciara was napping, he'd tiptoed upstairs, taken his trusty Rossi completely apart and thoroughly oiled every piece. After he'd reassembled it and loaded six rounds into it, he'd listened to the reassuring *whirr-tick-tick* of the spinning chamber, then snapped it shut with a flick of his wrist. Paranoid? he'd asked, sliding the revolver onto a high shelf. Probably, he'd answered, but better safe than sorry….

Hopefully, he'd never have to use it. But just in case, every now and then he rehearsed his trip upstairs to fetch it. He was in the kitchen now, fixing breakfast, when he went over it again. If he took the stairs two at a time, he believed he could get into the closet and back downstairs again in thirty seconds flat. If he could figure out a way to explain it to Ciara, he'd practice physically as well as mentally.

She had asked for a bowl of corn flakes this morning, and he topped them off with a sliced banana and cold milk. He'd put strawberry slices in her orange juice, to surprise her when she finished it off. He'd plucked a rose from the shrub beside the back fence, too, broke off the thorns and tucked its stem into her napkin.

"When I'm on my feet again," she said when she saw the tray, "I'm going to spoil you so rotten, you're going to stink!"

"My mom used to call me a little stinker. Maybe she's clairvoyant?"

"She's a mother, and mothers know things."

"Is that right?" He settled in his recliner and waited for Ciara to tell him what she knew about their baby. *Their* baby. *His* baby. She'd said so in the middle of the night, when she thought he was asleep.

"I know, for instance, that this baby is going to be brilliant and musically gifted and kind and…"

"How do you know all that?" he asked, chuckling good-naturedly. "Did the Baby Fairy tell you?"

"Make light of it if you must," she sniffed, "but it's all very scientific, actually."

"Scientific?"

Ciara began counting on her fingers. "You're very intelligent, and I'm not exactly a dull bulb, so the baby *has* to be smart." She held up a second digit. "I play a pretty mean piano, and you play just about every other instrument God ever created." The ring finger popped up. "And the way you've been taking care of me, well, if I didn't already know you were a kind, big-hearted man before I was quarantined, I know it now. Isn't it natural to assume our baby will have a blend of our finer qualities?"

He merely sat there a moment, nodding as he assessed what she'd said. Ciara hadn't mentioned one trait that even closely resembled Chet Bradley. And why would she? It's your kid….

"You know, when you put it that way, why wouldn't our kid be terrific?" He smiled. "But I hope he looks like you."

"And I hope he'll have your *character.*"

Chuckling, he nodded at the plaques and awards hanging on the fireplace wall. "Don't you mean my reputation? I've won—"

"'Reputation is what men think you are,'" she quoted. "'Character is what God and the angels know about you.'"

She had fixed him with that no-nonsense, all-loving

stare of hers, so he couldn't very well argue with her, now could he? And so he said, "Well, this *character* is gonna go down to the end of the driveway and see which shrub our paperboy has hidden the newspaper under this morning. And then he's gonna refill his coffee cup, and put up his feet, and make like a man of leisure till he's read every last page."

Ciara patted the mattress. "I'd like to ask you a question first...."

She'd been behaving strangely all morning. Till now, he'd chalked it up to her condition, to cabin fever, to being forced to stay off her feet. Mitch perched on the edge of the sofa bed. "Ask away, li'l lady," he drawled.

"When are you going to tell me where you were, when we're both old and gray?"

He frowned. "Where I was?"

"You know perfectly well what I'm talking about."

She wasn't teasing. He could tell by the lift of her left brow, by the slight narrowing of her wide eyes. Their hands, flat on the sunflowery sheets, were nearly touching. He inchworm-walked his forward until his forefinger rested atop hers. "The case, you mean...."

"Where were you? Why didn't you write, or call?"

"I tried, remember?"

She rolled her eyes. "So you've said. Didn't you wonder why, if you wrote so many letters, I never answered them? Didn't you think it was strange, that after one little fight, I'd completely write you off?"

"Didn't seem so little to me."

Ciara sighed. "It was the first time we'd ever disagreed about anything." She crooked her finger around his. "You didn't expect us to spend our whole marriage in a state of harmony, did you?"

Mitch shrugged. "My folks never fought."

"Maybe you never heard them fight, but they disagreed,

I'm sure. Every married couple does. It's normal. It's natural. It's…unavoidable."

He met her eyes. "I guess…I guess I just hadn't gotten used to the idea."

"We did sort of rush things, didn't we?"

Their eyes locked on a thread of understanding. "Do you still think it was a mistake?"

The pain in her voice was matched only by the agony shining in her eyes. Mitch pulled her to him. "Sweetie, I've *never* thought it was a mistake. From the moment I first saw you, I knew…."

She pressed a palm to each of his cheeks, her eyes searching his with fierce intensity. "Then why did you let them send you away? Why would you go undercover, and leave me here to wonder where you were… how you were?"

"Because I'm a proud, thick-headed, know-it-all."

Her brow crinkled with confusion. "A know-it-all?"

"I'd been hearing about Pericolo for ages. I knew it was going to take some fancy footwork to get him. The agency wasn't about to send some rookie in there to nab a guy like that. I guess I felt sort of proud they'd picked me."

"I see," she said softly, nodding.

"Well," he shrugged, "that, and Bradley made it pretty clear that if I didn't go *in,* I was on my way *out* at the Bureau."

"You could have found another job…what made you so sure I'd still be here when you came home…*if* you came home?"

"I wasn't." He exhaled a heavy breath. "Till recently, that is."

She leaned against the pillows and hid behind her hands. "I must need a nap already, because I'm not following you."

"I thought…." Mitch licked his lips. He wished she

hadn't pulled away, because nothing felt so reassuring, so comforting as having her in his arms. He looked at his empty hands, filled them with hers. "I thought maybe you found a way to replace me."

A tiny, nervous giggle popped from between the tightly-clenched fingers that hid her face. A second passed in utter silence. She folded her hands in her lap. "Replace you? How?"

"Bradley." The word ground out of him like a monosyllabic growl.

"Bradley?"

And then the light of understanding gleamed in her eyes. Ciara gasped, touched her fingertips to her lips, shook her head. "Mitch…you don't mean…." Her brows lifted and her eyes filled with tears. "You thought…." She bit her lower lip. "You thought I had…."

"Just look at you, trembling and tense. Forget I ever said anything. I'm a total idiot." He tried to gather her in his arms.

"Stop it," she said, one hand up like a traffic cop. "Just give me a minute to wrap my mind around this thing." Ciara took a deep breath. After a moment, she rested crossed arms on her ample belly. "What had I ever done to make you think such a thing?"

"Nothing. And I didn't think it. Not once in the whole time I was gone." He held up both hands in a gesture of defensiveness. "I knew I'd have a price to pay for leaving the way I did, for staying gone so long, but I figured we could work it out. I figured eventually, we'd…."

She lifted her chin. "What changed your mind?"

He took a deep breath. "Aftershave."

Ciara rubbed her eyes. "You're not making any sense…."

"Bradley's brand. In the medicine cabinet in the master bathroom.

She inclined her head. "Bradley's brand," she repeated, more to herself than to Mitch. And then she began nodding, tapping a finger against her chin. "So *that's* why he insisted on going upstairs that day...."

Mitch rested a hand on her thigh, and listened.

"He came over one day to see if I needed anything...and to tell me you hadn't been in touch, as usual...and acted as if he'd heard a noise upstairs. Drew his weapon and everything!" Lips narrowing with suspicion, she added, "Now I understand why he spent more time in our room than...."

"When?" Mitch demanded. "How long ago?"

"Right before you came home." A note of alarm sounded in her voice, and panic brightened her eyes. "Why?"

"Because it had been part of his plan all along. We were both pawns in his little game of 'kill two birds with one stone.'"

"What?"

"He used me to get rid of Pericolo, so Chambro could take over and Bradley's pay-offs would continue. He never figured I'd survive being underground with a maniac like that, and when I did...." He emitted a low groan of frustration. "And he used you to drive me over the edge."

"By planting the aftershave."

Mitch nodded.

"What I don't understand is why you believed I could have done such a thing."

He met her eyes, still damp from her bout with tears. "You're a beautiful woman, Ciara. Beautiful and warm and loving...." He shrugged helplessly. "You saw my mom's prized roses. She spent hours tending them every week."

"They're spectacular, but what do they have to do with...."

"She says the lovelier a creature of nature, the more time and attention it needs."

"I don't know whether to be flattered at being compared to a rose, or insulted that you think I'm so high maintenance."

"Not high maintenance, Sweetie, just deserving of some tender loving care."

"I suppose I can't fault you for doing the very same thing I did, can I?"

"Me? When would I…."

"I didn't know where you were, what you were doing. For all I knew, you'd been sent undercover to guard a beautiful singer, like in the movie that came out a couple years ago, where the bodyguard fell in love with his charge…."

"I never so much as looked at another woman," he said, hand forming the Boy Scout salute. "I swear."

"And I never looked at another man," she responded, mimicking the gesture. "So tell me, what changed your mind?"

"How do I know that baby's mine, you mean?"

She gasped again, and hugged her tummy. "You thought our baby…? You thought…*Bradley?*" Ciara shuddered. "Now I *am* insulted. How could you think so little of me, Mitch? Was it because I fell for you so quickly? Was it because I let you talk me into getting married after only a three-month courtship? Was it because…?"

"I already told you why," he said, grasping her hands. "I'm an idiot."

When she blinked, a silvery tear broke free of her long lashes, landed on the back of her hand. Mitch kissed it away. Kissed away the tears remaining on her cheeks, in her eyes. "I'm sorry, Ciara. About everything. If I could go back in time and do it all over, I'd…."

"Would you still take the assignment?"

"Not if I knew then what I know now."

"What do you know now?"

He cupped her cheeks in his palms. "That—cliché as

it sounds—I love you more than life itself, and nothing, no one, is more important than you." He wrapped her in his arms. "I can't live without you, Ciara. I'm so sorry for everything I put you through. It's all my fault you're in the shape you're in."

"Is that what you think?" she asked, pulling away.

"How else do you explain it?"

"Didn't Dr. Peterson tell you there's no known cause for this condition?"

"Well, yeah, but…."

"And didn't he tell you there's no predicting who it'll affect and who it won't?"

"Yes, but…"

"But nothing. It just happened, and you know what?"

"What?"

"I think it was a blessing."

"A blessing! To be practically flat on your back for over a month, worrying every minute whether…."

"It brought you closer to me than anything could have. And Mitch," she said, voice softened and warmed by tears, "it taught me so much about you."

"About *me?*"

"That's right, Daddy." She smiled. "It taught me that, despite the fact that you wear a big gun to work, and despite the fact that you talk tough, you're as gentle as Mary's little lamb. I couldn't have chosen a better husband and father if I'd ordered him from a catalog. I love you, you big idiot!" she teased, and kissed him soundly.

"I love you, Ciara."

"Now why don't you get the morning paper, and I'll 'scissors-paper-rock' you for the sports section."

Grinning, he headed for the door. He was on the porch when he said, "Do we have a new paper boy?"

"Not that I know of. Why?"

"Because the regular kid likes to chuck it into a shrub

or halfway up the crabapple tree, and today it's lying smack in the middle of the driveway."

"Stop complaining," Ciara called from the living room, "get that newspaper so we can see how the Orioles did in last night's game...."

"Good morning, Mitch," sang Mrs. Thompson. "And how are you on this beautiful morning?"

"Couldn't be better," he said, stooping to pet her toy poodle. "How're ya doin', fella?" Mitch ruffled the dog's curly ears. "Tell me, how is it that you're always so cheerful?"

The old woman smiled brightly. "I'm seventy-two years old, lived through five wars, the birth of three kids, eight grandchildren and two great-grandchildren. I buried two husbands and a business enterprise or two. After surviving all that, the world seems like a happy, peaceful place. Why wouldn't I be cheerful?"

"I like your outlook," Mitch admitted. "And I like your pup, here, too." Standing, he added, "I'll bet he could last a year on one bag of Chester's dog food."

"You'd be surprised how many Kibbles my little Bruno packs away." She clapped her hands, and the poodle leaped into her arms. "Isn't that right, sweetums? You eat Mummy right out of house and home, don't you?" Mrs. Thompson unclipped Bruno's rhinestone leash and draped it around her neck, then put the dog back onto the ground. "He hates to be tethered," she explained, heading for the porch. "How's that pretty little wife of yours today?" she asked, one foot on the bottom step. "I must say, she looked lovely yesterday. And you take such good care of her!" She patted her stomach. "By the way, the cookout was splendid. That potato salad of yours was scrumptious. Maybe you'll share your recipe...."

"There's a huge bowl of the stuff in the fridge. You'd be doing me a favor if you took some of it off my hands."

She grinned. "Oh, that would be lovely!"

He started for the house. "I have a memory like a colander. If I don't do it now—"

"Bruno, you leave Mr. Mahoney's paper alone now, you hear, before I—"

Mitch had no time to react. He looked back in time to see bits of smoking, flaming debris raining down from the sky.

In a heartbeat, he was beside the old woman. "Mrs. Thompson, are you all right?"

"I'm fine," she said, as he helped her sit on the top step of her porch, "but where's Bruno?"

He'd been on his way back inside when the explosion had cracked the peaceful July morning—hadn't seen what happened. But the last thing he'd heard was Mrs. Thompson, scolding the dog. If that was the case—

Act fast, he told himself. Ciara is inside alone....

"You sure you're okay?" he said.

Nodding, Mrs. Thompson clung to the wrought iron railing.

Mitch breathed a sigh of relief as he spied the dog, shivering under an azalea bush. "Found him," he called, pointing.

"Bruno," Mrs. Thompson cried, clapping her hands. "Bruno, you come here this instant!"

The dog was on her heels in an instant.

The old woman gripped the wrought-iron rail so tightly that her knuckles turned white. Mitch helped her to her feet and guided her through her front door.

"Just sit tight, Mrs. Thompson," he said. "As soon as I check on Ciara, I'll come back to see how you're doing."

"Yes, that would be best. You must go to Ciara. I'm perfectly fine," she said.

"Now then," she said, as he dashed out the door. "Lighten up! You don't want to frighten Ciara with that sour expression, do you?"

Frightening Ciara was the least of his worries right now. *Saving her*—from whomever was trying to even a score—*that's* what he was worried about....

Chapter Twelve

No one had made an outgoing call since the telephone woke them earlier that morning. Mitch dialed "star sixty-nine" and waited for the operator to identify the caller. "The last number to call your line was 410, 555-1272," said the smoothed-voiced recording. He scribbled the digits on a sheet of scrap paper and handed it to Bob Knight, the lead investigator from the Howard County Police Department.

Knight was tall and wiry, with coal black eyes and a shock of thick, nappy hair. "Maybe you oughta tell me about this case you were workin' on, Agent Mahoney."

Mitch snuck a peek at Ciara, who had been listening intently. "I'm cool as a cucumber," she said, crossing both arms over her chest. "And I agree with Officer Knight. It's high time we heard about this case you were working on...."

Mitch studied her calm face, her relaxed demeanor. He had to give it to her; she'd kept a tight rein on her emotions after the blast, and he knew that couldn't have been easy. Not for a woman whose feet left the floor if someone walked into a room and surprised her....

Ah, what a mother won't do to protect her young, he thought wryly.

"Really, Mitch," she added, trying to sound more convincing, "I'm fine. In fact, I think it'll be good for me to hear it…finally."

"The night I left here," he began, sitting beside her on the sofa bed, "I went straight to headquarters."

Knight made himself comfortable in Mitch's chair. "Go on…."

"Bradley was at my desk when I got there. He had Giovanni Pericolo's file and my undercover identity with him." Shrugging, he cut to the chase. "He told me the Bureau locked Pericolo up, but they couldn't stop Pericolo from doing business."

"It's sad but true," the cop agreed. "Guys run drug rings from prison every day."

Ciara sighed heavily. "And this is the man you were 'up close and personal' with for seven months."

Mitch nodded. "I posed as an accountant. Kept his books."

"How'd you get inside?" Knight wanted to know. He'd stopped taking notes. His interest was personal now.

"We busted one of Pericolo's right-hand men for trafficking, cut a deal with him. He'd get me into Pericolo's organization, we'd let him stay outside the federal pen."

"It's a miracle you're still with us," Ciara said, her voice trembling slightly. "You see why I was so afraid? Do you understand what—"

He squeezed her hand. "Yes. I admit it. I'm in a dangerous business."

"That's putting it mildly," Knight said. "You've got your neck in a noose every time you go under. Why don't you come to work for us? I happen to know we need a few educated, well-trained guys, right here in Howard County."

"Do you send men undercover?" Ciara asked.

"Uh-huh, but it's rare, and even then, only the narcs and homicide guys do stuff like that. What your husband, here, would be doin' would be relatively safe, all things considered."

"'Relatively safe'?" Ciara's brow furrowed with confusion. "'All things considered'?"

"Nothing comes with a guarantee these days, little lady, least of all a cop's safety. Every time you pull a guy over for speeding, you wonder if—"

Mitch saw her frown with resignation and roll her eyes, as if to say Where have I heard that before? and decided it was time to change the subject. "So what's your take on this, Knight? Based on what you've already got, that is."

"Well, whoever set the bomb wasn't an expert, that's for sure."

"How can you tell?"

"For one thing, amateurs always want to use too much explosive. It's like they think if a gram will go "Pow," then an ounce is sure to go 'Boom!' But they don't take that into consideration when they're putting the rest of the thing together. It was sheer luck it went off at all."

Knight took a deep breath and got to his feet. "Well, I've done all I can do here for the time being." He handed Mitch a business card. "Give me a call if you can add anything that'll help. And give some thought to ditchin' the agency and comin' to work for us."

Mitch tucked the card into his shirt pocket, shook the officer's hand. "I'll do that. Thanks, Knight."

"I'm putting round-the-clock protection on you guys." He chuckled. "Till the Feds bully their way in and take over, anyway. I hear they like to take care of their own."

"You hear right."

"Yeah, well, that ain't nothin' to be proud of, way I see

it. Doesn't make much difference what the emblem on your badge says, we all took the same oath."

He looked at Ciara. "So when's that baby of yours due?"

"A week, maybe two…*never,*" she said, rolling her eyes.

"I have three young'uns myself, five, six and seven. My wife just takes it in stride. Except for the big tummy, you'd hardly know she was havin' a baby at all!"

"I hope next time I'll be that way, too."

Mitch walked Knight to the door. "Can she hear us from here?" the cop mouthed when they reached the foyer.

Mitch nodded.

He grabbed Mitch's forearm and leaned in close. "Stay away from the windows," he growled softly, "you hear?"

"No way. When did they find the body?"

At the mention of the word *body,* he saw Ciara's needle hover over the cream-colored linen square she held.

"I'm not surprised," Mitch said, "considering. Still, it seems a shame. He was a good agent…once."

He watched as she tried to pretend she wasn't listening. What was it his Italian grandma used to say when he pouted? "You face, she gonna freeze-a that way!" The old wives' tale seemed to fit Ciara's present condition….

"He did what?" he asked Parker. "You've gotta be kidding." Shaking his head, he said, "Ironic, isn't it?" Then, "Yeah, I'll kick in ten bucks, but who's gonna see it? Yeah. Okay. Thanks for calling."

"Who was *that?*" she asked the moment he hung up.

He slumped onto the edge of the sofa bed, flopped back on the pillow beside hers and linked his fingers behind his neck. "Parker. Down at headquarters. They found Chet Bradley…."

"Found him? I didn't even know he was missing. Did the Bureau send him undercover, too?"

"Hardly," Mitch groused. "He's been workin' both sides of the street for years now. That's why I got sent to Philadelphia."

She put her needlework aside, snuggled against him. "I don't get it."

He'd never told her about his set-to with Bradley, right there in their living room. If she had known the guy had broken into their house, planning to murder him… Mitch didn't want to think about what might have happened.

"He worked a case, couple years back," he explained, "busted Pericolo for possession of cocaine, distribution, the whole nine yards. But the slimeball got off, thanks to our sophisticated immigration system. Anyway, it seems Bradley decided he could make a few quick bucks if he didn't turn in all the evidence. If he sold what he held aside on the street." Mitch took a deep breath. "The fool taste tested his own merchandise, got himself hooked but good and ended up having to make a deal with Pericolo."

"Chet Bradley?" She seemed surprised, then shook her head. "Well, he's a liar, why not a coke-head, too?"

Mitch turned slightly to read her face. If the news had secretly upset her, she was doing one fine job of masking it. He stared at the ceiling again. "He started doing odd jobs for Pericolo—muffing up investigations, losing evidence, running errands…."

"And Pericolo provided him with the cocaine."

"Uh-huh. Had himself a four-hundred-dollar-a-day habit at the end. You know how many favors a guy has to do to satisfy an addiction like that?"

"But why did he send you to Philadelphia? Were you involved in that drug bust all those years ago? Did you know something that would—"

He shook his head. "He had a falling out with Pericolo, and the boss man cut him off, cold turkey. Bradley was desperate to ensure his supply, so he cut a new deal…with Eduardo Chambro, Pericolo's next in command."

"How do you know all this?"

"Seems his upbringing got the better of him, and he made what you might call a deathbed confession." Mitch shook his head. "Nobody thought much of Pericolo, it seems. Chambro would have taken over years ago if he hadn't been scared witless of the guy."

"But…if Chambro was on Pericolo's side, what did he have to fear from him?"

"Plenty, believe me. I saw Pericolo waste a guy for interrupting a phone call. Heard that he'd done the same thing to men who dared to question his judgment or entered his office without knocking. The man had no heart, no soul, I tell you. Life meant nothing to him…except his own."

"So the lieutenant made a deal with Chambro," she said, bringing him back to the point. "How did you fit in?"

"He called me the best man on his team. Said I was perfect for the job. Not to sound arrogant, but he was right, and he knew it. The deal he cut with Chambro was to get me inside so I could take Pericolo out of the picture. And when Chambro took over…"

"He'd continue to supply Bradley with bribes," she said, thinking out loud. "A lot of things make sense suddenly."

He rolled onto his side. "Things like what?"

She met his eyes. "I had no reason to believe his lies. I'm ashamed to say I wanted to. It was easier to hate you that way, for leaving me here alone, for not getting in touch, for not being with me when—"

He pulled her to him. "Sweetie, I'm sorry you had to go through all that alone. Hindsight is twenty-twenty—I guess it got to be a cliché for good reason…every word of it is true—but if I had known then what I know now—"

"You would have come home that night? You wouldn't have accepted the assignment?"

"Exactly," he said firmly and without hesitation. "How could I have left my beautiful wife, pregnant or not? No amount of glory is worth a sacrifice like that."

"My dad said something like that the other day," she told him. "He said no sacrifice is too great when it's made for love."

"Smart guy, your dad." He kissed her cheek.

"Were you ever in any danger in Philadelphia? From Pericolo, I mean?"

He thought of that first night, when Giovanni had asked him to choose a card. "If you had picked a black card, you'd be a dead man now."

"Not really," he fibbed. "I was acting as a numbers man. A pencil pusher. A four-eyed geek. I suppose I didn't look like much of a threat, so—"

"Didn't look like a threat!" she stopped him. "As big and muscular as you are? As handsome and intelligent and—"

"I'd better get to work on those door frames," he said, laughing. "Any more of this flattery and my ego won't fit through the door."

"Mitch…"

"Hmm?"

"That explosion was intended for you, wasn't it?"

Every muscle in him tensed. Tell her the truth, and risk sending her blood pressure sky high. Tell her a lie and risk the trust she's beginning to put in you again. "It's possible," he said carefully.

"Who do you think was responsible…if you were the intended victim, I mean?"

"Truthfully?"

Ciara nodded.

"I have no idea.

"I suppose Pericolo might have had *one* loyal follower, but I don't think so. And it can't be Bradley, unless he's operating from the grave." Eyes and lips narrowed, she exhaled a sigh of frustration. "It could be anyone you ever arrested, or a family member of someone you locked up, or…"

"Sweetie, it's not good for you to get worked up over this. We're safe."

"For now. How long can that last? The cops won't hang around here forever. Whoever planted that bomb will wait until they leave, come back and finish what he started."

She voiced the fears that had been on his mind every moment since the explosion.

"Ciara, let's not talk about this now. It's not good for you to get upset, honey."

"You can't sweep it under the rug, Mitch. It's bigger than both of us. You can't deny it anymore. Like it or not, you have responsibilities now, to me, to this baby of ours. You can't just keep running off, playing cops and robbers. Not when it can backfire, blow up your family!"

He sat up. "Ciara," he said, his voice stern and scolding, "this isn't doing you any good. Let's—"

"Hiding from it isn't doing me any good, either," she said, sitting beside him. "Have you given any thought to what Officer Knight said?"

"Quitting the Bureau, you mean, to become a Howard County cop?"

She nodded, the barest hint of a hopeful smile playing at the corners of her mouth.

"Yeah. I've thought about it," he said dully. "I've thought about how I'd like to stop arresting nationally renowned criminals and start writin' speeding tickets. I've thought how nice it would be to give up apprehending drug lords and murderers, and spend my time shooing teenagers off the street corners after 11:00 p.m. instead." On his feet now, he added, "I'd be about as happy as your dad has been all these years, pretending that what I'm doing is what I *want* to be doing."

"But, Mitch," she said, her eyes welling with tears, "what about the baby and me? What will we do, if something happens to you?"

The smiling, the laughing, the playfulness…it had all been an act, and he'd known it all along. Worse, he'd *let* her put on the act, because it had made it easier for him to deal with his own guilt.

She was a tough little thing, and he knew if it weren't for everything that had happened—this illness, being confined to bed, the explosion—she wouldn't be crying right now. And he felt like a heel for being the one to put tears in her beautiful blue eyes. But she had asked him a straight question, and after all those months of silence, deserved to hear a straight answer. But did you have to make it *that* honest? he asked himself. He could blame the very same occurrences for his thoughtlessness, but the truth was he had no excuse for behaving like a self-centered lout.

And she deserved better than that.

He climbed back onto the sofa bed, took her in his arms. "Aw, sweetie. Seems all I ever do is apologize for hurting you. Sometimes I wonder why you married me. I'm sure as heck not very good for you." And the awful thing was, he believed it was true.

Ciara gripped his forearms, gave him a little shake. "You *are* good for me!" she insisted, her eyes blazing with unbridled affection. "You're the best thing in my life, if you want to know the truth. *That's* why I married you. That and the fact that I love you like crazy."

She felt so good, so right in his arms. She was the most beautiful woman he'd ever seen, the most affectionate and loving. Why wasn't it enough? Why did he feel he must have her *and* the Bureau to be happy?

"I did some thinking last night," she said softly, "about something Dad said at the cookout yesterday."

"You're all flushed, sweetie," he said, all but ignoring her. "Lie down, will you, before something—"

She did as she was told, but continued talking. "I know how unhappy he's been all these years, sacrificing the job he loved for his family. But he seemed to have derived some sort of satisfaction for having done the right thing. That's why he said no sacrifice is too great, if—"

"If your love is strong enough?"

Ciara nodded. Then she grabbed his wrists, forced him to place his hands on her stomach. "*This* is what's important, Mitch. *This* is your future. I know you're a good agent, one of the best. Of course the Bureau recognizes that and appreciates who you are and what you do…."

She placed a hand alongside his cheek. "But, Mitch, the FBI doesn't *love* you! If you die, they'll add your name to the already-too-long list of agents killed in the line of duty. They'll give me some sort of medal to lay on your grave, another plaque to hang on the wall. And by week's end, another agent will take your place." Her voice trembled, and fresh tears filled her eyes when she said, "*I* won't be able to replace you, Mitch, not if I live to be a hundred."

What *was* so all-fired important about his precious agency? he asked himself. *Why* couldn't he just give it up, walk away from it, without looking back?

She was right about one thing—he had a lot of thinking to do.

His big hands bracketed her face, his thumbs wiping the tears from her cheeks. "I don't deserve you," he said after a while.

"You deserve the best that life has to offer, which is why I intend to try and be the best wife who ever lived." She managed a tremulous smile, her voice whispery. "I love you, you big lug! Can't you get that through your thick, Irish skull? I love you, and I don't want to live a day of my life without you."

"I'm half Italian, don't forget," he said in a feeble attempt to lighten the mood, change the subject....

"And so am I."

He was aware of her scrutiny, aware that she wanted— no, needed—to hear him say he'd leave the agency. In truth, Mitch wished he *could* say it, because he wanted and needed to comfort and reassure her. Guilt ached in his chest like a huge painful knot. He looked away, feeling restless and uncomfortable with the fact that he couldn't tell her what she wanted to hear.

Ciara's small hand cupped his chin, turned his face and forced him to meet her eyes. Her tears were gone now, and she spoke slowly, with careful dignity. "You don't have to make up your mind right now. You have two weeks of R and R left. Please say you'll use that time to think about it, at least."

Mitch set his jaw. He could give her that much, couldn't he?

It was quietly disturbing to even consider leaving the Bureau, and his stomach knotted with tension. His voice began as a hushed whisper, then he spoke in neutral tones. "I'll give it some thought," he promised, his mouth tight and grim.

"And some prayer?"

"And some prayer."

"Thank you," she said, gently, serenely. "Thank you."

When she snuggled close, he felt the rhythmic pounding of her heart against his chest, and the strong, sharp kicks of the baby against his stomach. "*This* is what's important," she had said.

And it was.

* * *

For the first time in days Ciara put aside her secret needlework project and spent every moment, it seemed, making lists.

She had spent hours fixing up every room of the house, and it showed. But for a reason she couldn't—or wouldn't—explain, she hadn't done a single thing in the nursery. And now, it seemed, she was in a frenzy to get it all done before the baby came.

She insisted that Mitch sit beside her and help her pick out the furniture for the baby's room. Everything had to be neutral, yet stimulating, a concept which thoroughly confused him. "Nothing frilly or girlie, but nothing too strong or masculine, either," Ciara explained. "Colors capture babies' attention and help them learn faster."

They decided on a pale oak crib and ordered a dresser, changing table and toy box to match. He suggested the teddy bear wallpaper border. "Lots of color, without being masculine or feminine." Rather than repeating the print in the baby's bedding, Ciara ordered bright red sheets, a deep blue quilt, fluorescent yellow curtains and an emerald green bumper pad.

Portable phone in one hand, department store catalog in the other and list in her lap, she placed the order. "For an extra twenty-five dollars," she told him, "they'll deliver it tomorrow. Should I tell them to go ahead?"

It was by far the happiest he'd seen her since returning from Philly—small price to pay, in his opinion, for her pink-cheeked complexion and wide smile.

The next day when everything arrived, Mitch had the deliverymen put the boxes into the white-walled room across from the one he shared with Ciara. When they were gone, he took one of the chaise longues from the deck and dragged it upstairs, outfitting it with a downy quilt and pillow. And once he had her settled comfortably in it, he hung the wallpaper border and continued to focus on it as he hung brackets and rammed rods through the pockets of a pair of tailored curtains.

Then it was on to a more interesting—and difficult—project: assembling the crib.

"This manufacturer must be from Timbuktu or something!" Mitch growled. "I can't make heads or tails of these instructions. And what're all these nuts and bolts for? There aren't half as many holes to stick 'em into!"

"Sweetie," she said, repeating what he'd told her a day earlier, "it isn't good for you to get so worked up."

He shot her a narrow-eyed smirk. "Careful, lady," came his mock threat, "'cause I'm the guy in control of the cheesecake…."

Amazingly, she seemed to know what fit where without ever having so much as glanced at the directions. And once he got over the humiliation of being bested in a construction project…by a woman…the crib went together in no time flat.

She had him rolling the thing to every conceivable spot in the ten-by-twelve-foot space, and finally settled for putting the crib against the only blank wall in the room. The changing table, she decided, looked best under the window, and the dresser simply *had* to stand on the short wall, just inside the door, with the toy box right beside it.

Ciara clasped her hands under her chin when it was finished. "We'll have to get another catalog," she gushed, "and fill that toy box to the brim!"

"That's what Christmas and birthdays are for," he muttered, hanging the last picture on the wall.

"Oh, don't be such a Grinch," she scolded playfully. "Besides, his *birth* day isn't very far off, you know…."

Mitch tried to read her face, but couldn't tell if the silly expression was part of her excitement at having completed the nursery, or some strange way of masking pain. "Are you okay?" he asked, kneeling beside her chair.

"This has been driving me crazy for weeks. Now that it's done, I feel so much better!"

The doorbell rang, and Mitch grinned. He couldn't have timed it better if he'd tried.

"You didn't order in from Chiaparelli's, did you?" Ciara asked, narrowing one eye.

"Nope. Now you stay put, while I see who it is."

How the women for the baby shower had all managed to arrive at the same time boggled his mind. Leave it to Gina to get a bunch of women organized, he thought, grinning.

Gina had her back to him when he opened the door, and Mitch would have bet his last nickel that folks clear on the other side of the street had heard her severe "Shh-hhh-hhh-hhh!"

Silently he waved the ladies inside, nodding and smiling as they passed, each carrying a brightly wrapped package. "Get back upstairs," Gina whispered, "and turn on a radio or something so she won't hear us putting up the decorations."

"How will I know when to bring her down?"

"I'll send Chester up to fetch you," she whispered, smacking his bottom. "Now git! Before I take a broom to the seat of your pants!"

He ducked into their bedroom and turned the clock radio on full blast before returning to the nursery. "Who was it?"

"Wrong house number," he fibbed.

"Wrong—"

"Somebody looking for the Smiths. I think they were on the wrong street. I hope I didn't get them lost…." And without another word he scooped her up and carried her into their room.

"Goodness, Mitch," she said, hands over her ears, "aren't you a little young to be experiencing your second childhood? What's with the loud—"

"Didn't you ever get an itch to dance?" he asked, spinning in a dizzying circle, still carrying her. "Listen to that," he added, swaying to and fro in time to the music. "Ain't it a shame? They just don't write 'em like that anymore."

"I think you must have clunked your head on something while you were putting the furniture together," she observed, giggling. "You're acting very—"

She cocked an ear toward the doorway. "What was that? Did I hear voices downstairs?"

"Maybe...I left the TV on in the family room." He danced her farther from the door, danced her back again and kicked it shut.

"Put me down, you big nut," she scolded, "you're starting to perspire. I'm not exactly a featherweight these days. All we need is for you to develop a hernia right—"

"I'm fine," he interrupted. "Now stop being a spoil-sport. Who knows when we'll get another opportunity to go dancing?"

"What's that noise?" she asked, a finger aloft.

Mitch plunked her gently on the bed and turned off the radio. "Scratching?" He opened the door. "Hey, Chester. What're you doin' up here, old boy?" He ruffled the dog's thick coat, then hoisted Ciara in his arms once more and hurried down the stairs.

"Mitch, I wish I knew why you're acting so—"

Her eyes widened as both hands flew to her mouth. "Balloons, streamers, cake," she said, taking it all in, then seeing the women. "When did all of you— How did—"

Giggling, she buried her face in the crook of his neck and whispered, "How's my hair?"

"Can you believe all these wonderful presents?" she asked, holding up a tiny terry cloth jumpsuit. "We'll have enough diapers to last for months, and all these T-shirts and booties and..."

He'd been stuffing wrapping paper and bows into a gigantic lawn and leaf bag when he noticed she'd stopped talking. Mitch peered over his shoulder, surprised to find her crying. Dropping the trash, he wrapped his arms around her.

"I'm so lucky," she sobbed into his shoulder. "I have such good friends and so many wonderful relatives, and you…you're the best husband any woman could ever hope for!"

"But those are good things, sweetie. Why are you crying?"

She settled down a bit to say, "Because… because…because I'm so happy, that's why."

"I sure will be glad when this baby gets here," he teased, handing her a tissue, "'cause you're costing me a small fortune in blotting materials!"

Giggling, she blew her nose. "You could always buy stock in the company…."

He popped a kiss onto her forehead. "That's what I like, a woman with business sense who isn't afraid to cry."

"I hate crying," she admitted, sniffling. Then, eyes wide with panic, Ciara added, "What if I never go back to the woman I was before I got pregnant? What if I've turned into a big fat crybaby forever? What if—"

"What if I start hauling some of this loot up to the baby's room while you take a nap. You're looking a mite pooped, if you don't mind my saying so."

"You know, I think I'll take you up on your offer," she said, snuggling under the covers. "Two parties and a bomb blast in three days can be exhausting!"

He plucked a trash bag from the box and chucked a load of stuffed animals into it, filled another with miniature shorts and hats and shoes, and dragged both up the stairs behind him. It isn't like her to give in so easily to a suggestion to take a nap, he told himself. And she did look paler than usual….

Should he call Donna? Peterson? His mother? What could they do that you're not already doing? And the answer was, Nothing.

He continued making trips upstairs until every gift had a new place to call its own. She'll be happy to know the baby's toy box is filled to the brim, he thought, smiling as he left the last of it. Mitch stood in the doorway, arms crossed over his chest, and looked at the nursery. Soon, a baby boy or girl would call it home. Soon tiny cries would wake them from a sound sleep, demanding food or a fresh diaper or a dose of affection.

The telephone interrupted his reverie, and he crossed the hall to answer it in the master bedroom.

"Hey, Parker," he said, "what's up?"

"Well, I have the answer to your question, for starters."

"Yeah?"

"Bradley's blood type is AB Negative."

The news made him weak in the knees, and he sat on the edge of the bed. The card in his wallet said he was O Positive. And according to Donna's chart, Ciara was O Positive, too. Peterson had "typed" the baby weeks earlier, so they'd have a plentiful supply on hand in case of an emergency…and the baby's blood matched his mommy's and his daddy's.

His mommy's…and his daddy's!

How could he have ever doubted her? He felt terrible about it now.

The heat in his cheeks and the buzzing in his ears had usually accompanied bad news. Not this time. *Thank you, Lord,* he prayed. *Thank you!*

"What did you need that information for?" Parker wanted to know.

"Uh—confidential at this point," Mitch replied curtly. He wasn't lying. He'd no interest in sharing his suspicions about Ciara with anyone.

"Gotcha," Parker said.

"You said the info was 'for starters'?"

"Well, it'd be nice if you'd fill us in once in a while, Mahoney. How's that gorgeous wife of yours?"

"Tired, but holding her own. I think it's going to be soon. Very soon."

"Want some friendly advice?"

"Sure…"

"Get all the shut-eye you can, while you can, 'cause once that little one gets here, you're gonna need a dictionary to remember what *sleep* means."

Sleep? Mitch thought. *I don't know what that is* now, what with all that's been going on around here. Chuckling, Mitch thanked him and hung up. Then he headed down the stairs to climb into bed beside his sleepy wife and try to take Parker's advice.

"Mitch," Ciara whispered, shaking his shoulder. "Mitch!"

He draped an arm over her middle. "Mmmm?"

"I think I heard something…."

"Where's Chester?"

"Right here at the foot of the bed. There it is again…in the kitchen…."

"Can't be," he muttered, opening one eye, "there are half a dozen cops outside. Houdini couldn't get past 'em undetected." He yawned. "But I gotta admit," he said, wiggling his hips against hers, "I like the benefits of comforting a frightened—"

"Did you hear that?"

He laid a finger over her lips and nodded, then held the finger in the air, as if commanding her to listen.

"What do you—"

One sharp look from his worried eyes silenced her. "Don't say another word," he instructed, his whisper hoarse and stern. Mitch handed her the phone, where he'd taped Bob Knight's cell phone number. "You hear anything funny in there, call him. Okay?"

Wide-eyed, Ciara nodded. She grabbed his hand. "Please," she said, a hitch in her voice, "be careful…."

Trying to appear cavalier, he sent her a wink.

"Mitch," she added as he got to his feet. "I love you."

"Love you, too," he whispered, and headed for the stairs.

He took them two at a time, as he'd planned, then ducked into the closet and grabbed the Rossi. *Lord,* he prayed, switching off the safety, *I think we both know I'll use it if I have to. Don't let me have to….*

Mitch crept back down the stairs and peered around the double-wide doorway leading from the foyer to the family room. Hiding the gun behind his back, he caught Ciara's eye. "He still in there?" he mouthed.

Ciara nodded.

Thumb to his chin and forefinger to his ear, he pantomimed, "Did you call Knight?"

Another nod.

He blew her a kiss and headed up the hall. It seemed to take hours, rather than seconds, to reach the kitchen. Since he could see the reflection of a dark-haired man in the black glass oven door, the man could see him, too. Mitch flattened himself against the wall, heart hammering as he tried to plan his course of action.

Where are those confounded County boys? he wondered. They must have been asleep on the job. How else had this guy penetrated their line of defense? It happened so quickly, he never saw it coming…the karate chop that sent his service revolver clattering to the hardwood floor. He gave it a solid kick, sent it careering to the end of the hall. If I can't reach it, neither can—

A fist crashed into his jaw, killing the thought.

In the next seconds, amid the flurry of fists and arms, Mitch managed to grab hold of the man's T-shirt.

Pericolo's men never went out in public without a shirt and tie. But who was he to complain; the soft, cottony fabric of the T-shirt was a whole lot easier to grasp than a starched white collar. In a heartbeat, Mitch wrestled the intruder to the floor, straddled him and attempted to disable him with a wrestler's hold.

The high-pitched whimper made him stop just long enough to look at the face he'd been beating.

A boy's face.

David Pericolo's face.

Mitch pinned the kids' wrists to the floor. "What are you doin' here?" he demanded.

"You put my father in jail," he said haltingly, his lips swollen and bloodied. "'Eye for an eye,'" the boy added. "'Eye for an eye.'"

Bob Knight burst through the back door just then, and three uniformed officers came in on his heels. "Cuff him," Knight ordered, "wrists *and* ankles."

Shaking, Mitch got to his feet and leaned both palms on the kitchen table to steady himself. "Meet David Pericolo," he said to Knight.

"You'll pay," David whimpered, as Knight's fellow policemen secured the handcuffs.

"Get him out of here and keep him quiet," Knight barked, shaking a big fist in the air.

Once they'd dragged David off, kicking and screaming, Knight closed the kitchen door. "You okay, buddy?" he asked, patting Mitch's back.

"I'm fine." His gaze shot daggers into the cop. "How'd he get in here, anyway? Your boys oughta be ashamed of themselves."

Knight shook his head. "That number you gave me…the one you star sixty-nined?"

Mitch nodded.

"Pericolo's…car phone."

"I see."

"Heads are gonna roll for this one," Knight said, "trust me."

"You're just lucky nothing happened to my wife."

At the mere thought of her, Mitch tensed. "Ciara—" He ran into the family room and gathered her in his arms. *Thank God she's all right.* "You okay, sweetie? How are you feelin'?"

"Not so hot," she said in a small, shaky voice. "I've already called the hospital. They're expecting us." She buried her face in his shoulder. "Oh, Mitch, I was so scared. I thought…I thought…."

"Shhh," he soothed, stroking her back. "Nothing happened, and—"

"*This* time." She sat back, eyes bright with tears, and faced him down. "You're not a cat, Mitch. You don't have nine lives." Her lower lip quivered when she added, "If you were, I imagine you'd have used up at least six of them by now. How much longer do you expect your luck to hold out? How much—"

Gripping her stomach, she winced with pain.

"Ciara, sweetie, what is it?"

She met his eyes. "It's time, that's what it is…."

She was right. It was *time*. Time to stand up and act like a man. Not a gung-ho, macho, hot-doggin' FBI agent, but a man, who took his responsibilities seriously. He only hoped it wasn't too late….

Ciara took a deep breath and said on the exhale, "Could we…could we continue this later, do you think?" she said, smiling past clenched teeth. "Because if it's all the same to you, I think I'd rather have a baby right now."

Epilogue

Ciara snuggled deep into the pillows on her hospital bed, smiled contentedly into her newborn's face. "Your daddy went to get me a cup of soda," she cooed, kissing the tiny fingers that had wrapped around her thumb. "He'll be back any minute now."

And when he comes back, she thought, I'm going to tell him that it doesn't matter to me *what* he does for a living or where he does it; all I care about is that he's happy, and healthy, until the Lord calls him home.

She closed her eyes, hoping to blink away the horrible scene that had taken place hours ago. Until the sounds of the life-and-death struggle penetrated her brain—when she knew and understood that she could lose him, right there in her very own kitchen—Ciara had not realized just how much she loved having him in her life. *Whether you have a week or a year or a lifetime more with him,* she told herself, *you'll enjoy every moment, and thank God for it!*

How could she say that she loved him, really loved him, and demand that he give up the Bureau? He had worked too long, too hard, to leave it all behind now.

No doubt she would keep a careful eye on the clock

until he arrived home from work safe and sound, but she would lose no sleep over his absences, because faith would see her through. "When I'm afraid, I will look to the Lord," she paraphrased Micah, Chapter Seven, Verse Eight. "I will wait for the God of my salvation, and He will hear me."

The coins dropped into the machine with a metallic *chink-chink-chink,* and Mitch pressed the button that said All Natural Orange Juice. That oughta hold her over till they bring her supper, he thought, nodding when the can hit the tray with a hollow *thud.*

Those hours in the delivery room, when it was touch and go for a while, he knew what he had to do. You could have lost her, he reminded himself, but you didn't, and you'd better thank God for that!

Ciara had asked him to think about changing jobs. He could tell by the way she'd phrased the question that she fully intended to stand by him, regardless of his answer. He also knew that, even if he decided to stay with the Bureau, she would never do to him what her mother had done to her father. And you haven't earned devotion like that…yet….

While the nurses were getting Ciara and the baby cleaned up, he pretended to need a breath of fresh air. Instead, he placed a phone call, straight to the director's office. The director took the call, not so surprisingly, considering what Mitch had just accomplished on behalf of the agency. He would put in his resignation, here and now.

"What can I do for you, Mitch?"

"Well, I have a big favor to ask, sir."

"If it's within my power, it's yours. We owe you that much, son…."

Wait till Ciara hears the news, Mitch thought later, grinning. Merely imagining her reaction caused him to quicken his pace down the corridor. That and the fact that he couldn't wait to hold his firstborn in his arms….

"I'm so proud of you. You're the bravest woman I've ever known."

Ciara giggled. "You act like I'm the first woman on earth to have given birth."

"You're the first woman to give birth to *my* child." How good it felt to say that, and know for certain that it was true. Mitch knew that he would spend the rest of his life making it up to her for so much as *thinking* that she could have betrayed him.

"She's so beautiful," Ciara sighed. "Just look at her, Mitch."

"She's beautiful 'cause she takes after her mommy."

She met his eyes. "What are we going to call her? I didn't think up many 'girl' names—everybody kept saying 'he' and 'him' and 'his,' and I guess I got caught up in it myself."

"How 'bout Carrie, for old-time's sake?"

She branded him with a playfully hot glare. "You think I want a reminder, right under your nose, of your first love? No way, José."

He kissed the baby's round little head. "She smells so sweet. We could name her after a flower…Rose or Tulip or Daisy…."

"I'm glad you're having fun with this. At least *one* of us should be, I suppose."

"I want her to have a strong name. Something memorable. Like Hannah or Eden or Shana."

Ciara nodded. "Now that's more like it. Let's look them up in my baby book…."

Mitch dug around in her overnight bag. "It opened to the *M*s," he said, narrowing one eye suspiciously, "all by itself."

"Well, I have a confession to make," she said, flushing. "I *did* sneak a peek at a *few* girls' names…just in case…."

"Is that so?" He placed the book on the edge of the bed. "Let's see if I can figure out which name you chose." His thick finger ran down the pulpy paper page. "'Mildred' means 'gentle strength,' but I don't think so. 'Misty, Mitzi, Molly,'" he recited.

Suddenly, he thumped the book. "I know which name you picked."

"Which?" she asked, eyes twinkling with mirth.

"'Worthy of admiration,'" he quoted, then said with meaning. "Miranda."

"Do you like it?"

"I love it." He took the baby from her arms, held the tiny bundle tight against him and kissed her soft pink cheek. "Now," he said, drawing his big face close to his daughter's tiny nose. "I'm going to read you your Miranda rights. Number one—you have the right to have a healthy, happy daddy all the days of your childhood—number two—you have the right to the bravest, most loving mommy in the world—number three—you have the right to—"

"Mitch, what are you talking about?"

"I'm talking about my new job. I've been thinking," he announced, "and you're right. I've built up a lot of seniority at the Bureau. I can retire earlier if I hang in there…."

She lifted her chin and smiled.

Lord, I love her grit and determination, he said to himself. She thinks she's in for a lifetime of same-ole, same-ole, but wait till she gets a load of this:

"I talked to the director, not half an hour ago."

"The director? *Of the FBI?*"

"Hey," he said, looking wounded, "don't act so surprised. He takes calls from agents who bring in the big tuna…."

Ciara stroked the baby's head. "Did you hear that,

Miranda? Your daddy has the big boss's ear." She wiggled her eyebrows and bobbed her head coquettishly. "Ooh-la-*la*…. So why did you call him?"

"To quit."

Her eyes widened.

"But he begged me to stay. He's putting me in charge of assignments, Miss Smarty Pants…or should I say *Mrs.* Smarty Pants."

She wasn't smiling when she said, "Sounds dangerous."

"Yeah. I guess it does," he said, squinting one eye. "But it isn't. It's the best of both worlds. I don't have to take a boring desk job, but I won't be on the front lines anymore."

Her eyes brightened. "You won't?"

"I'll have to do some minor investigating, so I'll know which agents should work on what cases, but I won't have to go undercover ever again."

She gasped. "Never?"

"Never. Probably won't ever fire my weapon again, except on the gun range."

"Never?"

"Never." Balancing Miranda in the crook of one arm, he slid the other across Ciara's shoulders. "So what do you think of that, pretty Mommy?"

"I think God works in mysterious ways."

"How do you mean?"

"Well, you know the story 'Gift of the Magi' don't you?"

Mitch nodded. "The one where the guy sells his watch to buy combs for his wife's long hair, and she sells her hair to buy a chain for his watch?"

"That's the one. It's a direct parallel to us, don't you see?"

He gave it a moment's thought, then said, "Ahh,

because you were willing to live the rest of your life in fear, so I could be happy, and I was willing to give up the job that made me happy, so you wouldn't worry."

"Exactly! Neither of us has to make a sacrifice. God has seen to it we *both* have our heart's desire. It's a miracle, Mitch. He has given us a bona fide *miracle*."

"I can't very well deny that, now can I?" He slid the tray table aside, and laid Miranda in her mother's arms. "But let's make that miracles, *plural,* because I'm lookin' at two more, right this minute."

Ciara smiled sweetly. "There's a present for you…in my bag."

"Another present, you mean," he said, one hand on his daughter's head. He dug in her suitcase, pulled out the needlework project she'd been working on for weeks. "Except for your nightie, this is the only thing in here."

"That's it."

Mitch handed it to her.

"I'm going to have it framed and hang it over our bed."

"Lemme see this thing," he said. To Miranda he added, "It's been a big secret, for weeks." He turned it around, read aloud: "I am my beloved, and my beloved is mine."

"From the 'Song of Songs,'" she explained.

"From the bottom of my heart," he said, and kissed her.

She saw a wistful look and then a radiant smile come across his face. "Mitch, what is it?"

He met her eyes. "It suddenly struck me," he said, grinning happily, "I'm a daddy!"

* * * * *

Dear Reader,

When people ask where I got the idea for the Suddenly! series, I tell them, "It came to me—suddenly!" Seriously…I was perched outside the yogurt shop, eating a chocolate swirl cone drenched in rainbow sprinkles when a handsome man sat down beside me. Totally captivated by the beauty in his arms, he was oblivious to everything around him.

"First baby?" I asked. Without looking away from his baby girl's face, he nodded. His loving, awestruck smile reminded me of the way my uncle looked as he recalled the day he found out *he* was going to be a daddy.…

One of many soldiers aboard an aircraft carrier, Sam was on his way home from World War II. "I was standing at the rail, looking out to sea," he said, "thinking of my sweet Margie." Except for a weekend pass, Sam had barely seen Margie during the past two years. "The last time I'd seen her," he said, "she was slim as a dime." Imagine Sam's surprise when he stepped off that boat to find that Margie "looked like she'd swallowed a watermelon!"

What must it have been like, I wondered, to find out in such a sudden and surprising way that you're going to be a father?

The answer conceived the idea that gave birth to the Suddenly! series. If you enjoyed *Suddenly Daddy,* please drop me a note c/o Steeple Hill Books, 233 Broadway, Suite 1001, New York, NY 10279. I love hearing from my readers, and try to answer every letter personally.

All my best,

Loree Lough

SUDDENLY MOMMY

Get 2 Books FREE!

Love Inspired Books,
publisher of inspirational fiction,
presents

Love Inspired

A series of contemporary love stories that will lift your spirits and reinforce important lessons about life, faith and love!

FREE BOOKS! Use the reply card inside to get two free books by outstanding inspirational authors!

FREE GIFTS! You'll also get two exciting surprise gifts, absolutely free!

GET 2 BOOKS

IF YOU ENJOY A ROMANTIC STORY that reflects solid, traditional values, then you'll like *Love Inspired*® novels. These are heartwarming inspirational romances that explore timeless themes of forgiveness and redemption, sacrifice and spiritual fulfillment.

We'd like to send you two *Love Inspired* novels absolutely free. Accepting them puts you under no obligation to purchase any more books.

HOW TO GET YOUR
2 FREE BOOKS AND 2 FREE GIFTS

1. Return the reply card today, and we'll send you two *Love Inspired* novels, absolutely free! We'll even pay the postage!
2. Accepting free books places you under no obligation to buy anything, ever. The two books have combined cover prices of at least $11.00 in the U.S. and at least $13.00 in Canada, but they're yours to keep, free!
3. We hope that after receiving your free books you'll want to remain a subscriber, but the choice is yours— to continue or cancel, any time at all!

EXTRA BONUS
You'll also get two free mystery gifts!
(worth about $10)

FREE!

Return this card promptly to get
2 FREE BOOKS and 2 FREE GIFTS!

YES! Please send me 2 FREE *Love Inspired*® novels, and 2 free mystery gifts as well. I understand I am under no obligation to purchase anything, as explained on the back of this insert.

About how many NEW paperback fiction books have you purchased in the past 3 months?

❏ 0-2	❏ 3-6	❏ 7 or more
E5TW	E5T9	E5JM

❏ I prefer the regular-print edition **105/305 IDL**

❏ I prefer the larger-print edition **122/322 IDL**

Please Print

FIRST NAME

LAST NAME

ADDRESS

APT.#

CITY

STATE/PROV.

ZIP/POSTAL CODE

Visit us at
www.ReaderService.com

▲ Detach card and mail today. No stamp needed. ▲

(LI-2F-10R2)

The Reader Service— Here's how it works:

▲ If offer card is missing write to: The Reader Service, P.O. Box 1867, Buffalo, NY 14240-1867 or visit www.ReaderService.com ▲

BUSINESS REPLY MAIL
FIRST-CLASS MAIL   PERMIT NO. 717   BUFFALO, NY

POSTAGE WILL BE PAID BY ADDRESSEE

THE READER SERVICE
PO BOX 1867
BUFFALO NY 14240-9952

NO POSTAGE
NECESSARY
IF MAILED
IN THE
UNITED STATES

Chapter One

Jaina read the anguished expression on her mother's face and held the baby boy tighter. "What do you mean," she whispered, "his mother is gone?"

Rita ran a trembling hand through graying hair. "I mean, she *isn't here*."

Seemingly oblivious to his mother's absence, the baby filled his hands with Jaina's long dark curls.

"Did you look out back?" Jaina's father wanted to know. "In the parking lot?"

"Yes, Ray," Rita sighed, "I've looked everywhere."

Blowing spit bubbles, the child wrapped Jaina's gold chain around a stubby forefinger and cooed. "Well, I'm sure she'll be right back," Jaina said. "She couldn't have left without this precious little—"

"I found this in the ladies' room." Rita slid a note from her apron pocket. "She isn't coming back."

"What!" Ray thundered. "You mean she walked off and left this boy with total strangers? How does she know we're not murderers or…"

He stomped toward the counter. "Well," he growled, "how far could she have gone?" He pressed the receiver to his ear. "I'm callin' the cops, and I hope they throw the book at her. People like that don't deserve to have kids."

Jaina's dark eyes filled with tears and her heart ached for this abandoned child who clung almost greedily to her. She would likely never have a child of her own, but if God saw fit to reverse her physical condition and bless her with a baby, she couldn't think of any reason sufficient to walk away from him...to leave him with strangers.

"Ray, sweetie," Rita said softly, a hand on his forearm, "calm down. You'll frighten the boy. Besides, I promise you'll feel differently once you've learned what's in this note."

Their eyes met, then held for a moment on a look of understanding that linked them heart to heart.

He hung up the phone. "Okay, Rita. What's in it, anyway?"

She stood on tiptoe to kiss his chin. "There's just one way to find out, isn't there?" Turning to Jaina, she held out her arms and smiled lovingly. "Now, give me that dollbaby."

Jaina traded the baby for the slip of paper and took a seat at the counter, swiveling her red-cushioned stool until she faced the diner's parking lot. "It's so dark out there," she said, more to herself than to her parents. And staring through the mirrorlike black window, she added, "The weather reports are predicting a terrible thunderstorm. Where could she have gone, all alone on a night like this?"

"Where was that last bus headed?" Ray asked.

"I think the driver said he was headed for Chicago," Rita answered.

Jaina crossed the room and peered through the screen door. "There's lightning off to the north. I hope she's all right...."

Ray slipped his arms around his wife, hugged her and the baby she held. "C'mon back and sit down, sweetie," Rita said, "and read the note."

Silently, Jaina returned to the stool and took a deep breath. "'Dear Jaina,'" she began, "'I came to Ellicott City to meet my uncle for the first time. He's a lawyer on Main Street. I was planning to ask him if he'd take care of Liam for me. But I overheard him on the telephone, yelling at the top of his lungs. Something about a baby being an albatross around his client's neck. I couldn't leave my boy with a man like that!

"'I had thought he was my last chance at finding a good home for Liam. He's my only living relative. If I couldn't leave Liam with him, I didn't know what I was going to do!

"'And then God reminded me how kind you were yesterday when the bus stopped at your diner…the free meal, the way you played with Liam, the cheese and crackers you packed up for us to take with us when we left….'"

Jaina met her mother's damp brown eyes, her father's misting gray ones, and swallowed hard. It wasn't difficult, remembering the sad-eyed girl whose pride made her pretend she'd lost her wallet rather than admit she had no money for food.

"You okay, honey?" Ray asked, handing her a glass of water.

Jaina nodded, thanked her father and, after a quick sip, continued reading. "'I prayed harder than I did when I found out I was dying of leukemia.'"

Gasping, Jaina pressed a palm to her chest. "Dying?" she repeated. "But she couldn't be a day over eighteen!" Tears burned behind her eyelids as she looked into the baby's innocent, unsuspecting face. She took another drink.

"'The doctors say I only have a few months to live at best. Seems I spent my whole life trying to act grown-up, and here I am, talking like one. I think I would have been a good mom, if only…well, anyway, none of that matters now. The important thing is that the Good Lord led me to you. I've had to travel light, coming all this way on a bus. You'll find a couple of outfits in Liam's bag, some of his favorite toys and his birth certificate. Now that I know he'll be taken care of, I can go to the Lord in peace.'"

With her free hand, Jaina covered her eyes.

"You want me to finish it, honey?" Ray offered.

She met his loving eyes and smiled slightly. "No. It's okay, Dad. I can do it." She focused on the young woman's round-lettered script and began again.

"'My picture is in the side pocket of the diaper bag. When he's old enough, please tell Liam that I never would have left him if things had been different. You're probably thinking that I'm a terrible mother, that there must have been something I could have done besides leave Liam with strangers. You'll just have to trust me, the way I'm trusting the Lord.

"'When my own mother died, I learned firsthand all the terrible things that can happen to a kid who doesn't have a family. I don't want that kind of a life for Liam. You told me you don't have any children and that it wasn't likely you ever would. I could see in your eyes how much you want a baby and I could tell by the way you held Liam and talked to him what a good mother you'll be.

"'You're probably a little afraid right now, finding out that you're suddenly a mommy. I remember how it felt the first time I held Liam in my arms. I was barely seventeen and was I ever scared! But then he looked at me with those big blue eyes of his, and I fell in love.

"'Everything that's happened these past few days is proof to me that God wants you to be Liam's mommy. For one thing, the bus shouldn't have broken down. The driver said it had just been overhauled before we left Chicago. For another, he promised we'd be back on the road in no time, but we were stranded for hours while the mechanic worked on the engine. See? God put me in your diner long enough to get to know you. How does it feel to be part of God's plan? Don't worry, Jaina, you'll be a wonderful mommy. If I wasn't sure of that, I wouldn't be leaving Liam with you.

"'Thank you, Jaina, for what you're about to do for me…and for Liam. I know you're going to do it because, well, you just have to! Sincerely, Kirstie Buchanan. P.S. He hates strained peas, loud music and thunderstorms, and he loves to watch cartoons on TV.'"

The hand that held the note dropped limply into her lap. "I feel like I've just run a four-minute mile," Jaina said, sniffing.

The adults slumped, sad and emotionally spent, into the nearest booth. For several moments, no one made a sound save Liam, who sat in the middle of the table, babbling contentedly as he tried to depress the buttons on the tabletop jukebox.

Jaina broke the silence. Patting her father's hand, she said, "I think you're right. We should call the police, report this, get them to start looking for Kirstie. Only after they find her," she said, squeezing his hand, "we'll keep her right here with us so she won't have to spend her last days alone."

Liam popped the salt shaker into his mouth, shook his head and grimaced at it.

"We're duty bound to try and find her," Rita agreed, gently prying it from his fingers, "but Kirstie doesn't want to be found."

Ray heaved a deep sigh. "Where I come from, this wouldn't be a problem. Folks don't need cops and judges and lawyers to tell 'em what's the right thing to do."

"Then I wish we were in Abilene, Dad."

Ray dumped the contents of the baby's bag on the table. A blue flop-eared bunny, a red squeeze toy shaped like a fire engine, a brown teddy bear, a plain white envelope. Squealing with glee, Liam grabbed the truck and bit down hard on it, snickering when it squeaked. "A picture and a birth certificate," Ray said, shaking his head at the envelope.

Jaina picked up the birth certificate. "Liam Connor Buchanan," she said aloud, "born November 2 to one Kirstie Ann Buchanan." She patted the baby's hand. "Seven months old."

"Big for your age, aren't you?" Rita observed, running her fingers through his hair.

"What's that his mama wrote on the back of the birth certificate?" Ray wanted to know.

Jaina turned it over, found that Liam's immunizations were up-to-date. "'Nine pounds twelve ounces, twenty-one inches long,'" Jaina said, reading the youthful script, "'forty-two hours of hard labor.'"

"She would have been a good mother," Rita observed as Jaina slid the girl's wallet-size color photo from the envelope.

"Such a beautiful thing, and so *young,*" Jaina whispered, running a thumb over Kirstie's image. "I wonder how long she's been an orphan," she asked no one in particular, "and how she came to be alone in the world?"

Rita smiled. "Reminds me of your publicity photo, Jaina." Sighing, she added, "Seems like only yesterday that you sang for your supper."

Traveling from city to city, singing for a living had been fun and exciting, until…. "Let's not talk about that part of my life. Why don't we dwell on positive things, like the way Uncle Jesse's gift was a blessing in disguise…."

Her father shook his head. "Blessing indeed. This diner is more work than it's worth. I don't know if he did you any favors, leaving you this place in his will."

Liam grabbed for Kirstie's picture, effectively changing the subject. Jaina held it out for him to see. "Yes, that's your mommy," she told him. "Isn't Mommy pretty?"

"Mmumm-mmumm?" he repeated, touching a fingertip to his mother's image. Jamming the finger into his mouth, he grinned flirtatiously at Jaina and, crawling across the tabletop, snuggled into her arms. "Mmumm-mmumm," he said, a dimpled hand on each side of her face.

Her heart lurched as she looked into his wide, trusting eyes. *Sweet Jesus,* she prayed, *is he calling me Mommy?*

As if he'd read her mind, the baby rested his head on her shoulder. "Mmumm-mmumm," he muttered with a satisfied, sleepy sigh. "Mmumm-mmumm."

Jaina closed her eyes and thought of the morning after the accident, when the somber-faced doctor told her that to save her life, they'd been required to perform emergency surgery…. Liam might well be her only chance at motherhood. But she couldn't keep him.

Could she?

"It's an awfully big responsibility," Ray responded, "and you already have your hands full, what with running the diner and all. We could help some, but with your mother's heart condition…"

Jaina hadn't realized she'd spoken her thoughts aloud.

Rita's gaze met her daughter's, held it for a long, silent moment. Then, head on her husband's shoulder, she said softly, "But, honey, she's had so many disappointments. If she wants to do this—if the courts will even *let* her do it—we ought to help her." She grabbed her husband's arm. "I'll be careful, I promise."

"Mother," Ray warned lovingly, shaking a beefy finger under her nose, "don't start with me."

"It's a moot point," Jaina inserted, "because I can't keep him."

Liam's lower lip poked out. Ray's broad shoulders sagged. "Aw, would you look at that? It's like he understands." He ran a hand through thick hair that was going gray at the temples. "Well, folks, I don't know *what's* best here." And looking from his wife to his daughter, he said, "Let's pray on it."

With Liam sitting on the table in the circle of their arms, the adults joined hands, bowed their heads and closed their eyes.

"Lord Jesus," Ray's deep, resonant voice beseeched, "open our hearts and minds so we'll know what You have in mind for this young'un. Give us the wisdom to recognize Your will…and the strength to do it."

A moment or two passed before he added, "Call Skip, Jaina. He'll know what to do."

Rita's dark eyes widened. "But…but Skip works for Social Services. He'll—"

"Exactly. More'n likely he's come nose-to-nose with a problem like this before. He'll know what to do." Big calloused fingers tenderly tucked a shimmering blond curl behind Liam's ear. "Besides, Skip's our girl's best friend. He wouldn't steer her wrong."

Rita stroked the baby's silky cheek. "So precious, so perfect." Then, in a lighter, brighter voice, she ventured, "Maybe they'll let us be his foster family. It's the least we can do since we're going to deny Kirstie her last wish."

"We're *not* denying it, Mom. She asked me to take care of Liam, and that's exactly what I intend to do. I only want what's best for him."

"Kirstie was right, you know," Rita observed, raising one dark eyebrow. "You're a natural-born mother. *You're* what's best for him, if you want my opinion."

"Now, Mother, is that a tear I see?" Jaina asked.

Rita swiped at her eyes. "Of course it isn't." She held up a finger to silence her daughter's objection. "Don't tell me you can't keep him because you haven't the time. You made time to feed those baby robins every hour on the hour this spring. And what about that little squirrel you rescued last fall?" Rita laughed softly. "Why, it seems ever since you were old enough to walk, you've been bringing home stray critters." She began counting on her fingers. "Let's see…there was the sparrow that fell from its nest, and the bunny whose mama was hit by a car, and the kitten someone had thrown by the side of the road. And remember the time you brought home a skunk? You couldn't have been more than six. You said it was lost in the woods. Oh my, I thought we'd never get the stink out of your hair!"

Jaina sat back in the booth and smiled. "I'd been nagging you that whole summer to camp out in the backyard. That night, *you* suggested it!"

The threesome laughed softly at the fond memory.

"Why the sudden change of heart, Mom?"

Rita's cheeks flushed and she folded her hands on the table. Jaina had seen the pose before, many times. Her father often said her mother was "just a little slip of a thing." But when she set her jaw and squared her shoulders that way, she seemed as strong and immovable as a man twice her size. She had no intention of responding to the question, Rita's tight-lipped, closed expression told Jaina.

"Liam isn't a puppy or a kitten," Jaina persisted. "I can't keep him like some stray animal. There are laws, and he has family right here in Ellicott City. We have an obligation to—"

"Our only obligation is to Liam and Kirstie. She didn't want her uncle to have him."

If Jaina had married, if she could have had children, would her mother still be so intent upon keeping the abandoned child with them? "You're afraid Liam might be your only chance at being a grandmother, aren't you?"

Rita blanched. "I, uh, well, of all the ridiculous…" she sputtered.

Jaina's heart ached when she read her mother's face. Rita detested dishonesty, even tiny white lies told to protect others. The fact that she was avoiding giving Jaina a straight answer was proof enough that Jaina had uncovered a well-hidden truth…a truth that made Jaina painfully aware that her own sad and sorry past had affected her parents, too.

"…it's just that the longer I look at him, the more I like him," Rita was saying, "and the more I like him…" She heaved a deep sigh, shrugging. "We'd be better for him than strangers."

"But Mother," Ray pointed out, "as far as this young'un is concerned, *we're* strangers."

Rita's brow furrowed and she stared down her husband and daughter. "I suppose *someone* has to be the voice of reason." She shook her head. "How can you two be so hard-hearted at a time like this?"

Jaina and her father exchanged exasperated glances before Ray said, "Rita, honey, I'm sorry as sorry can be that we never had that house full of kids we talked so much about before we got married. But the doctor made it clear that your poor li'l heart couldn't take the stress of another pregnancy. Why, I nearly lost you when Jaina was born. Much as I wanted those young'uns, I wanted you more."

Rita crossed both arms over her chest and sent him a loving smile. "I love you, too." Then on a more serious note, she questioned, "But what does any of that have to do with Liam Buchanan?"

Ray shook his head. "I think our girl here is right— partly anyway. You want Jaina to keep him so you can get a whack at raisin' another little one." He slid an arm around her shoulders.

Rita pursed her lips and tapped a forefinger against her

chin, squinting her long-lashed eyes. "Why does the name Buchanan sound so familiar?"

"It's not that uncommon a name, but I've been wondering the same thing," Jaina admitted. "But you haven't said anything about Dad's comment, Mom."

Rita propped her chin on her fist, smiling at the baby. Suddenly, she sandwiched Jaina's hands between her own. "It's that nonsense the doctor spouted all those years ago, isn't it?"

Jaina raised a dark brow in warning. "Please, Mom, don't." Not once in twenty-eight years had she spoken to her mother with anything but respect, but this subject was off-limits, and her mother knew it.

"What happened was *not* your fault, Jaina. How many years are you going to punish yourself for it?"

She hung her head. "If I live to be a hundred," she said, her voice barely audible, "I'll never atone for it."

"But, sweetie, you were…" She bit her lip. "That awful man. What he did to you…" Rita scowled and shook her head.

Her father grated out an opinion of his own. "He's a butcher, and if I ever get my hands on him, I'll—"

"Mom, Dad, please…"

But Rita pressed on. "You were barely twenty at the time. That doctor wasn't God. He said—"

"I'll never forget what he said." Jaina's voice sounded cold and distant even to her own ears. "'There's less than a ten percent chance you'll ever have children.'" Despite her bravado, the word "children" stuck in her throat. Jaina took another sip of water.

Rita ran a hand through her gray-brown curls and tried again. "There's still a chance you *will* have children."

"He said it'd take a miracle for me to have a baby. You heard it yourself."

"You'll never convince *me* of that." Rita scowled.

"What that man did to you is unpardonable. You should have sued his socks off. You should—"

"Mom, please." Jaina wearily shook her head. "We've been through all this hundreds of times. I didn't take Dr. Stewart to court because I had no proof that he botched the surgery. It would have cost a lot of time and money and heartache, and for what? A few measly dollars? Money wouldn't repair me. Money wouldn't give me the baby I've always wanted."

For a long moment, the only sound in the diner was the steady *drip-drip-drip* of the leaky faucet behind the counter. Then her father began to drum his fingers on the tabletop. Rita arranged and rearranged the salt and pepper shakers like squat glass pawns on a Formica chessboard. Liam yawned.

And Jaina breathed an exasperated sigh. "It's getting late."

Rita leaned across the table and pressed a palm to her daughter's cheek. "Jaina, sweetie, everything you do has gentleness and sweetness written on it. That's why you're still bringing home bugs and birds and turtles and…" She looked toward the ceiling as if the help she sought was to be found up there. "You were born with a mother's heart because you were *born* to be a mother. God wouldn't have given you a heart like that if He didn't plan for it to happen someday. Don't you see?"

"What I see," Jaina said, acknowledging that if she'd made the right decision that fateful night, her mother would have had the grandchildren she so richly deserved, "is that you're disappointed in me."

"That isn't true and you know it!"

But it was true, and she did know it. "Then let's drop the subject, okay? Let's bury it and never dig it up again. Because, even if I *could* have a baby after what Dr. Stewart did to me, what man is going to want a woman with a limp, a woman who's all scarred and twisted and—"

Gently, Ray cupped her chin in his big hand, compelling her to look into his eyes. "Sure you have a scar or two, but I look at 'em as pockets."

"Pockets?"

"You need extra pockets to fit all the love you have inside you. If a man don't see that, well, he's plumb blind." He smiled tenderly. "I told you when you woke up from the operation and saw all those scars—" he swallowed hard "—I told you that one day the right man would come along, and when he does, he won't care one bit if you have a few scars because he's gonna love *you*, the girl with a heart as big as all outdoors."

Jaina sent him a trembly smile. That's what he'd said all right, and she'd known even in the thick of pain and agony that he'd meant every word. If only she could believe him, maybe her future wouldn't seem so empty, so bleak. If only she could find a man like *him*. But what were the chances of that in this world where beauty and perfection were second only to wealth and social position?

She looked at Rita, whose eyes had always lit up at the sight of a baby, a toddler, a small child. It had been a mistake, a cruel joke to play on her mother…behaving for even those few moments as though they might be able to keep Liam. Because if she'd been meant to be blessed with motherhood, would God have let the accident that rendered her barren happen in the first place?

Ray broke the silence. "Jaina's right. It's getting late. Let's hit the road, Mother. We'll pray on it tonight, figure out what the Good Lord wants us to do next. His answer will be there, I believe, after a good night's sleep."

Cooing and smiling, Liam hugged Jaina tighter. It dawned on her, as her arms instinctively wrapped protectively around him, that she'd be changing his diapers, feeding him a bottle, tucking him in…at least for tonight. First thing in the morning, though, there'd be other kinds of duties: a trip to the doctor to confirm his apparent good health, a call to Skip, another to the police….

Somewhere deep in her soul, Jaina felt the stirrings of long-forgotten yearnings. For as long as she could remember, she'd wanted a house full of children. It was hard, very hard, convincing herself that she might well be holding in her arms the only chance she'd have at motherhood.

"Oh, just look at them, Ray," Rita whispered, lower lip trembling. "She *wants* to be a mommy to this little guy, and he's crazy about her, too." In a louder voice, she said to Jaina, "God is at work here, sweetie. Can't you *feel* it?"

God indeed, Jaina thought bitterly. *Where was God's work when I needed it?* Jaina leaped to her feet, and with Liam firmly attached to her hip, she grabbed a cleaning rag and began polishing already gleaming tabletops. "What I feel has nothing to do with it. His mother will be back. Of course she will. She'll get a few miles up the road and start missing him—how could she *not?*—and by morning, she'll be—"

"But, sweetie, she's dying."

As painful a burden as her infertility was, it paled before the thought of giving birth, only to know you're going to die and leave a precious baby behind. "Maybe the doctors made a mistake. Maybe Kirstie misunderstood the diagnosis. Maybe—"

"Maybe you're grasping at straws. Remember my friend, Mary?" Rita asked. "The doctors said she had some rare strain of leukemia. One day she seemed healthy as a horse, the next she was gone."

Ray stood, then held out a hand to his wife. "Come on, Mother. Let's go home. Jaina can close up shop."

"I'd take him in myself—"

"Let's not even discuss it, Mother. You know you're not able to care for an infant." Jaina moved Liam to her other hip, then ran a hand through her hair. "Honestly, Dad…what are we going to do with her?"

Smiling halfheartedly, he shrugged. "I've been lookin' for the answer to that one for thirty-one years."

Jaina's lips formed a taut line. "Liam has an uncle right here in town. When he hears what's happened, I'm sure he'll—"

"If his mother felt she had to leave him with a total stranger rather than his only living relative…" Rita extended her hands palms up and gave her daughter a look that said, "What does *that* tell you?" Frustration made her shake her head. "I wish I knew why Buchanan is so familiar. Something in the news, seems to me…."

Her mother was right. A headline story, if Jaina recalled correctly. "I'll call Skip soon as I tuck Liam in. He'll know what to do."

Her mother was out of the booth and at Jaina's side in an instant. "You'll be sorry if you do that. Before you know it, you'll be all wrapped up in legal red tape, and court proceedings, and official documents, and a judge will…"

The mention of court papers and judges jogged Jaina's memory. She'd read an article a week or so ago about an attorney who'd defended a well-known surgeon for malpractice. Thanks to a series of legal loopholes and expert-witness testimony, the jury could not convict, and the doctor who'd bungled a patient's surgery got off without so much as a slap on the wrist. She'd have to check a few back issues of the *Howard County Times,* but Jaina felt sure the lawyer's name had been Buchanan….

"You aren't listening to a word I'm saying, are you?"

Jaina was so deep in thought that she never heard the question. Her heart went out to the injured woman who had taken that doctor to court…and her anger grew as she recalled the lawyer who had used the "system" to injure the poor woman further by getting the surgeon off the hook. "Sorry, Mom."

"As I was saying…things like trust and faith aren't born into a person. Those traits aren't passed down from generation to generation like the color of your eyes and hair. Frankly, I wish they *were* inheritable because maybe then you wouldn't be such a pessimist!"

Liam rested his head on Jaina's shoulder, and she automatically began swaying to and fro as if she'd been rocking him that way his entire life. Her mother's accusation hung in the air like a dusty cobweb. Jaina hadn't always been a pessimist. She'd had faith once, plenty of it, before that dreadful night. Right up to the moment of impact, she had prayed for Divine intervention. But her prayers had not been answered. Perhaps it was the Lord's way of telling her He did not approve of the way she'd conducted herself. How else was she to explain that God seemed to have turned His face from her at a time like that?

"I'm sorry if my feet-on-the-ground attitude is such a disappointment to you," she said, meaning it, "but I prefer to put my trust in things I can count on, like working hard and keeping my head out of the clouds." Her normally soft, warm voice tightened with weary resignation. "I'll keep Kirstie's baby, but only until she comes back."

"She isn't coming back and you know it."

Jaina shrugged. Much as she hated to admit it—for Kirstie's sake as well as Liam's—something told her that her mother was right.

Mother and daughter had apparently reached a stalemate and stood facing one another in stony silence. Jaina's father broke the quiet with a blustery announcement.

"Seems our boy here is about to fall asleep."

Jaina chose to ignore his "our boy" reference. Despite his earlier protestations, her father seemed as enamored of the baby as her mother. She was about to warn her parents not to get any more emotionally involved when her mother said, "On our way back to the diner in the morning, we'll stop off at the grocery store, buy Liam more disposable diapers, some baby food, cereal—"

"Well, don't buy too much," Jaina cautioned, "because this is a very temporary arrangement at best." She rubbed noses with Liam. "Isn't that right, cutie?"

"Mmumm," Liam said with an emphatic nod of his head.

The tiny bell above the door tinkled as Ray pulled it open. "G'night, honey. See you bright and early."

"Bright and early," she returned, locking the door behind them, and then to Liam, "with fifteen grocery bags full of stuff and all for you, whaddaya bet?"

Grinning, he grabbed her ears. "Buffoo," he said, "buffoo!"

Jaina blew kisses against his cheek. "Buffoo yourself," she said, laughing as she turned out the lights.

But the playful behavior did nothing to block the warning that echoed in her head. *This baby is not yours, Jaina. This is a temporary arrangement at best. Temporary…*

The contents of her bottom dresser drawer lay in a heap at the foot of her bed, and Liam lay snoozing contentedly on the downy quilt she'd lined it with. Jaina had tried to sleep in the bed with the baby in the drawer on the floor beside her. But it had seemed so far away that she'd tossed down her comforter and cozied up beside his makeshift crib to watch him sleep.

It had been a mistake because, just as his young mother had predicted, Jaina fell feet over forehead in love with Liam Connor Buchanan.

She'd had every intention of calling Skip the moment

she closed the door to her apartment. But there had been a myriad of excuses. It was after ten. The baby needed a bath. She had a load of laundry to do. She hadn't eaten since lunch. Telling herself she'd phone her pal first thing in the morning, she'd snuggled up beside Liam, fully intent upon sleeping there all night long.

But she hadn't slept a wink. Instead, she'd watched his every move.

She looked at him now as gentle breaths sighed from him with barely a sound, the corner of his mouth lifting occasionally in the beginnings of a soft smile. *What are you dreaming about, little one?* she wondered. *What sweet pictures do you see?*

Dozens of times during the night, she'd reached out to tuck a wayward blond curl behind his ear, to pull the clean white T-shirt down to cover his fat little tummy, to marvel at the long, lush lashes that dusted his pink cheeks. *Do you miss your mommy?* she'd asked silently when he'd wrapped his hand around her finger. *Of course you do.* She could only hope the Almighty would see fit to give Liam a short memory so the pain of separation would quickly fade away. Still, Jaina knew this much: if by some miracle, she *was* allowed to keep him, she would abide by her unspoken promise to Kirstie Buchanan. She would show Liam his mother's photograph often and tell him about the loving young woman whose last thoughts had been of him and him alone.

Jaina pictured Kirstie, tall and lithe, with gleaming waist-length blond hair, huge blue eyes and a quick, easy smile made all the more remarkable by the reasons that had brought her to The Chili Pot in the first place. With a child to worry about, she didn't belong here, and she certainly didn't look as if she belonged in a cancer-treatment program.

Jaina could imagine Kirstie on a high school stage,

doing a top-notch performance of Juliet, or Bianca, or Lysistrata. She'd be a marvelous actress, Jaina thought, because she'd certainly succeeded in hiding the sadness that must have prompted her trip from Chicago in search of the uncle she'd never met.

Had she been married and quickly widowed, or had Liam been born out of wedlock? How had Kirstie supported Liam all these months? And who had minded him while she worked to keep a roof over his head and food in his belly? Kirstie had done a fine job caring for him, and the proof was in the baby's rosy, dimpled cheeks, his sweet and calm disposition, his clean-as-new clothing.

"You were taking a terrible chance, Kirstie," Jaina said, tucking the sheet under his chins for the hundredth time, letting her knuckles gently graze the boy's cheek. She'd caught herself doing that a lot. It was becoming a habit, this stroking and tickling and kissing, a habit that would be hard to break. "You were taking a chance, leaving this precious gift with me. How did you know I'd do right by him?"

Something Rita had said time and again as Jaina was growing up echoed in her mind now. She'd been burning with fever, and on one of Rita's many trips to her bedside, Jaina had asked, "Mom, how do you know what to do for me?" Her mother had perched lightly on the edge of her bed and smoothed back Jaina's bangs. "A mother knows instinctively what's best for her child." She'd said it so matter-of-factly, Jaina believed it. And she believed it to this day. Whether a big-toe blister, a broken wrist or a bout with the flu, her mother had always known exactly what to say and do to comfort her daughter. "How do you know *I'm* capable of love like that?" Jaina asked Liam's missing mommy.

Kirstie had known, Jaina realized, because like Rita, the girl operated from a base of deep and abiding faith. Could this stranger have more in common with her mother than Jaina did? Could she have shared something with Rita… something that was only a dim memory to Jaina?

Maybe Mom's right. Maybe God is giving you a chance at motherhood through Liam….

Jaina blinked and shook her head. "Don't be ridiculous," she chided herself. Still, she wouldn't complain too terribly hard if Skip's advice was that she should keep the baby…at least until a suitable foster family could be located. It made perfect sense, really, since the boy had already been abandoned once.

Jaina sighed, thinking of the recurring dream she had at least once a week since the accident. It had been a mistake to get into Bill's car, and she'd recognized that right from the start. The error in judgment was something she'd have to live with for the rest of her life, and the dream was her mind's way of dealing with the ugly fact that if she'd listened to the silent warning that had gonged in her head that night…

But she hadn't listened.

Jaina glanced at the calendar page.

June 22.

Her heart thundered and her pulse pounded. What could it mean that Liam had come into her life eight years to the day since the accident?

She eased away from his side and tiptoed into the kitchen. Five thirty-five, if the glowing green numerals on the microwave clock were correct. She'd preset the coffeemaker for five-thirty and now inhaled the pleasurable aroma that filled the air. A cup of steaming hot coffee would be the perfect distraction.

Curiosity more than anything else prompted her to slide the phone book from the shelf under the kitchen counter. Plopping it onto the faux chopping-block surface, she opened it to the yellow pages and turned to the Lawyers listing. Her forefinger passed quickly down the column.

"'Baker, Beckley, Bloom, Brown,'" she read softly. The voice froze in her throat as her finger came to a halt beneath one name. "'Connor L. Buchanan, Specializing in Criminal and Divorce Law,'" she whispered, "'371 Court House Drive, Ellicott City.'"

The baby's full name is Liam Connor *Buchanan....*

Her heart clenched with dread. She'd been hoping this search wouldn't turn up anything but more questions, and that those questions would require further research, which would take time. Although she'd tried to rationalize it as attending to small details, it was a stalling tactic, she knew, nothing more—a stratagem that would buy her a few more precious hours with Liam.

"Well, that was smart, Jaina," she muttered. "Now that you've found him, you don't have any choice but to call him."

Or did she?

Buchanan had no idea his niece had been to see him or that she'd decided against leaving her baby in his care. *And what he doesn't know won't hurt me.*

Jaina glanced at the clock. Five forty-three. Ordinarily, she'd be at work, preparing for the breakfast rush. It was really too early to phone most places of business. On the other hand, if she called now and he wasn't in, she could leave a message. And of course he wouldn't be in. *Then the ball is in* his *court. If he doesn't call me back, I'm off the hook.*

Jaina grabbed the phone and quickly dialed Buchanan's number.

She'd expected a secretary's recorded voice to recite a series of instructions for leaving a message. Instead, a vibrant baritone answered, "Connor Buchanan here."

Jaina wished she'd given at least a moment's thought to what she'd say if a human being answered. But who'd have thought a lawyer would be in his office at this hour? "Um, uh, Mr. Buchanan?"

"Yeah."

Jaina blamed the early hour for his abrupt tone of voice. She cleared her throat. "This is, uh, my name is, um, I'm Jaina Chandelle, and I, uh…"

A brief pause, then, "And you *what,* Miss Chandelle?"

He'd all but barked the question. If he talked that way when Kirstie stopped by, no wonder she was afraid to leave Liam with him!

"I have to be in court by nine," he continued, his low-pitched voice harsher still, "and I'm in the middle of pre-paring a brief."

Jaina didn't know what had caused his attitude, but she'd had about enough of it. "Then let *me* be brief," she snapped. "I have something important to discuss with you concerning a relative of yours."

She heard a frustrated, exhausted sigh. "For your edification, I have no living relatives, Miss Chandelle—*if* that's your name—so save the con job."

"Con job? This isn't—"

"Look, I've had it with these nuisance calls. Thanks to caller ID, I've got your number…in more ways than one. I wasn't born yesterday, Miss Chandelle. Either you're casing the joint, or—"

"Casing the joint? You think I want to *rob* you?"

"Either that, or this is a clear-cut case of telephone ha-rassment. Now I'm gonna give you some free advice. I've earned my reputation as a hardnose. You want to find out why, just bug me again."

"Bug you? *Bug you!* I didn't call you to—"

He chuckled quietly.

"I was only trying—"

The chuckle became a full-fledged laugh.

"You're *laughing* at me? When the only reason I was calling was—"

"Wait a minute," he interrupted, his voice softer now. "I wasn't trying to ridicule you—"

But Jaina never heard Buchanan's apology because she'd hung up the phone. She hurried over to the infant seat set up on the countertop to scoop a now wide-awake baby into her arms. "Guess it's time we called my old buddy Skip," she said, blowing a raspberry onto Liam's cheek.

And her heart soared at the sound of his merry giggle. Quite a contrast to his uncle's rasping complaints…

"What's the big frown about?" Pearl McKenzie asked in her motherly fashion. "You haven't even had my coffee yet this morning."

Connor shrugged one shoulder. "I got a strange call this morning."

She rolled her eyes. "Well, unpleasant as they are, you ought to be used to things like that now. Don't these pesty people have anything better to do with their time?"

Connor leaned back in his chair and met the older woman's eyes. "Wasn't like the usual ones, and despite being a pest," he said, grinning slightly, "*she* had a very pleasant voice."

The white-haired woman raised a brow. "You don't say?"

Connor held up his hands in mock surrender. "Now don't get any ideas. I can assure you I have no designs on a stranger who calls me at five-thirty in the morning."

"Five-thirty! What did she want at that hour?"

He shrugged the other shoulder. "Something about a relative."

Pearl dropped her considerable bulk into one of the chairs across from his desk. "Of *yours?*"

He nodded.

"Hmm…"

He met her eyes, narrowed his own. "Hmmm *what?*"

"Well," Pearl began, tapping a pencil against the file

folder in her lap, "I was just wondering…" She dipped her head lower, looked at him over the rim of her purple-framed reading glasses. "Do you suppose this woman has anything to do with the girl who was in the office yesterday?"

"The rude little brat who ran out of here without rescheduling, you mean?"

"The one who ran out of here as if she had a pit bull snapping at her heels, I mean…thanks to the way you were going at it on the phone with the district attorney."

He recalled the argument he'd had with Andy Nelson. He had really lost it, he recalled. Connor sat forward, clasping his hands on the desktop. "What did you say the girl's name was?"

Pearl stepped into the outer office, then returned with an appointment book. "Kirstie Buchanan. I remember because she spelled her last name exactly the way you do. Yes, yes, here it is." She removed her glasses and used the earpiece as a pointer. "Says here she wanted to talk to you about a custody matter." Sliding the spectacles back into place, she cooed, "Oh, and you should have seen that little fella. Cute as a bug's ear, and my oh my, what a flirt! You want me to call this woman? Ask her to come in?" Pearl added.

Connor winced, remembering the way he'd spoken to her on the phone. Somehow she'd gotten the impression he was poking fun at her, when in reality, he'd been laughing at *himself* for being so all-fired certain she'd been another one of the prank callers.

If Kirstie Buchanan was indeed related to him in some way, and the caller had some information about her, it could only involve Susan. He hadn't heard a word from or about his missing sister in nineteen years. The girl Pearl had described was the right age to be Susan's daughter…. He'd had a private detective on the case for such a long time that he'd forged a strong friendship with the man. But two years ago, he'd called off the search. Connor preferred not to think about the reasons why Susan couldn't be found.

"No, I'd better schedule this one myself."

"Better make it snappy, then," Pearl suggested with a nod toward the clock. "You only have half an hour to get your ornery self down to the courthouse." Standing, she placed the message on his desk, then headed unceremoniously toward the door. "So," she began, one hand on the doorknob, "you think she sounded cute, eh?"

"Cute? Nobody is cute at 5:30 a.m. Now do me a favor and get me the Chandelle…I mean the Adams file, will ya?"

"Sure thing, Mr. B."

He heard her snickering as she closed the door. Shaking his head, Connor picked up the phone and dialed. He counted five rings and was about to hang up when a woman answered.

"Good morning. The Chili Pot."

He'd only heard it once, but he'd have recognized that lovely voice anywhere. "Miss Chandelle?"

A slight pause, then, "What do *you* want?"

He'd cross-examined plenty of witnesses who'd pulled this kind of stunt; it was apparent to Connor's practiced ear that Miss Jaina Chandelle was putting on a hard-gal act for him. But even her best efforts at toughness hadn't dulled the music in her voice.

"First of all," he began, "I'd like to apologize for being so abrupt with you earlier—"

"Po-ta-to, po-tah-to," she snapped. "You say 'abrupt,' I say rude."

She was quick-witted and feisty. He liked that. Smiling, he said, "Touché. Not that it's any excuse, but I get a lot of prank phone calls, some of them rather nasty. Unfortunately, I assumed yours was another one of them." He hesitated. "And, in all fairness, you have to admit it was a bit early for a business call…."

Connor tensed as he listened to the moment of silence. Had she hung up? He hoped not because… He relaxed some when she said, "I suppose you're right. Sorry."

"You haven't done anything to apologize for," he admitted. "But let me get to the point. I have to be in court—"

"At nine. So you said during our last conversation," she finished for him.

Chuckling despite himself, he continued, "I'd like to schedule a meeting with you, to discuss this, er, this relative of mine."

"When?"

"Any time after one."

"Today?"

"Yes…if that's convenient for you—"

"Hold on, will you?"

He listened to the sounds of muffled whispering—a man's voice, another woman's…a baby? Connor dismissed the disappointment simmering in his gut. *Too bad, fella,* he told himself. *The lady's married…and she has a kid.*

"I can be there at one-thirty."

At her request, he gave her directions to his office. And though he'd done it hundreds of times for hundreds of clients, it seemed to take longer to explain the route to Jaina Chandelle than it had ever taken before.

It wasn't until Connor had hung up that he understood why. For a reason he couldn't explain, he hadn't wanted to end the conversation. When he returned the receiver to its cradle, he frowned at the feelings bubbling inside him. *How can you miss someone you don't even know?*

Chapter Two

Hᴉs secretary's voice crackled through the intercom. "Oh, Mr. Buchanan…Miss Chandelle is here."

He didn't have to see Pearl's face to know what that singsongy voice was all about. She was likely wearing her matchmaker grin again. Sometimes, Connor wished he'd remarried for no other reason than to quell her desire to find his Miss Right. Pearl's heart was in the right place—he had to give her that—but she'd never even come close to introducing him to the woman of his dreams. If she thought Jaina Chandelle was that woman, well, this time his secretary had *really* missed the mark.

He wondered if she'd look anything like she sounded. He hoped not, because if she did, he was a goner for sure. Connor stood, stuck out his chin and straightened the knot of his silk tie. After the way he'd spoken to this…to Miss Chandelle earlier, he was determined to show her he could behave like a civilized gentleman. He strode purposefully toward the door and flung it wide open. Smiling as she breezed toward him, he extended a hand. "Connor Buchanan, Miss Chandelle. Can I get you a soda? Some coffee?"

"No thanks," she said, matching his firm handshake, "I'm fine."

You most certainly are, he thought, eyes following the long, slender fingers all but hidden by his own beefy ones, to the gentle curve of her shoulder, to the graceful slope of her neck. "Please, make yourself comfortable," he said, meeting her gaze as one hand indicated the chairs facing his desk and the other closed the door. He noticed as she passed that she was limping. Had she sprained her ankle? he wondered.

"So, you can be charming, I see…when you have a mind to."

Connor supposed he had that coming but chose not to respond to it. "It's a real sizzler out there today, isn't it?" he asked as she sat in the wing chair nearest the door. Afraid you might need to make a quick getaway? he asked her silently, his grin a bit wider.

"Ninety-eight *is* unseasonably hot for June, but you know what they say about the weather in Maryland. Wait five minutes and it'll change."

Connor chuckled and settled into his tufted leather chair. "They say the same thing about Ireland."

"Oh, and do they now?" she asked in a lilting brogue.

Ordinarily, first meetings, whether personal or professional, made him restless and uncomfortable, so Connor didn't understand how she'd managed to make him feel so quickly at ease…and on his own turf yet. "When I phoned this morning, you answered, 'The Chili Pot.' I'm curious. What sort of establishment is that?"

She laughed softly, and he found himself unconsciously leaning forward to put himself nearer the delightful sound.

"My parents and I like to say we're in the restaurant business," she said lightly, "but The Chili Pot is a diner, plain and simple. Like the one in that movie, you know? It belonged to my father's brother. Uncle Will never married. He always said I was like the daughter he'd never had, so he left it to me in his will." She tilted her head to add, "I'm surprised you haven't heard of it. It's been written up dozens of times over the years, and it's been right there on Route 40 since the late fifties."

He'd been dying to know if she was married. Thank you, he said silently as he saw his opening. "It's just you and your parents who run the place? What does your husband do for a living? He's not involved in the business?"

Her cheeks reddened and she stared at her hands. "I'm not…I don't have a husband."

She couldn't be more than twenty-five, he thought, so why does she seem ashamed to be single?

"You'll have to stop by some time…"

His question had unnerved her—though he didn't know why—but she'd pulled herself together quickly. He liked that, too, because he'd had enough of women who needed to be the center of attention, who felt sorry for themselves, who said they wanted men to treat them like equals…until a tire needed changing or a bill needed paying. "Maybe I'll just do that," he agreed. Nothin' could be finer than to be in Jaina's diner, he hummed to himself.

"…to try my chili," she finished. "The *Baltimore Sun* food critic called it 'awesomely hot.'" She gave a proud little nod of her head as if to emphasize the point, her eyes widening.

Those eyes—now that's what I'd call awesome, he decided, a smile growing on his face. Wa-a-y too much for a first meeting… Folding his hands on the desktop, Connor cleared his throat and reminded himself why he'd set up this meeting. "I don't mean to be rude, but…"

She cocked a finely arched brow as if to say, "Again?"

"…but about this relative of mine?"

She sat up straighter and unzipped her purse. "Yes. Of course. I'm sorry. I certainly had no intention of wasting your time." She bristled slightly, as if she, too, had forgotten for a moment why she'd come here. "You'll find I have a tendency to ramble, but I'm not easily offended," she said, breaking into a nervous smile. "If you catch me at it, feel free to nudge me back on track."

What made her think they'd be together often enough for him to notice such a thing? he wondered.

She took a deep breath and plunged in. "It's like this. A young girl came into the diner yesterday. Turns out she's your niece. She brought her little boy with her. I thought at first he was twelve, thirteen months old, but he's only seven months. He's quite big for his age."

His niece? Was that even a possibility? "Must run in the family. I'm big for my age, too." He smiled.

And so did she. "I'm afraid we're not talking egos, Mr. Buchanan."

Connor laughed.

"As you'll see when you read this—" she slipped a sheet of folded paper from her purse "—your niece was in my diner the day before yesterday, as well." She bit her lower lip and sighed before continuing, "Since I don't know how to preface or explain the rest, I'll just let the note speak for itself."

He reached across the desk to accept it, mindful of the worry lines that now creased her brow. Heart pounding, Connor slowly unfolded it. What made her so certain the girl was his niece? "You're behaving as if this is a matter of life or death, Miss Chandelle," he said, fighting the urge to frown. "I'm sure once we get to the bottom of this, we'll find it isn't all *that* serious."

"Please, call me Jaina. You make me feel like a prissy etiquette teacher with your 'Miss' this and your 'Miss' that." She took a long, slow breath before adding, "Besides, I have a feeling we're going to be seeing a lot of one another."

One corner of his mouth lifted as he made mental note

of this second reference to their future together. His pulse also quickened in response. He'd always been drawn to tall and willowy women, with long blond hair, fair skin, pale eyes. They'd been glamour personified with their painted fingernails, made-up faces, designer suits. The reaction he seemed to be having to this petite brunette surprised him, since she was everything they weren't and nothing like the types he thought he was attracted to.

"I don't mean to sound melodramatic, but this *is* a life-and-death matter—" she nodded at the note "—as you'll soon see."

Because she didn't seem the type for histrionics, he decided to take her at her word. Smoothing the note on his desktop, he began to read it aloud. "'Dear Jaina,'" he read, "'I came to Ellicott City to meet—'"

She held a finger in the air to silence him. "Would you mind very much reading it to yourself?" Jaina smiled sheepishly. "I'm a big believer in first impressions, you see, and I don't want you to get the idea I'm a crybaby."

"A crybaby?" he echoed. "Why would you…?"

Heaving another deep breath, she pointed at the note and gave him a look that said, "You'll see."

Simultaneously, they both sat back—Buchanan to read, Jaina to watch him.

From his gruff telephone manner, she'd expected him to be much older, her parents' age at least. Technically, Connor was Liam's great uncle, since he was Kirstie's mother's brother. It was impossible however to think of this man as elderly or doddering in any way. Jaina guessed him to be in his early to mid-thirties. She hadn't pictured him as tall or broad-shouldered, certainly not good-looking. If there had been any doubt in her mind that Connor Buchanan, Esq., was Liam's uncle, his appearance cast it aside, for the lawyer's eyes were the same deep shade of blue, fringed by long, dark lashes. Liam's blond hair was several shades lighter than Buchanan's. She didn't know if Liam would develop an adorable cleft in his chin to match his uncle's, but something told her that when the baby matured, a smile would produce a dimple in the very same spot on Liam's right cheek, too.

She noticed the thick golden mustache above Buchanan's lip quaver slightly as a deep furrow creased the space between his well-arched brows. Had he gotten to the part where Kirstie said she didn't want a man like him raising her son? To the passage that explained *why* she was trying to find a home for her son in the first place? Or had the overall mood of the note caused his mouth to turn down at the corners?

She watched him run long, thick fingers through gleaming, wavy hair, listened to the frustrated sigh that rasped from his lungs. If she'd known him better, Jaina might have been able to determine whether he had angled a hand over his eyes to cut the glare from the window or to hide the threat of tears.

Her heart ached for him. The note had made *her* cry, and she hadn't been related to Kirstie. The girl might have been a virtual stranger to Buchanan, but she was blood kin to him nonetheless. He must have just learned that her short time to live had convinced her to believe she must leave her helpless baby boy behind. The effect of the news was apparent on his somber face, in the slight quaking of his big hands. She resisted the urge to reach out and comfort him, say something to soothe his obvious distress. *Don't forget…this guy isn't your friend,* Jaina reminded herself. *He's the enemy, the man who's probably going to fight to keep you from adopting Liam.*

Adopting Liam?

Jaina felt a bit fickle even considering such a thing. Skip had warned her about getting emotionally involved. In all likelihood, he'd said, in a few weeks, when the paperwork had been filed and processed, she'd be forced to give him up. She couldn't have admitted it to her best buddy because he'd diagnose her certifiable if he knew she'd fallen this much in love with the child after just one night.

Buchanan's yellow pages ad said he specialized in criminal and divorce law. Did he know enough about adoption to represent himself? Or would he hire a colleague who specialized in that area?

She'd made the decision earlier to keep Liam—at least, she'd decided to *try*—despite her conversation with Skip. "Babies of this age require special care," he'd said. "The couple I'd normally place him with already has more than enough to handle." Somewhere across town, Skip was pushing through the paperwork that would allow Jaina to keep Liam until a more permanent arrangement could be made.

Preferably with a relative.

Handsome as he was, the man on the other side of the massive mahogany desk must have a dark and devious side. How else could he have decided to help that conscienceless doctor who'd made all the newspapers? "Birds of a feather," said the sages. Should a man like Buchanan be allowed to adopt a defenseless seven-month-old baby, just because he was blood kin? You'll learn soon enough, little Liam, she thought, that you can choose your friends but you can't choose your relatives.

She hadn't realized how intently she'd been studying him until he looked up from the note. He'd been visibly moved by the news, as evidenced by his inability to focus, the slight quaver of his lower lip and hard set of his jaw. But then, lawyers had to be good actors to convince juries to cast their votes in favor of their clients, didn't they?

Buchanan cleared his throat. "It appears the two of us are facing a quandary," he said, his voice fraught with emotion.

"Quandary?" She uncrossed her legs and planted both feet flat on the floor. "I'm afraid I don't—"

"Says here that Kirstie…that my niece provided you with her son's birth certificate."

He seemed disturbed by his reaction to the letter and compensated for it by jutting out his chin and adjusting the knot of his already straight tie. He swallowed—to hide the tremor in his voice?—and held up both hands as if surrendering, then closed his eyes.

Well, he's not praying, she told herself, *not a man like him.* Jaina chalked up his behavior to some caveman-type attempt at regaining control of the situation.

"I don't suppose you brought it with you?" he asked, looking directly at her.

A second ago, he looked for all the world like a little boy lost. Yet, with nothing more than a minor adjustment of his posture, he'd assumed a composed and professional demeanor. "The birth certificate, you mean? As a matter of fact, I did," she said, a bit taken aback by his chameleonlike behavior. Jaina withdrew the envelope from her purse and handed it to him. "I haven't had a chance to photocopy it, so I'd appreciate it if you'd…"

He emptied the contents onto his desktop, the little-boy-lost expression returning to his face as he studied the photograph of his niece. Drawing his generous mouth into a thin, taut line, Buchanan abruptly stood. There was nothing to do but….

She watched him turn next to the birth certificate and holding it, he strode from the office. She wondered where he'd taken the official document…and why.

Glancing around the room, Jaina found herself strangely comforted by the bloodred hues of the Persian rug, the deep greens and pale creams in the plaid draperies, the masculine scent of a caramel-colored leather couch and matching wing chairs, the burnished gleam of mahogany.

It was a gray day, the kind that promised refreshing showers, but so far, nature had not delivered any such respite from the early-summer heat. The afternoon's bleakness filtered through the many-paned window behind Buchanan's desk, shrouding the room with a dreary light. Jaina took the liberty of turning on the green-globed floor lamp behind his high-backed armchair. Immediately, the room glowed with diffused iridescence. The heavy bronze figurines on the mantel, the legal volumes that filled the ceiling-to-floor bookshelves, even the bust of Julius Caesar on the credenza, took on a faint and pleasant verdant hue.

The light also gleamed from a brass picture frame on his desk. Jaina crept closer to get a better look. "Kirstie's mother," she whispered, heart beating in time to the mechanical *tick-tock* of the carriage clock. If not for the hairstyle and vibrantly colored shirt reminiscent of the late seventies, the young woman could have been Kirstie herself.

"Entertaining yourself?"

The sudden sound of his baritone startled her so badly that Jaina dropped the picture. Its heavy frame chipped the credenza on its way to the carpet, where it landed amid the tinkling of breaking glass. Jaina was on her knees in an instant, picking up glittering crystal-like fragments and tucking them into an upturned palm. "I'm so sorry. I never meant to… I saw the picture, and it looked so much like Kirstie that I wanted a better look. I'll replace the frame—"

"Don't worry. I have others," he said, smiling gently.

She knew she was rambling but seemed powerless to stanch the flow of words. This man had the power to take Liam from her. "I'm sorry," she said again, noticing for the first time a small dent in the mahogany. "Oh my," she fretted, "would you look at this? I can't believe I…that

I…" She ran her fingertips over it. "I've refinished several antiques. And I'm pretty good at it, if I do say so myself. If you'd like, I could bring my woodworking kit over some day when you're not busy or when you're in court and repair the—"

Buchanan got down on one knee beside her and gently wrapped his large hands around her wrists, effectively silencing her. "Miss Chandelle…Jaina," he said softly, calmly, "it's all right. It's more my fault than yours. You wouldn't have dropped the picture if I hadn't scared you half to death."

His gaze fused with hers, and she thought for a moment that he intended to kiss her. Her heart pounded with fear and dread as every muscle and joint stiffened. When his head lowered and his eyes narrowed slightly, she followed his stare to the palm of her hand.

"You've cut yourself," he said quietly. Slowly, their faces lifted, their eyes met. They knelt on the fringed carpet trim for a long moment, not moving, not saying a word. Buchanan stood, helped her to her feet and led her to the window. Cradling her hand in his, he turned it up to the light. "Doesn't look too serious. Hold still now, while I…"

She watched his brow furrow with concentration and concern as he leaned in for a closer look. She hadn't been this near a man since that horrible night. *Strange,* she thought, *that I can hear my heart pounding in my ears, but I can't make out a word he's saying.* Was it because she hadn't slept last night that her head was spinning? Or because she hadn't eaten in nearly twenty-four hours? Had the tension of this meeting caused her dizziness? Might it be the sight of her own blood, gathering in a tiny puddle in the palm of her hand, or the nearness of him that made her knees go weak and wobbly?

She inhaled the crisp, masculine scent of his aftershave, felt the dry heat of his warm hands wrapped around hers. Part of her knew he meant her no harm; part of her could think of nothing except the last time a man had gripped her wrists, had held her hands, had breathed minty breath into her nostrils….

Jaina closed her eyes and tried to focus on the here and now. *He isn't Bill,* she chanted mentally. *He won't hurt you. He isn't...*

The pounding in her ears turned to ringing, then to gurgling, as if she'd been suddenly submerged in a pool of water. Buchanan seemed to be moving in slow motion…plucking a tiny shard of glass from her palm… dropping it into the brass wastebasket beside his desk…taking a white handkerchief from his back pants pocket… pressing ing it gently, gently against her wound.

"Just a little cut," she heard him say, his voice taking on the grinding, guttural quality of an old record being played backward. "Barely a scratch. A little scrape that won't even need iodine."

If it wasn't any more serious than that, why did she feel hot and cold at the same time? Why was she breathing as if she'd just run a five-minute mile? Why had her hands begun to sweat? And why was she powerless to still their trembling?

If she could find her voice, she'd tell him to let go, take a step back, give her space to breathe. *He's not Bill,* she told herself. *He won't hurt you. He...*

"Jaina…"

Connor Buchanan's voice, not Bill's. *He's close, so close. So why does he sound so far away?*

By now, the room was spinning, and she reached out for something, anything, to steady herself. It was his hard, muscular forearm she grabbed onto. Should she hold on and endure his nearness, or let go and fall down?

"Ah, Jaina, you're looking a little pale."

The worry in his voice penetrated her frenzied fog. Was his concern genuine? She didn't know because she couldn't see his face, couldn't focus on anything in the spinning, reeling room.

Then, strong hands gripped her waist, eased her into a softly cushioned chair. One of those hands, cool and smooth and steady, cupped the back of her neck, forcing her to rest her face between her knees.

"Deep breaths, Jaina," he instructed, repeatedly stroking her back. "Get some oxygen into your lungs, some blood to your brain."

Mechanically, she did as she was told.

"That's the way. Nice, steady breaths. You're gonna be fine, just fine…."

The dizziness was passing, the trembling easing, and she was able to think a bit more clearly at last. *So why can't I sit up?*

Because Buchanan's hand, pressed against her back, prevented it.

"Easy now," he coached. "Atta girl."

"You can let go now," Jaina said, words muffled by her denim skirt.

"Oh. Sorry." He let go and, with a hand on each of her shoulders, helped her sit up.

Their faces were no more than six inches apart, he facing the window and she facing him. Even in the cloudy light that eked through the glass, his eyes seemed so big and bright. A shudder passed through her when he blinked and she made note of long, dark blond lashes and clear blue irises.

She almost said aloud, "No, don't," when he narrowed his eyes and muttered, "Remind me never to sneak up on you again. You put the fear of…" He hesitated, frowned, then licked his lips. "You really had me going there for a minute."

Funny thing was, she believed him. Who'd have thought a lawyer, who defended society's worst, could be so kind?

"You okay?" he asked, strong fingers combing her damp bangs back into place.

Jaina nodded. "I feel like a little fool, damaging your whatchamacallit, your…thingamajig, swooning like some kind of—"

"I'd like a copy of your thesaurus," he interrupted, chuckling, "'cause it's gotta be more interesting than the one I've been using."

Jaina smiled shakily, ran a hand through her hair and, wincing, looked at her still-bleeding palm.

"I'll buzz Pearl." Buchanan reached for his phone. "That woman is prepared for any emergency. She'll have a bandage and some—"

She grabbed his forearm. "No. Please, don't. I'm embarrassed enough. One witness to my display of weakness is one too many."

He perched on the edge of his desk and regarded her carefully. "The color is coming back into your cheeks. I think you'll live." The words were no sooner out of his mouth than he seemed to realize the inappropriateness of them, considering the content of Kirstie's note. Beneath the ruddy complexion, his cheeks reddened slightly.

"I've wasted far too much of your time already," Jaina said, changing the subject. "Besides, I told my folks I'd be away an hour or so. It's been a long time since they've been alone with—"

"A baby?"

Jaina nodded. "Yeah," she said dully, reminded of the reason for her visit, "a baby." She shook her head and sighed. "I know it's ridiculous after just twenty-four hours, but I really miss the little guy."

He went on as if he hadn't heard her. He handed her

photocopies of the note and the birth certificate. "I feel like a first-class heel for scaring Kirstie off yesterday. She overheard one humdinger of an argument, and I'm afraid she got the idea it's my normal personality." One side of his mouth lifted in a wry grin and he spread his arms wide. "I'm not so terrible, am I?"

On the one hand, she felt she had good reason to believe he was so terrible, when she considered the malpractice suit he'd won and that was just *one* case! On the other, he'd been so gentle with her, so kind and sweet and…

But she couldn't admit either of those things straight out, not to the man who stood between her and Liam. Jaina chose her words carefully. "I don't suppose 'fee, fi, fo, fum' is a regular part of your vocabulary."

His smile softened. "I have a friend who's a private investigator. If he can find Kirstie, will you vouch for me?"

Would Jaina tell the girl it had all been a terrible misunderstanding, that her uncle was goodness personified? She honestly didn't know. "When we realized that she'd left, I told my parents we should try to find her so she wouldn't have to spend her last months…" The next word froze in her throat.

"Alone?"

Jaina nodded.

His expression warmed. "You mean…you'd have taken her in? Just like that? You would've cared for a total stranger until…?"

"Well, of course I would!" she said, rescuing him from having to finish the dreadful sentence.

The blue eyes darkened as his brow furrowed. "How very kind of you."

What was going on in that handsome head of his? What had changed his mood *this* time?

"There isn't much I can do to alter the outlook for Kirstie, but my nephew's future has yet to be decided."

His nephew.

So, Buchanan was drawing boundary lines, was he, and daring her to cross them? Would he have issued the same cold challenge if he'd known Jaina had never run away from one in her life? "Kirstie made it perfectly clear that—"

"She's barely eighteen—*dying*—and completely alone in the world." On his feet now, he began to pace back and forth behind his desk. Then he stopped abruptly, pressing both palms on his desktop and leaning over it. "Nothing she said under the duress of these conditions can be taken seriously."

Oh, you're good, Buchanan. I'll give you that. I'll bet juries just love you. She matched his tone decibel for decibel. "I hope you aren't saying Kirstie wasn't of sound mind when she wrote that note, because she looked sane and reasonable to me." She hesitated, then lifted her chin and boldly added, "And I'm *perfectly* willing to testify to that fact."

He straightened, crossed both arms over his chest. "You must be *perfectly* healthy, too, because you sure did make a fast recovery."

If you weren't so perfectly *arrogant, you might be* perfectly *gorgeous!* Jaina thought. Was he accusing her of faking the fainting spell? What sort of woman did he think she was? "What?" she protested.

Either he hadn't heard her or had chosen to ignore the question. "I wasn't aware you had a degree in psychology, Miss…er…Jaina."

She didn't like the way he stood there, towering over her. Fighting the last of her wooziness, Jaina got to her feet. "I don't need a degree in psychology to know an unbalanced person when I see one. Kirstie was as…" She narrowed her eyes. "I was about to say she was as rational as you, but you're obviously not rational, or you wouldn't be—"

"*I'll* determine her health, mental and physical," he asserted, all but ignoring her, "if and when I find her."

Perhaps if she appealed to his sensitive side… *Please, God, let him* have *a sensitive side.*

"Mr. Buchanan, you haven't had much time to absorb all this information. Why don't you give yourself a day or two, let it sink in while your friend looks for Kirstie. And while you're waiting, maybe you'll give a thought or two to what Kirstie is going through. I mean, it couldn't have been easy, physically or emotionally, to make that long trip from Illinois to Maryland with a baby, especially on a crowded bus. But she did it because she was desperate to find a good home for Liam before…"

Before she dies.

Try as she might, Jaina couldn't make herself complete the sentence.

"I'm thinking of nothing *but* what she's going through…what she's *been* going through. Which is why I want to find her. I want to make sure she'll get the best of—" he spread his arms wide "—the best of *everything.* We're minutes from Johns Hopkins after all, where the country's top doc—"

Jaina held up a hand to silence him. "I haven't lived my life on another planet, Mr. Buchanan. I've heard a thing or two about the great work they do at Johns Hopkins." She clasped her hands to her waist. "I hope you find Kirstie, because I have a feeling she'll need all the help the hospital's specialists can give her." She returned to her seat, took a calming breath. "Until then, may I make a suggestion…in the best interests of Kirstie *and* her son?"

Buchanan headed back to his own side of the desk. "I'm all ears."

"Won't you let Liam stay with me, for now at least? He's been through so much in such a short time. It would only confuse him to move again so soon." She smiled nervously. "He's happy with me…you're more than welcome to come see for yourself."

A thumbnail between his teeth, Buchanan regarded Jaina through hooded eyes as he contemplated her suggestion. After a while, he buzzed his secretary. "Pearl? What's my schedule like for the rest of this week?"

Her voice crackled through the speakerphone. "Have you forgotten? You leave this evening for that conference in New York."

Buchanan exhaled an exasperated sigh. "That's right," he said, more to himself than to Pearl. "I *did* forget, what with all this baby stuff and—"

"Your speech is typed up and ready to go," Pearl continued, "and I've booked you on a flight leaving BWI at eight o'clock. All you have to do is go home and throw a few things in a suitcase."

"You're the best, Pearl."

The secretary chuckled. "Sure thing, Mr. B."

Hanging up, he swiveled his chair until he faced Jaina. "You've been in touch with the authorities, I presume?"

"Yes. I called Social Services and—"

"Good." He nodded somberly. "They have no problem with your keeping the boy?"

The boy? Jaina swallowed her disapproval. *"The boy" has a name.* "They're fine with it," she said emphatically.

He studied her face for what seemed an eternity. "I suppose you're right. If I interfere at this juncture, it might possibly traumatize him." Buchanan steepled his hands beneath his chin. "All right, Jaina, I'll take you up on your generous offer. For the time being at least, Liam can stay with you." He shoved his chair back and stood. "I'll be back in Baltimore on Friday. We'll start the preliminaries first thing the Monday morning after that.

"Meanwhile," he continued, walking toward the door, "I'll get my investigator started on the search for Kirstie.

I'll make him photocopies of her note and the baby's birth certificate, too. That ought to help with his search."

"Speaking of which," Jaina said coolly, "if I'm going to take care of Liam, I need the original birth certificate…just in case anything should happen."

He winced. "You're right. I never thought of that." He traded the copies for the originals.

Right now, Jaina wished with all her heart that she hadn't called him. There didn't seem to be room in his schedule *or* his heart for a baby boy. Liam needed a full-time parent, not a man whose career obligations came ahead of "baby stuff." And there was that matter of the caliber of people he defended….

"Well," she said, forcing a smile, "let's not forget that you're big for your age."

Chuckling, he nodded and opened the door. "I'll call you from New York so you can introduce me to Liam via the telephone."

She stepped into the outer office. He needed to understand that she intended to take her mothering job seriously for as long as it lasted. "Keep in mind he's only seven months old. Call before eight o'clock or he'll be fast asleep."

Buchanan raised a brow. "What a fortunate boy to have such a fastidious guardian in his corner."

Despite her better instincts, Jaina felt warmed by his compliment. She did her best to hide her reaction and offered only a small smile in response.

"You sure you're okay to drive?" he asked. "You're not still dizzy or anything, are you, because I'd be happy to—"

"I'm fine, thank you." She headed for the exit. "And Liam will be, too," she flung over her shoulder.

"I never said he wouldn't be."

That stopped her dead in her tracks. "So you'll be calling tonight?"

He nodded.

And so did she. Aiming for the elevators, she added, "Talk to you later, then, Mr. Buchanan."

"Jaina?"

She turned. "Yes?"

"Call me Connor. Makes me feel like a prissy etiquette teacher, what with all your 'Mr.' this and your 'Mr.' that."

She smiled and pressed the down button.

"Did the picture frame land on your foot?"

Jaina sighed inwardly. Hard as she had tried to hide it, he'd seen her limp anyway. How else was she to explain the pitying expression on his handsome face?

She'd always been one to confront things head-on, and saw no reason to hide from his concern. "Thanks for asking, *Connor,*" she said, deliberately emphasizing his name, "but no, the frame didn't cause my limp."

There seemed to be nothing left to say, so she pressed the first floor button.

"I'm sorry for asking," he apologized in a gentle tone. "That was stupid of me," he added, though his concern had been genuine. "Maybe someday you'll tell me how...."

The elevator doors hissed shut, closing off the end of his sentence.

Connor cleared the remainder of broken glass from the carpet, then carried Susan's picture to his desk. He couldn't stop thinking about the wide-eyed fright that had registered on Jaina's face when he barged into the office earlier. Since she didn't look like the type who'd be bowled over by a little blood, he assumed something from her past, something horrible and terrifying, must have been responsible for her behavior.

"He's not Bill. He won't hurt you." She'd chanted the words under her breath, saying them out loud without realizing it. Who's this Bill guy? Connor wondered, and what did he do to make her so afraid of being near a man?

He leaned back in the chair, one hand tucked behind his head as he stared at the camera-frozen image of his older sister, his only sibling. He knew by what Kirstie *hadn't* said that Susan was dead and buried. How long ago she'd died and of what, he didn't know. Might never know. He closed his eyes. *Not now,* he cautioned, shaking his head. *Don't react to it now. You don't have time.*

He brought to mind Kirstie's photo, the one she'd asked Jaina to show Liam. If he'd had the chance to see it, he could compare it now to his sister's image. As it was, he'd have to content himself with a photocopy of the letter and Liam's birth certificate. Unfortunately, his sister and her daughter had more in common than a striking physical resemblance. Both had given birth while in their teens, and each would have met their Maker way ahead of schedule, leaving a motherless child behind.

He had no proof, of course, that Kirstie had not married Liam's father. But if she had, would the girl have traveled halfway across the country in search of a total stranger... someone to care for her boy?

Connor felt the heat of tears burning behind his eyelids. He hadn't reacted this way two years ago, when he'd given up all hope of ever finding his sister. Hadn't reacted this way nearly two decades ago, when Susan had run away from home after their parents found out she'd gotten pregnant out of wedlock. He remembered how they'd frightened her, wondering if she could ever atone for her sin.

Hundreds of times, he'd wondered why she'd never contacted him. He chalked it up to her overprotectiveness. Susan had no doubt decided that she'd better stay out of the picture for his sake, knowing that their self-righteous parents would have viewed his communication with her as a betrayal of all they believed in and stood for. They'd have made his life miserable. Well, he'd been miserable anyway, so what had Susan's sacrifice accomplished, except to leave a cavernous hole in his life and a nonstop ache in his heart?

Connor swiped angrily at his traitorous, tear-reddened eyes. Had his beloved Susan lived alone and died alone? Nah, of course she hadn't. She'd always been a ray of light in the dark world his harsh and judgmental parents had created for him. She'd been that way with neighbors, kids at school, total strangers. No doubt, wherever she had chosen to live her life, she'd made friends. Lots of them. He could only hope they were with her at the end.

And Kirstie—the niece he didn't even know he had until Jaina Chandelle introduced him to her by way of a brief note—a pretty young girl with everything to live for, including an adorable son. What kind of world was this, where an eighteen-year-old girl could be taken by something as ugly and vile as cancer?

The answer didn't satisfy him.

The same kind of world that turned your parents against their own flesh and blood because she'd made a flesh-and-blood mistake. Whoever said life ain't fair knew his stuff, he decided.

Connor ticked off all the things that might have been different if…

If Susan hadn't gotten pregnant.

If he'd been able to find her after she'd left.

If Kirstie hadn't heard him shouting on the telephone.

Of course, the only reason he even had his list of ifs was because he'd met Jaina.

Jaina… Her image flashed in his mind.

She was totally unlike the many other women who'd had a way of meandering in and out of his life, his ex-wife in particular. Miriam had been a spoiled "wanna-be rich" girl who was happiest aboard cruise ships, in Caribbean cabanas, on England's shores. She wanted nothing but to live the good life, draped in furs, bangled in gold and jewels, boasting an address in horse country. How had she known, when they'd met at the tender age of seventeen, that Connor would be her ticket to a house full of expensive possessions and a well-stamped passport? It wasn't until he asked her to prove her numerous singsonged "I love yous" by giving him the children she'd promised that he realized her words were nothing but lies, told to ensure a full travel itinerary. "*Why* don't I want children with you?" she'd asked lightly. "It's really quite simple. I don't think you'd make a good father."

The answer hurt worse than any injury he'd suffered to date. What had made him believe that sooner or later, after he'd satisfied her hunger for trips and treats, she'd realize he *was* father material after all? Naiveté? Bullheadedness? Blatant stupidity?

And then one day, his wife had come to him in that coolly detached manner that was distinctly Miriam's and told him she was going to have a child. Why wasn't she shouting for joy? he'd wondered. Why wasn't she leaping in jubilation? No matter, he was happy enough for the both of them. A baby, at long last!

Less than two weeks later, her agonized moans woke him in the middle of the night. He spent the next morning in the hospital's chapel, seeking the strength he'd need to be supportive of his wife. The doctor had found him there, and sitting beside him on the hard wooden pew, he'd explained that Miriam's IUD had caused the miscarriage.

"What IUD?" Connor had demanded. "My wife and I don't believe in birth control."

"I'm sure that as an attorney, you understand that doctor-patient confidentiality prevents me from discussing any details of your wife's—"

"Do you mean to say I have no say in whether or not she used artificial means to prevent pregnancy?"

"I'm afraid that's something you're going to have to discuss with her."

Connor vowed then and there, looking into the doctor's sympathetic eyes, that Miriam had hurt and humiliated him for the last time.

He had taken her home from the hospital and helped her to bed, brought her cup after cup of Earl Grey, brewed the way she liked it and served in a Wedgwood cup. It hadn't been easy, behaving like the devoted husband, because now he had proof that she did not see him as a man, as the head of their household. He began to understand that her secrecy had been a lie, a blatant betrayal, and it had killed their marriage just as surely as her choice of birth control had killed their child.

Miriam did not cry over the loss of the baby. In fact, it seemed not to have affected her at all, emotionally. Within days of the miscarriage, she was back on her feet, laughing, planning shopping trips and vacations, ordering a new sofa for the parlor and shoes from an exclusive New York shop.

She had lied by omission when she'd instructed her doctor to insert the IUD, just as every "I love you, honey" had been a lie. He knew that now. If she'd ever loved him, even a little, wouldn't she have seen that he was suffering, that he was grieving over the baby's death? If she'd loved him at all, wouldn't she have seen how much fatherhood meant to him?

Connor had kept track of the weeks and months, and on the day that the doctor had predicted would have been the baby's due date, he'd driven miles into the country and parked in a secluded spot beneath a willow tree, then stared for hours, dry-eyed, at the Victorian-style farmhouse he'd purchased months ago. He'd planned to bring

Miriam here as a surprise after their baby was born. It was his dream house—the perfect place for his new family, where a child could run free, maybe even have a pony.

He didn't fight Miriam a month later when she asked for a divorce. Didn't grieve when the final papers were delivered. It surprised him, when she was gone, that he didn't miss her, not a bit. They'd shared a home, a bed, a life of sorts for nearly ten years after all….

Instead, in the wake of her leaving, Connor experienced a solace like none he'd never known, a peace he hadn't thought possible in this world. If yoking himself to a woman meant giving up that hard-won tranquillity, he'd gladly spend the rest of his days alone. And so, he had not been deeply involved with a woman since. The moment it began to look as if a woman was expecting him to make a commitment to the relationship, he'd ended it.

Every lawyer should be forced to live with a woman like Miriam, he often told himself, for what she'd done to him had left him callous, rigid, insensitive…characteristics that made him a ruthless, determined-to-win attorney.

Connor hadn't shed a tear when his father died of a stroke five years after the divorce, nor when a heart attack took his mother a year after that. His parents had been cold, withholding people who hadn't shown him or Susan a moment of warmth. They hadn't abused their children physically, nor had they neglected them. In fact, anyone on the outside looking in would have commended Bert and Edie Buchanan for providing their son and daughter with the best of everything…everything but the knowledge that they were loved.

He hadn't cried two years ago when he accepted the possibility that Susan did not want to be found. He'd made the decision to stop looking for her matter-of-factly, from a levelheaded, feet-on-the-ground position.

Until now, he'd convinced himself he had inherited the

same gene that made his mother and father frosty, hard-hearted, unreachable. How else could he have suffered so many losses without shedding a single tear?

Until now, he'd never known how much he needed to grieve.

Connor gave in to it. Great, racking sobs shook his body as a lifetime of unspent tears rained down his face.

He didn't know how long he sat there, bawling like a child. He only knew that if not for Jaina, he might have spent his whole life thinking himself abnormal, uncaring, *dead* to such emotions.

But she had breezed into his life, blowing warmth into the pockets of cold aloneness with nothing more than her concern for his nephew.

He didn't know why an unfettered single woman would want the responsibility of raising someone else's child, but Jaina wanted Liam; Connor read it in her eyes, heard it in her voice. If she could love the boy that deeply after just one day with him, how much more would she love him in a month? A year? A lifetime?

He admitted that if she hadn't contacted him, he'd never have known his niece had come looking for him in the first place, wouldn't have known that he had blood kin on this earth at all.

Why, he asked himself, had she risked losing her only opportunity to keep Liam? *Because she's the kind of person who believes in doing the right thing, even when it costs her.* That's *the kind of woman you* should *have married, Buchanan. The kind who puts the needs of others ahead of her own. You might have even had a kid or two by now…or half a dozen if…*

If…

There it was again. One of the smallest words in the English language, yet oh, how large its implications.

Something about her called to everything manly in

him. He had a feeling that Jaina had a capacity for love and caring and nurturing like no one else he'd ever known. She might be petite, but he could tell by the way she walked and talked that her strength of spirit more than compensated for whatever limitations God had placed on her body. He liked that, too, and found it far more attractive than the practiced demeanor of a woman who took her physical gifts for granted. She'd probably be the kind of woman who kept an orderly house and cooked rib-sticking meals, who'd make her man believe he'd hung the moon. He'd spent a total of perhaps forty minutes in her presence; how could he be so certain, after such a short time, that she'd be good for him, good for his life?

You're losin' your mind, that's why, Buchanan, he thought, shaking his head. *Finding out you've got family has you living in a fantasy world.*

He sat up, straightened his shirt and tie, wiped his eyes with the hankie he'd used on Jaina's palm. The tiny spot of her blood caught his attention. Remembering the way she'd pulled herself together, despite whatever trauma had put her into the tailspin to begin with, he pulled himself together now.

He shrugged. Sniffed. Knuckled his eyes.

He made himself focus on the boy and wondered what Liam would be like. Jaina had said he was big for his age. Would he be blond and blue-eyed like his mother and grandmother? Would he have Susan's even-tempered disposition? Or might he have inherited his great-grandfather's quick ire? His great-grandmother's judgmentalism? Connor's own heartlessness? *If there's any justice in this world, every one of the bad traits skipped a generation, because life is gonna be tough enough for the kid.*

He took a deep, shuddering breath.

And did Liam cry quickly and easily? Or was he stoic and brave?

Connor could hardly wait to find out.

Funny, he thought, sniffing one last time, *that a full-grown man can have so much in common with a baby.* Except for the other, each of them was alone in the world.

He'd been powerless to help Susan. Hadn't been able to help Kirstie. If he found her—another if—he doubted he could do more than make her last days comfortable.

But he *could* make a difference in Liam's life.

He could, and he *would.*

He had a family at long last.

Family!

Connor would move mountains, fight beasts bare-handed, take on every official in the state of Maryland, if need be, to adopt this child he'd never met. He didn't have to *meet* the boy to know he loved him, didn't have to *see* him to know he'd protect him till his own dying breath.

And he'd do it, no matter what—or whom—it cost him.

Chapter Three

"Hi, Jaina. It's—"

"Connor. I know." She cut a quick glance at Liam, lying on his side in the middle of her living room, sucking his thumb and poking a stubby finger into the quilt's colorful rainbows. Her heart lurched with love for the sleepy boy…and with fear at the sound of the voice of the man who would attempt to take him from her. "So, how's New York?" She asked the question lightly, casually, as if she hadn't noticed that he didn't call last evening as he'd promised.

"Same as always…dirty, crowded, noisy."

Jaina wondered about the feelings of protectiveness and pity that automatically rose inside her when she heard the exhaustion in his voice. *You shouldn't be feeling anything for him but mistrust. Remember what Skip said.*

"Sorry I haven't called sooner. It's been a circus up here. I haven't had a minute to myself since I stepped off the plane."

Did he really expect her to believe he couldn't have found one moment to check on Liam's welfare? Following Skip's instructions, Jaina jotted the time and date of his call in a spiral tablet. From now on, every moment the lawyer spent with Liam—in person or on the phone—would be logged in Jaina's Buchanan Book. So far, he was playing right into her hands. She could only hope he'd continue behaving as though everything in his life took precedence over the baby.

Feeling a little two-faced, she put an extra lilt into her voice. "It's a shame they're keeping you so busy. You ought to take advantage of being in the Big Apple. See a play. Tour the museums. Stroll down Times Square. Do something touristy."

"I have a client with business interests in New York. I'm up here once a month, minimum…"

Jaina scribbled that fact in the tablet.

"…and I wouldn't do any of those things even if I *did* have the time."

When his tone switched from exhausted to disgusted, Jaina got a mental picture of him, wrinkling his nose at the idea of doing anything fun. "So you've never seen *The Phantom?*"

"Nope."

"Cats?"

"No."

"Why not?" she asked, genuinely incredulous.

"I'd rather sit in my room, watch the news and order room service than watch a bunch of supposedly sane adults romp around a stage dressed up like cats," he replied in a cutting tone.

Jaina's brow rose a little higher. Kirstie was right. He *is* a mean old grouch. And she might have said so if Skip hadn't cautioned her to treat Buchanan with kid gloves… at least until after the preliminary hearing.

"Oh, well I guess musicals aren't your thing," Jaina replied lightly.

"Got that right," he grumbled.

"So, did your audience like your speech?"

He chuckled. "Nobody threw rotten tomatoes, and I didn't hear any snoring. It went all right, I guess."

She reminded herself what else Skip had said. "It'll be harder for him to take Liam if he *likes* you." She'd started working with the public at seventeen when, to pay her way through college, she began singing and playing guitar all around the country. Jaina's easy manner at the mike earned her a reputation for having what was generally referred to as "stage presence." *Just pretend he's some guy in the audience, celebrating his birthday.*

"What was your speech about?" she asked. Skip's advice had very little to do with her interest; *everything* about Connor Buchanan fascinated her, from the beautiful smile he so rarely exhibited to the fact that he, too, seemed to know how to "work a crowd."

"Well, it was called 'The Importance of Effective Closing Arguments.'" There was a long pause before he added, "I seem to have a talent for them, according to the media."

"Why? Because when you're at your best, you can turn a jury around, even at the last minute."

There was another long pause. And then he said, "Been reading the papers, I see."

Jaina thought of the case she'd read about—the surgeon who still had his license thanks to Connor Buchanan's "talents." Suddenly, she didn't care what Skip had said about biding her time, about buttering up the lawyer. "Would you like to talk to Liam?"

A moment of silence ticked by as if he might be considering it. "Nah, it's after ten, and I don't want you to wake him."

At the mention of his name, Liam reached for her. "Mmumm-mmumm," he said, lifting his arms. "Mmumm-mmumm."

Buchanan cleared his throat. "He's still up?"

"Yes."

"I thought you said his bedtime was eight."

She sighed at his scolding tone, stroking Liam's hair. "It is, usually. But tonight we went to the park after supper, had some ice cream. Between the long walk, the swings and the slide, plus the extra chocolate sprinkles, he's a little wound up." Worried that Buchanan might read "too permissive" into the way she was caring for Liam, she quickly added, "But it usually doesn't take him more than ten minutes to fall asleep." Just for good measure, she tacked on another truth. "Especially if I rock him with a lullaby."

Another moment of silence. "How do you manage the, uh, quality mothering when you have a diner to run?"

Skip had predicted this question, too, and warned her that Buchanan would try to make the judge see her as a success-oriented businesswoman who couldn't—or wouldn't—make room in her busy schedule for a baby. "I'm already interviewing to hire extra staff and a full-time manager at the diner. I also have my parents to baby-sit anytime I need help. Liam is number one on *my* priority list. Would he be on yours?"

"I think I can make a case for that."

"But that's not the question, Counselor." Lifting Liam from the quilt, she settled into the rocker with him. Immediately, he grabbed the phone cord. "No, no, sweetie," she said, gently disentangling his fingers from the coils, "don't put that in your mouth."

"So, can I talk to him?"

Jaina could have sworn she heard apprehension in his otherwise sure-of-himself voice. Apprehension, and maybe a tinge of uncertainty. "I have to warn you, he doesn't say much, but listening amazes him."

This oughta be fun, she told herself, holding the phone

to Liam's ear. A one-way conversation between a defense attorney and a defenseless baby.

"Hey, Liam. Whatcha doin', li'l buddy?"

The child turned his head toward the voice, scraping a fingernail over the tiny holes in the earpiece.

"You bein' a good boy, Liam? Huh? Are ya?"

The baby furrowed his brow. "Dih-dih?" he asked Jaina, pointing at the phone. "Dih-dih-dih?"

"I'm gonna come see you tomorrow," she heard Buchanan say. "What do you think of that? Maybe we'll go to the zoo, see the big ol' lions and tigers, even ride the train."

She'd expected the lawyer to sound stiff and stern, not animated and friendly. Then Jaina remembered he'd behaved similarly when she nearly fainted dead away in his office. But was the warm, gentle demeanor genuine, or rehearsed like his jury-turning closing arguments?

Liam tried his best to stuff the entire phone into his mouth. When it wouldn't fit, he lost interest entirely and focused on Jaina's dangly wolf earrings, which suddenly held far more baby appeal. Then, just as quickly, he spotted the wooden pull-toy truck her father had made him and did several deep knee bends in her lap, pointing toward the quilt. "Mmumm-mmumm. Mmumm-mmum!"

"Sorry," she said, taking the phone. "His attention span is fairly short, especially at this time of day."

"He sounds terrific. I can't wait to see him."

Her mouth went dry and her palms grew damp. He'd been away for days, had promised to call yesterday, then didn't. Now, suddenly, after a brief conversation with Liam, he wanted to see him? *I don't like this. Not one bit.*

"How's tomorrow?"

Her heart thudded with dread. Saturday had always been The Chili Pot's busiest day. She pictured his quiet, elegant office, comparing it to the nonstop hustle and bustle of the diner. He didn't know a thing about the restaurant business and would likely see all the activity and noise as a chaotic mess. And as an unsuitable place to raise a traumatized, abandoned child. "It's a lot quieter midweek, between lunch and supper," she suggested. "If you stop by, say, on Wednesday afternoon, I can give you my undivided atten—"

"It isn't going to be a social call, Jaina, so you needn't worry about entertaining me. Besides, it isn't you I'm coming to see."

She clenched her jaws together so tightly, her gums ached.

"If the plane lands on time, I should be there by one."

Why had he asked to see Liam tomorrow, Jaina wondered, when his attitude made it perfectly clear it had been an order, one he fully expected her to follow?

"I, uh, I bought a little something for him."

She imagined a Statue of Liberty key chain, an Empire State Building mug, an I Love New York baseball cap, things completely inappropriate for a seven-month-old and probably purchased in his hotel's gift shop. "How thoughtful."

"You doing okay?"

"I'm doing just fine," she said, her voice thick with defensiveness. "I've had to juggle my schedule a bit so that Liam gets my best at all times, but—"

He harrumphed.

Time to terminate this conversation, she told herself, *before you say something that gives him the excuse he needs to take Liam away from you now.* "Have a safe flight."

"Will do."

"See you tomorrow."

"Okay," he said. "Gotta go. I have a call waiting." And he hung up.

Jaina stared at the dead receiver for a moment. Of all the arrogant, pompous—

"Dih?" Liam asked, pointing at the phone. "Dih-dih?"

Fear gripped her heart. It sounded an awful lot like he was saying Da-da. No, you're just imagining it, she assured herself. But the baby was clearly responding to Connor. Had the baby somehow sensed that he and Buchanan were related? Had he recognized something in the man's voice that told him they were family? She picked him up, then hugged him protectively, possessively. "Time for bed, little one," she cooed into his ear. "You've got a big day tomorrow."

Jaina tucked him into the crib she'd gotten from Ronnie's Rent-All and turned out all but one dim lamp. And after dragging her bentwood rocker closer, she did what she'd been doing for five consecutive nights. She slid her hand between the bars and let Liam hold on to her forefinger. If the night ran true to form, he'd fall asleep in minutes, snuggled against her hand, and long after slumber overtook him, she'd continue to watch him until drowsiness overtook her, too.

Jaina woke, wincing at the discomfort of the cramp in her hand. When she sat up in the rocker to flex it, she noticed another knotted muscle in her neck. *How long have I been asleep?* she wondered, stretching as tall as her five-feet-three-inch frame would allow. A glance at the glowing red numerals of her alarm clock answered the question. Buchanan had called shortly after ten and talked all of five minutes. She'd put Liam to bed immediately after his uncle hung up. It was now one thirty-five. No wonder she was stiff and sore. She'd been out for nearly three hours!

Taking a deep breath, she raised and lowered her shoulders, rolled them forward and backward, tilted her head left, right, left again. The alarm clock blinked as it changed to one thirty-six…a silent reminder that its radio music would come on in less than four hours.

In less than *twelve* hours, Connor Buchanan would arrive.

She tiptoed over to the crib, leaned on its oaken rail and smiled. She'd tucked a light blanket around him earlier. He must have kicked it off when he rolled over. Grinning, Jaina shook her head. How can you be comfortable in that position? she asked him silently, covering the round rump that protruded into the air, the pudgy fingers splayed on Winnie the Pooh sheets. She patted that well-diapered little behind…and wondered about the sob that ached in her throat.

It hadn't even been a week since his mother's disappearance. If not for Skip's influence, Jaina didn't know what might have become of Kirstie's innocent little boy. Since the demand for suitable foster parents was far greater than those available, Liam would likely have ended up in some impersonal, overcrowded children's ward. Surely, if that had happened, the doctors and nurses on duty would have given him the best they could, despite the demands of their busy jobs. But a hospital is a place for sick people, not for abandoned youngsters. The day after Kirstie's disappearance, Jaina had taken Liam to a pediatrician recommended by Skip. "The only thing wrong with this baby," the doctor had said, "is that he has no family."

Well, that wasn't entirely true. He had Connor Buchanan….

But despite the age-old cliché, blood wasn't always thicker than water. And the proof—at least in Jaina's mind—was the lawyer's cavalier attitude toward Liam's well-being.

How could he have gone off to New York, knowing

Kirstie's little son would be in the care of strangers, without checking on him from time to time? For all he knew, Jaina *was* the overambitious career woman Skip had described, who'd put business ahead of the child's welfare. How did he know she even *liked* children? What made him so certain she wouldn't abuse or neglect the baby? Why did he believe Liam would be in safe hands?

Blind faith must run in the Buchanan family, she told herself, remembering the trusting way Kirstie had left Liam at the diner in the first place. Odd, she told herself, because faith was primarily a spiritual thing, and Buchanan didn't seem the religious type....

Liam sighed in his sleep, a delightful, musical sound that made Jaina's heart throb with love. She hadn't known it was possible to love this deeply in such a short time. Indeed, she didn't know it was possible to love this much at all!

If she was the one who'd given birth to him, she might have understood the all-consuming tenderness she felt for him. If she'd held him in her arms in the delivery room, nursed him, sung him lullabies in their hospital room, she might have had an explanation for the overwhelming fondness beating in her heart. If she'd watched him thrive and grow as she showered him with attention and affection as he struggled to sit up and then to crawl, eager to learn about the world around him, she might have comprehended the powerful sense of devotion she'd developed toward him.

But he'd been with her less than a week. Was there something wrong with her, that she'd so quickly succumbed to this innocent baby's charms? Could there have been such a void in her life that she'd be so utterly filled with love for this tiny being?

There was no denying how lonely she'd been until he came into her life. Lonely for someone to care for, someone to be needed by, someone to spend years of pent-up love on. How strange that she didn't know it, didn't recognize it for what it was until Liam came into her life. He'd filled the emptiness in her soul, in her heart. But what had she done for *him?*

Any foster parent could have provided him with safe surroundings, healthy food, wholesome activities, a clean diaper when he needed it. If Skip had been able to find a home that wasn't already overrun with children, that's exactly the kind of care Liam would be getting. It was only because her best friend believed Liam would suffer less anxiety and disruption if he remained with Jaina as the investigation surrounding his permanent placement continued that she'd been given this time with him.

Jaina wondered if her mother could be right…that Liam was God's reward for her stoic acceptance of her barrenness.

Jaina padded into the kitchen and poured herself a glass of lemonade, then unlocked the back door and stepped out onto the porch. Standing at the rail and looking beyond the parking lot, she could see rolling hills, pastures and farmland, a fence here, a barn there.

As a child, she'd moved every other year on average, from apartment to apartment on air force bases between New York and California. It had been fun and exciting—meeting new people, seeing new sights, learning new things—yet Jaina had always dreamed of living in a place surrounded by acres of grassy, tree-lined knolls. Since owning The Chili Pot, she'd been saving every spare dime, intent upon making her dream a reality. For the time being at least, she must be satisfied with her vision of the two-story farmhouse she'd someday call home.

It would have a wraparound, covered porch. She'd paint the railing and the floorboards white so the bentwood rockers flanking the front door would be clearly visible from the road, telling passersby that the house and its views were thoroughly and frequently enjoyed by its owner.

There'd be lots of tall, narrow windows, where she'd hang gauzy white curtains that would billow gently in the summer breezes, a gray-with-age split-rail fence, lined by black-eyed Susans, and a winding flagstone path that would lead visitors from the crushed-stone driveway to her red-enameled front door.

Ancient trees would shade the house, creating a cool canopy on sizzling August days and a place for birds to build their twiggy nests in the springtime. Out back, she'd plant a garden and grow vegetables for freezing and canning, enough for friends and neighbors, as well as a few to set out on a table near the road, where a sign would invite city folk passing by to partake in nature's country glory.

If she had that place now, she'd certainly have a better chance at being allowed to adopt Liam. What judge could refuse her, when the home she'd provide for the boy would have a tree house, a swing set, a pond for catching toads, a stream for snagging fish, and a big, bright bedroom overlooking it all.

She had always been happy in her modest apartment above the diner. Soon after moving in, she'd torn off layers of peeling wallpaper and painted the whole place a creamy off-white. She'd taken up the green shag rug, refinished the mellow oak floors and laid down the Persian rugs her family had collected when stationed with her father in faraway places. She'd scrubbed years of grease and grime from the windows and replaced the heavy draperies with tap-topped curtains she'd sewn herself. She'd furnished the rooms with an eclectic mix of comfortable traditional-style pieces, family heirlooms and some interesting old "finds."

But there was only the one bedroom. And no backyard. The only way to reach the apartment was by way of the long, narrow staircase at the back of the diner. Worse... whatever noise was going on downstairs could easily be heard through the floorboards. Then once the sun went down, the chili red neon sign she'd had crafted by an Ellicott City glassblower beamed steadily, casting an orange glow over everything in the living room.

The diner was open 7:00 a.m. to 7:00 p.m. every day except Sunday, but it took two hours to get ready for the public and two hours to clean up after the last customer had gone home. Would a child-care specialist see this as a stable home for a growing boy...or as a virtual three-ring circus?

She should have bought that little farm she'd found last year, she scolded herself, instead of being such a perfectionist. It hadn't been such a bad place; a little time and elbow grease would have turned it around, just as her efforts had improved the apartment.

But the house had been a rambling ranch, not a stately Victorian. In place of a cozy wraparound porch, there was a concrete slab near the front door. She couldn't hang a tree swing from the branches of the pathetic sapling in the side yard. The house had a contemporary modern kitchen and two equally sleek bathrooms. And the only antique that would have fitted into the low-ceilinged, narrow-doored house was the player piano she'd found at the Westview flea market.

But the price had been right, and considering that it was situated less than a mile from The Chili Pot, the location couldn't have been better. With a farm to her right and woods to the left, she'd have at last those wide open spaces she'd yearned for while living on cramped air force bases.

"You're such a tomboy," her mother would lament when, as a girl, she'd come home with cuts and bruises sustained in a rousing game of touch football. "What a wild one," her father would exclaim when Jaina slunk into the house with holes in the knees and seat of her jeans...holes put there by reckless slides into home plate. She'd always been a spur-of-the-moment girl, a do-it-now, worry-about-it-later kind of kid.

Except about that house. To make that dream come true, Jaina had been more than willing to wait.

It had been that very mind-set that prompted her to get onto her first stage in response to a dare from Skip and sing with Bobby Pierce and his four-piece band. If she had known her guitar wasn't tuned to scale, she'd never have agreed to stand at the mike and croon the tune she'd written all by herself. Somehow, Bobby's lead guitarist provided backup to her little ditty, and when the song ended, it had been the plaudits of the musicians that gave her the incentive to repeat the performance again the very next week. She had a natural talent with the guitar, they'd said; she could go places with a voice like that, they'd insisted.

And she had. After signing with Artists' Corporation of America, her agent had booked her all over the country. It had been after a benefit performance in Chicago that a record producer approached her about signing a contract. She'd gone to Nashville with the grandfatherly gentleman, done a stint with the Grand Ole Opry and cut a record.

The tune went national, and within the first week, radio stations from coast to coast were broadcasting "Lovin' Arms," the song she'd written about the love of her life, drummer Bill Isaacs.

She'd met Bill during that first year of touring the country, when the agency scheduled her to do a show at a college in Virginia. She'd been slated as the feature act, and Bill headed up the backup band. They had clicked both musically and personally, and when the gig ended, they'd arranged to meet as often as possible.

Like everything else she'd done in her life to that point, Jaina decided in a snap that she loved him, despite his heavy drinking and bouts of bad temper. Her devotion, she'd told herself, would give him the incentive to quit.

And then one night, when his band wasn't booked, Bill drove from Illinois to Wisconsin to spend a weekend with her so they could discuss their future. And in a snap, she knew if he asked her to marry him, she'd say yes.

He had shown up nearly an hour late. If she'd known he'd been drinking, she'd never have gotten in the car with him, but Bill was good at hiding his drunken state. As she later realized, Bill was good at hiding so much of his real personality from her. Or, was it only that she chose not to see his weakness?

As she walked toward the car, something warned her not to get in. She hesitated a moment, and Bill called to her. Hollered at her belligerently and honked the horn. Everything in her warned her not to get into the car with her wild-eyed boyfriend.

In a snap, she'd cast caution aside.

And she would pay for that mistake for the rest of her life.

You're paying for it now, she thought dismally, *big time! If it hadn't been for that night…*

Fear seized her soul.

What if Connor found out about that night? It wouldn't matter one whit that you were totally innocent of any wrongdoing and that the records have been expunged. A lawyer like Connor Buchanan will pounce all over that black mark in my past and use it to take away Liam so fast it will make my head spin.

Jaina gave the view a last forlorn glance and went back inside. After locking up, she stuck her empty glass into the dishwasher and headed for her room. On the way to the extra wide four-poster, she stopped beside Liam's crib.

He'd kicked off his covers again, and she gently pulled them up. Tears filled her eyes. As she watched him sleep, Jaina did something she hadn't done in a very long time.

"Dear Lord," she whispered, "I want to do Your will, and I want to keep Liam." Softly, her fingertips traced his cheek. "Please help me find a way to do both."

Her father had been an early riser ever since his air force days, when he'd get up before dawn to climb into a cockpit and "test drive" the latest, fastest, most powerful fighter planes. "I'm at the market," read the note propped against the carving board. "See you by six. Hugs and kisses, Dad." He'd been penning the same words every day for all the years they'd run The Chili Pot together.

The name on the diner's deed said Jaina Clarisse Chandelle, but she had never considered herself sole proprietor. Without her father's keen eye for picking only the best fruits, vegetables and meats, and her mother's knack for creating delectable sweet treats, Jaina's menu would be sparse indeed.

The rest of the staff, she believed, owned a piece of the place, as well. Take Eliot, for example. It had been a risk, hiring the cook; with nothing more than the say-so of Pastor Cummings, she'd given the ex-con a job, knowing full well that he'd spent the past three years at Jessup on charges of car theft. To this day, he proclaimed his innocence, but guilty or not, in Jaina's mind the man had served his time and deserved a chance to prove he'd righted his life.

It had been one of the smartest business moves she'd ever made, and the proof could be found in the crowded lot, where vehicles with license plates from West Virginia, New York, Delaware, Virginia and Maryland's Eastern Shore parked every day of the week. It was one of the best personal choices, too, because in the six years he'd worked for her, the stocky black man had become one of her dearest, most trusted friends.

Hiring Billie had also required a leap of faith. She'd come to Jaina's attention thanks to the pastor's youth rehab program. Billie had been drawn into a gang and couldn't see a way out, until Pastor Cummings had come into her life. A youthful offender, she'd been arrested for shoplifting, truancy, driving without a license and a few other minor offenses. In the pastor's program, she'd decided to turn her life around, get a job and leave the gang. Now Jaina was determined to help her anyway she could. In Jaina's opinion, Billie was the best all-round waitress in the tristate area. She could keep a twenty-party order straight without writing down a single word and balance six plates on one arm while carrying four cups and saucers, stacked one atop the other, in her free hand.

Eliot's cousin, Barney, a recent graduate of Cummings's Say No To Drugs project, could operate and repair every piece of equipment in the diner, from the twenty-slice toaster to the industrial-size dishwasher, from the extra large stove and grill to the walk-in freezer.

And Joy, who had hung out with Billie on one of Baltimore's meanest streets, rounded out the diner's offbeat employee roster.

Until now, Jaina hadn't given much thought to the things they'd done before joining the Chili Pot family. But Connor Buchanan changed all that. Skip had warned her that if Buchanan discovered the dubious résumés of her employees, he'd use them against her in court.

There was a chance, she supposed, that he'd be as broad-minded as Pastor Cummings, the way she and her parents had been. But then, they'd had reason to be understanding. Her friends deserved *at least* as much of the fairness and open-mindedness that she'd been given since her release from Jessup.

Would he be fair and open-minded? Jaina was in no position to take chances. Not when Liam's future was at stake.

She crumpled her father's note and tossed it into the trash can. "Dad ought to save himself the bother and carve the message into the countertop," she told Liam. Secretly, she'd have been disappointed if he did, because when she came downstairs from her apartment every morning, finding his brief note was like running into an old dependable friend.

"What're you lookin' so down in the dumps about?" Eliot asked. He'd already toasted several loaves of bread and now stood at the stove, flipping sausage patties in a giant iron skillet.

"Liam's uncle is coming to meet him today."

"A big-time lawyer in The Chili Pot?" the cook said, shaking his head. "There goes the neighborhood!"

"Fortunately," she countered, laughing, "he'll only be here a short while. I don't think he'll drag down the property values in an hour or two."

"Well, he gives you any trouble, you send him to *me*," he said, slathering butter onto the last slice of toast. "*I'll* set that legal beagle straight!"

Jaina patted his shoulder. "Thanks, Eliot."

"Hey, what're friends for?"

Billie barged into the room, balancing a plate on one palm. "They're for saving us the last wedge of lemon meringue pie, that's what friends are for," she said around a mouthful. "I love ya, big guy!"

"Aw, now don't go gettin' all mushy on me, girl. I only set that piece of pie aside 'cause I couldn't stand to throw it away."

"I forgot," the waitress said, smiling sarcastically and rolling her heavily made-up eyes, "how much you hate to waste food."

"Don't you sass me, missy, or I'll put you to work choppin' onions. You know what that does to your mascara."

Her blue eyes widened. "You wouldn't!"

Eliot smirked. "I would, and you know it."

Billie faced Jaina, pretending she needed protection. "Help?" she said in a tiny, wavering voice.

"Don't look at me," Jaina said, holding up one hand as Liam inspected the other. "I just write the paychecks. He's in charge of the kitchen…or the onions at least."

Billie chucked Liam's chins. "How's our widdo boy? Did him sweep wike a wock? Did him have boo-tee-ful dweems?"

"Don't talk to him that way," Eliot scolded. "You'll make a sissy out of him. Besides," he added, "I read someplace that it takes young'uns twice as long to learn proper English if they have to learn two languages."

Billie grabbed the salt canister. "What?"

He held up one finger. "English," he said as a second finger joined the first, "and baby talk."

Using her hip to open the swinging door, Billie harrumphed. "When did *you* get so smart?"

"Didn't get smart," he called after her. "Was *born* smart."

"Yeah, yeah, yeah," she said from her side of the door. "And it's gonna snow on the Fourth of July."

Eliot met Jaina's eyes.

"I know, I know," she said on a sigh. "You think she's getting too big for her britches."

"If she spent a little more time on her feet, waitin' tables," he hollered, "and less time warmin' the stools at the snack bar…"

"I heard that, Eliot!"

"Are you two at it again?" Rita asked, waltzing into the kitchen. "Honestly, I feel like I'm back teaching kindergarten again, refereeing all of your squabbles!" She held out her arms, and Liam spilled into them. "How's my boy? Did you sleep well, sweetie?"

"Connor Buchanan will be here at lunchtime," Jaina said matter-of-factly.

Rita's eyes widened and her mouth dropped open. "You invited him *here?* Jaina, what were you thinking?"

"I was thinking we'd better keep him happy so that maybe—Lord willing—he'll see how good we are for Liam and won't throw a monkey wrench into the works and ruin our chances for adoption." Her heart raced as she said it because Buchanan had probably already set his investigative team to snooping into her background.

Rita looked at Eliot. "I guess if you're going to dream, you may as well dream big, right?"

Eliot looked from Jaina's frowning face to Rita's mistrustful expression. "Ladies," he said, carrying his egg tray to the stove, "I have scramblin' to do, so if you'll just excuse me…"

"Chicken," Rita grumbled. "Go ahead, leave me here all by myself."

"I learned long time ago, it ain't smart to take sides. Not when it puts you between two women!"

Rita clucked her tongue, then said to Jaina, "I finally figured out why Buchanan's name is so familiar." She handed Liam a long-handled spoon to chew on. "There was a big article about him in—"

"The *Howard County Times*. I know."

Eliot turned away from the stove long enough to ask, "What did he do? Cheat on his bar exam?"

"Worse," Rita explained. "He defended a doctor whose botched surgery cost a woman the ability to have children. He got the man off."

The cook put his back to the women. "Nothin' wrong with that," he grumbled. "Man's innocent 'til proven guilty. Least, that's what the writers of the Constitution intended for folks in this country."

Jaina stiffened but said nothing. Eliot didn't know about her past so he couldn't possibly realize how deeply his comment had affected her. What he didn't know couldn't hurt her; she'd learned the hard way that when people found out about the accident, things changed. They took a step back. Smiled the way one might smile when speaking to the very young—or the very old. Spoke with a patronizing tone as though they believed anything they said might cause her to snap.

"What's this lawyer fella gonna say when he finds out what your employees were up to before they started working here?" Eliot wanted to know. "You reckon he's gonna use it against you in the adoption proceedings?"

She had never been one to sugarcoat things. "I'm sure he'll try, but he won't get very far. You and Barney, Billie and Joy have turned your lives completely around. If anything, knowing about you will *help* me, not hurt me."

Eliot's brow furrowed. "How do you figure that?"

Jaina grinned mischievously. "Well, my goodness, if I can make honest citizens out of the likes of you guys, think what I can do with an impressionable kid like Liam!"

"Oh, so now you're taking the credit for our reform?" he teased.

Her grin became a gentle smile. "Only if Buchanan forces me to, and even then, only on the witness stand." She took a deep breath. *It's* my *past that'll hurt me in court, not the Chili Pot employees'.*

"Enough blabbing," Ray ordered good-naturedly, dumping a fifty-pound sack of potatoes on the floor. "Let's get this show on the road. We open in fifteen minutes!"

As usual, eighteen-wheelers, pickup trucks, motorcycles, cars and assorted minivans had already filled the graveled parking lot. They opened the doors at seven, and by quarter past, all the booths and tables in the diner were filled.

Joy took care of the Minnesota family heading for Washington, D.C., and the young Maryland couple who planned to spend the afternoon at Baltimore's National Aquarium. Billie handled the truckers and bikers sitting at tables near the window, Jaina waited on retirees and construction workers lining the snack bar, while Rita monitored the cash register. Barney saw to it that a steady supply of squeaky-clean dishes lined the shelves below the counter, and Ray did double duty as busboy and setup man.

They'd worked it out to a fine science, easily satisfying hundreds of hungry patrons a day, thanks to Ray's "Get 'em in, fill 'em up, move 'em out" policy. If the dishwasher had decided to malfunction any other day, the Chili Pot team would have handled the setback with quiet efficiency, and more than likely, nary a customer would have noticed.

But the machine sprang a leak at precisely the same time as the main drain developed a clog. Barney hadn't touched the central water valve in so long, it took five minutes to locate and turn it off. Meanwhile, the black-and-white-tiled floor seemed to float beneath several inches of foamy, antiseptic-scented dishwater.

The crew tried valiantly to sop up the mess, slinging long-handled string mops, towels, aprons…*anything* they could get their hands on. Customers tiptoed through the suds, their sneakers and sandals and work boots squishing as they made their way to the cash register and out the door. A pigtailed redhead of perhaps five fell *splat* on her behind, raining water on everyone in the vicinity.

"I can't get up, Mommy," she whimpered. "The floor's too slippery."

As her mother held out a hand to help, she joined the

girl with a watery *sploosh.* "George," she called, "give us a hand, will you?" To his credit, the poor man tried. A second later, he, too, hit bottom.

"Danny's making fun of us," the little girl whined, pointing at her brother. "Make him stop it, Mommy."

"Danny," the woman warned, shaking a bubbly finger in her son's direction.

The boy clamped his lips together to stanch his laughter. But his efforts were of no avail. His snickers and snorts soon had the rest of the patrons laughing right along with him.

Jaina, balancing Liam on one hip, stepped cautiously toward the wet-bottomed threesome. "I'm so sorry," she said, extending a helping hand to the mother. "Your breakfasts are on us." And as if to punctuate the offer, she became the fourth, turning the damp human triangle into a neat, if soapy square.

Liam slipped from her arms and began crawling through the frothy water, stopping now and again to slap at the foam. His giggles blended with the rest of the happy din.

Connor stepped back onto the wood-planked porch and looked up at the sign. It said The Chili Pot all right, he thought, frowning as he went inside. He didn't know which was wetter—the floor, the diners, or the staff. *Talk about a tempest in a teapot,* he mused, smiling slightly as he looked for Jaina amid the tumble of soggy, cheery people.

His smile froze when his gaze came to rest on the baby on the floor, sitting in a diaper-deep puddle, spattering his own happy face with the droplets that flew from his hands. The baby had Susan's blond hair and his own blue eyes. Liam? he wondered, his mustache tilting in the beginning of another smile.

But what was the child doing in the middle of this

mess, unsupervised? And what *was* the mess anyway? It looked like soapsuds, and if it was, they could get into the baby's eyes and—

"Dih-dih-dih," Liam squealed, flapping his arms like a bottom-heavy bird. "Dih-dih!"

Since Liam had been looking straight at Connor when he'd said it, all heads turned, gazes zeroing in on the only dry person in the diner. Connor was the center of attention, but he didn't even notice.

As he moved slowly, woodenly, across the room, his feet seemed weighted down by far more than the water that had seeped into his Italian leather loafers. If he didn't know better, he'd have to say the baby seemed pleased to see him. *But how can that be, when we've never met?*

Chili Pot patrons cleared a path for the tall, muscular man in the dark suit, but Connor didn't notice that, either. The closer he got to Liam, the harder his heart pounded, and when at last he was within reach, he got down onto one knee, seemingly unaware of the inch-deep water, and scooped the baby into his arms. "Hi there, little guy," he said, sliding a crisp white handkerchief from his breast pocket. "What're you doin', taking a bubble bath, or do they have you swabbin' the deck?" he added, blotting Liam's hands and dripping blond curls.

The child looked deep into his eyes as if searching for some clue to a riddle. He popped a fist into his mouth. "Dih-dih," he muttered around it. "Dih-dih."

Lost in the deep blue intensity of Liam's gaze, Connor felt as though he was in a trance. Mesmerized, he stood, balancing the baby on his hip as he blinked silently, unable to tear his eyes from the child's angelic face.

Her voice came to him as if through a long, hollow tube. "Mr. Buchanan? I mean, Connor?"

Hugging Liam a little tighter, Connor turned. He knew before she came into his sight who had called his name.

She looked lovely, despite her waterlogged jeans and sneakers, despite the drops raining from her cinnamon curls and clinging to her long, lush lashes.

He swallowed hard, then gritted his teeth, fighting the feeling of powerlessness that was washing over him. He was here to meet his nephew, to establish a routine visitation schedule—as his friend, Judge Thompson, had advised—not to get all googly-eyed over Jaina Chandelle.

"What's the big idea," he demanded, "of leaving the child all alone in the middle of this slop?"

Chapter Four

"I realize how this looks," she said, hands twisting in front of her. "You're probably thinking he might have gotten soap in his eyes."

"But—"

"And you may think he could have fallen facedown in this mess—kids can drown in half an inch of water, you know. He might have—"

"I haven't said—"

"But I had an eye on him every minute," Jaina defended, tucking a damp and droopy curl behind one ear.

"So did I," Rita announced, stepping up beside her daughter.

Ray stood on Jaina's other side, his defensive stance indicating he'd been watching, as well.

Eliot crossed both arms over his broad chest. With a nod of his head, he indicated the kitchen, which was no more than five feet away. "I was right there the whole time."

Joy knocked on a nearby tabletop. "This is my station."

"And this one," Billie said, pointing to the tables across the narrow aisle, "is mine."

The last muffled voice, coming from somewhere under the counter, belonged to Barney. "And I was right here."

"Mmumm-mmumm," Liam said, smiling and waving at Jaina. He leaned forward, nearly tumbling from Connor's arms as he reached for her. "Mmumm-mumm, Mmumm-mmumm."

Connor turned so the baby would be farther from Jaina rather than closer. A second or two ticked by before Liam turned, too. He looked into Connor's face, an expression of confusion and slight mistrust registering in his now serious blue eyes, as if he was wondering why the man who had seemed so friendly would now want to keep him from his mmumm-mmumm. Undaunted by the added distance between him and Jaina, Liam threw his body toward her. Connor winced slightly as though the child's actions had hurt his feelings.

But he did not hand the child over.

"Don't you know anything about babies?" Billie snapped. "Can't you see he wants Jaina?"

"Yeah," Joy agreed. "Give him to his mommy."

Both Eliot and Barney took a careful step forward, their assertive stances telling Connor they were prepared to do whatever it might take to rescue Liam from this stranger. His eyes narrowed and darkened as he searched each serious face.

A moment of silence passed as the row of defensive men and women moved closer. Connor stood his ground. "I'm the boy's uncle," he said through clenched teeth. "What's wrong with you people?"

"Don't make any difference if you're the Pied Piper," Eliot said, "if the kid wants Jaina…."

What's with these people? Connor wondered. He looked at Liam, who had been temporarily distracted from wanting to be in Jaina's arms by the intensity of the verbal sparring. The baby frowned as he studied his uncle's serious face, then stuck a damp, chubby finger into his mouth. "Dih," he mumbled around it. "Dih-dih?"

One look at the little fellow had been all it took to stir a strong territorial reaction; the child was *his* flesh and blood, not these strangers', and the last thing he wanted was to hand him over on some infantile whim. And yet that was exactly what Liam seemed to want. The questions warred inside him: satisfy his own need, or the baby's? He'd never been in a position like this before and didn't quite know what to make of it. Because the real question—in everyone's mind, it seemed—was what was best for *Liam?*

The baby answered for them by giving one last squeal, then diving toward Jaina. Connor's eyes darkened even more as he handed the baby over. "This place is a madhouse. How do you expect to—"

Jaina, hugging Liam and smiling into his face, held up a hand to silence Buchanan. "We've had a minor emergency, that's all. The dishwasher sprang a leak, and the main drain is clogged, so there was no place for the water to go." She met his eyes to say, "I know it seems like a madhouse right now, but things like this don't happen every day. In fact," she said, looking around at her friends for support, "ordinarily, our Chili Pot is a pretty quiet place."

"I'll say," Eliot agreed.

"Downright dull," Billie put in.

"Boring," Joy said.

Ray gave a yawn and Rita stifled one as if to prove it.

Connor met each pair of eyes in turn. "Now why do I find that difficult to believe?"

If Liam *had* been in any danger, it was apparent any one of them would have fought to the death to save him. That fact should have riled him further. So why was he feeling strangely calmed and satisfied?

He pocketed both hands. "I'd call you a 'see no evil, hear no evil, speak no evil' bunch," he said, a half smile slanting his mouth, "but there are too many monkeys... and too many monkeyshines."

Rita stood as tall as her five-feet-two-inch frame would allow and lifted her chin. "We're a family, Mr. Buchanan, and families stick together."

Family. The woman couldn't possibly know what the word meant to him. His smile vanished as he ground his molars together to hide his discomfort. "Right or wrong?"

She narrowed her dark eyes and rested a fist on her hip. "I can only answer half your question since we haven't done anything wrong. We believe what it says in the book of Jeremiah. 'Walk ye in all the ways I have commanded you, that it may be well unto you.'"

"And blessed are those who are blameless," he translated another verse, "who walk in the law of the Lord." He gave her a hard stare. "But unless they've rewritten the Scriptures, Mrs. Chandelle, none of us is blameless...except Jesus."

Rita's mouth dropped open in silent shock.

"What's the matter?" Connor asked Jaina's mother. "Surprised I'm a believer?"

"Well...well, yes, frankly," she stammered. "I suppose I am."

A loud sucking sound captured everyone's attention. "That's got it!" Barney hollered. "The main drain's cleared!" Within minutes, a few puddles were all that was left of the miniflood.

"Mom, why don't you take Liam and Mr. Buchanan up to my apartment while the rest of us clean up this mess. I can't afford for the tiles to lift and loosen and—"

"Of course you can afford it." Rita took Liam. She gave Jaina a look that said, "Watch what you say around this guy, will you?"

"There's lemonade in the fridge upstairs," Jaina told them, heading for the kitchen, "and I baked chocolate chip cookies last night."

Connor didn't miss the understanding expression that connected mother to daughter. It told him they shared a love, deep and abiding, that allowed them to read one another's thoughts, to sense one another's feelings. A spark of envy shot through him for he'd never known love like that, not as a boy and certainly not as a man. Another spark—determination this time—flashed through him. *Liam deserves to be loved like that, and I'm going to see to it that he is!* he silently vowed.

Rita started for the stairs. "Take your time, sweetie," she called over her shoulder. "We'll be just fine." She gave Connor a look that defied him to challenge her and added, "Won't we, Mr. Buchanan?"

Connor's brow furrowed slightly. "Sure. Why wouldn't we be?"

"If you'll just follow me…"

At the bottom of the steps, Connor wiped his feet on a mat that said, "Hi! I'm Mat!" Smiling, he climbed the highly polished wood steps and thought of the moment that Jaina had spotted him in the diner. He could think of only one reason she'd seemed so terrified at the mere sight of him. *Brace yourself, Buchanan. She's going to fight like a mama tiger for that boy.*

His attention was immediately diverted by the paintings that lined the left side of the stairway. Landscapes—farms, mostly—all signed JCC. Though each was a different size and shape, nestled in its own unique frame, one thing repeated itself in every picture: a two-story farmhouse. *His* house!

Did she really think he'd fall for such an obvious plot to gain his approval? Did she honestly believe he wouldn't see through her attempt to win him over?

You're not making sense, man, he chided himself. *No sense at all.* There had to be two dozen paintings here, he began to reason. Even if she'd had time to find out what kind of house he lived in, she hadn't had time to put it into all these paintings, not with running a restaurant and taking care of Liam.

Liam.

He looked up, saw that the baby was staring directly at him. The child wasn't smiling. Nor was he frowning. Rather, he seemed content to merely study the man in the soggy-cuffed pants whose shoes squished with every step. "Who are you?" his big blue eyes seemed to ask, "and what is your interest in me?" Even if Liam had been seven years old instead of seven months, Connor couldn't have explained. How would he describe a feeling so deep and so intense that he himself didn't understand it?

Rita dug in her pocket and came up with the key to Jaina's apartment. "Well now," she said, stepping inside and gently depositing Liam in a fifties-style playpen, "would my boy like a bottle of juice?"

"Dih," he responded, pointing at Connor. "Dih?"

She pulled dry baby clothes from a bureau drawer and began stuffing Liam into them. "Isn't this a pretty dresser?" she said, more to herself than to Connor. "Jaina bought it just last week at a yard sale. Had no idea what she'd keep in it." She gave Liam's tummy a playful poke, smiled warmly when he giggled in response. "And then this little fella came along. I'd say it was the Lord's hand at work if you hadn't—"

Botched up Jaina's plans to be a mommy? he finished silently.

Rita clamped her lips together, then smiled stiffly. "How about a nice glass of lemonade? Jaina makes it fresh-squeezed, you know."

He did his best to mask his annoyance. Fresh-squeezed?

In this day and age? Yeah, right. "Lemonade sounds great," he said, his big hand ruffling the baby's golden curls. "Can't recall when I last had fresh-squeezed."

"Keep an eye on him while I pour, will you?" she asked, handing Liam to Connor.

And while she rummaged in the kitchen, Connor meandered around the apartment. "I'll bet you can't find a speck of dust in this place even if you gave it the white-glove test," he whispered into Liam's ear. But it didn't have the look of a room that had been recently scrubbed to impress him. Rather, it seemed to Connor that Jaina lived by the old adage that everything should have—and be in—its proper place.

She'd managed to make the huge space seem intimate, cozy even, by arranging overstuffed sofas and chairs in the center of the room. She'd offset the almost antiseptic white walls and cream-colored upholstery with bright pillows, candles, more artwork....

Here in the living room, as in the stairway, her paintings were of country settings, and the Victorian had found its way into each. In some, the house dominated the canvas; in others, it occupied a background space. Connor stepped up to the one hanging above the player piano. "Look at that, Liam," he said softly, pointing. "See that pretty house?"

It sat in the upper right-hand corner, high on a rocky hillside, and though it was barely larger than a postage stamp, the detail was incredible. Lace curtains hung in every window. Twin bent-willow rockers sat on the covered, wraparound porch, a brass door knocker gleamed from the red front door, a gray-striped tabby lay curled up on the welcome mat, and a cardinal perched on the white picket gate. Except for the cat and the bird, it was *his* house, right down to the rope swing in the giant oak out front. It had been there when he'd bought the house, and although he had no kids—and doubted he ever would—he couldn't bring himself to take it down.

He'd gone to great pains to keep his home address and phone number private. How had she managed to find out where he lived…*how* he lived—in such a short time? She just couldn't have. She hadn't had time to dig up the information and create dozens of paintings in the limited time they'd known one another. So how did she know so much about his house?

It was the most amazing, uncanny coincidence of his life. Or was it a sign of some kind, one he should pay attention to? His cynical side shook off the notion.

"Well, she's no Rembrandt," he told Liam; "but she ain't bad, is she?"

The baby wasn't in the least bit interested in Jaina's artwork. Wasn't interested in Connor's critique, either. Kicking both feet, he reached for the piano keys. "Mmumm-mmumm," he said. "Mmumm-mmumm."

Connor sat on the piano bench and placed Liam's fingers on the keys. "Ready for piano lessons, little guy?" he asked, chuckling.

"Dih." With surprising deftness, Liam gently depressed the keys one at a time. "Dih," he said again as the pleasant notes drifted throughout the apartment.

Connor's eyes were drawn back to the picture. She couldn't have known it was his house. If she had, she wouldn't have put it on a hillside in one painting, in a valley in the next, on a rocky outcropping in another.

Something happened to him as he sat there, gazing at Jaina's creation, something simultaneously wonderful and frightening. He'd gotten the same sensation when she'd nearly fainted in his office and he'd held her in his arms for the tick in time it had taken to help her to a chair. He'd put his hands on *her,* so why was *he* feeling touched?

The sensation washed over him again, the feeling that

she'd known him, and he her, for a long, long time. He'd never experienced anything quite like it before, didn't know if he *liked* the experience. For even while the connection made him feel as though he belonged, it made him feel vulnerable, out of control.

He shook his head, held Liam a little tighter, kissed the top of his head. *Get hold of yourself, man,* he cautioned himself, *'cause one thing is certain. If you want to win in court, you'd better stay in control.* Complete *control at all times.*

Connor stood and headed for the French doors on the opposite side of the room. Outside, a wide deck overlooked a thick stand of yellow and white pines that swayed in the steamy breeze. Liam, who'd caught sight of a toy in the playpen, began to bounce up and down. "Buffoo?" he asked, a finger aiming in the direction of the desired plaything. "Buffoo?"

He put the baby back into the playpen, and the child grabbed what appeared to be a hand-carved wooden truck. An assortment of new toys surrounded him. If she'd brought in a playpen, no doubt she'd also secured a crib, a high chair, a car seat…everything a social worker would deem necessary to care for a baby Liam's age. Connor ruefully shook his head and lifted one eyebrow. He had to give her credit. She was good, real good. She'd gone to a lot of trouble to make herself look like a woman who deserved to win a Mother of the Year trophy. Either that, or…

Did he like and admire her…or didn't he?

"Dih-dih," Liam said, holding up his arms.

Connor picked him up again. "Can't make up your mind whether you want in or out, eh?" he asked, gently chucking the baby's chin. "I know the feeling."

Liam offered him the truck.

"Say, this is nice. Where'd you get it?"

"My husband made it for him," Rita explained. She'd entered the room, holding a baby bottle in one hand, balancing a tray on the other. "He's very handy. Fairly artistic, too."

"So that's how Jaina comes by her talents." He nodded toward the paintings. "Did she study art in school?"

Rita giggled. "No, no. Didn't have time for art lessons. Everything you see is the result of God-given talent."

"Can't help but notice that the same house is in every picture. Is that where she grew up?"

Liam, having seen the bottle, began flapping his arms. "Buffoo. Mmumm. Dih!" he said, reaching for it.

Laughing softly, Rita took the baby from Connor's arms. "No, but she would have loved to. It's her dream house."

"Her…"

"Her dream house. You dream, don't you, Mr. Buchanan? Every Sunday, she combs the real-estate section of the newspaper, looking for something that even comes close." She headed for the bedroom. "One of these days, she's going to find it. I wouldn't be the least bit surprised if when she does, she sells The Chili Pot and spends the rest of her life painting and growing flowers."

Connor pocketed both hands and nodded. He could almost picture her in that house, long, thick hair tied up in a ponytail as she stood, paintbrush in hand, at her easel, fresh-cut flowers from her garden in vases all around her…. He'd bought the place, held the deed to it, but could it have been intended for *her?*

"Would you like to see where Liam sleeps, Mr. Buchanan?"

He blinked himself back into the present, then followed Rita through the arched doorway. Several things—from the sensible way she'd dressed each time he'd seen her to her obvious belief in hard work—made him believe the furnishings would be plain and simple. Instead, an ornate four-poster dominated the space. A mahogany chifforobe and matching bureau stood side by side against one wall, a small writing desk and chair against another. A thickly napped blue Persian rug dominated the center of the gleaming hardwood floor, while wide-slatted wooden blinds covered the double-hung windows. Here, as in the living room, she'd brightened the backdrop of creamy white walls with multicolored afghans, lamp shades and knickknacks.

Liam's crib stood beside her bed, and next to it, a low-seated, broad-backed rocker. The beady black eyes of a fuzzy teddy bear peeked out from the baby blanket folded neatly over one chair arm. He could picture her sitting there, tucking the blanket around Liam, who'd be snuggled against her bosom, chubby fingers wrapped around her slender ones, hugging the bear as she rocked him to sleep.

It was a lovely picture.

Too lovely.

Cut it out! he scolded himself. *You don't even know the woman.*

Rita snapped the blinds shut, throwing the sunny room into chocolaty darkness as Liam settled in for his afternoon nap.

Connor followed her back into the living room. "Should I close the door so our talking won't keep him awake?"

"He sleeps like a log."

She said it like a woman who knew Liam well. A pang of guilt shot through him. *He* was Liam's blood kin; *he* should be the one spouting everyday facts about him.

When she'd come into the room earlier, Rita had placed the tray, bearing a plate of cookies and two glasses of lemonade, in the center of the coffee table. She leaned down and helped herself to a cookie and a glass, settled on one end of the couch and tucked her legs up under her. "Have a seat, Mr. Buchanan. Jaina won't be much longer, I'm sure." Smiling fondly, she shook her head. "She can't stand to be away from the baby for more than a few minutes. Sometimes it seems like he's permanently attached to her hip!" A soft, motherly chuckle punctuated her statement.

He settled into the overstuffed chair, where he could see the bedroom doorway. "I may not have been the first to admit it, but I'll admit it now. Jaina's been good for the boy. It's obvious she's doing everything she can for Liam. I don't know how I'll ever repay her."

Rita's smile vanished, and in its place she wore an angry frown. "Repay her?"

"I assure you, I didn't mean that as an insult. I only meant that I appreciate what she's done...what she's doing—" he glanced at the bedroom doorway "—at least until the legalities are finalized."

The woman lifted her chin. "You sound awfully sure of yourself, Mr. Buchanan. How can you be so certain the courts will appoint *you* Liam's legal guardian?"

He shrugged. "I'm his only living relative. It's been my experience that in cases like this—"

"Please don't take this the wrong way," she interrupted, "you being a lawyer and all, but I know you've read Kirstie's note. She made it clear where she wanted her son to live." Rita tilted her head slightly to add, "Doesn't that matter to you at all?"

Connor leaned forward, balanced his elbows on his knees and clasped his hands tightly in the space between. Only then did he meet Rita's eyes. "Please don't take this the wrong way, *you being Jaina's mother and all,* but we can do this one of two ways. The easy way, or the hard way."

There was no question in his mind that Mrs. Chandelle understood his meaning. He watched as she glared openly at him, lips trembling as she struggled to keep a civil tongue in her head.

The door opened, then closed quietly. "I see you've put Liam down for his nap," Jaina said, breezing into the room. "It's a little early. But then, he had quite a morning, so I suppose it's all right." She smiled at Connor. "Did you two have a nice visit before he conked out?"

He had made up his mind on the way over here to take a hard-line approach toward the woman who wanted to deprive him of a life with Liam. Despite his resolve, he returned her friendly smile. "We had a few minutes."

"Isn't he the most precious thing you've ever seen?"

Her eyes sparkled, her smile sweetened, her voice sang. His back stiffened in reaction; he'd been the unwilling victim of womanly charms before. Had been the victim of not-so-charming wiles, too. He'd learned the hard way that smiles, tears, pouts and venomous glares could be turned on and off like a water faucet to ensure that the so-called "lady" would get her way. He didn't know why Jaina wanted Liam, but she did. To stop the ticking of the proverbial biological clock? To fulfill some typically female need to win?

Looking into her open, honest face, Connor was forced to acknowledge another possibility, another *probability:* she genuinely loved the baby.

He'd dismissed his earlier suspicions about her. He considered character judgment part of his business, and she didn't seem the type who would deceive him. Well, he wouldn't hurt her, either...if he didn't have to.

Connor didn't relish the idea of waging judicial war against this diminutive woman who seemed to care so deeply for his nephew. She either loved him, he thought, or she'd missed her calling and deprived Hollywood of one of the world's greatest actresses.

She glanced at his half-empty glass. "Would you like a refill?"

Connor blinked. Met her eyes, and again smiled against his will. "No. It was terrific, but I've had plenty, thanks."

She sat on the other end of the sofa. "Well, what do you think of him?" Grinning like a proud mama, Jaina enthused, "Isn't he adorable? And what a smartie! He'll be talking and walking long before other kids his age, I just know it. And the doctor—"

"The doctor?" he interrupted. "Is everything all right?"

Jaina waved his concern away. "Of course it is. I didn't mean to scare you. It's, well, he'd been through so much, what with the long trip and all, that I thought it would be a good idea to bring him in for a checkup." She shoved a damp curl behind her ear. "I mean, what if something was wrong and Kirstie was too distraught to notice?"

"Wrong? Like what?"

She shrugged. "Nothing serious, really, but a milk intolerance, for instance." Another shrug. "It's such a relief knowing he's perfectly, one hundred percent healthy."

Milk intolerance? He'd never even heard of such a thing. Under the same circumstances, Connor doubted he'd have thought to take the baby to a pediatrician. A male versus female thing? he wondered. He'd heard the age-old theory that mothers were natural-born nurturers. Not that he knew it from personal experience, his mother being as cold as she was and all…. "How many people know about Liam? In a professional capacity, I mean."

"The doctor—" she began counting on her fingers "—and the police, of course."

"The police?"

"Sure. Liam was exhausted that first night, so the very next morning, I called a friend of mine—he's a social worker with the Department of Social Services, you know—to find out what I should do. Skip came right over, told me to call the police so there'd be a record of how the baby came to be in my, ah, possession."

"You have a friend with the Department of Social Services?"

Jaina nodded. "I've known Skip since…" She hesitated. "For years," she finished carefully.

Connor made note of the way her smile faded and the bright light in her eyes dimmed during her moment of hesitation. She was hiding something…something that seemed to be causing her a great deal of discomfort, and he aimed to find out what. He had enough familiarity with adoption proceedings to know they were rarely cut-and-dry. Just as in custody cases, folks would sometimes fight ruthlessly over a child, with both sides willing to wage full-scale, no-holds-barred war to win. Connor didn't like the idea of putting Jaina through that. But if that's what it took…

Because he was a practical man, if nothing else. Sure, he owned a fifteen-room house on a three-acre property in one of Howard County's most prestigious neighborhoods. And true, his legal practice provided him with more money than he could spend in his lifetime.

But he was divorced. Had developed a bit of a reputation for being a ladies' man. Even his peers called him a shark because he'd defended clients accused of the most heinous crimes—spousal abuse, murder, kidnapping—and secured acquittals more often than not.

He was realistic enough to know he'd have a fight on his hands, trying to beat a woman like Jaina Chandelle in a courtroom. If the judge issued his decree based solely on outward appearances, she'd win hands down. Pretty and petite, with an angelic voice and the smile of a saint, she was a hard worker who could prove to the court that she had an army of friends and relatives standing by to help if and when she needed it.

The way he saw it, if he wanted Liam—and Connor wanted him more than anything—he had no choice but to use every weapon at his disposal. And the secret she harbored, he believed, might very well be the deadliest weapon of all.

He'd faced enough hostile witnesses in his day to know how far to push, how hard, and when. This was not the time for confrontation. "So," he said, smiling, "what does this Skip person say your chances of adopting Liam are?"

Her gentle expression hardened, and Jaina sat up straighter. "He advised me to keep you away from Liam, if you want to know the truth," she snapped, "but I didn't think it was fair, to you or Liam."

Connor expelled a bitter chuckle. "Not fair? Why?"

She seemed amazed he needed to be told something so obvious, so elementary. "Because you're *family,* of course."

That word again. Connor bristled as it echoed in his ears.

"I may be cutting my own throat to admit this," she began slowly, "but I happen to love that little boy more than I imagined it was possible to love another human being. You can ask my mother. I didn't want to keep him…at first."

That surprised him, and he said so.

"It's true," Rita confirmed. "She was dead set against the idea."

"But…why?"

Focusing on her hands, clasped tightly in her lap, Jaina took a deep breath. "I…I have my reasons," she said softly. Lifting her gaze to his, she continued, "It was past closing time when Kirstie left the diner. I couldn't shuttle him off to some institution that late at night." Sighing heavily, she closed her eyes. "It was supposed to be one night. Just one night."

"You don't have to tell him any of this, sweetie," Rita interjected, patting her hand. "He's—"

"He's Liam's uncle," she stated matter-of-factly. Jaina sandwiched her mother's hand between hers. "He deserves to be a part of the boy's life."

"So what made you change your mind?" Connor asked quietly. "About keeping Liam, I mean."

She gave him a whimsical smile. "He did." She cut a glance toward the bedroom where the baby was napping.

Rita gazed lovingly at her daughter. "She didn't have a crib that first night, so she dumped her clothes out of a dresser drawer and lined it with a quilt. And would you believe this girl spent the night on the floor?"

"Because I couldn't leave him," Jaina defended.

Connor's eyes narrowed. He hoped they'd rehearsed this little skit just for him because if Jaina was sincere… "But you'd only be, what, three or four feet away."

"I know. But everything about him fascinated me. The way his chest rose and fell when he breathed, the way he puckered his lips now and then, the sweet little sounds he made… He was just so…beautiful!"

There's a time and a place for everything, he reminded himself, biting back anger that seemed to have no source, yet pulsed through him like jolts of electricity. "So you're intent on taking this to court."

In place of the smile was a look of strength and determination. "I know it sounds silly after just a week with him, but I don't have any choice."

Connor stood. "Then I hope you have a good lawyer."

Rita frowned. "Good lawyer? Ha! I believe that's the best example of an oxymoron I've ever heard."

Jaina turned to her mother with a warning glance. "Mom, please…"

Connor ignored Rita's insult. "I only meant that legal battles can be lengthy and expensive, Mrs. Chandelle."

"I have the rest of my life," Jaina asserted, standing and looking at him hard. "As for money, I've saved a little for a rainy day."

He acknowledged that he'd be doing his own research, that he'd be representing himself. The hearing would cost him next to nothing, but Jaina...

Guilt hammered inside him as Connor walked toward the door. "I'll get started first thing in the morning, then."

"Started?" Rita asked. "Started on what?"

"Paperwork. Call my office and let Pearl know who your lawyer is, so I can mail him the filings."

Jaina stood near the door, wringing her hands in front of her. "Will your...your paperwork spell out where Liam will stay in the interim?"

"It will." For motives he could neither name nor understand, he felt like a heel for causing her even a moment's fear. "Don't worry, I won't bother filing for temporary custody because the judge more than likely will decide Liam should stay right where he is, until the final court date anyway." He met her eyes. "Frankly, I think that's best for him, all things considered."

She nodded, then sent him a trembly smile. "I appreciate your honesty, Connor." Jaina extended a hand.

Connor hesitated, unable to believe she could bring herself to do such a thing under the circumstances. She had a surprisingly strong grip for a woman her size. Another item on his "Reasons To Like Jaina Chandelle" list.

"I just want you to know," she said, "that if I win, you'll always be welcome here." She straightened her shoulders. "I hope you'll extend me the same courtesy if you—"

"If he wins," Rita snapped, "Liam loses."

Again he pretended he hadn't heard Rita's barb. He was still holding Jaina's hand and could barely believe it when he heard himself say, "You can see him anytime you like.

That goes without saying." One of the first rules a defense attorney learns is to keep his strategies to himself. So why had he exposed so much of his plan to the enemy?

She released him and stuffed the hand he'd held into her apron pocket. "Would you look at me?" she asked, running her other hand through still-damp curls. "I'm a soggy mess. What must you be…?" Biting her lower lip, she sent him a nervous smile. "You won't use this against me in court, will you?"

He returned the smile. "What…that as for your being a mother, I think you're all wet?" Jaina nodded, and he read the hopeful expression on her face. "I fight to win, and usually I do," he admitted, "but I believe in fighting fair. If I win, it'll be because I deserve to. Dirty tricks will not be on the agenda." His earlier thought—of using her secret against her—resurfaced in his mind. *Dirty trick,* he asked himself, *or semantics?*

She opened the door. "I'll call your office, then, once I've hired someone."

"Good. And I'll call you to arrange another visit with Liam soon." He glanced toward the bedroom. "He's quite a kid."

Jaina agreed. "Speaking of kids…have you had any luck locating Kirstie?"

"The investigator I hired did some computer tracking, found out who her doctor was. She'd been going for treatments twice a week before coming to Maryland." He looked at Jaina, at Rita, then Jaina again. "She hasn't been back."

Rita's hands flew to her mouth. "Oh, no. You don't suppose that means…"

Connor slowly shook his head. "I don't know…I hope not."

Jaina laid a hand on his forearm. "We'll all pray that you find her." She squeezed the arm gently. "She needs to be with family at a time like this."

There was that word again. Connor stepped into the hall.

"If you find her, will you let us know?"

He nodded. "Sure thing."

This wasn't the way he'd intended for things to go. Not even close. He'd planned to leave here, feeling secure in the knowledge that he'd made her see how futile it would be to fight him for Liam. And what had he done instead? Advised her to get a good attorney!

He started down the steps, stopped, then turned to face her. *Say something businesslike,* he told himself, *something to end things on a professional note, like "Don't wait too long to get a lawyer."*

He met her big dark eyes—eyes still damp with concern over his niece's disappearance—and was reminded of what she'd told her mother. "He's Liam's uncle," she'd said in her no-nonsense way. "He deserves to be a part of the boy's life." The memory of that killed the last of his resolve.

"Thanks, Jaina," he said instead.

"For what?"

You really don't know? he asked silently. *For being you!* "For the lemonade, the hospitality, letting me see Liam…."

With him now two steps down from the landing, they were eye-to-eye. She smiled. "Anytime. When Liam becomes mine, I know I'll need to provide a place at my table for his closet kin. You know where to find him. No need to call first, because—"

"I'm family?" He didn't miss her hopeful statement.

"Exactly."

It was as though someone had sneaked up behind him and nailed his shoes to the step. Connor couldn't seem to make himself turn away from her warm gaze.

"Well," she offered, rescuing him, "I'd better change into some dry clothes and get back to work."

He hurried down the steps. "Thanks again."

"No thanks necessary," he heard her say as he stepped into the diner, "but you're welcome all the same."

"'Fear not, for I will be with you,'" Connor recited Isaiah quietly to himself, "'the rivers shall not overwhelm you, and when you walk through fire, you shall not be burned, nor will the flame consume you.'"

He wondered if, within the pages of his Bible, he'd find a passage that assured him protection against falling in love with the enemy....

Jaina locked up The Chili Pot and turned out the lights as Liam babbled nonstop in her arms. She felt Connor Buchanan's presence as she climbed the stairs. Though there was no physical evidence that he'd been in her apartment, it seemed he'd left a sliver of himself here, a fragment there, to remind her of him.

Soon, she'd be standing toe-to-toe with him in a courtroom, fighting for Liam. The dilemma: how to defend herself against a man she genuinely liked.

Though she considered herself a peaceable sort on the whole, Jaina had participated in her share of disputes, debates, and arguments. Calm, reasonable discussion, she believed, could only take place between rational, mature individuals. If an adversary didn't respect her right to express an opinion, she wouldn't respect his. She'd never started a fight, but she'd never run from one, either. "If you have right on your side," her father had always asserted, "you can't lose."

But was she right to fight for Liam?

Or did Buchanan have right on *his* side?

"'The way of the righteous is level,'" she quoted Isaiah. "'Thou dost make smooth the path of righteousness. In the path of judgments, Lord, we wait for Thee.'"

As she got Liam into his pajamas, he cooed and gurgled

contentedly. She felt as though he'd been a part of her life *all* of her life. Taking care of him had seemed natural and normal—routine—and no more work than brushing her teeth or combing her hair. What would her world be like without him, now that she'd grown so accustomed to having him near?

She couldn't bear thinking of the possibility.

If she lost the court battle, would Buchanan really allow her to remain a part of Liam's life? Why should he? She wasn't blood kin.

But he *had* to, she thought, biting her trembling lower lip. "I'll just have to believe in the power of hope," she said softly. God had promised to be her steadfast anchor, her forerunner, her refuge, hadn't He?

After filling a baby bottle with milk, she microwaved it for a few seconds to take off the chill, screwed on the top then shook it well. Nestling in the chair where Buchanan had sat mere hours ago, she held Liam close.

He wrapped both hands around the bottle, sucking greedily from the nipple. "'Hush, little baby, don't say a word,'" she crooned. "'Mama's gonna buy you a mockingbird.'"

Smiling with his eyes only, Liam continued to drink.

"'And if that mockingbird don't sing, Mama's gonna buy you a diamond ring.'"

She finished the song, and another, and halfway through the third lullaby, his eyelids began to flutter as he struggled to stay awake. But soon his jaw relaxed and he let go of the nipple, setting a gurgling stream of tiny bubbles loose in the bottle. Jaina got slowly to her feet, tiptoed into the bedroom and eased the baby into his crib. He stirred slightly, then settled into a peaceful sleep. She gazed at his sweet face and tears filled her eyes. "In my heart, he's already mine, Lord. If You truly don't want me to have a child of my own, please know that I'm available for this one."

Several years ago, in an attempt to comfort and console her, her pástor had suggested she read Psalm 113: 9. The verse had not given her hope, had not provided solace as she fretted about whether she'd ever marry and have children like a normal woman.

She found solace in God's Word, and in doing His work, teaching Sunday school, helping to prepare children's services, preparing food for the potluck suppers and labeling products to be sold at white elephant sales and volunteering for the pastor's various rehabilitation programs. Helping others, she discovered, kept her mind off her past and her lost dreams.

Now, with Liam safely sleeping in the next room, Jaina took the black leather volume from the shelf and found the verse. "'He gives the barren woman a home,'" she read softly, "'making her the joyous mother of children. Praise the Lord!'" The verse that had once been the source of bitter tears now gave her hope as she took heart in the possibility that with Liam she had a chance, at least, at motherhood.

Carrying the Holy Book to the overstuffed chair, Jaina did something she hadn't done since she was a little girl.

Every night before turning in, instead of getting on her knees and asking the Lord to bless her parents, her stuffed animals, her teacher, like so many other Christian children, she'd sit on the edge of her bed, the Bible in her lap and, closing her eyes tight, let the book fall open on its own. Her forefinger would draw an invisible spiral that started above her head and stopped on a crisp, gilt-edged page. Only then would she open her eyes to read what she believed to be the verse the Lord had chosen for her and think about how the passage fitted her life.

When she opened her eyes this time, Jaina's finger was resting on Genesis 2:18. "'It is not good that the man should be alone.'" She closed the book, opened it again, read the first verse she saw. "'Oh that his left hand were under my head,'" she read from the Song of Songs, "'and that his right hand embraced me!'" Another flip of the wrist provided a line from Proverbs. "'House and wealth are inherited from fathers, but a prudent wife is from the Lord.'"

This wasn't working the way it used to, Jaina thought, smiling wryly at every romance-related passage. She decided to give it one more try. This time, the Bible opened to Ecclesiastes, 4:9. "'Two are better than one, because they have a good reward for their toil. For if they fall, one will lift up his fellow; but woe to him who is alone when he falls and has not another to lift him up. Again, if two lie together, they are warm; but how can one be warm alone?'"

She had a strange feeling these verses *were* messages from God. But why? And what had He intended her to learn from them?

Jaina reread the last verse. "'Two are better than one…'" Did it mean that together, she and Connor would be better for Liam than either of them could be alone?

The thought struck a reverberating chord in her heart. Strange as it seemed, the idea *did* make sense….

Stop it, she commanded herself. *Stop being a silly, overly romantic girl! Grow up and face the music. If you want this child, you're going to have to fight for him.*

Still…the idea of raising Liam *with* Connor instead of against him had a certain appeal that she hadn't thoroughly embraced. For one thing, if they had a…*relationship*…he might not be so certain to dig up her sorry past.

Jaina hadn't felt much like reading the Bible since the tragic night that had changed the course of her life. Her faith had been badly shaken, her trust all but snuffed out, because the way she saw it, God had gone back on His word. He'd promised that if she believed a thing strongly enough, it would be done. Well, she had believed He would help her, so why hadn't He? Confused, angry, afraid and hurt because she believed He'd abandoned her, she'd turned from Him. Until now, nothing had seemed important enough to encourage her to reestablish a relationship with Him.

Liam's well-being was important enough. It was more important than *anything*.

She wanted so badly to be his mother—legally, not just in her heart. But she also loved him enough to want what was best for him. Was *she* best for him, a woman with a tainted past? Or was Connor Buchanan?

All her life, she'd heard that the surest way to solve a problem was to lay it at the foot of the cross. Jaina closed the Bible and returned it to the bookshelf, confident for the first time in a week, because it was right to leave the matter in the Lord's capable hands.

Something told her that sooner or later, God would let her know what He wanted her to do—fight for Liam, or step aside and let Buchanan raise the boy, or suggest the "togetherness" idea.

Her father had a favorite Bible verse. "He will not let you be tempted beyond your strength, but with the temptation will provide a way of escape, that you may be able to endure it."

She would adopt First Corinthians 10:13 as her own chosen verse. Because, she admitted, slipping into bed, if the Lord decided it was Buchanan who should parent Liam, Jaina was going to need all the strength she could muster.

Chapter Five

J aina ran a hand through perspiration-matted hair and said a quick prayer of thanks that he'd phoned instead of dropping by as she'd suggested. Her evening of weeding the flower beds out back had cost her one bruised knee, two broken fingernails and a scraped palm. She hadn't minded Skip seeing her this way when he'd come over earlier, so why did it matter what Connor Buchanan might have thought of her appearance? She searched for a reason she could live with. *Because Skip's opinion of you won't affect the judge's ruling, that's why.* There was a lot of truth in that, but not the whole truth....

"Sorry to be calling so late," he said, breaking into her thoughts, "I thought I'd take a chance Liam might still be up."

If she didn't know better, she'd say he sounded lonely. But how could that be? she wondered. He was...he was *Connor Buchanan!* "I'd wake him for you, but he's had quite a day. I bought him one of those big blue wading pools, and he splashed away the whole afternoon. And tonight, he had his first gardening adventure."

He chuckled. "I'll bet he dug in for all he was worth."

Jaina giggled. "Those petunias didn't know what hit them. I found dirt in crevices I didn't even know he *had!*"

They chatted about the heat and humidity, about the Orioles' chances of playing in the World Series, about the Ravens' star quarterback sustaining an injury that might keep him from supporting his team in the fall.

"So, what do you guys do to celebrate the Fourth of July?"

Jaina thought she detected a note of hopefulness in his voice but couldn't determine if he "hoped" to have Liam all to himself, or "hoped" she'd include him in the family's plans. "We have all sorts of traditions," she said. "For one, we start the day with a red, white and blue breakfast."

"Red, white and blue?"

"Raspberries, blueberries and whipped cream on our pancakes. Then we head for the parade. No matter where we were stationed, Dad always managed to find us a marching band and a majorette. Then it's home again for hot dogs and burgers on the grill. And once our bloated bellies deflate a bit, it's off to the fireworks."

"Sounds like fun."

The hopefulness in his voice had turned to disappointment, she detected. Surely he didn't really expect her to invite *him.* Her mother would probably ring her neck for asking, but…

"What do *you* do on the Fourth?"

There was a long pause before he said, "Once in a while, I take Pearl up on her invitation to spend the day with her family."

"Only once in a while?"

"She has four kids, eleven grandchildren and four great-grandchildren."

"Goodness, she doesn't look old enough to be a great-grandmother! What's her secret?"

"She claims to walk two miles a day, and her kids tell me she reads like it's going out of style."

"If that's what keeps her so young and alert, I'm going to walk and read more, starting right now!"

Connor laughed. "She's a dynamo all right."

"So…why would you ever avoid spending time with a woman like that?"

"Because she's got a huge family. Sometimes it seems like half of Ellicott City is packed into her yard."

"But…that sounds wonderful."

"It is, in a way." He hesitated. "But it's hard being around all those people when you're not related to a single one."

Connor Buchanan, big news-making attorney, wishing for a family? Jaina couldn't believe her ears. Surely he had parents, siblings other than Kirstie's mother… "I only spoke with Pearl once, and the conversation was admittedly brief, but I got the distinct impression she's the kind of woman who goes out of her way to make folks feel like part of things. I'm sure if she knew you were feeling uncomfortable, she'd—"

"She's a doll, and I know she means well. Trouble is, the more effort she puts into making me feel a part of the family, the more obvious it is that I'm *not*."

She heard him take a deep breath.

"We didn't do picnics and cookouts and parades when I was a kid. Ever. I don't know how I could miss something I never had but…" He paused. "Family stuff scares me to death."

He was either genuinely miserable or doing an excellent job of faking it. But why would he pretend? Some of her most pleasant memories were rooted in family gatherings. No one should be deprived of such happiness. "Why does it scare you?"

If not for the sound of his sigh, she might have thought he'd hung up. "Because," he said, breaking the lengthy silence, "sometimes I wonder if it'll ever be mine to enjoy, except from the sidelines."

If he was anything like her father, Buchanan would rather die than discover he'd made her feel sorry for him. She knew how to comfort her father at times like this, but Jaina had only exchanged a few words with Connor Buchanan. She wanted to say something soothing, but she didn't know him well enough to choose the right words. What if what she said insulted rather than reassured him?

Hold your tongue, Jaina. You can't risk riling him.

But even as she thought it, Jaina knew the reason she didn't want to hurt him had nothing to do with the adoption case. She didn't want to hurt him because she was beginning to feel a strong emotional attachment for him. Already.

He began to chuckle softly.

"What's so funny?"

"You."

Me? "But I didn't say a word."

"It wasn't what you said. It's what you *didn't* say."

"I don't get it."

Another long moment passed. "Maybe I'll stop by to see Liam on the Fourth. Just for half an hour or so."

Pursing her lips, Jaina ran the options through her mind.

She could say it wasn't a good idea for him to see Liam on such a busy day. She could tell him to come on over just for a while as he'd suggested.

Or she could do what she knew to be the right thing, the Christian thing. "Look, why don't you plan to spend the day with us? I'm sure Liam would love it, and I could use help lugging him around. He's a solid little guy even if he is only seven months old, you know."

He was holding the phone with his left hand. She knew because the quiet was so complete she could hear the ticking of his watch.

Finally, he said, "The whole day?"

"Why not?"

Again, silence.

What if he has plans? she asked herself, feeling her cheeks redden. *He's a good-looking, successful guy. Maybe he's turned Pearl down because...* "If you...if you have a date, feel free to bring her along," she said. It surprised her a little to admit how difficult it had been to say that. Surprised her a lot to admit to feeling jealous. Jaina forced a note of cheeriness into her voice that she didn't feel. "The more, the merrier, I always say."

"I don't have *plans,*" he said, overemphasizing the last word. Then, in a softer, almost pleading voice, "Are you sure it'll be all right?"

He reminded her of the seven-year-old she'd found wandering the Columbia Mall a couple of weeks back. She'd stayed with the boy until Security found his mother. He'd fought tears the entire time, repeatedly apologizing for being such a bother. "Why wouldn't it be all right?" she asked Connor.

"Well...I get the feeling I'm not one of your mother's favorite people."

Put a hammer in the man's hand, Jaina told herself. *Can he hit the old nail on the head, or what!* In this case, a fib was far kinder than the truth, and so Jaina said, "She doesn't know you very well, that's all."

"Neither do you."

He loved Liam. At least, she was pretty sure he did. How else could she describe the look that came over his face whenever the baby was around? "I know enough."

"What can I bring?"

"Just yourself, and a big appetite. Mom always goes overboard with the potato salad."

"Okay, then. What time does the parade start?"

"Nine. But it's in Catonsville, and that's a twenty-minute drive from the diner. You'd better be here by at least seven."

"What!"

"You want a red, white and blue breakfast before we stake out curbside seats, don't you?"

Chuckling again, he said, "Yeah, I guess so."

"Then be here by seven. The diner is closed for the holiday, so we'll have the whole day to ourselves."

"I'm looking forward to it. I'll bring the gift I bought for Liam in New York. I left it in the car last time I was there and forgot to get it in all the, uh, confusion."

She remembered the stern, disgusted expression that had darkened his handsome face when he saw the soggy hullabaloo in the diner. "I'm sure he'll love it, whatever it is."

"It's kinda big."

She'd pictured the trinkets folks generally brought home from New York, most of which could fit in a shirt pocket. "How big?"

"Your height, and maybe three times your width."

"Good grief, Connor!" she said, half-laughing, "a toy that big for a baby this small? What were you thinking!"

"Truth is, I *wasn't* thinking."

"When you get here, come to the back door. It won't be locked."

"Gotcha."

"By seven, then."

"Right. Seven."

Jaina hated to hang up, but she couldn't for the life of her understand *why.* "G'bye," she said.

"Bye."

They seemed to be enmeshed in a contest of wills, each daring the other to hang up first. Grinning mischievously, Jaina said, "See you day after tomorrow." She quickly added, "Of course, you're welcome to stop by, or call, or both, before that."

"I know."

"They're calling for rain on the Fourth, you know. Maybe you should bring a jacket."

"Gotcha."

She smiled. "Connor?"

"Yeah…"

"Hang up, okay?"

He chuckled. "Okay."

And he did.

Jaina cut the connection and hung up, glancing at the calendar. A day and a half till the Fourth of July…

She pictured him in his crisp gray suit and sodden wing tips, slogging through the inch of water that had flooded the diner floor. He was kinda handsome, if you liked the button-down type. Did he own any casual clothing… sneakers, shorts, a T-shirt? She hoped so, because wouldn't he look funny at the barbecue in a dapper suit?

Her smile faded as she realized she faced a much more serious question. How would she tell her mother she'd invited the fox into the henhouse? We might not even have to leave the diner to see fireworks, she thought, grinning halfheartedly.

By accepting the invitation, Connor was effectively deep-sixing any case he had against her for being an unfit guardian. He shouldn't like her. Didn't want to like her. Had no reason to like her.

But he did.

She'd been taking such good care of Liam. Showering her parents with love and respect. Treating the men and women who worked for her like family, and from what he'd seen in the moments before Rita led him upstairs to Jaina's apartment, her customers got the same treatment.

Hard *not* to like a woman like that, he thought, tapping his pencil against the legal pad he'd been doodling on, especially with those big brown eyes and a smile that could melt a polar ice cap.

Connor didn't know why he'd accepted her invitation. Visiting Liam was one thing—how else could he ensure the child would get to know him?—but spending a major holiday with Jaina Chandelle was another matter entirely.

He had feelings for her—a hard fact to admit.

But *why?* Because he was lonely? Connor didn't think so. He'd been lonely for years, and it had never inspired him to willingly lay his head on a legal chopping block. *And that's exactly what you'll be doing if you don't get your emotions in check,* he warned himself.

Did she realize that when she aimed that loving, motherly smile at Liam, she made Connor want to fill that dream house of hers with children…*their* children? Did she understand that the sound of her laughter reminded him of birdsongs and wind chimes and a myriad of other delightful, musical things? Did she know that when he looked into those big brown eyes of hers, he wanted to take her in his arms and kiss her?

Connor sighed. She'd stirred up a vat of trouble, that was for sure. Trouble with a capital *T* if he didn't get a handle on his emotions…

Maybe *she* hadn't stirred up the feelings. Maybe what he felt was merely the result of decades of feeling like an outsider. Maybe seeing her with Liam, dispensing maternal warmth and affection…maybe *that* was what had awakened his incredible yearning to start a family of his own.

He remembered the natural, easy way she'd plopped Liam onto her right hip and dotted his chubby cheeks with a hundred sweet kisses. Connor had wanted to stick his head between hers and Liam's to find out for himself if those pink lips felt as soft as they looked.

And what about the time he'd watched her comb

slender fingers through the baby's curls? What would it be like, he'd wondered, to have those hardworking yet tender hands rearranging *his* hair?

Once, when Liam had started to fuss for no apparent reason, she'd cuddled him close and looked deep into his eyes. "Aw, don't be grumpy, sweetie," she'd cooed. "Let's see your beautiful smile. That's it! Where's that shiny new tooth of yours, huh?" Her lovely voice alone would have been enough to soothe the child, but her hands and her lips had gotten into the act, and in no time the baby's whimpers became happy giggles. Standing on the sidelines with his hands in his pockets, Connor had had to force himself to stop wondering what life might be like if she loved *him* that much.

She was everything he'd ever wanted in a woman, and then some. What was wrong with him anyway, that he'd never been able to attract someone like her, someone stable and secure, someone who seemed to like him for who and what he was rather than what he could buy her, or what he could do for her, or where he could take her?

But *was* she so different from all the other women he'd known? *Did* she like him for himself?

Or was the gentle, caring way she treated him directly related to the fact that she wanted something from him?

Liam.

Oh, Lord, he prayed, *don't let it be that.*

Connor closed his eyes and conjured up her image. She was so tiny that the top of her curly-haired head barely reached his chin. His fingertips would probably meet if he wrapped both hands around her waist. He had a dim childhood memory of Christmastime, when his grandmother roasted chestnuts in the fireplace; the sheen and glow of their mahogany shells had fascinated him. Jaina's hair was exactly the color of those chestnuts.

She didn't seem strong enough to lift a basket of feathers, but he'd seen her heft a fifty-pound sack of potatoes as if *it* were the basket of feathers. And her hands... He'd exchanged handshakes with men whose grip didn't possess such power and strength. And yet she'd touched his arm so gently, so tenderly when he told her there'd been no word about Kirstie, that if he hadn't seen it, he might not have known she'd touched him at all. To have that sweetness aimed in his direction...

Knock it off, Buchanan! Running a hand through his hair, he took a swig of coffee. *Best thing to do is stop focusing on her and start focusing on what's good for the kid.* Made perfect sense, since sooner or later, he and Liam would be sharing the house.

The house...

Her mother had told him about Jaina's dream. *You oughta just marry her...make her dream come true and avoid a court battle at the same time.*

The idea struck him like lightning, knocking him back in his chair. Talk about comin' out of left field... He swiveled to face the windows. The view of parked cars, shaded by saplings, was hardly distracting enough to push the concept from his mind. *Marry her? Are you out of your ever-lovin' head?*

But he couldn't shake it loose.

For the rest of the day, when he least suspected it, thoughts of Jaina pummeled his mind. As he was scheduling a meeting with Judge Thompson, he suddenly envisioned her on his front porch, smiling and waving goodbye as he headed for the office. Instead of writing "Tuesday, 2:30" in his appointment book, he'd called out, "Pearl, did you get those tickets for the Toronto Blue Jaina...uh...the Blue Jays game?"

He called a client to inform him about a postponement, then had a mental picture of Jaina standing in the foyer of his house, arms spread wide in welcome when he came in from work. He almost said "Ah, but it's good to be home," into the answering machine. While dictating a letter for Pearl to type, he imagined Jaina snuggled on the sofa, reading to Liam. He had to rewind the tape and erase the line that went something like "I couldn't have ordered a better life if the Sears catalog had a 'Terrific Wives' section."

And when he imagined her in his kitchen, feeding Liam mashed potatoes and strained carrots, he nearly slammed his fingers in a file drawer.

If he kept this up, he thought, reaching for his coffee, no self-respecting judge would let him adopt a goldfish, let alone a kid.

The telephone rang, startling him so badly he nearly overturned his mug. "Yeah?"

"Hey, Buchanan. How're things?"

Connor balanced an ankle on a knee. "Fine, O'Dell, and you?"

"Well, there's good news and there's bad news. Whaddaya want first?"

He could almost picture Buddy O'Dell, the potbellied, Dallas-born private eye whose impish grin seemed painted on his face. "The usual," Connor said.

"Okay, bad news first." O'Dell proceeded to fill Connor in on the search for Kirstie. He'd reached a dead end at a small hospice in a Chicago suburb. She'd been in Lombard as recently as last week, the detective explained. Rumor had it she'd gone to Milwaukee to spend her last days with a friend. "I followed that lead, but either the friend isn't home or she's avoiding me. I have a couple feelers out in Racine and Kenosha in case they're headed south on their way back to the hospice."

Connor nodded sadly. "If we don't find her…"

"I know, Boss, I know."

There was no mistaking the sympathy in the man's voice. Connor stiffened his back. "So what's the good news?"

"It's about the lady who has your great-nephew." Connor listened as O'Dell rattled some papers. "Says here that once upon a time, she was a singer. Toured the U.S. all by her li'l self with nothin' but a twelve-string guitar to keep her company."

"A singer?"

"Yup. Little over ten years ago. She was doin' pretty good there for a while. Folks musta liked her 'cause she made return performances in just about every place she was booked."

Connor couldn't seem to wrap his mind around that news. "A *singer?*"

"Uh-huh. She even cut a record. Made the top ten back in the late eighties. Then she dropped out of sight, just like that."

Connor heard the unmistakable *pop* of snapping fingers. "She quit? After a hit recording? Why?"

"Arrested."

Every muscle in his body tensed. "Arrested?"

"We must have a bad connection."

Connor frowned. "Why do you say that?"

"'Cause you keep repeating everything I say."

He cleared his throat. "Why was she, uh, arrested?"

"Seems the guy she was seeing at the time—drummer name of Bill Isaacs—was having some trouble with booze."

"Spare me the details, O'Dell. I get the picture." He'd been clamping his teeth together so tightly, he was beginning to get a headache.

"I don't think you do."

Connor ran a hand over his face. "There was an accident, wasn't there?"

"Uh-huh. Bad one."

Connor's heartbeat doubled. "Was Jaina hurt?"

"Yep. Spent a week in intensive care, another two in a private room, then six months in physical therapy."

Connor clenched his fists until the joints began to ache. "And then what?"

"A stint in the pen."

"What!" Connor clenched and unclenched his jaw. "She got in the car with a drunk. There's no crime in that. She probably didn't even know he'd been drinking till it was too late."

There was a considerable pause before O'Dell spoke again. "Seems she was in the driver's seat when the cops showed up. She claimed she was trying to drive back to the hotel when Isaacs lost it and grabbed the wheel, and… Well, the rest is in the report."

Connor replied with a deep sigh.

"Can I ask you a question, Boss?"

"You can *ask*."

"Are you sweet on this li'l gal? Not that I blame you, 'cause I've got a picture of her here, and she's right pretty, but…"

Sweet on her? Did he have to tack a Texas cliché onto everything he said? "This is business, O'Dell. Period. She's the lady my niece left her baby with. If I hope to adopt the boy, I need to know as much about her as possible."

"Didn't mean to pry. It's just that your reaction to the news was—"

"Believe it or not, even a coldhearted defense attorney like me can feel a pang of pity when he hears about the suffering of others."

"Yeah, well, whatever…" Then, "You want I should fax this stuff to you?"

"Do that. And Buddy?"

"Yeah?"

"Keep your mouth shut about this. I don't want the information falling into the wrong hands."

"Consider my lips zipped. You want me to head on home?"

"Nah. Give it a couple more days. Maybe we'll get lucky and one of your leads will turn up something on Kirstie." He breathed a deep sigh, then said in a gravelly voice, "I don't want her dying alone."

"I could always hire couple a locals. Three heads are better than one and all that."

"Whatever you think best," he said distractedly.

Connor hung up, then buzzed his secretary. "I'm expecting a fax," he announced when Pearl answered. "When it comes in—"

"I know, I know. Don't read it, don't touch it. It's top secret, right?"

"Right."

"I'll buzz you the minute it arrives."

After thanking Pearl, Connor spent a few restless minutes shuffling folders around his desk and pacing from one side of his office to the other.

Finally, Pearl entered with O'Dell's report. Connor nearly grabbed the papers from her hand. "Hold my calls," he instructed.

Connor quickly scanned the report, which included old news articles, police records and also records from Jaina's internment at Jessup. Connor didn't know how O'Dell had gotten them, but there they were. The date O'Dell had given him was emblazoned on his brain, and he aimed to find out all he could about the night of Jaina's accident. It took nearly an hour of cursoring, but he finally found what he'd been looking for.

According to an old article, Jaina had spent seven months in the hospital, and after her release, she'd spent another six at the Women's Corrections Center at Jessup.

There had been an operation, too. "Injured Convict Under Suicide Watch," that headline said.

Connor's heart pounded as he skimmed some medical records from her prison file. "Surgery performed by Dr. Thomas Stewart to correct internal injuries sustained in a head-on collision on Interstate 94 in June of this year may have rendered Jaina Chandelle incapable of having children… Chandelle was extremely depressed upon learning of her condition."

Rubbing his forehead, Connor sighed. "Poor kid," he said under his breath.

He quickly flipped through other pages, noting her description as a "model prisoner," then paused to skim Jaina's arrest record. The officer who'd taken the police report recorded that Jaina had claimed that Isaacs pulled the wheel away from her, causing the accident. Other than that, her "jacket" was clean. *One of those "guilty by association" cases, looks like to me,* Connor thought. He closed the file and set it aside on his desk.

He stared down at the file. *This* was the secret he'd suspected she'd been hiding. *This* was the weapon he needed to beat her in court. He should be feeling elated, confident. So why didn't he?

He tried to focus on his work again. But it was no use; he couldn't concentrate on anything but Jaina. O'Dell had called the report a bad news/good news kind of thing, but in Connor's opinion, there hadn't been anything good about it.

He sat back in his chair and linked his fingers behind his head. Until now, he hadn't really understood Jaina's deep and sudden attachment to Liam. But if she believed she'd never conceive a child of her own, it made perfect sense that she'd latch onto one that had literally been dropped in her lap.

And now he understood why that single case of his that she'd read about had pushed all her buttons.

But Connor had taken an oath on the day he became an attorney. In it, he'd sworn to fairly and honorably defend all citizens protected by the Constitution. He didn't believe in much these days, but he believed in that.

The harsh, unfeeling upbringing of his Bible-wielding parents had caused him to leave organized religion behind long ago; if his mother and father were typical examples of devout churchgoers, he'd just as soon not call himself a Christian. He worshiped privately in his own way and found, during his one-on-one sessions with the Almighty, that whether social, political, personal or religious, *any* issue could be put to the Golden Rule test. If *he'd* been brought up on similar charges, would he want to be stamped "guilty" without benefit of a fair trial?

Each time such a case crossed his desk, Connor forced himself to answer that question because how would he face the man in the mirror if he wasn't willing to give every defendant the benefit of the doubt? He firmly believed in the basic precepts of the Constitution. Among them, that no matter what crime a man is accused of, every U.S. citizen must be considered innocent until proven guilty in a court of law by a jury of his peers. Anything less, and anarchy would prevail.

His heart ached for Jaina. A familiar "I want to *do* something about that!" sensation plagued him, as it always did when he heard a story like hers. But, as usual, he felt paralyzed because, much as he wanted to right every wrong committed against the innocents of the world, he could not. The best he could hope to do, given his power-lessness, was to go back to basics: the Golden Rule.

If *he* had survived Jaina's ordeal, how would he want her to deal with *him?* Would he want her to back off, let him win Liam simply because he'd lived through some tough times? Or would he want her to treat him as an equal, with no more rights—and no fewer—than she had?

The answer was obvious. He would not add insult to injury by treating her like a victim because, in truth, she was anything but. She had turned tragedy into triumph, had risen above her past and emerged victorious. Out of admiration and respect for that, he owed it to her to treat her as an equal.

Besides, he wanted Liam to be a full-time, permanent part of his life. True, he'd mostly felt that way at the start because the baby was kin—his only connection to family—but within moments of his first encounter with the bright-eyed, smiling little boy, Connor had been captivated. Liam had stolen his heart, and there was no escaping that fact. The love he felt for the child was like none he'd felt before, and *that's* why he wanted Liam now. If he had to hurt Jaina to make Liam his...

He'd represented parties on a great many custody suits and couldn't recall one that hadn't been hard fought, that didn't end up causing hatred or, at the very least, bitterness between the parents. How could he even consider putting Jaina through that when he felt...

But exactly how *did* he feel about her?

Connor knuckled his eyes and sat up abruptly, knowing that to acknowledge the truth was tantamount to legal suicide. His head and his heart were clashing.

You're falling for her, old boy, falling hard, said his brain.

FallING, his heart asked, *as in "You're gonna"? Or fallEN, as in "Man, are you in trouble"?*

What's the difference? his brain demanded.

If you have to ask, answered his heart, *it's already too late.*

Dear Jaina,

I've been staying in Milwaukee with some friends that I met in the hospice. They told me a man has been poking around, asking a lot of questions about me. I told them to ignore him.

You're the only person I know who would have any reason to send someone looking for me, and I think I know why. It's because you don't want me to be alone right now. I'm not a bit surprised that you would go to such lengths to make my last days happy and comfortable. It's even more proof that you're exactly the right person to raise my little boy.

I know that some people will say I'm a terrible mother for leaving my son with a woman I had never met before. They just don't understand! I didn't want to leave him at all! So when they say it, you just tell them that in my heart you were never a stranger! Because as soon as I found out I was going to die, and Liam might end up in some of the same horrible places I grew up in, I spent hours on my knees, asking God to help me make sure that wouldn't happen.

I know it sounds crazy, but I believe He put me in your diner because He had chosen you to be Liam's new mommy. God wouldn't steer me wrong. Especially not at a time like this!

So please don't worry about me, Jaina, because I really am fine. I'm not in any pain, and I'm not afraid of what's about to happen because, as God said, "Your years will end like a sigh."

I think that it's a real blessing that Liam is so young. If he was older, I'd probably be all worried that he might miss me. As it is, I can go to Jesus without a care in the world for I know my baby boy couldn't be in better hands. Plus, I know that you'll help him understand why I did what I did, and that you won't let him forget me.

They say there's a special place in heaven for

people who do angelic things on earth. You are one of those people, Jaina. God bless you, and thank you from the bottom of my heart.

Kirstie Buchanan

Jaina thanked God that she'd had the presence of mind to put Liam to bed before opening the envelope. Though there had been no return address, she had immediately recognized Kirstie's unique handwriting, and something had told her the contents of the letter would not be easy to accept. She stared through her tears at the colorful balloons Kirstie had drawn in the upper left-hand corner. They seemed to bob and float on the page. She was far too young to meet her Maker, Jaina thought, sighing.

Kirstie was dying when she'd come into the diner. When she'd penned this message, the end was closer still. For all Jaina knew, the girl had already joined her Father in heaven. It seemed terribly unfair that a beautiful young woman should be separated from her child for any reason, but *this*…

If only Jaina could find her! She'd do everything in her power to make the girl comfortable, until the end came. And surely if Kirstie wrote a letter, or made a tape, outlining her desire to have Jaina raise Liam….

Why did life have to be so hard? she wondered.

But Jaina knew better than to ask why, because her own experiences had taught her that there were no satisfactory answers to questions like that.

Jaina had heard it said that human suffering was a test from God, that it must be endured so He might humble and discipline His children, to make them worthy to spend eternity with Him. *You need to take a lesson from Job,* Jaina told herself, *because he managed to accept all the anguish tossed at him without question or complaint.* Still…she wanted to believe there was a better way, an easier way for God to read Kirstie's heart than cancer.

Jaina went to the bookshelf and pulled down her copy of *Don't Blame God*. She'd purchased the book years ago while searching for healing of her own wounded spirit. The text had not brought her comfort despite the fact that she'd read it cover to cover several times. Maybe *this* time, she'd find the answers she sought.

The book opened automatically to page 179. "God cannot be blamed for sickness, disease, tragedies, and trials," Michalski had written, "any more than He can be blamed for sin."

He cannot be blamed for tragedy any more than He can be blamed for sin, Jaina reflected. If He created the universe and everything in it, didn't He also create sin?

No. Jaina couldn't pin that one on the Lord. He'd blessed His children with something He hadn't given a single other creature: free will. Unlike the beasts of the field and the birds in the sky, He expected His children to exercise that free will rather than act upon instinct. Crime was the direct result of the actions of people who chose to do evil. No one had forced Bill Isaacs to get drunk and then get behind the wheel of a car; no one had forced Jaina into his car that night. The accident that altered her life was no one's fault but her own, she reasoned, for she had *chosen* that path.

It wasn't as easy to explain something like cancer. The answer to that—if an answer existed—could only be found through prayer. A lot of it. But…did she remember how to pray? Did she even *want* to remember?

She'd been a devout girl, a prayerful young woman. But Jaina had not conversed with God in a long, long time. Not, in fact, since that night. Why would she, when she believed He didn't listen to her pleas?

Her fifth-grade Sunday school teacher had given this homework assignment: "Find a Bible passage you can call your own. Memorize it, so that when trouble comes your way, or you're afraid, or your faith is tested, you can recite it, and it will renew your strength."

It took hours of searching before Jaina had come across the verse in Psalms that had always soothed and calmed her, even on the stormiest of nights: "…when the waters of the sea roar, and the mountains shake with the swelling thereof, be still and know that I am your God, your refuge."

Jaina closed her eyes and huddled in a corner of the sofa, hugging her knees to her chest. Until that awful night, she'd believed wholly and completely that she was a child of God, that He loved her with all His might and would never leave her alone and unprotected.

Don't do that, she warned herself. *Don't let yourself remember….*

But in the blink of an eye, she was transported back in time to Menomonee Falls, Wisconsin, and the nondescript room management had provided as part of her week's pay for entertaining guests in the hotel lounge.

There was Bill's car, an old yellow boat of a thing that had been around since the late seventies. She'd thought it odd that he hadn't greeted her with his usual kiss to her cheek, but dismissed it. Bill was often withdrawn and surly when his band was out of work.

It wasn't until he steered the car onto the highway that she realized he'd been drinking. "Pull over," she said, "and let me drive."

He shot her a withering glance. "Nobody drives my baby. You know that."

"Yes, but you've been drinking, Bill, and I think…."

"I haven't had that much. I'm fine."

They drove in silence for a moment or two before Jaina turned in the passenger seat. "You have two choices, Bill Isaacs. Stop this car and let me out, or pull over and let me drive, because I have no desire to die in a…."

"Okay. All right. Calm down," he said, a hand in the air to silence her. Both brows rose as he considered his alternatives. One look at her no-nonsense expression seemed enough to convince him to steer onto the road's shoulder.

"Nice and easy now," he instructed as she made a U-turn and headed back for the hotel. "Hey, where you goin'?" he demanded, reaching for the steering wheel. "We haven't had our talk yet."

Jaina didn't know why the Lord would turn a deaf ear to her pleas. She only knew that if Bill continued jerking on the steering wheel, they'd end up….

When she came to, she couldn't feel anything from her waist down, couldn't see past the white-hot pain that filled her head each time she opened her eyes. She remembered the way Bill's big hand had clamped over hers on the wheel, the way trees and fence posts whizzed by at breakneck speed as the car lurched toward the ravine beside the road. Her screams were still echoing in her ears as she lay there, gasping, panting as those last terrifying seconds ticked through her memory in sickeningly slow motion….

The sudden jerk of the car as it tilted right, the sound of branches and rocks pummeling the undercarriage…

…the giant tree, looming closer, closer.

She had no idea a vehicle that could hum so quietly while on the road could make such a hideous sound upon impact.

Then blackness, and total silence.

Had it been minutes, or hours, that she lay there in the dark, paralyzed, terrified? Jaina only knew that at the sound of distant sirens, she began to cry tears of relief, softly at first. By the time the paramedics yanked open the door that groaned in protest, her sobs had blocked the questions hammering in her head: Where's Bill? Is he all right?

Two days later, Jaina learned she was being accused of

vehicular manslaughter. The authorities didn't believe her when she said Bill had jerked the wheel, sending the car careening out of control.

Jaina didn't know exactly when she'd stopped hating herself. The self-loathing was restricted to those times when she stupidly allowed herself to glance in a mirror. When she saw the scars twisting and turning across her abdomen, *then* she hated herself. *Then* there was no escaping the fact that in that moment in time, she'd made one terrible decision, and it had cost her the ability to have children…the one thing she'd always wanted more than anything else in the world.

She pressed a hand to her stomach. Even through her pajama top, Jaina could feel the disfigurement that would be a permanent reminder of that night. Thanks to the operation, performed in haste by a surgical resident mere hours after the accident, a child would never grow in her womb. They'd made the decision without discussing it with anyone—not her parents and certainly not Jaina—and the surgery that had saved her had, in her estimation, destroyed her.

She'd never been a particularly vain woman. Even now, as she ran her fingers over the thick, ugly scars, Jaina knew the deformity wouldn't have bothered her…if it wasn't a reminder that she'd never have her own children.

Liam whimpered in his sleep, rousing Jaina from the horrible memories. She ran to him, scooped him up, held him tight. "You're all right," she crooned into his ear. "I'll never let anything hurt you, I promise."

It's what she had expected the Lord to do that night— scoop her up in His Almighty embrace, put a stop to anything that could harm her—and promise that she'd always be safe in His protection.

She carried Liam to the living room and snuggled with him in the recliner. The Bible was still on the coffee table where she'd left it, open to the verse in Psalms that had given her such peace as a child.

Anger and disappointment made her turn her face from it. She focused instead on Liam's sleepy eyes. He was so much like the way she'd been before that night: vulnerable, innocent, completely dependent on bigger, more powerful beings for care and protection. But that night had changed her dramatically and forever.

Never again would she trust those who claimed to be wiser than her. Never again would she have faith in mere words. Actions, life had taught her, were stronger and more powerful than any promise ever made.

Except one. "You can always count on me, sweetheart," she said, kissing his forehead. "I *promise.*"

They had a lot in common, Jaina and this helpless baby.

He needed her.

And more than anything, she needed him.

Chapter Six

The phone was ringing when Connor unlocked the office door, and he fumbled with his keys, briefcase and file folders in an attempt to grab it before the answering machine picked up.

He glanced at the digital clock on Pearl's desk. Eight fifty-five. She didn't get in until nine sharp. He had this theory that she stood just outside the door every morning, tapping her toe and staring at the minute hand of her watch, waiting for it to hit the twelve before making her entrance.

"Law office," he droned, dumping his load on Pearl's armless chair.

"G'morning. It's Jaina."

As if she had to identify herself. He'd thought about her—and her past—long into the night. Connor's heart lurched at the sound of her musical voice. "I didn't expect to be talking to you until tomorrow morning."

"I didn't expect to be calling, but…"

He noted the careful pronunciation, the slow pace of her words. "Is Liam all right?"

"He's fine. In fact, he stood on his own for the first time last night."

Spoken like a true mother, he thought, grinning, proud of her boy's latest achievement. Connor felt a pang of guilt, knowing that her mothering days were quickly drawing to a close…thanks to the paperwork he'd filed the prior afternoon.

"The reason I called," she said slowly, "is because I got a letter from Kirstie in yesterday's mail. I thought maybe you'd like to…"

O'Dell had tracked the girl as far as Milwaukee but hadn't been able to get any further in his search for Connor's niece. Every night since she'd left Liam with Jaina, the last thoughts in his head before drifting off to sleep had been of Kirstie. Every night except *last* night, when he'd lain awake thinking of that article about Jaina…. "Does she say where she is?"

"No, she still doesn't want to be found."

"Does she say how she's doing?"

"She's doing all right. Why don't you stop by sometime today," she suggested gently, "and read it for yourself?"

He drew a quick breath through his teeth and winced. If only he could; it would be an opportunity to see Liam…*and* Jaina. "I wish I could, but I've got a packed schedule… back-to-back appointments before lunch, a hearing this afternoon. I can't come to The Chili Pot, but…"

He wondered if she was wearing her shoulder-length curls in a ponytail at the nape of her neck as she had the day the diner had flooded, or if she'd let it hang free, the way she'd worn it for the meeting in his office. *Wild and free,* he hoped.

Jaina ended the long pause. "But what?"

"But if you let me buy you lunch," he finished, "we could kill two birds with one stone."

"I suppose I could get away for an hour or so. Where should I meet you?"

"Ever been to The Judge's Bench?"

"No, but I've passed it a hundred times when I've been on Main Street looking for bargains in the antique stores."

Antiques. She had an eye for them all right, and a flair for knowing how to show off their finer qualities, as evidenced by the way she'd scattered them throughout her apartment. Maybe one of these days, he'd bring her to the house, see if she'd be interested in helping him fix it up....

Very recently, thoughts of her had distracted him from his work. Now, the image of her, arranging and rearranging things in his house was having the same effect.

"When?"

"When what?"

"When should I be there?"

"Oh. Right." He adjusted his tie as if that would set his mind straight. "Why don't I call you when I wrap up my last appointment, so you won't end up waiting...in case the meeting runs overtime."

"That'll be fine." It was her turn to hesitate. "Is this...is this a fancy place?"

He didn't believe there was a woman alive who didn't ask that question when invited to a new restaurant. He smiled, picturing the way Jaina might dress for work: kicky little skirts or blue jeans, but with a bright scarf or a strand of colorful beads for added flair. "A black robe will be fine."

She laughed softly. "Not that I have anything against basic black, mind you, but maybe I'll just wing it."

"I can tell you this. You'll stand out like a sore thumb if you wear anything dressy."

"It's just...I thought with a name like The Judge's Bench, it'd be crawling with guys and gals in suits and ties and Italian loafers, you know?"

"Nah. Just ordinary folks like you and me." He felt a bit strange saying that because, in his opinion, there was nothing ordinary about Jaina Chandelle.

"Good. Then I won't have to change."

"Call you around noon, then."

"Okay. And Connor?"

"Hmm…?"

"Just so you won't worry…Kirstie says she's not alone. She's getting some medical care, too."

Then why couldn't Jaina wait until tomorrow to show him the letter? he wondered. "Don't *you* worry. I won't."

Connor was still sitting on the corner of Pearl's desk, staring at the receiver, when the secretary breezed into the room. "You have to talk into the end with lots of holes," she said in a scolding tone, "before anything will come out of the other end."

He blinked. "Morning, Pearl." Squinting, he wrinkled his nose. "Er, what did you say?"

Pearl shoved her purse into a drawer and grabbed the phone from his hand. "Never mind," she said, hanging it up. She opened the appointment book. "I'll pull the Adams file for you. They won't be here until nine-thirty. You have plenty of time to go over your notes."

Nodding distractedly, he gathered his things and headed for his office. He stopped in the doorway. "Pearl?"

"Hmm?"

"Would you get me the Adams file? They'll be here soon, and I want to go over my notes."

Frowning, she propped a fist on an ample hip. "Sure thing, Boss." Then, pursing her lips, she studied him through narrowed eyes. "You okay, Mr. B.?"

"Who, me?" He smiled. "I'm fine." He knitted his brow. "Why do you ask?"

She shrugged. "No reason, just asking."

He sent her a halfhearted smile, then disappeared into his office.

"If I didn't know him better," Pearl muttered, "I'd say he's been bitten by the lovebug."

"Did you say something, Pearl?"

"Sometimes we old folks talk to ourselves, that's all."

But he didn't hear a word she'd said. Pearl knew it because the last thing she saw before pulling out the top drawer of the filing cabinet was Connor Buchanan, staring off into space, thick mustache slanting above a silly half grin.

She rummaged in the drawer, withdrew a folder labeled Adams. "Here you go," she said, handing it to him.

He met her eyes. "Isn't that incredible? I was just about to buzz you, ask you to bring me this very file."

Shaking her head, she raised one brow. "Just doin' my job, Boss." And as she closed the door, Pearl put a hand over her mouth and giggled softly. "I hope he's not planning to drive anywhere today," she said under her breath, "'cause I don't think the insurance company covers fender benders caused by bug bites."

With Liam safe in his playpen in the far corner of her room, Jaina prepared for her lunch date. She hadn't been out with a man in nearly two years, unless she counted going to the movies with Skip as a date, and she didn't. But then, this wasn't a date, either. *Because Connor Buchanan doesn't care a fig for me!*

She looked at the rumpled pile of clothing in the middle of her bed. Jaina had tried on every summery outfit she owned, as well as a few that would be more appropriate in the spring or fall. *You should have stayed in the diner till it was time to leave,* she scolded herself, *because then you'd have been too busy to think about anything so silly as what you'd wear.*

Jaina slumped to the floor and leaned against the wall. What would he think of a woman whose clothes were more suited to McDonald's than a fashionable café in town? But what did Connor Buchanan's opinion of her wardrobe matter? *Liam* was the reason he'd come into her life, and Liam would be the only reason they'd continue to communicate.

Liam, and for a little while longer, Kirstie….

She thought of the way he'd sounded when she told him about Kirstie's letter. The joy and relief in his voice made it clear that he really cared about a girl he'd never met…a girl he hadn't even known existed two weeks ago. As well he should, considering that Kirstie had been his beloved sister Susan's daughter. But how did he feel about the fact that Kirstie would soon be gone, and the only family he'd have left in the world came in the form of a tiny, gurgling package called Liam Connor Buchanan?

If only she could get a message to Kirstie! Jaina would love to tell her that she'd made a terrible mistake about her uncle. Because though Connor might have appeared to Kirstie as grumpy and mean, he was nothing of the kind. He had a giving nature, and the proof was in the way he behaved around Liam.

She'd seen plenty of men attempt to communicate with babies. Most seemed to feel it wasn't macho to make silly faces and noises. And then they wondered why kids didn't react well to them! It was no surprise that Liam had taken an immediate liking to Connor. But then, any man willing to speak two octaves higher than usual—while wiggling his brows and making funny noises—was pretty much guaranteed a happy and affectionate response.

He'd be a wonderful father someday, she thought. Jaina's wistful smile gave way to a worried frown as she thought of his desire to be a father to Liam. But hopefully, not any time soon.

Buchanan was young, vital, handsome. Why hadn't he married, had a few children of his own? she wondered. If he had a wife and family like most other men his age, maybe he wouldn't be so intent on having Liam.

The door opened, providing a much needed escape from her frightening reflections.

"Hey, girl, what's shakin'?"

"Skip! What are you doing, stopping by in the middle of a workday? Is this where my tax dollars are going?" she teased.

"You need to get a new writer, pal, 'cause that joke's gettin' old." He chuckled. "Say…I'm gonna be here around lunchtime. Since I'm with Social Services, what say I offer you *my* services. Whatcha doin' for lunch?"

Ordinarily, she'd have jumped at the chance to spend an hour or two with her best friend. "Today?"

"No," he said teasingly, "the second Tuesday of next month."

"I'm sorry, Skip, I'd like to, but—"

"Why am I always the last to know about your love life?"

"If I ever *get* a love life, you'll be the first to know," she said dully. "This isn't a date." The words had spurted from her mouth so quickly, even she didn't believe she'd actually said them.

"Hmm, what was that old line out of Shakespeare? Something like me thinketh thou protesteth too mucheth?"

She took a deep breath and started over. "Seriously, it's a business lunch."

"What kind of business?"

"Well, I got a letter from Kirstie Buchanan yesterday and—"

"The girl who dumped her baby in your diner?"

Jaina frowned. "She didn't 'dump' him. She wrote to let me know she's doing fine. She didn't want me to worry."

"Mighty big of her," he grumbled, "considering it's *she* who oughta be worrying…about whether or not her kid's okay, about whether or not you're a serial killer, about—"

"Skip," she interrupted, "be fair. You know the circumstances as well as anyone. Kirstie is barely more than a child, herself, and she's dying. What did you expect her to do?"

"Oh, lemme see, I dunno. Put him into a home with two loving adults, where maybe he had a chance of becoming a permanent part of a real family?"

"You don't have to be so sarcastic. You read the letter. Her own mother died when Kirstie was young, and the poor girl got bounced around by the system for years. She didn't want that for Liam."

There was a long pause before he muttered, "I don't know why you're mad at *me*. I don't make the rules. And I know the system isn't perfect. Besides, I haven't really been looking for foster parents. I thought you wanted—"

Jaina sighed heavily and rolled her eyes. "Then I wish you'd told me that before. Every time my phone rings, you know, I think it's going to be you—"

"Thanks a heap, kiddo. Didn't know you cared so much."

"You didn't let me finish. I was about to say that every time the phone rings, I'm afraid it's you, calling to say you *have* found someone to keep Liam until—"

"Until the final adoption hearing is scheduled?"

"Yes. Until then. I'm really nuts about him, Skip, and every day that he's with me, I love him more." She sighed again. "How do foster parents do it?"

"Do what?"

"Take a child in, treat it like their own, then hand it back whenever Social Services snaps its collective fingers."

"To my knowledge, we've never done *anything* collectively. But to answer your question, it's just as hard for foster parents to give up the kids we place with 'em as it'll be for you to give up Liam. The difference is, it's something they accept because it's part of the job, which is to do what's best for the child."

His matter-of-fact comment seemed to freeze the blood in her veins. It may have been good advice, but it sure did hurt.

She chose to ignore his dig. "Do you really think that I'll have to give him up?"

"Yes…and I think *you* think so, too."

Jaina might have denied it if a sob hadn't choked off her words.

"When there's a healthy, well-adjusted relative in the picture, the court awards that party custody…if that's what the person wants."

A glimmer of hope sparked in her. "What do you mean…'if that's what the person wants'?"

"Well, sometimes a cousin, a grandparent, whatever, will go for guardianship instead of full parental rights, either because the kid's parents are still in the picture, or maybe because they're in some sort of bad trouble and the relative is hoping that when things straighten out, the kid can go back home to them. And sometimes, folks plain don't want the expense and bother."

"But…but Liam doesn't *have* anyone except for—"

"Exactly. So if Buchanan wants to adopt the kid, they're gonna let him. He's a close blood relation, and the way the state sees it, a kid is usually better off with family than anybody else. Face it, pal. You're fighting a losing battle. As long as he hasn't killed anybody lately, Connor Buchanan, Esq., is gonna be a daddy in a little while."

"But he isn't married, and his schedule is frantic, and he lives alone, and—"

"Change the 'he' to a 'she', and you could be describing yourself," he gently reminded her.

"I have my parents to help me. And loads of friends. Who has Buchanan got?"

"Not 'who,' but 'what.' He's got money. I don't mean to sound vulgar, Jaina, but whatever he doesn't *have,* he can *buy*. He has, as they say, 'the wherewithal' to take care of the child."

She ran a hand through her hair. "Is that the reason you wanted to go to lunch, Skip? To rain on my parade?"

"Course not, but…" He paused, then patted her hand. "Okay. Here's my honest, professional opinion. If Buchanan wasn't in the picture, I'd bet my last paycheck the judge would let you adopt, considering—"

"Considering what?"

"That his mother left the…left Liam with you and wrote that heart-tugging note and—"

"You really think Buchanan will win?" she broke in, unable to get her mind off a comment Skip had made moments ago.

"It's rare, *real* rare, for a woman in your position to get custody."

"It's rare, but it happens from time to time, right?"

She could tell from Skip's expression that he was torn. Part of him wanted to help her by not offering any false hope, while another part couldn't resist the pleading look in her eyes.

"Well, I shouldn't be telling you this—it wouldn't be right to give you false hopes—but a couple years back, I handled a similar case. Remember that woman who found a baby in the trash can behind her apartment building?"

The story had been in all the papers and on the TV news for days, Jaina recalled.

"Well," Skip continued, "she brought it to the hospital, and the whole time the docs and nurses were checking its health, she stayed right there. When they gave the little guy a clean bill of health, she told 'em she wanted him."

Jaina said, "I don't remember how it turned out."

"She got him."

"Was she…?"

"Wasn't married, owned a cleaning service, lived alone…the works."

"Oh, Skip," Jaina sighed, "do you think…?"

"See, this is just what I was trying to avoid. Listen to me, Jaina. *That* kid didn't have a relative waiting in the wings, so unless you're planning to get rid of Buchanan, it's apples and oranges." A few moments of silence ticked by before he said, "So, who are you having lunch with? Your lawyer?"

"No…"

"It's high time you started planning a strategy, to discuss the girl's letter and all. Who'd you hire? Maybe I know him and can put in a good word."

"I don't have a lawyer yet."

"Jaina! What're you waiting for?"

"When I need one, I'll get one. I'm hoping that in the meantime, Buchanan will realize I'm in a better position to—" The sight of him smacking his palm against his forehead silenced her.

"I can't believe this," Skip said. "Don't tell me your business lunch is with—"

"Yes, Connor Buchanan."

"Are you out of your ever-lovin' mind? Consorting with the enemy? You have no chance of beating him in court, and you're gonna—"

"Hold on a minute, *pal*. 'No chance'? Just a minute ago, you said I had a slight chance. Which is it? C'mon, 'fess up. You know how important this is to me."

He moaned quietly, then said, "Jaina, don't do this to me."

"A little thin-skinned, aren't you, Skip? Especially since I'm still wiping the dirt off my face."

"Huh?"

"After you rubbed my nose in it," she explained, impatience ringing in her voice.

"I didn't mean things to sound that way at all," he said. "It's just that we've been good friends a long time, and I'd like it to stay that way."

She rolled her eyes. "Really, Skip," she said on a mocking laugh, "what could you possibly have to say that would threaten our friendship?"

"All right, but don't say I didn't warn you." He took a deep breath. "You're doing the right thing for all the wrong reasons. This attachment you have for Liam? In my professional opinion, I think you've turned him into a substitute."

"Substitute? For what?"

"For the babies you think you can't have," he said quietly.

As her heart thundered, Jaina's free hand clenched and unclenched. *The babies I think I can't have?* She would have shot his opinion down if the words hadn't frozen in her throat.

"It's perfectly understandable, but it isn't healthy, not for you *or* for Liam. You'll only end up brokenhearted again."

"Again?"

"The way you were when Bill…when he—"

"You haven't had any trouble speaking your mind so far. Go ahead. Say it. When Bill died and left me to pick up the tab."

"Stop it, Jaina. That's not what I meant and you know it." He breathed an exaggerated sigh. "Look, I have a meeting with my boss and I haven't even pulled the case histories yet. Can I call you later so we can finish discussing this?"

"We've already finished discussing it."

"There you go again."

Jaina emitted a low growl of frustration. "What does *that* mean?"

"You can't hide from the truth because it'll find you every time."

"What truth am I hiding from *this* time, Dr. Freud?"

Skip chuckled. "Go ahead, insult me if it helps." He cleared his throat as if preparing for the seriousness of what he was about to say. "When they take Liam from you—and it's pretty likely they will—it's gonna break your heart. *Those* are the facts, and pretending they don't exist won't make them go away."

Go away. That's *what I'll do. I'll take Liam and head out of town.* No, that wouldn't solve anything. Not for Liam, certainly not for her.

She bit her lower lip to stanch the sob aching in her throat. It seemed as if Skip was deliberately trying to hurt her. But why? Why had he told her the story about the woman who'd adopted the baby she found in a trash can? Why give her some small hope to cling to, then retract that hope entirely?

"I know I'm being rough on you, Jaina, but what kind of friend would I be if I lied to you? I know how these things play out. I see it everyday." He paused, looking as genuinely contrite as she'd ever seen him. "Would you have preferred it if I lied to you and said it was all going to work out just fine?"

She shook her head. "No… I guess not. At least now I know what I'm up against." Then, in a stronger voice, "Are you coming to the parade with us tomorrow?"

"Wouldn't miss it for the world."

"According to my watch," she said, forcing a lilt into her voice, "you have to get ready for your boss."

A slight pause, then Skip said, "You know I love ya, don't you?"

Her eyes filled with tears, but she managed to say, "Yeah, I know." But she didn't know anything of the kind. She seemed to have made a habit of developing close ties with men who were bad for her. "You don't want to be late. Now get going."

"See you tomorrow," Skip said cheerily, and left.

Jaina glanced over at Liam, sitting in the middle of the playpen, trying to decide between his squeaky red fire engine and the yellow plastic dump truck she'd bought him. She cried softly as Skip's warning reverberated in her ears. She didn't want to lose Liam.

That first night, as she lay on the floor beside him, a thousand worries had kept her awake. Did he understand, in some instinctual way, that he'd been abandoned? Did he sense that his mother was dying? And if he did, Jaina had wondered, how would she assure him he'd be well cared for, always? Because what did she know about babies? Would she know if, when he cried, his tears were from hunger or gas…or fear?

When he woke fussing the next morning, Jaina couldn't explain it, but something had told her that a clean diaper and a sweet song was all it would take to calm him. And it had. From then on, knowing when he needed a nap or if a hug was called for seemed as natural as inhaling and exhaling. In just two weeks, he'd become the center of her world.

One of the hardest things about having been told she might never be able to have children of her own was the fear that if she adopted a baby, as everyone advised her to, she couldn't love the child as deeply or completely as a baby she'd given birth to herself. Jaina's feelings for Liam were proof that love for a child could be all-encompassing and all-consuming, no matter what. If she couldn't keep him…

The accident hadn't killed her, but it had come close. Neither had the subsequent physical therapy—though at times, as she struggled to regain the use of her legs, she thought it might. And somehow she'd managed to keep body and soul together, even after stepping into the hideous orange jumpsuit at Jessup. Those six months had changed her forever, had hardened her in so many ways. Being tough, she learned early, was the only way to survive. Innocent? Guilty? What did it matter to women who'd been sentenced to two, five, *twenty* years? Jaina got through it by dipping into a reserve of inner strength she hadn't known she possessed. It never ceased to amaze her that no matter how many times she went to it, the well always seemed just full enough to provide the fortitude to go on despite the hardship. Only recently had she come to realize that it had been kept full by the love of Almighty God.

But how deep *was* it? How much more could she take from it? The ultimate test, she believed, lay just ahead. If Skip was right, if Buchanan succeeded in taking Liam from her, it would require so large a draft of courage and endurance, that the well might just run bone-dry.

When Connor called, as promised, to tell her he was leaving for the restaurant, he thought she'd sounded sad. That was odd, he told himself, remembering their brief conversation, because she'd seemed pretty up when she phoned him earlier. Could it be that she knew what he'd been up to? That he'd had a detective on her heels? That he'd started the machinery to take the baby from her?

Perhaps this motherhood thing was beginning to wear thin. She'd lived a full and busy life before Liam came along; maybe the added stresses and strains of taking care of him day in, day out, were proving to be too much. Which, in his opinion, would be a blessing in disguise because Connor wasn't looking forward to taking the baby from her.

He set the scene in his mind: Jaina, teary-eyed and trembly-lipped, arms outstretched as he walked away with his bawling nephew. His heart beat double time and he winced, forcing the picture from his mind. He ran a hand through his hair. If thinking about it made him feel like such a heel, what was it going to be like when the real thing happened?

And it *was* going to happen because he intended to raise that boy as his own. He didn't want to fight her; that would mean dredging up her past. He knew hers was just the kind of story that media vultures were always hunting for. And he'd do everything in his power to prevent that, but...

He spotted her just then, crossing the street from the parking lot to the restaurant. Thoughts of fighting her were forgotten as he smiled unconsciously. Connor liked the way she walked, head up and shoulders back, each fluid stride causing her glistening chestnut brown curls to bounce a bit. Somehow her slight limp did nothing to distract from her grace. She raised a hand to tame wind-blown bangs, frowning slightly when they refused to cooperate. She'd worn a jean skirt cut a few inches above her knees, topped by a white summer-weight sweater. He noted a brown braided-leather belt around her slender waist and matching sandals on her tiny feet. Cinderella couldn't have looked as pretty at the ball, he thought.

She saw him then, at the table on the other side of the window, smiled and raised a hand in friendly greeting.

He stood to remove his jacket and hung it on the back of his chair. "I hope you haven't been here long," she said, settling into the seat across from him. "I left as soon as we hung up."

"No, not at all," he said. "I've only been here a few minutes." Connor hadn't felt this awkward since high school, when he asked the homecoming queen to accompany him to the spring dance. "I have to admit, even if I'd been here an hour, it would have been worth the wait. You look lovely today."

Jaina blushed, then fanned her face with the menu. "I, uh, the air conditioner in my car isn't working very well. I think it must need servicing. Freon. Something…" She took a quick look around the place, ran a finger down the food list. "You've eaten here before. What do you recommend?"

"They make a mean crab cake, and their pizza isn't half-bad, either."

She took a sip of water from a squat, red-rimmed tumbler. "There's no price beside the crab cake platter." Narrowing her eyes, she leaned across the table. "'Market price.' What kind of nonsense is *that?*" Clucking her tongue, she lifted her chin. "Mine is 9.95 year-round, period."

Chuckling, Connor waved the waitress over. "I'll have a glass of iced tea. Jaina?"

She laid the menu beside the small butter plate. "Make it two," she said. Then, looking around conspiratorially, she wiggled her forefinger to summon the woman closer. "How much are the crab cakes today?"

The waitress looked left and right. "Eight ninety-five," she whispered, "and they come with French fries and a side of coleslaw."

Jaina's brows rose. "Wow, a whole dollar less than mine."

"Well," Connor said, "you know what the sages say."

"You get what you pay for," they said in unison, laughing.

As the woman left to get their drinks, Connor commented on the weather, and Jaina repeated last night's Orioles score. He asked if she'd heard about the dockworkers' strike. She wondered if he'd seen the article about the president's latest diet. Once the waitress had delivered their tea, Jaina opened her purse and sat back, smiling a bit.

"What?"

"This feels strangely like déjà vu. Except the last time

I did this," she said, pulling the letter from her purse, "we were in your office."

"True." He cocked a brow. "How'd you sleep last night?"

"Fine, thanks, and you?"

"Like a rock, as usual. Did you have breakfast?"

She tilted her head to the side and looked at him curiously. "Why…yes."

"Good."

Jaina nodded slowly. "Ahhh, I get it. You're worried I'll pass out again," she observed, grinning mischievously, "and make a scene in front of all your lawyer friends."

He chuckled. "They've already observed a young woman in my company making scenes. Then again, a swoon would be a refreshing change."

Her smile faded. "I apologize for that business in your office. I wish I could explain it. Sometimes the strangest things remind me of…" Eyes wide, she bit her lower lip, then hid behind the menu. "So, you say you've had the crab cakes here?"

Though she'd left her remark unfinished, he knew where she'd been headed, thanks to O'Dell's report. And because of what he'd read on his own, he understood for the first time that he must have said or done something that day to remind her of the accident. Whatever it had been, *that's* what prompted the fainting spell. He shrugged one shoulder. "I've had better, but then, I've had worse."

She nodded again, and he took a swallow of his tea. He'd heard enough testimony, both in private quarters and on countless witness stands, to know what went on inside a women's prison. He'd always felt many differing emotions when listening to ex-cons tell their stories. Some he thought deserved exactly what they'd gotten. Others he'd believed couldn't possibly have deserved the punishment meted out in a court of law. But he'd always managed to keep his reactions to himself, to keep a safe emotional distance, because they'd all been virtual strangers.

But he knew Jaina. Knew her well enough to believe he might be falling in love with her. That anyone had used and abused this diminutive lady caused a roiling that started deep in his gut and ended at his tightly clenched fists. The muscles of his jaw flexed and his eyes narrowed. If he could've gotten his hands on that Bill guy, he'd have… *You're a hypocrite, Buchanan,* he told himself, heart pounding with shame, *because what you're planning is going to hurt her more than—*

"Connor? Are you all right?"

He met her dark eyes, reading genuine concern on her pretty face. Connor wrapped his hand around the glass of tea. "I'm fine. Why?"

Jaina blinked several times before answering. "You looked…" She grinned. "You looked like you were ready to commit a homicide." Jaina feigned a look of terror. "Not a very smart place to murder someone, what with all these cops and judges and prosecutors around."

He chuckled.

"So, who was the victim—me?"

The question made him sit up straighter. "Why would I want to hurt you?"

She laid the envelope beside the web-covered candle in the center of the table. "Because I'm going to fight you for Liam."

Connor licked his lips. Nodded. He took another sip of the tea. "I can think of less messy ways to stop you."

He saw the fear that widened her big brown eyes and winced inwardly. *Well, you knew this wasn't gonna be easy,* he told himself.

"You wouldn't kill me to get Liam," he said, and seeing the mischievous grin that lifted one corner of her mouth, added, "would you?"

Narrowing her eyes, Jaina wiggled her brows. Smiling gently, she reached across the table and touched her index fingertip to his forehead. "That's for me to know," she said, her thumb cocking a pretend gun, "and you to find out."

"Wow," he said, laughing. "I can't remember when I've last heard that 'me to know' line. Not since third grade, I'll bet."

"'You make me feel so young,'" she sang, forefingers waving in the air.

His smile diminished a little in response to her singing. It had lasted a second, perhaps less, but it had been enough to make him want to hear more. He could almost picture her, microphone in hand, eyes closed, standing in the spotlight and crooning a ballad. "So tell me," he asked, nonchalantly picking up the letter, "how's my little man today?"

"Terrific. Did I tell you he's learned to stand?"

"That must be a sight," he said, sliding Kirstie's note from its envelope.

She scooted her chair back. "He uses the coffee table for balance, gets into a standing position, like this." Jaina stood beside the table, oblivious to the curious glances of nearby diners, spread her feet shoulder-width apart and assumed the position. "His arms go up and down like he's going to take off, then he leans forward, bobbles back and forth, side to side, and *plop!*" Air whooshed from the cushion as she landed on the seat of her chair. "Good thing his bottom is well padded!"

Jaina lifted her shoulders in a dainty shrug. "I declare, you just gotta love him!"

Unfolding Kirstie's letter, he wondered what it would feel like to have her saying that about him. "What do you think…should I read this before or after we eat?"

"Maybe it'd be best if you waited." She inclined her head, studying his face for a moment. "You don't seem like the type who has a weak stomach, but…"

He returned the letter to its envelope. "As my old granny used to say, I'm as strong as an ox."

Jaina clasped her hands beneath her chin. "Is she still with you?"

Connor shook his head, then took a sugar packet from the tray on the table and folded all four corners down. "No. She died when I was about twelve."

"Any grandparents left at all?"

He unfolded the corners. "Nope." And meeting her eyes, he asked, "You?"

"I'm afraid it's just my parents and me."

He folded the corners in the opposite direction. "No siblings?"

"Mom has a heart condition. She didn't find out until she was in labor with me. From what I hear, the delivery nearly killed her. The doctors told her if she got pregnant again, that'd be the end of her." Jaina took a deep breath, staring out the window for a moment. "So she had her tubes tied, and that was that."

He shook his head. "That's too bad. Would your parents have wanted any more kids?"

Jaina met his eyes. "Dad wanted four, she wanted six. The thing was, they'd have needed ten kids in order for both of them to get their way."

She smiled, but it never quite made it to her eyes, he noticed. Something dark and sad glittered in the brown orbs, something akin to bitterness.

"Yeah, it would have been nice to have brothers and sisters," Jaina admitted. "But my mother's alive, and so far she's healthy." She swirled the clear plastic straw around in her tea, setting the ice cubes to tinkling against the glass. "I used to think I'd like four or five myself."

Her long lashes, dusting her cheeks as she stared into her drink, reminded him of the woolly caterpillars that appear in the fall, signaling winter's approach. "Used to?"

Jaina stared into the whirlpool she'd created in the tumbler. A spark—anger? regret?—glittered hard and cold in her usually warm eyes. "Things happen, you know? If you don't go with them, they'll knock you flat."

And you know something about that, don't you? It took all the strength he could muster not to leap from his chair and wrap her in a big protective hug. His heart ached for her, for all she'd suffered and survived, because good people like Jaina shouldn't have to endure such hardship.

"So, are you folks ready to order?" The waitress stood beside the table, looking from Connor to Jaina, order pad in one hand, ballpoint poised in the other.

Connor's eyes never left Jaina's. "Two crab cake platters. Broiled, not fried. And onion rings instead of French fries."

"Need refills on your tea?"

He continued staring into Jaina's face. "Sure."

"Back in a jiff," she said, and left them again.

Something told Connor to fold his hands on the table, the way his fifth-grade teacher had taught him, to keep him from fiddling with his pen or the corners of his textbook. But he didn't listen to the warning. Instead, he reached out and grasped Jaina's hand, then gave it a gentle squeeze. Under the circumstances, it was the best he could do because he couldn't very well admit that he'd found out what she'd lived through and admired her for it. Maybe someday…but not yet.

He half expected her to withdraw her hand and tuck it out of sight in her lap. Jaina surprised him by placing her free hand atop his, effectively sandwiching his hands between her own. Smiling sweetly, she gave his knuckles an affectionate little pat, and he read it as a silent thanks for his understanding.

Her fingers felt smooth, cool, soothing, against his skin. He wanted to rest the fingertips of his other hand on her delicate wrist, walk them up her slender arm and pull her close, closer, until he could press a kiss to those smiling lips.

As if she could read his mind, her lips spread into a wide grin. "You're good, Buchanan. I'll give you that much."

He gave her a puzzled look. "Good? Good at what?"

She arched a brow and tilted her head, before shooting a taunting glance his way. "Distractions are probably very influential with members of a jury, but they're not quite so effective with the unsequestered."

One corner of his mustached mouth rose. "I don't get it."

The warm light in her brown eyes cooled. "Romancing me isn't the answer. I love him, and if I have to, I'll fight for him."

He'd been so lost in the moment, he hadn't caught her meaning until now. Then, as understanding dawned, he tightened his grip slightly and asked softly, "What makes you think I'm romancing you?"

Jaina's heart thundered suddenly in response to his question. The challenge in his words was matched only by the impact of his intense gaze. She withdrew her hands, hid them in her lap. "I'm sorry," she said quietly. "That was out of line."

Connor crossed his arms over his chest and sat back. "No. I'm the one who's sorry."

She tried but couldn't make sense of the peculiar expression that had hardened his features. She watched him pick up the envelope, then pretend to be engrossed in the postmark.

"So, Kirstie's still in Milwaukee, I see."

Unable to speak, Jaina only nodded. She'd grown accustomed to keeping an arm's length from men. Pulling away had become a knee-jerk reaction. Clothing hid her scars, but she was aware of them always, and could feel them even through bulky sweaters. If she let a man hold her hand, he might think it was all right to pull her into a casual hug. What if, as his fingers rested on the small of her back and his thumbs pressed against her stomach, he felt the scars? Jaina didn't know what she'd do if she read disgust—or worse, revulsion—on his face.

Keeping a safe emotional distance served another purpose. People tended not to look too closely at folks they didn't care about; if she let a man into her heart, he might just see everything else.

But she hadn't withdrawn from Connor's touch. Hadn't *wanted* to, and that surprised her. It was something she'd give some careful thought to at home later, when she was alone....

"Here ya go," the waitress sang out, depositing their plates in front of them. "Ketchup? Mustard?"

"None for me," Connor said. "Jaina?"

"No thanks." Jaina smiled up at the woman.

"Okay, well, just flag me if you want to see the dessert menu."

Their eyes locked as they replied in perfect harmony, "Just coffee, please."

The waitress gave them her best "the customer is always right" smile and walked away.

They made small talk as they dined, discussing everything from the weather to the high cost of living in Howard County, Maryland. Connor finished eating first, and the way he laid his knife and fork on his plate reminded her of the ceremony made famous by naval academy cadets. They'd stand facing one another, sabers crossed high as a newly married fellow student and his bride walked beneath the shimmering steel archway. Marriage? What was she doing thinking about *marriage?*

They were on their second cup of coffee before Connor picked up the envelope again. "Well," he breathed, "here goes. Shall I read it aloud?"

She shook her head. "I've read it a dozen times already. I'll just take this opportunity to find the ladies' room."

A gentleman to the hilt, he half stood as she rose from her chair. "Don't be long," he said, nodding toward the letter. "I might need you to hold my hand."

He wasn't kidding. She could see genuine apprehension in his blue eyes. "You know," she said, sitting down again, "I think I'll just take advantage of Miss Manners's newest rule and reapply my lipstick right here at the table." She slid a compact from her purse, popped open the lid and glanced into its small oval mirror. "Well, what do you think of that?" She snapped it shut again. "I don't need a touch-up after all."

The look of relief on his face sent her heart into overdrive. Jaina didn't know how to react to that, either, and hid her surprise by pretending to sip coffee from the thick earthenware mug.

She sat back and watched him scan the neatly penned lines of Kirstie's letter. For some time now, she'd been questioning her feelings for him. Did she think of him nearly every hour of the day—and quite a few hours of the night—because he might take Liam away from her? Or was the baby's delighted reaction to him the reason Connor seemed to be constantly on her mind? Were the memories of his compassionate reaction to her dizzy spell in his office what prompted the soft sighs and the quickened heartbeat that accompanied thoughts of him, or had remembering the way he'd clowned for the baby caused the response?

How do you feel *about him?*

She'd posed the question at least a thousand times in the weeks since Kirstie left Liam at The Chili Pot. If he truly was everything he appeared to be—warm, thoughtful, caring of his nephew—she could love him. But if he was the kind of man who could take Liam from her...

Chin resting in her palm, she'd been staring out the window, only half-seeing the people who sauntered past the restaurant. The sound of rustling paper roused her from her reverie, and she glanced up in time to see Connor struggling to stuff the letter back into its envelope.

Was that a tear in his eye? And was she mistaken or had his lower lip trembled?

Yes, the content of his niece's letter had obviously moved him deeply. His valiant effort to hide his emotions moved *her*. Dozens of times, her mother had said, "A man wears pride like a badge of courage." Jaina averted her gaze so that when he looked her way, he wouldn't know she'd seen his moment of vulnerability. He'd likely view it as a moment of weakness; she'd seen it as proof of his capacity to love.

Love.

It explained everything, including the question she'd asked herself a thousand times.

And created a list of new questions yet to be asked.

Chapter Seven

Connor walked Jaina to her car, relieved her of the keys, and unlocked it. After climbing inside, he revved the motor and turned the air conditioner to full blast. "Keep me company for a few minutes while it cools down in there," he said, slamming the door.

Because she'd hoped there would be a reason to extend their time together, she didn't bother to remind him that her car's air conditioner had been on the blink. She felt safe and protected in his company. Strange, since he was the one person who could do her the most harm. She leaned back on the sedan's fender and glanced up. "Looks like rain. I sure hope the weather does whatever it's going to do tonight. I'd hate to see the Fourth of July festivities get washed out."

"Me, too. I've never had a red, white and blue breakfast."

Laughing, she said, "Mother Nature can control the parade and the fireworks, but she can't dictate what I'll do in my very own kitchen!"

"Seven at the latest? Rain or shine?"

Crossing her arms in front of her, Jaina gave an assertive nod. "Yep."

Connor shrugged out of his suit coat, hooked the collar

on a forefinger and slung it over his shoulder. "I didn't figure you for a four-door kind of girl," he said, patting her car's roof.

"What sort of girl *did* you figure me for?"

"I dunno. I guess I saw you in something sporty and low-slung, with a convertible top. Or maybe one of those four-wheel-drive things."

Almost from the day she got her learner's permit, she'd wanted a shiny red four-wheel-drive vehicle. "And why's that?"

He loosened his tie and unfastened the top button of his shirt. "Because you seem too easygoing, too down-to-earth for a sedate sedan."

Connor draped the jacket over his forearm and began unbuttoning one shirt cuff. The coat nearly slid to the pavement several times before Jaina intervened. "Funny you should mention that," she said nonchalantly, neatly folding the sleeve back once, twice, then smoothing it. "I've always wanted a Jeep. Or one of those goofy-looking things the army guys drive."

"A Hummer?"

"Right!" She unbuttoned his other cuff. "The only thing I like better than off-roading is horseback riding…mainly because it's quieter."

"Horseback riding, eh?"

"If I do say so myself, I was quite the little equestrian when I was a girl."

"Did you compete?"

She breathed an indignant huff. "You mean, you didn't see the trophy on the mantel in my living room?"

"Sorry," he said, smiling. "I must have missed it."

"I don't see how." She finished rolling the second sleeve. "It's three feet high." She patted the cuff. "All set!"

The tawny mustache tilted above a rakish smile. "Thanks. You're a natural-born caretaker, aren't you?"

Jaina didn't know if it was the weather or his compliment that sent a rush of heat to her cheeks. She tore her gaze from his blue-eyed admiration, pretended to be interested in the sidewalk sale in front of a shop up the street. "I wonder if they still have that sideboard?" she said. "I've been drooling over it for ages. It'd be perfect for my front hall. Every now and then I check to see if the price has dropped."

His grin broadened. "Let's check it out." He reached into the car, turned off the motor, then he gestured for her to lead the way.

Jaina had never liked walking in front of anyone because it only called attention to her limp. She would have said Connor hadn't noticed it, but he'd asked if she'd sprained her ankle that day as she left his office. Either he didn't mind it, or he was one fine actor!

They walked side by side in companionable silence until they reached the storefront, where Jaina continued her charade of being interested in the items on display. "I have a set of these," she said, pointing to the spire-shaped salt and pepper shakers. "They don't hold much, but they look so pretty when the table's all set for dinner."

"They'd look great in your house."

"My apartment, you mean."

"No. I mean your house. The one in all your paintings."

Her flush deepened. "Good grief. You noticed them?" She hid her face behind her hands. "It was a birthday surprise. Mom hung them all up one day while I was at the market." Jaina came out of hiding to add, "It's embarrassing as can be, but what could I say after she'd gone to all that trouble?"

"Embarrassing? I think they're very good."

She rolled her eyes. "Please." And then, "Funny how therapeutic something like painting can be when…" A hard little laugh punctuated her unfinished sentence. "I'd never picked up a paintbrush before…" She shook her head, then started again. "Before I knew it, I was surrounded by paintings. Big ones, small ones, rectangles and squares and ovals…" She laughed softly. "I used to watch that guy on PBS. You know the one…with the bushy red hair?"

"'And a happy little tree lives right here,'" Connor said in a perfect imitation of the television artist.

"That's the one!" She giggled. Sighed. "I'd stand there watching him, trying my best to duplicate whatever he was working on that day." She shook her head and gave a wry little smile. "Strange the way that house popped up in everything I did."

"Not so strange. It's your dream house, isn't it?"

One hand flew to her throat. How did he know that? And then it dawned on her. "My mother talks too much sometimes."

"Funny thing," he continued as if she hadn't spoken, "how much that house looks like mine."

"You have a dream house, too?" she blurted.

"I don't know how dreamy it is, but it's where I live."

Jaina gasped. "You live…you live in a house like the one in my paintings?"

Connor nodded. "Wanna see it?"

Her eyes widened. "Now?"

"Why not?"

"Well…well," she stammered, "for starters, I thought you had to attend some kind of hearing this afternoon."

He glanced at his watch. Frowned. "I've got exactly twenty minutes to get back to the office, pick up the files and head over to the courthouse."

"Well, then," she said, smiling, "you'd better get a move on."

"I could pick you up after work, drive you and Liam over there. If you're not busy, that is."

Me? Busy? Jaina almost laughed out loud. She didn't know what had inspired the invitation, but it pleased her nonetheless. Did he want to show Liam the room he'd be sleeping in? Or did he want *her* to see it so she'd know firsthand how well he could provide for the baby? Either way, Jaina's curiosity was piqued. "I'll bring supper," she volunteered, "so Liam won't get off his schedule."

He began walking backward toward his own car. "Pick you up at five?"

"We'll be ready." She watched him climb into the sleek silver sports car. If it hadn't looked like rain, would he have put the top down? she wondered. And then something else occurred to her, and she half ran toward his car. "You'll have to leave your car at the diner."

He leaned out of the driver's window to ask, "You have some objection to foreign models?"

"There's no back seat in this thing. Where would we put Liam's car seat?"

Connor pursed his lips. "Good point." Grinning, he added, "See? It's like I said…you're a natural-born caretaker."

She'd almost asked it the last time he'd paid her the compliment. *What have you got to lose?* she asked herself. "If you really feel that way, why do you want to take Liam away from me?"

Jaina felt his gaze sweep over her face. When his eyes met hers, he said, "I don't *want* to take him, Jaina. I *have* to." She was about to ask why again, but thought better of it as he revved the sports car's powerful engine. "See you at five," he called out, then drove away.

The answering-machine light was blinking when they walked into his kitchen. Still reeling from the similarity between his house and the one she'd dreamt of for as long as she could remember, Jaina watched as Connor reached for the Play button and Liam tugged his earlobe. "Easy, little guy," Connor said, gently prying open the baby's fingers.

She thought of what he'd said just before he'd driven away from the parking lot earlier. A fierce possessiveness overtook her, and Jaina stepped up and held out her arms. "Here," she said, "I'll take him while you do that." Liam's shirt had ridden up, exposing his round tummy, and Jaina adjusted it.

Connor read aloud the bold black letters on the front of it. "'Actually, I'm a rocket scientist.'" And laughing, he played the message.

"Better be careful," a gravelly voice said, "because when you least expect it, you're gonna get yours!"

Scowling, Connor flushed. "Don't tell me *this* is starting again."

"What's starting again?"

He shook his head, jerking a thumb over his shoulder at the phone. "Threats."

"You've been threatened before?"

"Only a few thousand times." He shrugged. "Actually, that one was tame compared to most. It sorta goes with the territory."

She frowned. "I presume you've notified the police."

"Yeah. And I'll give you three guesses what they said."

"They want to assign someone to guard you?"

He perched Liam on his shoulders. "Ain't she the sweetest, most innocent li'l thing you ever did see?" he asked the baby.

"Well, at least they must be going to guard you part of the time," she pressed. "Right?"

Connor shot her a crooked grin. "Gosh, you're cute when you're being naive."

Jaina felt a blush creep into her cheeks. "Then...they're going to increase the patrol cars that pass by your—"

He hissed a stream of air through his teeth. "Don't make me laugh. I'm a defense attorney, remember? I'm the guy who puts their collars back on the street."

Liam heard the hissing sound Connor had made and tried his best to emulate it.

"But...but you're so isolated, way out here in the country. Are you safe, all alone like that?"

"So far...and I'm keeping my fingers crossed."

"Then why aren't you doing something about it?"

Connor unfolded the portable playpen she'd brought along, and Jaina put Liam into it. Together, they emptied the mesh bag that held his toys. The baby squealed with glee as stuffed animals and rubber balls rained down upon him.

"How 'bout a glass of lemonade?" he asked.

"I'd love some."

"I have to warn you...it isn't fresh-squeezed," he bantered.

While he put ice cubes into glasses, Jaina poured. "You can't change the subject that easily, Connor."

He heaved a deep sigh. "It's a long story."

"Liam doesn't have to be in bed until nine. We have four hours by my watch." She put their glasses on the kitchen table, sat, then crossed her arms over her chest. "I'm listening...."

He took the seat across from her, leaned both elbows on the pine surface and, for the next half hour, compelled her attention with the tale of his life in the courtroom, first as a prosecutor, then as a defense attorney. "Didn't matter much which side of the courtroom I was on; in the opinions of the defendants, I helped some, I hurt some."

Jaina wondered whether or not to tell him she had been a defendant. "This is a free country, certainly they're entitled to their opinions. But what they're doing is wrong. And what's that old adage? 'Two wrongs don't make a right.' You can't let them get away with this just because you feel sorry for them."

"It isn't pity, Jaina. It's guilt."

"Guilt? But you were only doing your job!"

"True, but I'm not God. What if, in a few cases that I prosecuted successfully, the defendant really didn't deserve to go to prison? If the evidence said otherwise I had to do my job. Still, my presence is a constant reminder of their years behind bars."

She studied his face and saw that he meant it. The more Jaina learned about Connor Buchanan, the better she liked him. If only there was some way to convince him to let her keep Liam. If only there was a way they could share him.

"If you're in danger…so would Liam be…if he lived here."

He considered that for a moment. "You've got a point. But he doesn't live here."

"Yet." She brought the subject back to the phone call. "How do you know so much about how they feel?"

He stared at his hands, folded on the tabletop. "I was a prosecutor before I became a defense attorney. The things I saw and heard…" He shook his head and gave her a long, penetrating stare. "And how is it you can be so forgiving?"

Jaina flinched. "I…I…I'm afraid I don't…"

He leaned forward, both hands now pressing down on the tabletop. "Yes you *do*." He cupped her hands in his own. "You understand perfectly, because you lived it yourself. Why aren't *you* bitter and angry? Why don't *you* blame all men for what one man did to you?"

She began to tremble. It started in her fingertips, then reverberated to her limbs, her shoulders, her hips. Surely he could feel it, as tightly as he was holding her hands. *He knows about…* But *how* did he know? Had it been something she'd said or done? Was the past written on her face like a scarlet letter? One thing was sure: if he knew about the surgery, he knew everything that had led up to it, too. Jaina's heart thundered, because if that was true, Liam was as good as gone.

"Who told you?" she asked, her voice a thick, hoarse whisper.

He broke the intense eye contact and, staring at their hands, said, "I just know, okay?"

Jaina glanced at Liam, playing happily in the playpen. "I should start supper. He'll be hungry soon." She stood, then nervously began rummaging in the cooler she'd filled with Chili Pot food. "I think we'll start with a nice salad, and then we'll have some of Mom's famous minestrone before we eat the spaghetti. There's a wedge of cheese-cake in here somewhere," she rambled, jostling jars and plastic containers around. "I'll let you set the table since this is your kitchen and you know where things are. If you'll just get me a saucepan so I can heat the—"

In a heartbeat, it seemed, he was beside her, gently en-circling her wrists with long, strong fingers. "Jaina," he breathed, "don't."

Don't what? she wanted to demand. Unable to meet his eyes, she focused on their hands. *What must he think of me?* she wondered as her trembling intensified.

Connor lifted her chin on a bent forefinger. "Look at me."

Slowly, she raised her gaze.

"I'd never hurt you, not in a million years."

You're going to take Liam from me, and that'll hurt worse than anything I've ever...

There was a hitch in his voice when he asked, "Do you believe me? That I'd never intentionally hurt you, I mean?"

The same instinct that could have saved her—if she'd listened to it that night with Bill—pinged inside her now. For a reason she couldn't explain, she wanted to say "Yes,

I believe you," for no reason other than that he seemed to
need to hear it. But it was a lie. He would hurt her, *intentionally*, when he took Liam. Jaina looked into his eyes,
sparkling with expectation and hope.

She nodded.

Connor looked toward the ceiling and heaved a great
sigh. "Thank God," he whispered, his voice quaking,
"thank God."

Slowly, he lowered his head. That time in his office…
she'd worried he might kiss her. This time, she knew he
would. In the instant, that tick in time before it happened,
thoughts churned dizzyingly in her mind….

For the first time since they'd met, she saw him as
more than the savvy legal shark whose no-holds-barred
approach to law had likely won him a thousand cases. It
was evident in his square-shouldered stance, his no-
nonsense gait, his matter-of-fact voice, that he was a man
unaccustomed to losing. Until now, she believed he
viewed Liam as the trophy to be won at the end of a long,
arduous battle, or property to be claimed, like a lost dog
or a wallet that had fallen from his pocket.

When Jaina read the yearning in his crystal blue eyes,
she was reminded of the reason he'd offered for having
avoided most of his secretary's get-togethers. Adopting
Liam wasn't about ownership, she realized. And it wasn't
about winning, either. It was about love, about family,
about the need to feel he *belonged*. With nothing more
than a forlorn expression, he'd awakened feelings in her
she didn't know could exist.

He stood a head taller than her, outweighed her by at
least fifty pounds. Clearly, he didn't need her protection.
And yet protecting him was precisely what Jaina wanted
to do. She felt compelled to stand in front of him, to defend
him against anyone who threatened him.

She guessed him to be in his early thirties, and by all

outward appearances, he seemed to have done a fine job taking care of himself physically. The house, though sparsely and plainly decorated, was spotless, the yard around it as manicured as a golf course. Yet she wanted to cook for him, clean for him, turn this house into a haven that would welcome him at the end of a long, hard day.

And though she could tell by the taut set of his lips and his lantern jaw that he was trying hard to hide it, Connor looked sad and lonely, and she wanted to wrap her arms around him, whisper soothingly into his ear that everything would be all right…that she'd *make* everything all right.

She was surprised by the tenderness welling up inside her. For one thing, she'd never felt anything like it before; for another, *this* was the man who wanted to take Liam from her. To feel such things for him…

Yes, he was going to kiss her.

And she welcomed it!

When his arms slid around her, she felt the protective wall she'd spent years building around herself begin to crack. He pressed her to him, gently, tenderly—as if the action was, for him, more a gesture of comfort than passionate need—and the wall crumbled around her feet.

His hands, so strong and sure as he tended to her cut that day in his office, trembled now as he embraced her. She felt the thrumming of his heart, steady and sure against her chest, and the faint quaking of his fingers as he combed them, slowly, lovingly, through her hair.

He leaned back slightly, holding her at arm's length, and silently searched her face. She read his soft gaze and understood that he saw her not as a scarred woman with a limp, not as a woman with a sordid past, but simply as a woman, a *whole* woman, with yearnings and dreams that matched his own.

Jaina had thought that, in her twenty-eight years,

she'd experienced every emotion known to humanity... love, hate, fear, gratitude. She'd accepted others at face value many times, but she'd never experienced it herself. Not like this. It was new, brand-new, this wonderful sensation that came with knowing that someone who wasn't obliged by blood ties to accept her unconditionally, as her parents did, *accepted* her, scars and limp and history and all!

Overwhelmed with gratitude—to God? to Connor? Jaina didn't know—she felt her heart begin to pound. Hesitantly, she lifted a hand to trace his beard-stubbled cheek with the backs of her fingers. Oh, what a face it was. Square-jawed and high-cheeked, it was hard angles and raw planes, completely masculine. And yet, beneath the thick sandy blond mustache, a tenderhearted smile, and in the bright blue, long-lashed eyes, a shimmering tear.

She wiped it away with the pad of her thumb, smiling shakily through tears of her own. A silent prayer of thankfulness whispered in her heart, and she bowed her head, humbled by the breathtaking freedom Connor had given her. Freedom from feeling she'd been tainted by the violence of that fleeting, long-ago moment. Freedom from believing that the sharp edge of that instant in time had cut her out of the normal things in life, had destined her to spend her life alone, remembering, reliving, regretting her immature, injudicious decision....

It seemed as natural as breathing to press her cheek against his hard, broad chest, to wrap her arms around his narrow waist. Jaina stood in the shelter of his embrace and reveled in the utter peace that surrounded her.

Connor kissed the top of her head, her temple, her cheek. His eyes met hers, and she read the longing there. The same pining beat in her own heart, and she willed him with her gaze to continue, to touch her lips with his.

But she couldn't speak past the sob that blocked her voice.

Since her release from prison so many years ago, every time a man had let her know, by his expression, by taking her in his arms, by saying point-blank that he wanted to kiss her, fear had made her stiffen, step back, call a quick halt to anything that might lead to emotional or physical intimacy. What if the same poor judgment that had allowed her to get into the car that night had also affected her ability to discern between the right man…and another like Bill? And what if he was with her only because he believed her to be defiled to the point that she'd be, as several had put it, "easy pickin's." Equally fearsome, what if, in those rare instances when the man had no knowledge of her disgrace, he found out about it and judged her contaminated?

She had no such things to fear from Connor. He'd spent the bulk of his career dealing with the worst society had to offer after all. He'd have gone into another area of the law if he didn't believe every murderer, robber and rapist had an inalienable right to be considered innocent until proven guilty. He would not judge her sullied. At least, not until all the evidence was in.

And he knew. The evidence *was* in!

The knowledge made her feel safe. Secure. Sure.

His tenderness that day in his office, the gentle way he handled Liam, the respect he showed her mother—despite the fact that Rita was always so hard on him—was rooted, Jaina believed, in a good and decent heart that beat strongly with compassion and thoughtfulness. She sensed he was the type who'd teach his children to pray for those less fortunate, who'd help them learn to field a grounder, and who'd sit proudly in a dark auditorium while his youngster massacred Beethoven's Fifth. Patiently, lovingly, he'd assist with homework and mean it when he recited timeworn clichés like "The world is your oyster" and "Look before you leap" and "Sticks and stones may break your bones but…"

She had never been the bold and brazen type. Despite the fact that she'd gone onstage, wowing audiences, she'd always been a bit shy. It was almost as though the microphone and the guitar had been props that helped her believe some invisible barrier existed between her and the crowds. Like the clown who hides behind his makeup and the politician who hides behind his speech writers, Jaina hid behind her talent.

No one was more surprised than Jaina when she bracketed his face with both hands, her thumbs drawing lazy circles on his cheeks. Holding his gaze, she slid her hands to the back of his neck, guided him near, nearer, until she felt his warm breath on her lips, until she felt the softness of his mouth against hers.

A dizzying swirl began churning inside her, eddying through her being, until her heart beat like a war drum and her pulse pounded like a jackhammer. She *wasn't* damaged goods, *hadn't been* ruined forever by that night. Connor knew—she didn't know how, but he *knew* about her sorry past—and yet he wanted her. It was a glorious, miraculous feeling. Her pastor had been right when he'd advised her to stop ridiculing herself for feeling so afraid every time a man got too close. "None of them has been the *right* man," he'd said. "When the mate God has chosen for you comes along, fear is the last thing you'll feel."

Connor Buchanan was that man!

Groggy with joy, Jaina began to laugh and cry at the same time. *Thank you, thank you, thank you,* she repeated—to God? To Connor? Both?

"Oh, Jaina," he gasped, hands on her shoulders, "I'm sorry. I'm so sorry that I got carried away. I don't know what's wrong with me." He grimaced as though in pain. "And I promised…I swore you'd always feel—"

Shaking her head, she placed her fingertips over his lips to silence him. Her tears had sent him the wrong message, she realized. "Shhh," she managed to say, "it's…it's not you. I'm…I'm not crying because…I'm afraid," she haltingly replied. "It's…because I'm…*relieved!* I thought…I was…that something was wrong with me."

He looked into her eyes, and as understanding dawned, he drew her close. "Ah, Jaina," he said, "there's not a thing wrong with you. *Nothing.*" He cupped her chin in a palm, and with a perfectly straight face, said, "Well, there's *one* thing wrong with you…."

She bit her lower lip and braced herself for the awful truth.

"You're not mine."

Skip darted into the kitchen. "I thought I'd *never* get you alone," he whispered. "Awright, Jaina, 'fess up. What gives?"

She met her friend's green eyes and said in her best Southern belle voice, "Why, Skip darlin', whatevah do you mean?"

He regarded her with a sidelong glance. "Connor Buchanan, that's what I mean. He's been makin' cow eyes at you all day long. What's goin' on between you two?"

Her heart pounded at the mere mention of his name, just as it had all through the long, lonely night. "I think the great generals would say we've declared a truce." She licked her lips and smiled, thinking of that kiss…. "Connor and I have decided it's in Liam's best interests if we try to get along."

"So it's *Connor* now, is it?" He raised his dark eyebrows. "That sounds very cozy."

She didn't like his insinuation. "Don't be ridiculous. We're…we're—"

"Friends?" The sarcasm in his voice rang like an Oriental gong.

"We're becoming friends. Yes."

"Aha. And my old Aunt Bessie is a horse."

Jaina clucked her tongue. "Shame on you, Skip. Bessie can't help it if she's a bit overweight."

He frowned. "You can't distract me that easily, pal. I know what's going on between you and our attorney friend, and if you ask me, you're making a big mistake."

"First of all," she snapped, "I *didn't* ask you." Propping a fist on her hip, Jaina added, "And secondly, it's obvious from this nonsense you're spouting that you haven't the foggiest idea what's going on."

"Oh, don't I? *That* guy," he said, thick forefinger jabbing the air, "is the only thing standing between you and permanent custody of Liam. And I've seen the way you look at that kid. I believe you'd do *anything* to keep him."

Her eyes widened and she gasped. His insinuation had become a full-fledged accusation. "We've been friends for ages. You know better than that."

He raised a brow. "I thought I did."

Leaning forward, she aimed a threatening digit at his nose. "Listen, *pal,* I'd never do anything so underhanded to get something I want!"

"Not even something you want as badly as you want Liam?"

She met his challenge head-on. "There's nothing I want badly enough to make me—"

He held up a hand to silence her. "Save it for the courtroom."

Jaina couldn't believe her ears. This wasn't like Skip at all. If she didn't know better, she'd say he was acting like a jealous suitor. Did Skip really think she was so desperate to keep the baby that she'd resort to…to *that?* Hadn't he learned anything about her in all the years they'd known one another? "I have hamburgers to make," she said flatly, turning away from him. "If you're going to help, wash your hands and grab some gloves. Otherwise…"

Connor entered the room, grinning and rubbing his palms together. "I'd be happy to help," he began. His smile faded as he took note of the surly expressions on their faces. "Sorry, guys. Didn't mean to interrupt." Walking backward, he headed for the door, hands up in mock self-defense. "I'll just—"

"No. *I'll* 'just,'" Skip interrupted, his voice brittle with bitterness. He shoved the screen door open. "You know what they say, two's company, three's a crowd," he grumbled.

"Skip, don't be silly!" Jaina's retort crackled.

The door slammed as Skip stomped down the steps.

"What was that all about?" Connor asked when Skip was out of earshot.

Jaina cut the end off an onion. "He thinks," she began, the blade hovering inches above the vegetable, "that I'm using my feminine wiles to trick you into letting me keep Liam." She quickly carved parallel slices three-quarters of the way through the onion, then deftly turned it ninety degrees and repeated the process.

Remembering the way she'd responded to his kiss, Connor swallowed. *Skip thinks she'd…*

He stopped himself. He didn't know Skip from a hole in the wall, so why should he take anything the man said to heart? He stepped up to the sink, turned on the faucet and tested the water temperature before grabbing the bar of soap on the counter. "So…are you?"

The knife split the onion in two, stopping with a dull *thunk* on the battered cutting board. She held his gaze for what seemed a full, agonizing minute. A slow, mischievous grin drew up the corners of her mouth, glittering in her dark, long-lashed eyes. "Am I *what?*"

He looked from her eyes to her lips, and it took every

ounce of control he could muster to keep from kissing her right where she stood. One side of his mouth lifted in a sly grin. He decided to rearrange the question slightly, see what her reaction might be if he caught her off guard. *Play it safe,* he decided, his smile broadening, *at least until she puts that knife down.*

"*Are* you using your feminine wiles?"

"No."

"Just as well," he said, though every male fiber in him wished she'd said yes. He shrugged. "'Cause what would a scheme like that get you in the long run?" Their kiss simmered in his memory. Anything she wanted, he admitted, regretting her quick denial even more. Anything she wanted.

She laid the knife on the cutting board and crossed her arms over her chest. "You, for starters."

"Me?" He chuckled. "What would you want with me?"

She tilted her head and raised an eyebrow. "If we were…*together,* I wouldn't have to fight you for Liam, now would I?"

He wished he'd known her longer, wished he knew her better, so he could determine if that flash in her eyes meant she was teasing…or not. Connor didn't want to believe she was like every other woman he'd known—capable of underhanded and deliberate manipulation—but there was too much at stake, and he simply couldn't afford to discount the possibility.

Despite his concerns, his grin broadened. "But, Jaina," he drawled, taking a step closer, "what would you do with me *afterward?*"

To his surprise, she said, "Why, I'd honor my marriage vows, of course. Which would be to your benefit."

Laughing, Connor moved closer still. "And why is that?"

She gave a nonchalant little nod of her head. "I'm right

handy with an iron for one thing, and you wouldn't believe how fast I can sew a button onto a sleeve. I believe cleanliness really *is* next to Godliness, and if I do say so myself, I'm pretty good in the kitchen."

If that kiss in my *kitchen is any indicator, I agree!* "So you're saying we should get married? Avoid the courtroom altogether?"

She picked up the knife again. "I'm no lawyer, but if I'm making any sense at all of Skip's advice, a stable, married couple would have an easier time trying to adopt Liam than two people who are—"

"Footloose and fancy free?"

"Cliché, but yes, being single will make it harder."

"Much harder."

He watched her turn the onion on its side so she could carve quarter-inch slices through the grid pattern she'd already cut into it. Tidy opaque squares avalanched onto the cutting board. "I guess your dad served some KP time in the service, eh?"

Jaina's hands froze. "Excuse me?"

"He's retired air force, right? I'm just assuming he did kitchen duty at some point in his military career and taught you that nifty little trick."

She looked at the cutting board, at his face, at the board again. "As a matter of fact," she said, her voice trembling slightly, "my father *did* teach me this nifty little trick." Jaina met his eyes. "But the only KP he did was during barbecues."

She straightened, and he read the pride in her stance and on her face. "He was a test pilot."

"I know."

Glaring, she all but slammed the knife down. "Of course you know." Her mouth formed a taut line as she pointed to a shelf above his head. "Would you mind handing me that bowl?"

Connor placed it on the counter, and while she filled it with chopped onions, he sighed inwardly. Her marriage talk had been a joke, nothing more, he believed. Which was too bad, since it made sense. A *lot* of sense.

It actually *would* make the adoption process a lot simpler if they were a couple. Besides, he could see what a wonderful mother she was. He wanted Liam, wanted him badly. But he wanted Jaina, too. *To be Liam's mother, of course....*

The mental pictures he'd gotten at the office—of her seeing him off in the morning, welcoming him home again in the evening, caring for Liam, for *him*—flashed through his mind. He'd dismissed the feelings those images had aroused. Feelings of warmth and comfort, of peace and passion. Feelings born of the knowledge that, in her eyes, whether rich or poor, he was *okay* just the way he was.

After discovering his ex-wife's betrayal, he'd made a promise never to get serious about another woman. There was no point since they all had a similar plan: lure him into their web with whatever deceitful means they deemed necessary, wrap him securely in their silken lies and leave him there to hang.

It had been a halfhearted promise at best. Because if he was honest with himself, Connor had to admit he'd been searching for the right woman all his life. If he'd listened to his own gut instincts, he'd have admitted way back then that Miriam hadn't been that woman; if he'd heeded his own good advice, he wouldn't have wasted all those years. Maybe now he'd have his dream—a devoted wife and a house full of rambunctious kids.

Why *not* marry Jaina? he asked himself. Then he'd—

"Tell me something, Connor."

"Hmm?" he said distractedly.

"How *do* you know so much about me?"

He repeated her question in his head. She'd been honest

with him—at least he *thought* she had been—and he saw no point in being evasive. "I hired a private detective."

Her glare intensified, and she faced him head-on. "A private detective," she echoed.

He nodded.

"So you know—"

"Everything," he finished. "And it doesn't make a bit of difference to me." It was true after all. He'd read the reports, and in his opinion, none of it had been her fault. And even if some of the blame *did* belong on her shoulders—and he refused to accept that as a possibility—she could be forgiven her mistakes because she'd only been nineteen or so at the time. In the years since then, she'd accomplished a great deal.

Rage blazed in her eyes. She turned abruptly away and grabbed a handful of raw hamburger. "Well, it's *going* to make a difference." She rolled the meat into a sphere, then slapped it flat between her palms. Setting the burger on a plate, she plucked off another lump of beef and smacked it into a patty. "How are you going to feel when the judge says you can't have Liam…because your wife is an ex-con?"

"Not a problem. I'll adopt Liam first, and *then* we'll get married."

"Slick, Buchanan," she said.

"Excuse me?"

"You get me to hand him over just like that, and once the papers are filed…"

He was focusing on the fact that she'd said "when," not "if." Then he noted her determined expression. He'd heard all his life that love was blind. Not till that minute did he realize it was stubborn, too. "If that happened, I wouldn't be thrilled," he admitted, "but…" Could he say it? Dare he admit how he felt? *But I'd feel like a lucky guy all the same, because I'd still have* you.

Practice makes perfect, he thought, knowing that he'd always made a habit of thinking first and speaking later. He'd always kept a tight rein on his emotions, something he was grateful for right now. Because what he wanted didn't matter. Much as he wanted—no, needed a life with Jaina—Liam needed a secure home, a stable parent *more*. If there was a chance, even a slight one, that her background might cost him a life with the child…

Connor cleared his throat. "I suppose you're right." Several silent seconds ticked by before he helped himself to a fistful of meat. "How many of these things do we need?"

He glimpsed the flicker of pain that glimmered in her dark eyes before she answered.

"Ten more oughta do it. 'Cause we have hot dogs and potato salad and baked beans and—"

She stopped speaking so suddenly that he wondered if maybe something had blocked her windpipe. He looked up in time to see her wiping her hands on a towel.

"I, uh, I'll be right back," she stammered. "Can you hold down the fort for a few minutes?"

"No problem," he said as she dashed away.

Before she'd run off, the room had seemed warm and sunny, despite the storm-threatening skies. As the door between the kitchen and the diner hissed shut behind her, Connor acknowledged that without her, his world was as dark and bleak as a windowless cell.

Jaina stood in the ladies' room, palms flat on the countertop. "What were you thinking?" she asked the woman in the mirror.

The answer was clear: she *hadn't* been thinking. If she had been, would she have suggested they get married? Would she so boldly have suggested she'd make some lucky guy a pretty good wife?

Not in a thousand years, she admitted. *Not in a* million *years.*

She turned away from the mirror and covered her face with both hands. *He knows what you are.* He knows, and yet he'd said he didn't care, that it didn't matter.

But how could it *not?*

There hadn't been much point in trying to keep her past a secret throughout her life; the accident and everything that had happened on the heels of it had been in the papers for weeks afterward. Like Eliot and Billie and Joy, she'd been forced to learn to live with the sneers and whispers that so often followed her when folks found out her past was not spotless. Some of her friends and co-workers really *had* been headed down the wrong path. Jaina, on the other hand, hadn't been guilty of anything but empty-headed gullibility.

To her knowledge, no one had tried to pass a bill that made foolishness against the law; if they had, six months in Jessup wouldn't have been nearly long enough because it had been blatantly stupid to get into that car with Bill! She'd suspected *something* was wrong that night and hadn't heeded her own inner warnings. That in itself deserved severe punishment, didn't it?

But when would she stop paying for her naiveté? Hadn't the injury, the months of physical therapy, the long, dark days in prison been enough? What of the supposedly life-saving surgery that had more than likely killed her chances of having children, leaving her stomach so contorted with scars it looked like a relief map? And what about the limp she tried so hard to disguise? How much more pain must she endure before she'd atoned for her transgression? When would she have done enough penance for her foolishness, and be set free at last from the humiliating, oppressive burden that was "the past"?

Jaina blotted her eyes on a brown paper towel and blew her nose. She couldn't remember the last time she'd felt so sorry for herself. In the hospital? During rehab? In Jessup? She sighed, remembering that long ago, she'd decided that self-pity was an ugly, egocentric waste of time and emotion. It had not furthered her recuperation, had not erased Bill's brutal death from her mind, hadn't wiped visions of the accident from her memory. And it hadn't cleared away the charges filed against her by the state.

Self-pity hadn't done her any good then, and it wouldn't do her any good now.

A verse she'd often read during her self-pitying days now came to mind. Jeremiah 20:7-18 had given her a sort of perverse comfort, for reading the ragings of that holy man, she'd felt less alone, less forgotten; if even God's chosen few had, from time to time, been furious with the Almighty, was she so different, for being angry because, in her mind, He'd let her down?

As a child, she'd learned that God loved all his children equally, no matter what. He had a capacity for love and mercy far beyond man's understanding, her Sunday school teachers had said, and promised to forgive and forget every sin…provided the sinner admitted culpability and confessed it with a contrite heart.

Connor, for all his insistence that her past didn't matter, was a flesh-and-blood man. She didn't know how long it would take, but sooner or later, she feared, he'd see how wrong he'd been and put a safe, permanent distance between them. It would break her heart when that happened, and she honestly didn't know if she could survive another crushing blow to her soul.

Jaina faced the sink again, patted her cheeks with cold water and ran now damp fingers through her hair. *He* had run his fingers through her hair last evening she remembered. And hiding her lips behind her palm, she tried to forget the sweet, soft kisses he'd pressed to her mouth.

She'd made a complete fool of herself, she acknowledged, and making a fool of herself was getting to be a bad habit. A habit she'd break, starting now.

Jaina stood as tall as her five-feet-three-inch frame would allow and took a deep breath. *You go out there and try to forget about that kiss, 'cause it's a sure thing he will.*

Maybe he could forget, but *she* wouldn't.

Because it was too late.

She'd already opened the door to her heart and let him in.

Chapter Eight

Liam lay sound asleep on his tummy, a thumb in his mouth, oblivious to the brightly colored explosions overhead. Jaina and Connor were on their backs on either side of him, their murmured oohs and aahs harmonizing with those of other spectators enjoying the fireworks.

"I've been giving a lot of thought to what you said earlier," Connor remarked.

Jaina got up onto one elbow, smoothed a wrinkle in the red plaid blanket beneath them. "What, specifically, did I say?"

Connor now, too, levered himself up. "That we should get married."

In the rainbow of light that drizzled from the sky with a prismatic glow, he watched her dark eyes widen, her full lips part, her delicate hand flutter at her throat.

"It…it was a joke," she stammered, her voice shaking. "I never intended for you to take me seriously."

Connor had a feeling that if it hadn't been so dark, he'd have witnessed a deep blush coloring her cheeks. In the time he'd known her, he'd learned that she found it difficult to stretch the truth even a bit. "That's too bad," he said. "I was really lookin' forward to telling all my pals down at the law library that the prettiest woman this side of the Mississippi proposed to me while—"

"Whom do you know west of the Mississippi?"

Laughing, he said, "I didn't take you seriously." But he hadn't thought of much else since, he admitted silently. It made sense. Perfect sense. They had a lot in common, for one thing. She was a terrific mother, for another. They both wanted what was best for Liam. Granted they didn't know each other well, but…

He'd been telling himself the idea only seemed so appealing because he didn't have the stomach to fight her. Here, now, gazing into her sparkling brown eyes, he admitted the truth: He didn't want to fight her…because he *loved* her.

He couldn't name the precise moment in time when he'd first realized it. That day in his office, when she'd breezed past him, trying like crazy to hide the limp? When he'd called her from New York, and she'd asked all those caring, wifely questions about his well-being? In the diner, when he'd watched her orchestrate the cleanup of the miniflood with calm finesse? Climbing her stairs, when he'd noticed the paintings of her dream house?

What about the horrible accident she'd survived…and everything that had been a consequence of it? And the way she'd defended him to her mother, saying he had a right to see Liam anytime he wanted to because he was *family*.

And her reaction to his kiss…

She'd seemed so tentative at first, so shy and uncertain. He loved the pluck and spirit that had moved her beyond her fear; it was the same drive and determination that had helped her survive an ordeal that might have crushed other women.

He loved the open-armed attitude that had allowed her to welcome an abandoned baby into her heart, into her life, as if he were her own. Loved her levelheaded matter-of-factness, her mind for business, her old-fashioned work ethic…

To put it simply, Connor loved everything about her, from her curly brown hair to her size-five feet. Pride prevented him from admitting it, though, because what if she didn't feel the same way about him? He believed there were just two things he couldn't survive at this point in his life: losing Liam, and losing Jaina.

He could only hope that in time—provided he could convince her to agree to his plan—she'd grow to love him, too.

It wasn't completely implausible, was it? Because throughout history, marriages of convenience had prevented wars, secured fortunes, saved businesses, ended family feuds.

If Jaina could admit she *liked* him now, there was reason to hope that someday she'd love him, too.

Wasn't there?

He looked at her, and his heart lurched with hopeful possibilities. It was certainly worth a try. Besides, he added, marrying her would certainly solve a whole slew of problems.

Connor slipped his hand behind her head, fingers playing in the soft waves at the nape of her neck. He didn't know how long he'd been staring into her eyes, lost in his moment of whimsy. He only knew that he wanted this beautiful, bighearted little woman. Wanted her to be Liam's mother. And if the doctors were mistaken—and he'd move heaven and earth if only he could prove them wrong—he wanted her to be the mother to his children, *their* children. But even if the medical professionals were correct, and Jaina could never have babies of her own, he still wanted to face all the joys and trials of life beside her, forever.

He smiled and, leaning forward, placed a light kiss upon her forehead. She'd closed her eyes as he drew near, and Connor backed away slightly to study her face.

He took note of thick, dark lashes, finely arched brows, the gentle slope of her nose. The fireworks' showy hues illuminated her lovely features, accented the soft, feminine roundness of her cheeks and the delicate point of her chin with shimmering, sparkling light that glowed scarlet to emerald to gold. It was as though the state fair's Strong Man had clutched his chest, tightening and twisting. Oh, how he wanted to wrap his arms around her and never let go.

Her lashes fluttered like miniature wings, sending his heart into a pulsing, pounding rhythm that echoed in his ears. He had snickered at the age-old cliché, borrowed and repeated too many times to count by men for whom poetry seemed like a foreign language, but when at last she opened her eyes and he gazed into the depths of those dazzling spheres, Connor understood for the first time what it meant to feel like a drowning man, caught in the powerful vortex of a whirlpool.

"We're missing the finale," he heard her whisper.

Finale? What did he care about eye-popping, eardrum-splitting thunderflashes? The real rockets were exploding in his heart.

Connor watched her profile, resplendent in the rich, radiant color reflected from the sky. Moments later, he, too, looked toward the heavens, pretending to be engrossed in the percussive display until Liam stirred between them.

The baby sat up and knuckled his eyes. Unfazed by the noise above him, he crawled into Jaina's lap and pointed at the booming bouquets above. Her smile, in response to his delight, was tender and sweet, her voice, in reply to his excited squeals, laughingly lively. She wrapped her arms around him, took his tiny hand and pointed it at the sky. If Connor didn't know better, he would have assumed they'd been together since the baby's birth.

That's where he belonged, Connor told himself.

And if he could find a way, that's where the little boy would stay.

Jaina woke to the trilling of the phone and mumbled a groggy "Hullo" into the mouthpiece.

"Hey. It's Skip. How ya doin'?"

"Fine," she said around a yawn. "And you?"

"Look. I won't beat around the bush. I called to say I'm sorry. I didn't mean to be so hard on you yesterday. Forgive me?"

One hand covering her eyes, Jaina shook her head. "Yeah, I guess so." She stretched, thinking of their argument. Had he called to pick up where he'd left off? Jaina hoped not. She didn't like confrontation, though Skip seemed to handle it fine. But then, she supposed, he was a counselor and trained to handle difficult emotional discussions.

"So," she asked now, stifling another yawn, "where'd you go after you left the diner yesterday?"

"Home." He cleared his throat. "I had some thinking to do."

Jaina chuckled. "Uh-oh. That's not a good sign. I'll bet you have a wicked headache this morning."

"I forgot how mean you can be first thing in the morning."

"If you don't tell me why you're calling at this hour…"

"Hey, be nice. I was up all night, thinking up ways to help you."

"Help me?" She stretched. "Help me what?"

"I kinda hoped you'd invite me over. You know, to discuss it in person."

She sat up, pressed her fingertips against her forehead

and glanced at the clock. "It isn't even five yet." Furrowing her brow, she added, "I thought you liked to sleep till noon on the weekends."

"I'm too excited to sleep. I want to run this idea by you, see if it cuts the mustard."

She swung her legs over the edge of the bed. "I have to shower and dress, feed Liam his breakfast. I suppose you could meet me in the diner in, say, forty-five minutes." She narrowed one eye to ask, "You sure it's not too early? Because I'd hate for you to fall asleep behind the wheel and—"

"Trust me," he insisted, "I'm wide awake."

She'd known him long enough to recognize excitement in his voice when she heard it. "Give me a hint. Did you get a raise? A promotion? Find the girl of your dreams?"

There was a considerable pause before he said, "I'll tell you this. It's about you."

Jaina laughed. "Me? What could I possibly have to do with—"

"Nothing. Everything. I mean…" He exhaled an exasperated sigh.

"You want me to have your favorite breakfast ready when you get here?"

"Are you kiddin'? I haven't had French toast in ages. I'll be there in *half* an hour!" An hour later, Jaina was helping her father unload the morning's delivery of milk when Skip blasted through the diner's back door. He grabbed her hand. "Come with me," he said, panting as if he'd run a marathon.

"Skip," she scolded gently, "I'm right in the middle of—"

"This is important, Jaina." He glanced at the rest of the staff and lowered his voice. "I need to talk to you in private." He gave her arm another tug. "It won't take long. I promise."

Her father gave Skip a quick once-over. "What's got you so riled up this morning, son? I don't think I've seen you this excited since…" His forehead furrowed slightly. "Why, I don't believe I've *ever* seen you this excited."

Jaina wriggled free of Skip's grasp. "I hate to be a party pooper," she said, tapping her watch, "but we open in less than an hour." She looked at Skip. "You've known this bunch of nuts for years. They're family. You can say anything in front of them." She went back to unloading the truck. A touch of impatience rang in her voice when she said, "Skip, would you please just spit it out?"

He took a deep breath. "I'm offering you the opportunity of a lifetime."

"What opportunity?"

"Me!"

"You?" Jaina frowned. "I don't get it."

"How long have we known one another?"

She shrugged. "We met in the third grade. If you don't count all the times Mom and Dad and I were transferred back and forth before we settled down here, I'd say twenty years."

"How'd you put up with him that long?" Eliot wanted to know.

"Sometimes it wasn't easy."

"In all the time we've known one another," Skip asked, "have we ever had a fight?"

They hadn't fought, Jaina admitted, because she'd chosen to overlook his bad behavior. "How 'bout the one we had on the Fourth of July?"

"I don't mean little stuff like that," he interrupted, waving her comment away. "I mean serious disagreements."

She gave the question a moment's thought. She hadn't considered his attitude toward Connor, toward her keeping Liam, "little stuff." Far from it.

But it seemed he'd taken her silence to mean they'd had no serious disagreements. "Of course not. I'm the most even-tempered man you know." Skip began counting on his fingers. "We both like baseball, hate sour pickles, and neither one of us misses the six o'clock news unless there's a national emergency."

Things she had in common with thousands of total strangers, she reflected. "So what's your point?"

"Well, you're not gettin' any younger—" he glanced at the baby "—and the ki…I mean Liam here is in a dandy fix."

Oh, no, she thought, her hard-beating heart rattling her rib cage, *I know where this is going.* Clasping her hands beneath her chin, Jaina closed her eyes. *Dear Lord,* she prayed, *let this be a dream, and when I open my eyes, the alarm will be buzzing….*

Of course he hadn't been serious. How could he *possibly* have been serious? For as long as she'd known him, Skip had been a tease. Maybe this was one of his practical jokes. Jaina hoped so, because if it wasn't…

She'd always tried to be a good friend to Skip, and he'd always been there for her, too. But marriage? To a man she didn't love? That wouldn't be fair to her or to Skip. Out of the question! Yes, she'd been accused of a crime, had served time for it, but Jaina believed that even *she* deserved a better life than that!

Connor couldn't believe his ears. He stopped dead in his tracks just outside the diner's open back door, unconsciously clenching his hands into tight fists, his molars grinding like unoiled gears. *Why, that little twerp is gonna ask Jaina to marry him!*

Even before taking his self-imposed vow to keep a safe distance from women, he'd never had reason to be jealous. Not even when his lady friends played the age-old game of passing off another man as Connor's competition. Each time they tried that tactic, it had failed miserably, and they'd stormed off in a huff when he failed to react to his so-called challenger as they'd hoped he would.

Well, he was jealous now!

He'd never been a violent man, and Jaina's old pal had never done anything to him. So why did he feel an over-whelming urge to punch Skip in the jaw?

Connor had stopped by the diner this morning to propose. He'd been up all night, thinking about how much sense it made. Despite the way she'd laughed off the idea. Perhaps he could convince her that marrying him was the best solution for everyone concerned.

Now he understood why Skip had stomped out of the diner yesterday. He must have interrupted his proposal. If he'd known he had a rival, he might have posed the question sooner. But he couldn't very well second-guess a man he'd never met before, now could he? And besides, Jaina had made a point of telling him that she and Skip had been buddies since childhood.

Well, he didn't like her buddy. Not one bit. He didn't like the way Skip looked at Jaina and he certainly didn't like Skip thinking she might even marry him.

Would Jaina say yes to Skip? he wondered as his heart hammered. Why was it so quiet in there?

"So anyway," Skip continued as if in response to Connor's thought, "I decided that I have what you need—and you're not so bad-lookin' yourself—and since we have so much in common, we could make a go of this marriage thing."

Connor was clenching his jaw so tightly that his teeth ached. As Skip's question reverberated in his head, his fists ached for the same reason. As did every other muscle in his body.

He thought the long, silent pause might kill him. "Why

doesn't she *answer?*" he whispered through his teeth, then offered up a quick and fervent prayer. *Please, God, let her say no.*

If he took half a step to the right, he discovered, he could see their reflections in the door's square, chicken-wired windowpane. He watched Jaina clasp her hands beneath her chin. "Oh, Skip," she said, sounding incredulous.

After a moment, he saw Skip put his hands on Jaina's shoulders. "So when do you want to do it?"

Jaina turned her head, and Connor could have sworn she had seen *his* reflection in the window, for it seemed that she was looking directly into his eyes. It was an eerie, uneasy feeling that set his heart to pounding again. He held his breath.

After another agonizingly long moment, she turned back to Skip. "Well, the paperwork has to be filed first...."

"Paperwork? For the justice of the peace, you mean?"

"To have you committed. You must be crazy if you think I'd marry you!"

Way to go, Jaina! Connor silently rooted.

"Well, seemed like a good idea in the middle of the night," Skip mumbled.

Connor had been up all night, too, imagining the rest of his life with Jaina. But did she consider *him* nothing more than a buddy, as well? Not that he had a problem with that—friendship was one of the most important components of a successful marriage, he believed—but he wanted more, much more, than just being her friend....

His secretary read three, four romance novels a week, and a year or so ago, Connor had picked one up. He'd selected a page at random, thinking he was in for a good chuckle, at least when he reached the parts where the passionate clichés began. But he hadn't so much as cracked a smile as he began to read.

Does she realize what she's *doing?* he wondered. Did she understand that her friendly greeting had done more than invite him inside? Was she aware that, as she plumped sofa cushions and poured hot tea to warm him, make him feel cozy and comfortable, *she had succeeded?* Or had it simply been an accident of fate, some curious coincidence, that her glittering eyes and lovely smile told him he'd always be welcome, wanted, accepted here, *despite* his unhappy past?

Connor had turned the page, uncomfortable with the fact that he had identified so closely with the story's hero. Perhaps a different passage would inspire the hearty laugh he'd expected.

It was more, so much more than his lips pressed to hers. It seemed they'd become one living, breathing being, united in heart and mind and soul by a thing as innocent as a kiss. She knew, as she stood in the protective circle of his embrace, that near him was where she wanted to spend the rest of her days. Because she also knew, as his hard-pounding heart thrummed against her, that he was a man capable of living and loving to the fullest…to the end.

He wanted to make Jaina feel like that, wanted to be the one who put stars in her eyes, caused her heart to beat hard and fast, and made her ache with yearning when he was out of sight.

"Let me know when you come to your senses," Skip said, heading for the door. "But then, I won't hold my breath…all things considered."

And if Jaina will marry me, I'll be shouting from the rooftops, Connor thought.

"But you haven't had your French toast," Rita pointed out.

"I guess I'm not hungry after all," Skip replied in a disappointed tone. "Thanks anyway, Rita."

Connor recognized the defeated tone in Skip's voice and even felt a bit of sympathy for the guy. Missing out on marrying Jaina was truly a loss. But rather than offer his condolences, Connor knew he'd better beat it.

He took one more longing look at Jaina's reflection in the window of the diner's back door. Even the wavy glass couldn't mar her sweet beauty. Quietly, he walked the block and a half to the parking lot where he'd left his car. In an hour or so, he'd return, broach the subject of marriage again.

And again and again, until she said, "Yes."

Besides she'd been the first one to bring up the subject, he reminded himself. She'd claimed it had been a joke, that she'd been teasing. But what was that lesson he'd learned in Psych 101? "There's a bit of truth in every joke."

He knew full well it might be a mistake to hang all his hopes on one lesson, learned so long ago. Revving the engine, he steered the sports car onto Route 40. As he merged into traffic, Connor considered all the pluses of his plan: Liam would have two parents, Jaina would have the baby *and* the house she'd always dreamed of, and he'd have the family he'd always wanted.

Jaina had been reading food orders for so long, it was second nature to her now. She hustled back and forth in the kitchen, helping Eliot fill platters and plates.

But her mind was not on her work.

She couldn't remember a time when she felt more confused. And there wasn't a soul she could discuss the dilemma with, now that Granny Chandelle was gone.

She had questioned herself intensively about this matter

of falling so quickly in love with Connor Buchanan.
Granny had always said, "Give a new love at least four
seasons, so you can test its durability." Oh, to have the
luxury of twelve leisurely months to define her feelings
for Liam's uncle. Did she feel this way *because* he was
related to the baby? Or were her feelings more personal
than that?

She'd left his office that first day thinking he was a nice
enough guy; he'd certainly been considerate when she'd
nearly blacked out. Still, he'd seemed indifferent to Liam's
needs, disinterested in how his own my-way-or-no-way
mind-set might affect Kirstie. Nice, yes, but opinionated
and stubborn, too.

Since then, she'd drastically altered her opinion. Now
Jaina saw him as an unbiased, flexible, caring man. If his
warm, devoted behavior with Liam didn't make him father
material, she didn't know what did. And surely the fact
that he refused to prosecute the woman who'd been ha-
rassing him was more proof what kind of man he was.

Certainly he could afford to live on some exclusive
Nob Hill, in an impressive, contemporary style of house,
with wide expanses of glass and filled with costly, one-of-
a-kind furnishings. Instead, he'd purchased a dilapidated
Victorian on the outskirts of town and refurbished it with
his own two hands.

When he'd given her what he called The Grand Tour
of the house, Connor explained how he'd sanded and refinished every window and door frame, every ceiling
molding, every chair rail and panel of wainscoting. He
showed her the wide-planked pine floors he'd preserved
along with the original wood dowels that held them in
place. She'd done enough to her apartment to know it had
been painstaking, time-consuming work. She had loved
every backbreaking, fingernail-chipping moment of it; he
seemed to have enjoyed it, too.

His pride and joy, he'd admitted, was the small sunporch, added when he'd finished with the inside, so that after a harrowing day at the office, he could sit and stare into the woods along the banks of the Patapsco River.

Connor wasn't at all stuffy and pretentious, as she'd expected him to be. He'd worn sneakers and well-worn jeans to the Fourth of July parade...and a T-shirt that read "My golf score would be great...if I was bowling." And when she'd learned that he taught law part-time at the University of Baltimore, she'd remarked, "A professor...I'm impressed."

"Don't be," he'd cautioned, a sly grin on his face. "The hours are terrible and the money stinks."

"Then why do you do it?"

His smile had softened and he'd said, "Doesn't happen as often as I'd like, but once in a while, I get a student who loves the law as much as I do." He'd shrugged. "Those are the ones who'll help me dispel the idea that lawyers are like vultures, feeding off the misery of others."

She'd smiled at that. "You don't strike me as the type who pays much mind to the opinions of others."

His blue eyes had widened and his brows had lifted, giving him an innocent, little-boy look. "Of course I care," he'd said. "At least...I care what *some* people think of me."

His intense scrutiny had unnerved her, so she'd focused on the plaques and certificates he'd hung in a dark hallway. "What are these?"

Normally, he was proud of his efforts, but somehow Jaina taking notice rattled him. She always rattled him.

Even in the dim light, she could tell her question had flustered him. He'd stammered and stuttered like a teenager on his first date, and if the light had been better, she was sure she'd have seen him blush like a schoolboy. "Oh, those," he'd said. "I've been working with the city's Stamp Out Illiteracy project for years."

Jaina pictured the baseball player who'd started the program; Connor resembled the sports hero even more than the star's younger brother who played for the same team. Tall and well built, Connor's thick-muscled shoulders and biceps were those of an athlete. She wondered what sports he might have played in high school and college. Quarterback? He was certainly big enough, smart enough. Goalie on a soccer team? He had the strength and agility.

She wondered what his favorite subjects had been. Math and science, maybe. He was such a quick thinker. She could easily see him as president of the student council, standing at the podium introducing festivities at an assembly. Surely *he* hadn't been the type whose shyness kept him from volunteering.

Or had it?

She didn't like admitting it—given the fact that she had actually wanted to say "Yes!" when he'd brought up the subject of marriage—but Jaina knew very little about Connor Buchanan. What kind of people had raised him? Had he ever been married, and if so, had it ended because he'd been widowed…or divorced? Was he a churchgoer? Could he try to be?

What Jaina did know about him, she liked.

He craved order in his life. What more proof of that did she need than the way he'd organized his kitchen cabinets: mugs on one shelf, tumblers on another; pots and pans stacked neatly, each with its own lid upside down inside it; spices and canned goods, like toy soldiers standing at attention, had been arranged in neat, alphabetical rows.

He was not a bully, as evidenced by the way he'd reacted to the Chili Pot flood. Finding Liam in the sudsy water had upset him, and he'd said so in a firm yet calm voice.

He'd treated her so gently that day in his office. Held

Liam with such tenderness. Spoke to her parents with respect, despite the fact that Rita resented him and made no secret of it.

And that kiss in his kitchen…

She'd been dreaming about it off and on for nearly a week now. The way he'd wrapped her in his arms had made her feel treasured, had awakened emotions she hadn't known possible.

One of the many things that stood out in her mind was the discussion they'd had about her limp. They'd barely gotten the blanket spread on the ground when he'd asked, "Do you mind if I ask you a personal question?"

"How can I answer that until I've heard the question?" she'd teased.

"You have a point," he'd agreed. "Let me preface it, then, by saying if it makes you in the least uncomfortable, feel free to tell me to buzz off, take a flying leap."

What could be so important, so serious, she'd wondered, that Connor had felt it necessary to apologize *before* he'd asked the question? "I might be forced to say mind your own business," she'd told him. "But buzz off? Take a flying leap? I'm afraid that just isn't my style."

Smiling, he'd gently deposited Liam in the center of the blanket, then sat down beside him. "Does your leg hurt very much?"

Only then did she understand. He wanted to know if she limped because each step was painful for her, or if the accident had caused so much bone and tissue damage that she couldn't walk any other way.

"The doctors were forced to remove a part of my thigh bone," she explained matter-of-factly. "It shortened my leg by nearly an inch." She paused to read his face. Satisfied he didn't feel sorry for her, Jaina continued. "Sometimes it bothers me a bit, but no more, I imagine, than anyone else if they've been on their feet too long."

"Good. I'd hate to think that accident had left you with pain to bear, too."

Too? she wondered.

"I mean," he quickly inserted, "you had so much else to contend with because of that…"

His gentle expression hardened, and hot fury blazed in his eyes. Jaina believed he must have read her face, seen the stunned reaction to his anger there, because he shook his head.

"Sorry," he said. "Do you get a lot of dimwits asking questions about it, or am I the first?"

"Children ask me about it all the time. It's refreshing, really, how open and honest they are. I wish grown-ups would ask how it happened," she admitted. "It'd be so much easier to take than their pitying stares."

"So I take it you don't think I'm *not* a dimwit," he said, chuckling. "I'm a *childlike* dimwit."

There's nothing dim about you, Connor Buchanan, she wanted to say. *Not your eyes, or your smile, or your charming wit.*

"Truth is," he said, "it's the only proof I have that you're human. Though I still think you're way too perfect for the likes of me." He smiled, then said in a halting voice, "So what's it going to be, Jaina? Are you going to marry me or not?"

"You're joking again, right?"

"I'm completely serious," he assured her. "But don't worry. You needn't answer right now. Give it some thought. I think you'll see it's the best solution for everyone."

She hadn't known what to say in response to that, and so she'd asked him to please pass her a soda from the plastic cooler they'd brought along.

For the rest of the day—and night—Jaina could think of little else. Connor had called his proposal a solution, but how could it be?

He knew everything there was to know about her, from the accident that left her scarred and, in all likelihood, barren, to the charges that had landed her in jail. He knew every detail, good *and* bad…

Considering all that, could he possibly want to marry her?

Besides, he didn't need Jaina on his side to adopt Liam. In fact, having her there might hurt his case. So why would he ask her to become his wife? The question rumbled in her head until her heart was reverberating with it, too.

Could it be that he loves you?

Instinctively, she tried to dismiss the idea as ridiculous. Silly. Too outrageous for further consideration. Just as immediately, it was back, bigger and more powerful than ever. She smiled slightly, considering the possibility that a man like Connor Buchanan—handsome, intelligent, successful, highly respected in the community and comfortably off financially—would have more than a passing interest in a woman who only had down-to-earth parents and an assortment of friends many would consider less than socially acceptable.

Not that she was ashamed of them. Jaina would have held any of them up for comparison against the so-called high-and-mighty muckety-mucks of the social scene. They had made some mistakes, but they'd learned from them and were God-fearing Christians, good to the bone. Still, he was obviously not interested in her because of her family background.

Or was he?

He as much as said he admired her work ethic. And he *did* say he liked the way she took care of Liam. She grinned, thinking, *He sure doesn't have any complaints about the way you kiss.* But then, it wasn't really fair to take credit for that since her behavior was nothing more than a reaction to *him.*

Until Liam came into her life, bringing with him his handsome relative, Jaina had resigned herself to living the rest of her life alone. Even if Connor did not love—would *never* truly love her—surely a marriage founded on mutual respect, affection and their love for Liam beat the prospect of life alone, hands down? Besides, being perfectly honest with herself, Jaina knew now that if Connor took Liam from her she would miss *both* of them.

Chapter Nine

When Pearl informed Connor that Judge Thompson's secretary had lost his petition for adoption he slammed down the phone. He could have Pearl run off another copy, but it was too late to get Judge Thompson's signature now. The old fellow and his wife would be leaving for Europe this afternoon to celebrate their fiftieth anniversary.

Fifty years with the same woman. Connor found it hard to believe any man could put up with a woman that long if they were all like Thompson's secretary. And they surely all *seemed* to be.

Well, that wasn't entirely true. There was Jaina….

His own parents had stayed together until their deaths, but he doubted they'd been happy in their nearly thirty-year marriage. Quite the contrary. They tolerated each other, and it was obvious to anyone with eyes and ears. Why couldn't they have been more like the Thompsons? Even a cynic like Connor could see that those two old people loved each other like crazy, and after half a century together yet!

Would he be a cynic still if he had a woman like Jaina at his side? If he had someone like her encouraging him, supporting his decisions, being a true helpmeet?

Connor blinked and forced himself to focus on the matter at hand. He glanced at his watch. It wasn't even eleven yet. He'd done the elderly gent a wagonload of favors; surely the man wouldn't object if Connor dropped by to get the required signature. He had to at least give it a try.

He depressed the intercom button on his phone. "Pearl…you saved my adoption petition on disk, didn't you?"

"Course I did."

"Change it to today's date, will you? And print out another copy."

"Don't worry, boss," she replied breezily. "I'll get right on it."

She had the document ready for his approval in less than five minutes. And five minutes after that, Connor was in his car, headed for the judge's house.

John Thompson lived in an old, established community on the outskirts of town. Elegant and stately, his house was emblematic of his lifestyle, complete with wrought-iron gates, manicured lawns, ornate flower beds. Connor parked in the circular redbrick driveway and headed for the front entrance.

"Well, if it isn't Connor Buchanan."

A quick look around told Connor the source of the deep baritone had originated from the rose garden. "Judge Thompson," he said, smiling and extending his hand. "All set for your trip?"

"I should hope so," the older man said, stuffing his pruning shears into a back jeans pocket. In a conspiratorial whisper, he added, "Millicent has had this thing planned for a decade!" Pumping Connor's arm vigorously, he said, "Good to see you, son. What brings you here?"

Connor held up the manila envelope that bore his petition for adoption. "I need your signature on this. I wouldn't bother you at home…especially not today…but…"

The judge ran a hand through his thick white hair. "C'mon, let's step inside, get out of this heat," he suggested.

As he followed Thompson into the house, Connor had to admit that the elderly fellow amazed him. Pushing eighty, the judge walked ramrod straight and quick as a man of forty. In every courtroom in the tristate area, he'd earned a reputation for having a mind sharper than a new-honed blade, and it didn't appear to be growing any duller with age. Connor had heard it said that what a man becomes in his old age is determined by the wife he'd chosen when he was young. If there was any truth to the old adage, Judge Thompson had chosen well.

"Now then," Thompson said once they'd settled in the library, "what can I get you? A glass of lemonade? Some iced tea?"

"Nothing, thanks." He slid the petition from the envelope. "I know you're busy, getting ready for the—"

"Nonsense," the judge interrupted, smiling. "There's nothing to do but call a taxi to take us to the airport." He held a forefinger in the air. "You're forgetting…I'm married to a woman who believes organization and planning are next to Godliness!" He clapped his hands together once. "Well, son," he said, settling into a buttery black leather recliner, "what can I do for you?"

"This petition for adoption we discussed last week…"

Thompson's brow furrowed. "It isn't like you, Buchanan, to say you're going to get right on something and then procrastinate. Especially something as important as—"

"You don't have to tell me. Your Mrs. Miller has already raked me over the coals for my shoddy work."

He held up a hand as if to silence Connor. "*My* Mrs. Miller? She doesn't get upset over… Wait. Let me guess. Dorothy misplaced it, didn't she?"

Connor averted his gaze.

And the judge sighed. "She means well, but I'm afraid Dorothy isn't the crackerjack secretary yours is." He relieved Connor of the envelope. "So tell me, how'd you get such a gem, if you don't mind my asking?"

"Just lucky, I guess."

"Please, please, take a load off," Thompson insisted, pointing at a matching recliner. Settling gold-framed half glasses on his patrician nose, he began perusing the document. "You're still determined to go ahead with these proceedings, I see."

"Yessir, I am." Connor's brows drew together slightly. "You don't agree?"

"I wouldn't say that. But I've done a bit of digging myself," he said as he thumbed through the papers. "This Chandelle woman who has your great-nephew… She's got quite a history, doesn't she?"

Connor swallowed. "Well, that's the way it appears at first glance, but…"

Thompson peered over his spectacles to say, "If the D.A. had brought a case like hers before my bench, I'd have laughed him out of the courtroom. It's as obvious as the nose on my face that the man was stockpiling guilty pleas to secure his own job." Thompson shook his head. "I hate to see injustice done. You'd think after all these years, I'd be inured to it, wouldn't you?"

Thompson had earned a reputation for being a straight shooter. It wasn't easy being forthright and honest in a world of loopholes and nepotism; if Connor could retire with a record like the judge's, he'd consider himself fortunate.

Thompson sat taller in his chair, aiming his clear blue gaze directly at Connor. "Are you a God-fearing man, Buchanan?"

The question rocked him. "Why, yes, I am. Why do you ask?"

"Most natural question in the world," the other man observed, "considering what you're proposing to do."

Connor leaned forward and rested his elbows on his knees. Smiling slightly, he said, "You're talking to a thickheaded Irishman, Judge. It might seem the most natural question in the world to you, but I don't have a clue what you're talking about."

"Thickheaded, my foot!" Thompson's gruff snort was quickly swallowed up by the carpeting and draperies in the well-appointed room. "I saw your bar exam scores. You were top of the class in every school you attended. Don't get me wrong. I find your humility charming. It's like my old grampa used to say, 'Woe to those who are wise in their own eyes and shrewd in their own sight.'"

"I prefer Proverbs myself," Connor said. "'Knowledge is a precious jewel.'"

Thompson nodded. "*Hundreds* of lawyers have stood in front of my bench over the years, and in my opinion, only a handful of 'em will ever amount to anything worthwhile. You know why?"

Connor shook his head.

"'Cause most of 'em are in it for the money. They don't love the *law,* they love what it'll *do* for 'em." He waved the paperwork under Connor's nose. "You believe in something far more powerful than the almighty dollar. I spotted that right off. It's just one of the reasons I've always liked you, Buchanan."

Chuckling, Connor said good-naturedly, "Coulda fooled me. Sometimes I thought if you'd been allowed to keep a loaded gun up there on that bench, you'd have used it…on *me!*"

The judge laughed. "I admit I was hard on you. But I was testing your mettle." One snow-white brow rose high on his wrinkled forehead. "You passed with flying colors, son. Those others…" His face contorted as if he'd inhaled an unpleasant odor. "You're in a league of your own."

The compliment might not have affected him had it come from someone he respected less. But coming from Judge Thompson, it was high praise indeed. Connor felt the heat of a blush creeping into his cheeks.

"If you're a God-fearing man, why are you going about this the hard way?"

"The hard...?"

"Why not just put it in God's capable hands. See what He wants you to do with it?"

Connor shrugged. "I'm ashamed to say I never gave it a thought."

"You're probably wondering what any of that has to do with your petition here, aren't you?"

"Well, frankly, yes."

"As I said, after you spoke to me about your great-nephew, I took it upon myself to do some checking on this young lady. Millicent and I have taken a few meals in her diner since then, I'll have you know. Fine woman, that Miss Chandelle. Hard worker, bright, good-natured..." He winked mischievously. "And mighty easy on a man's eyes, wouldn't you say?"

"I'd be a liar if I denied it."

"And a fool to boot!" The old man's laughter bounced off every wall in the room. Suddenly, the judge was all business. "Now give it to me straight, son," he said, giving the petition a shake. "What's this really all about?"

"I want to adopt the boy," Connor said.

"That's nonsense!"

Connor swallowed. He wished now he'd taken the judge up on his offer of a soft drink because his throat was as dry as sand. "I beg your pardon?"

"Don't beg *my* pardon. Beg that lovely young woman's! She's doing a Grade A job taking care of that youngster. I've seen it with my own eyes."

"But…but he's *my* nephew, my blood kin."

"No one's disputing that. I'm just remembering how well she handled it when her diner turned into a three-ring circus. Water everywhere…people falling on their posteriors… She'd make a magnificent mother if—"

"You were there?"

"You seem surprised." He slapped his knee. "Well, here's something else that'll surprise you even more. I was in The Judge's Bench recently, so I've seen the two of you together more than once. You're in love with that pretty little gal. Not that I blame you…."

Were his feelings for Jaina that obvious? Connor wondered.

"I'm sure you've heard the old saying, 'You can't have your cake and eat it, too.'"

Connor nodded.

"Marry that girl and you *can.* You'll have her and the boy, as well!"

"So you aren't going to sign the petition?"

"Course I am. You want to be the boy's father legally, don't you?"

Another nod.

"Then you'll need all the *i*'s dotted, all the *t*'s crossed." He strode to his desk, withdrew a gold pen from a side drawer and scrawled his name on the last page of the document. "Done! Now it only needs to be filed with the county records office, and providing there's no one who objects," he said, winking again, "you'll officially be a family man."

Thompson walked around to the front of the desk and handed the pages back to Connor. "Course, if you ask me, you're not really a family man until you have a wife to go with that youngster."

Connor slid the petition back into its envelope. "I don't know how to thank—"

"How old are you, son?" the older man asked, still towering over Connor.

He cocked a brow. What could his age possibly have to do with anything? "I'll be thirty-five in a few weeks."

The judge harrumphed. "Land's sake," he said, shaking his head, "I was married with four kids by that time. What in the world are you waiting for?" Thompson laid a fatherly hand on Connor's shoulder as the two men walked side by side into the sunny foyer. "They say free advice is worth what it costs you, but I'm going to give you some anyway."

Connor grinned. "I'd be honored to take it."

"The right woman only comes along once in a man's lifetime. If you let her get away, you'll regret it for the rest of your days." The judge opened the door. "Millicent and I will be back in early September. Give me a call. You can fill me in on the details."

Connor wished him a safe flight and a pleasant trip, then held up the envelope. "I don't know how to thank you."

Thompson gave one last wink. "By inviting me to the wedding so I can dance with the bride," he said, and closed the door.

As he drove away from the impressive estate, Connor couldn't get Thompson's words out of his mind. The judge had been right; life was fraught with regrets. Why add another to the already too-long list?

As soon as the adoption papers were filed, he'd visit Jaina, tell her exactly how he felt. Hopefully, she'd agree with him and say yes when he popped the question.

Jaina hadn't been in when he stopped by, so Connor asked Rita's permission to take Liam for a drive in the country. Had it been up to her alone, the answer would have been a terse no. Thankfully, Ray had been there, too.

Connor decided to stop off at the office first, to file his copies of the paperwork…and to show Liam off to Pearl. He heard the music even before the elevator doors opened. Standing in the waiting room, he teased, "You're not going deaf on me, are you?"

"Course not," she called from somewhere in his office.

"Then why is the radio turned up so loud?"

"Can't hear it when I'm in here. Besides, that song the DJ is playing is one of my all-time favorites. Has been for years."

Until that moment, Connor had only been half listening to it. Something about it sounded strikingly familiar. "Nice," he admitted, nodding as he sat on the couch across from Pearl's desk, "real nice."

Liam bounced up and down on his knee. "Mmumm-mmumm," he said excitedly, pointing to the stereo. "Mmumm-mmumm?"

He looked into the boy's eyes. O'Dell had told him she'd had one hit record. Could this be it, and had Liam recognized her voice?

"In your eyes, love," the singer crooned, "I see my future. When you smile, my whole world is at peace. When that old world starts closin' in around me…wrap your lovin' arms 'round me…"

It was Jaina all right. Either that, or there were two women in America who had deep, sultry voices. If he remembered correctly, she'd written the song herself.

"Kiss me soft, love, and let me hear you sigh. Only in your arms, love, do I feel free…so wrap your lovin' arms 'round me…"

Had she written it for that no-account Bill Isaacs? A surge of jealousy sizzled through him. Connor hoped not because, someday, he wanted her to sing it for *him*.

"I will love you until the day I die. I'll never leave you, never make you cry. I've just one dream for all eternity… that you'll wrap your lovin' arms 'round me…that you'll wrap your lovin' arms 'round me…"

Pearl bustled into the room, dusting the palms of her hands together. With a flick of her wrist, she turned off the stereo.

"No…don't," Connor said.

"The song was over anyway." She walked closer, then bent over slightly and rested her hands on her knees. "Well, what have we here?" she cooed to Liam. "I haven't seen you for such a long time, little fella. Lookin' good. Real good." Gently, Pearl touched the tip of his nose. "Do you have any idea the effect you've had on your Uncle Connor?"

One finger in his mouth, Liam peered up at her through long lashes and grinned flirtatiously.

"You've turned a grumpy old meanie into a young, happy man, that's what."

For the second time that day, a secretary had referred to him as mean. He couldn't have been that bad…could he? "Liam and I are going to take a ride in the country," he announced. "Soon as I stop by the house and change into jeans, I'm going over to Marriotsville Road to check out those horses for sale."

Pearl straightened up and crossed her arms in front of her. "You have the perfect place for them. All those rolling acres…that big red barn… It'll look like a picture postcard with a couple of beautiful horses grazing in the corral."

The only reason he'd considered the idea at all was because Jaina had told him in the parking lot after their lunch that she loved to ride. But he couldn't very well admit that to Pearl. If he did, her romantic matchmaking side would never let him hear the end of it. Connor was contemplating what he *would* say when the ringing phone rescued him.

"Mr. Buchanan's office. May I help you?" Pearl nodded, held one hand over the mouthpiece. "It's Mr. O'Dell," she whispered. And making a silly face at Liam, she added, "You want me to get a number? Tell him you'll call him back?"

The baby giggled at her, and Connor kissed his cheek. "Nah, I'll take it. O'Dell is usually to the point." He stood and handed Liam to her. "You don't mind, do you?"

Beaming, Pearl cuddled the baby to her ample bosom. "Mind? I should say not!" She pulled open a desk drawer as Connor headed for his office. "Look what your old Auntie Pearl has for you," she cooed, handing him a tea biscuit.

"Not too much junk food now," he said, grinning.

She never took her eyes from the baby as she waved his comment away.

He picked up his phone. "Hey, O'Dell," Connor said. "What's up?"

"Good news, bad news."

Connor sighed deeply. "Okay, let me have it."

"Good news first this time. I found your niece."

"Kirstie? Where?"

"Small hospital outside of Chicago."

"Have you seen her?"

"Yeah…that's the bad news."

"Not good, huh?"

"'Fraid not. You want to see her, better get here fast."

Connor felt his heart sinking as he jotted down the address and phone number of the hospital. "I'll be on the next flight to O'Hare. Can you meet me?"

"Sure thing. Just let me know when and where. And Connor?"

"Yeah?"

The man hesitated. "Never mind. Just hurry up, all right?"

They hung up simultaneously. "Pearl," Connor said,

stuffing the message slip into the breast pocket of his suit, "I need to be on the next plane to Chicago."

She stopped bouncing the baby on her knee. "But…but you have appointments up to here, both in the office and in court, and—"

"Make my apologies and reschedule what you can."

"O'Dell found your niece?" she asked, standing.

Connor nodded. "She doesn't have long." She handed Liam back to his uncle and riffled through her Rolodex. While she was dialing the airline, he said, "Reserve two seats."

"Two?"

"One for me, one for my boy here."

Smiling, she nodded understandingly.

"There's a plane leaving BWI in an hour," she said a few minutes later. "You might want to stop by your house and—"

"No time for that," he said, hoisting Liam up. "I'll stop at the store for some necessities. Whatever else we need I'll buy when we get there." Then, "Will you—"

"I'll call O'Dell, give him the flight number and arrival time. I'll call Jaina, too."

Connor gave Pearl a small peck on the cheek. "Thanks."

She pressed her fingertips to the spot he'd kissed. "For what?"

"For being a gem."

He left her there, blushing and looking puzzled, and headed straight for the airport.

"What do you mean, he came and took him away?" Jaina's heart beat double time as she slumped onto the padded seat of a booth.

"I mean," Rita said, "he said he was going to take him for a drive in the country. He promised to have him back by six."

Jaina glanced at the antique grandfather clock in the corner of the diner. Any minute now, it would strike eight. "Maybe they got hung up in traffic. You know how crazy that beltway can be on a Friday night."

"Nonsense," Rita said. "He's taken him away, and I don't think he'll be back."

"Have you called his house?"

"No."

Jaina hurried to the phone behind the counter and dialed Connor's home number. The answering machine picked up, and she left a brief message.

"He can be a real workaholic. Maybe he stopped by his office," she said, thinking aloud, "to pick something up, or drop something off, or—" Again, a machine intercepted her call. She hung up quietly and, leaning both elbows on the counter, hid her face in her hands. "I hope there hasn't been an accident." Horrible as the thought was, it seemed almost preferable to the alternative.

"He isn't home and he isn't in his office and there hasn't been an accident. I think you should call the police," Rita said, "because that no-good lawyer has run off with Liam!"

"Mother," Ray said, "calm down now. You know that it isn't good for you to get so excited."

"Well, pardon me all the way to town and back," Rita fumed, "for having a normal human reaction to this fiasco."

"Mom," Jaina said softly, "Dad's right. I can't believe Connor would…that he'd just *leave* without a word. I'm sure there's a reasonable explanation."

"You could be right, but I don't think so."

It wasn't like Rita to be so pessimistic. Jaina recalled the night Kirstie had left Liam in their care, when her mother had accused *her* of being cynical. *Think positively,* she told herself. *Anything else is unacceptable, intol-*

erable. Since her accident, it had been *Jaina's* nature to be distrustful. How many times had Rita called her a gloomy Gus, a doubting Thomas? And how many times had she excused her own negative behavior by saying that people deserved her cynicism?

Too many to count.

But Liam had changed all that.

Liam…and his uncle….

She refused to believe Connor had simply waltzed in and taken the boy away with a promise to return if he had no intention of doing so. There was a reasonable explanation for his sudden disappearance. There *had* to be.

Connor *couldn't* have done anything as despicably thoughtless as stealing Liam.

Because if he could, it meant she'd let herself fall in love with the wrong man…again.

Connor had never been so well looked after during a flight in his life. He knew without a doubt he had Liam to thank for the nonstop service. Even before the plane got off the ground in Baltimore, the baby had won the hearts of all the flight attendants. Upon their arrival in Chicago, one pressed a colorful sticker of gold wings to his shirt, while another propped a tiny cap bearing the airline's insignia onto his head.

As promised, O'Dell was waiting for him at the gate and drove him to the hospital. He didn't waste a moment explaining the situation to the nurse on duty, who insisted on taking care of Liam while Connor spoke with Kirstie's doctor.

Dr. Ginnan quickly updated Connor on her condition, explaining the type of cancer that was draining the life away from her.

"How long does she have?"

"Couple of days, a week at the outside."

"Is she in pain?"

"Well, we have her on a painkiller IV. She can dose herself any time she feels the need."

"That doesn't answer my question, Doc."

The physician sat back, folded his hands atop his abdomen. "Kirstie seems determined to tough this thing out." He removed his eyeglasses and placed them on the desk. "May I ask you a question, Mr. Buchanan?"

Connor nodded.

"She told us she had no family, made it clear she didn't want anyone notified of her condition. How did you find out she was with us?"

"She left her son with…" Connor did *not* want Dr. Ginnan getting the impression that his niece was a flighty girl, too immature to be a good mother. He had two heartrending notes to prove the contrary. "Kirstie left Liam with a friend who contacted me, and…" He shrugged. "I didn't want her spending her last days alone, so I hired a detective to find her."

The doctor pursed his lips and nodded thoughtfully. "I see," he said. He shoved back his chair and stood. "I'll let you see her now. Perhaps you'll be able to convince her to take advantage of the medications. There's really no sense in her suffering."

Connor stood. "Will we—her son and I—have unlimited access to her room?"

"Naturally. Have you seen her?"

"No. Not yet."

"Then let me warn you. She's very weak and pale, and she's lost a lot of weight."

On the way, Ginnan stopped at the nurses' station so that Connor could retrieve Liam, then led the way down a long, polished corridor.

It was quiet inside, so hushed that it reminded Connor of an empty church. After the warnings from O'Dell and the doctor, Connor had expected his niece to be attached to numerous monitors and feeding tubes. Instead, there was one plastic bag hanging from a tall metal stand beside her bed.

"Kirstie," the doctor said softly, laying a hand on her shoulder, "there's someone here to see you."

She saw Liam first, and her eyes instantly filled with unshed tears. Her pale cheeks flushed with sudden color, and smiling, she held out trembling arms. Connor gently deposited the baby beside her.

"Mmumm-mmumm." He seemed to sense that he must be gentle, and snuggled quietly up to her.

"Oh, sweetie, I can't believe you're here. Let Mommy look at you…." She kissed his cheeks, his forehead, his chin. "You're beautiful! I was right, Jaina is taking good care of you, isn't she?"

Jaina. Oh, how Connor suddenly wished she were here, her remarkably strong, peaceful presence bolstering him.

Only then did Kirstie seem aware that she and Liam were not alone in the room. "Uncle Connor?"

The doctor gave him a polite little nod of his head and quietly stepped out of the room.

"How did you know who I was?"

"I'd know you anywhere. Mom described you to me ten thousand times." She emitted a weak laugh. "I have to admit you're even more handsome than she said."

Connor scooted the bedside chair nearer and sat beside her.

"How did you find me?"

"I hired a private detective."

"That was *you?* I thought…I thought it was Jaina."

"I know. She showed me the letters."

"You and Jaina…you've met?"

Connor explained how, the day after Kirstie had disappeared, Jaina had come to his office. "I'm so sorry you overheard that argument. I wish you had stuck around, told me to my face what a mean old grouch I am."

Another feeble laugh.

"If you had," he continued, "I would have kept you with me, seen to it you had only the best care."

"They've been taking good care of me here."

"I see you have a morphine drip," he said, nodding toward the bag. "Do you use it often?"

"So Dr. Ginnan put you to work, too, did he?"

"I'm afraid I don't—"

"He wants you to talk me into using the morphine, right?"

She seemed far too perceptive for one so young, Connor thought.

Kirstie wrinkled her nose. "I don't like the way it makes me feel, all groggy and thickheaded. I want to be aware that I'm alive, right up to the last minute." She hugged Liam a little tighter. "Especially now."

"But, honey," he urged, his fingers gently caressing her forearm, "if you're in pain…"

"I'm fine." She met his eyes to add, "I'm sorry for acting like a spoiled brat that day…running away from your office like a big scaredy-cat. I should have known you weren't as mean as you sounded."

Connor couldn't help but chuckle at that. "You know, this is the third time today that women have told me I'm nasty, mean, grouchy, grumpy."

"Pity you're so tall…"

Still smiling, he rumpled his brow.

"…because if we could find a theater where they're doing *Snow White,* you could play the part of all seven dwarfs!"

Laughing, he shook his head. "My, but you're a lot like your mother."

"That's the nicest thing you could have said to me. She was a wonderful woman."

He wanted to talk about Susan. Wanted to ask the questions that had been stewing in his brain since the day she'd left home. But these were Kirstie's last hours.

"She always felt bad about the way she left. But she was afraid that if she contacted you, your parents would make your life miserable."

"That's what I figured. Sometimes," he said, "I wish she'd been more selfish."

"Why?"

"If she wasn't always worrying about me, maybe she'd have gotten in touch. It would have been worth a little aggravation from the folks just to know she was all right."

"She'd never have done that. Mom said if you ever found out where she was, you'd come to her. She couldn't let you do that."

The conversation was wearing the poor girl out. Her whispery, raspy voice proved it. "Shhh, sweetie," he said gently. "Why not take a little nap and—"

"I have one, maybe two days left on this earth. Please don't ask me to sleep away my last hours."

He swallowed, biting back the tears that stung his eyes. She laid a cool hand on his. "Mom said if you had come to Chicago, you wouldn't have gone on to college, or law school, or—"

"She knew about that?" he asked, incredulous. "How?"

Kirstie gave him a knowing grin. "She kept tabs on you for years. Remember Miss Bonita?"

A soft smile creased Connor's face. "The old lady who lived next door? If it hadn't been for her, your mother and I might have gone stark raving mad."

"She sent us articles and…and things."

He remembered the way the old woman had insinuated herself into so many family functions, pretending to be interested in his parents' religious activities. She'd attended his high school and college graduations. Had baked him chocolate chip cookies when he passed the bar exam. Quilted him a blanket when he got his first apartment.

"She never forgave them, you know."

"Our folks?"

Kirstie nodded. "She blamed them for your divorce. Said if they'd been good Christian parents like they pretended to be, they never would have let you marry that gold digger who broke your heart."

Connor snickered a bit at that. "Gold digger. I never thought of Miriam in quite that way before." He was having a hard time dealing with the fact that Susan had known so much about his life, yet he'd known next to nothing about hers.

He felt uncertain how to respond to this girl-woman. He'd come here to comfort her, not the other way around.

"Are you curious about how she died?"

Curious? Why, he was nearly *exploding* with the need to know. But he dared not admit it because Kirstie's worn-out body needed rest.

"She earned her living modeling. For catalog companies, for local store brochures. She even made a few commercials. Mom felt it was important to stay trim, especially as she got older, to stay ahead of the competition, you know? So her doctor prescribed a drug. She took it every day…." Her voice trailed off as she stared at some unseen spot across the room. "She did a lot of damage to her heart…"

Connor laid a finger over her lips. Certainly she didn't need to say it any more than he didn't need to hear it. The image of his dear Susan, wasting away, nearly broke his heart.

Kirstie mustered enough strength to push his hand away. "She died when I was twelve."

Ever so gently, he lifted her hand, pressed it to his lips. "If you knew where to find me, Kirstie, why didn't you call? I would have—"

"All I knew about you was what I'd heard…I thought you'd be too busy and too important to have time for me. And, I was afraid." Kirstie gave him an unsteady, mischievous grin. "What a little chicken, huh?"

He kissed her hand again, then tenderly brushed the bangs from her forehead. "Kirstie, you're the bravest girl I've ever known."

Liam sat up just then, met Connor's eyes. "Mmumm-mmumm," he said, patting his mother's other hand. He reached for Connor. "Dih?"

Kirstie began to cry, softly at first, then harder, until the sobs racked her puny little body. "What's wrong, sweetie? Are you in pain? You want me to call the doctor?"

She waved his concern away. "No," she sniffed, pulling herself together. "It's not that. It's just…I'm so happy…."

Connor leaned down, hugged her and Liam both. "Well, you sure have a funny way of showing it," he said, winking and tweaking her nose. He pulled a tissue from the box on her nightstand and blotted her tears. When her breathing returned to normal, he said, "Now, really, what was that all about?"

Kirstie exhaled an exhausted sigh. "I never thought I'd see him again," she admitted, lovingly stroking Liam's cheek. And meeting Connor's eyes, she added, "And I *never* thought I'd meet *you*." Another raspy breath rustled from her. "I have a family," she said, lower lip quivering as she grinned. "A *family!*"

It was a slow night in the diner. Rita and Ray were working in the kitchen, and the rest of the crew, sensing her need to be alone, were flitting about pretending to be busy. She'd just concluded a short prayer of thanks for her good friends when the bell over the front door tinkled.

Her mother had been certain Connor had stolen Liam, that he was off making the adoption legal. But Jaina refused to believe it. He'd been straightforward and honest with her to this point, had asked her to marry him, so they could raise Liam together. "He wouldn't do anything so underhanded," she'd said in his defense. She'd believed Connor would never knowingly hurt her. She trusted him. Yet, she'd been a poor judge of character before, putting her trust in the hands of a man who was undeserving of it.

While Jaina mulled over her worries about Liam and Connor, and tried to avoid checking the clock, a woman of perhaps sixty hustled inside. She looked vaguely familiar. Not until she plopped her suitcase-size handbag on the counter did Jaina recognize the wide, friendly smile. "You're Connor Buchanan's secretary, aren't you?"

"Name's Pearl, and I have a message from Mr. B."

"I've been trying to get in touch with him for *hours!* Where has he *been?* Is he all right? Is Liam okay?"

"And I've been trying to get in touch with *you,* to tell you he's left for Chicago. Your line was busy for the longest time here, so I decided to stop by on my way home, but the traffic was awful, and then my car overheated," the older woman rattled on. She stepped up behind the counter and helped herself to a cup of coffee. "You want some?"

Jaina nodded.

"Straight, or cream and sugar?"

"Just black, thanks."

Pearl poured a second cup, handed it to Jaina. She came around to the front again and straddled a stool. "Sit down, honey. Take a load off." Unceremoniously, she dumped three sugar packets and two cream containers into her cup. "He was just planning a little drive in the country," Pearl said, her spoon clanking against the mug as she stirred. "He came into the office to get another set of adoption papers."

"Adoption papers?" Jaina's heart beat hard with fear and dread.

"Yeah. The original petition apparently went missing and was never filed at the courthouse. Anyway," she continued, seemingly oblivious to Jaina's distress, "he was about to leave when Buddy O'Dell called."

"Who?" Was he another lawyer? Someone who'd help Connor take Liam away?

"Private detective…the one who found Kirstie."

"Who found…" So *that's* why he left the way he did. She *knew* there was a good reason! Her thoughts turned immediately to Kirstie. "She's dying, isn't she?"

Sipping her coffee, Pearl nodded.

"And Connor went to Chicago to be with her…to let her see Liam for the last time." She glanced at her watch. "He's probably with her by now."

She loved him more at that moment than she'd ever loved anyone in her life. He *hadn't* lied to her. She *hadn't* been wrong about him.

The grandfather clock struck the hour. Nine o'clock. The past three hours had felt like a lifetime. But Liam was safe. *Thank you,* she silently prayed. She pictured him, fast asleep by now. "What about the baby's food, and diapers, and—"

"Mr. B. said he'd buy whatever they needed when they got to Chicago. Don't worry, the little guy's in good hands."

Pearl was right, of course. Connor loved Liam at least as much as she did. Of *course* he'd take care of—

"He loves you, you know."

Jaina pictured his chubby little face, his dimpled little hands—

"He needs you, too. I've known him for years, and I tell you, I've never seen him so happy."

Known him…for years? But he's only seven months…

Jaina realized suddenly that Pearl was talking about *Connor*, not Liam.

Pearl rattled on, "I've seen him with plenty of women. Not a one of 'em made him happy. He didn't smile, least not with his eyes. And when he laughed, it was that fake thing folks do to be sociable, you know? Work, work, work…for a handsome young man, he just plain wasn't enjoying his life very much. But since he met *you*…" Pearl winked, grinning. "Since you came along, Mr. B. is a different man."

"That doesn't mean—"

"Honey, I'm going to be sixty-five on my next birthday, and I know love when I see it. And you can deny it if you want to, but I know that you love him, too."

Jaina stared at her hands. "I won't deny it," she said softly, "because I can't." She met Pearl's eyes. The woman believed what she'd said. A warm glow flowed through her as the shadows lifted from her heart. Exhaling a sigh of contentment, she reveled in the peace and happiness Pearl's words had given her.

Then a disturbing, agonizing thought smothered the pleasant feelings. What if Pearl was mistaken? What if the changes she'd seen in her boss had been caused by *Liam*, and not her?

That was it. That *had* to be it.

The idea raised a panic inside her like she'd never known. A chill black silence engulfed her as a pulsing knot formed in her stomach. To be jealous of Liam was unthinkable, unspeakable. What kind of horrible person was she?

She looked hastily away from Pearl, uncomfortable with the thoughts churning in her head, embarrassed that she'd professed her love for Connor to this virtual stranger. An oddly primitive warning whispered in her head as she considered the disquieting fact: She'd fallen in love with a man who would never love her in return.

She chewed her lower lip and pulled composure around her like a cloak, determined to sheathe her innermost emotions. Jaina stifled a bitter laugh. *Isn't it a little late to hide your feelings, now that you've confessed your best-guarded secret?*

His image floated through her mind, his name lingered on her lips—*Connor, Connor, Connor*—as she recalled every minute detail of his face, his touch, his voice…

One nagging thought refused to be stilled: Connor loved Liam. Loved Kirstie, too. If he could care so much—and he did care, deeply; she could see it in his eyes—for those two destitute children he'd known for such a short time, was it really too much to hope that Pearl might be right? Was it unreasonable to believe he *might* love her…if not today, then someday?

Jaina smiled, remembering a verse from Psalms: *My times are in Thy hand…*

Several chattering ladies entered the diner as Pearl rose to leave. "Get some rest," she said, chucking Jaina's chin. "He's gonna need to lean on you when he gets back. Gonna need you like he's never needed anyone before."

Chapter Ten

"Uncle Connor?"

Connor hadn't intended to doze off when the nurse took Liam for a walk, but...

He was beside her in a heartbeat. "What is it, sweetie? You okay? You need the doctor, or—"

She took his hand. "You have a birthday coming up. We should do something special to celebrate."

Chuckling affectionately, he patted her hand. "I'm too old to celebrate birthdays."

"Thirty-five isn't so old. What would make you say such a thing?"

"I've lived alone so long, I feel ancient sometimes, that's all."

"Liam is going to be good for you, then." An almost indiscernible sigh escaped her lungs. "Amazing, isn't it?"

"What's amazing?"

"The way God brings people together, exactly when and where they need each other most? I mean, if I hadn't overheard that argument in your office, I'd never have left Liam with Jaina, and then you two wouldn't have met." She managed a grin. "*She'll* be good for you, too."

Picturing Jaina, Connor smiled.

"I'm so happy Liam is going to grow up in a house with a mommy and a daddy who love each other. It gives me a lot of peace, knowing that."

He couldn't very well burst her bubble, now could he? In place of a response, Connor got her brush out of the nightstand drawer and began pulling it gently through her thinning blond hair.

"Feels nice," she sighed, closing her eyes. "Just the way Mom used to do it…." And then she was asleep.

She slept in fits and starts, he'd discovered; a moment here, five more there. He'd brush her hair all day long if he thought it would encourage some much needed peaceful sleep. As she dozed, Connor recalled the conversation they'd had in the middle of the night.

"Tell me about the girl of your dreams," she'd said.

"I don't have a—"

"Oh, yes, you do," she'd said, feebly shaking a finger at him. "We all have dreams."

He didn't know why, but the comment had made him think of Jaina's house. *His* house…

He'd leaned back, with Kirstie still holding tight to his hand. "Okay…here goes. For starters, my dream girl will have a lot of patience and a really big heart. She'll have to, to put up with the likes of me," he'd said, winking playfully. "Plus, she'll want a lot of kids to fill up the big old house we live in. And in order to keep us all happy and healthy, she'll be as organized as a marine drill sergeant."

"Blonde, redhead, or brunette?"

Oddly, though every woman he'd ever dated had been a blonde, the girl of his dreams had dark hair. Chestnut-colored, to be exact.

"Sort of auburn."

"What color are her eyes?"

That had struck him as strange, too, because the women

in his past—including the one he'd made the mistake of marrying—had had blue eyes.

"Brown."

"Is she tall?"

"Actually, she's rather short."

"Petite," she'd corrected teasingly. "Short girls like 'petite' better."

"Is there no escaping political correctness?" he'd asked, chuckling.

"Is she pretty, or sort of average-looking?"

"She's a livin' doll, with the voice of a songbird and—"

"She sounds just like Jaina."

Kirstie had been right, and the proud expression on her ashen face told Connor she'd known it.

"When are you planning to tell her?"

"Tell her what?"

"That you love her, of course!" She'd given his hand a small squeeze. "Men. You can be so exasperating sometimes! You can't put it off, you know. While you're waiting to share your big news, what if she goes and falls in love with someone else? Wouldn't that just *devastate* you?"

"That would be awful," he'd admitted, pretending he hadn't seen the teasing glint in her eyes. She was playing the old reverse psychology game, and he'd known it. But the thought of Jaina, in love with another man—even in his imagination—had been agonizing.

Suddenly, Kirstie awoke and gave his hand a hard squeeze, interrupting his reverie. "Uncle Connor…it's time."

"Time for what?"

"For me to go to Jesus."

He wanted to shout "Kirstie, no! Don't leave, not yet. Not when I've finally found family." But her sallow complexion, her faltering voice, the pain that lined her brow, told him he *had* to let her go.

"Would you find Liam for me? So I can…"

He patted her hand and kissed her cheek because he knew why she wanted to see Liam right now, and he didn't want to hear her tell him why. "Sure. Course I will. You just lie still, okay? I'll be right back."

He hesitated in the doorway.

"Don't worry," she said, "I'll hang on till you get back." And with a quavering smile, she added, "But…don't be too long…."

In the hallway, once her door hissed shut, Connor pressed his forehead to the wall. Tears filled his eyes. It was so unfair and unjust that she should be fading away like this. His fist pounded the cold tiles, once, twice. It was so cruel and—

"Mr. Buchanan?"

He scrubbed a palm over his face, turning toward the familiar voice. "Dr. Ginnan."

"Is everything all right with Kirstie?"

"Yeah. No. Well, she, uh…" He swallowed, praying for the self-control to get through this—for Kirstie, for Liam. Standing taller, he ran both hands through his hair, held them there a moment, then cleared his throat. "Kirstie sent me to find her son so she could…"

The doctor clamped a hand on Connor's shoulder. "So she could say goodbye?" he finished.

Connor nodded.

"Don't be ashamed of your feelings, Mr. Buchanan. Kirstie is a lovely, loving young woman. The disgrace would be if you *didn't* feel this way about being so close to losing her." He gave the shoulder a squeeze. "There's a chapel down the hall if you'd like to visit it."

Connor stared at the highly polished linoleum beneath his feet, thumb and forefinger rasping over his day's growth of whiskers as he tried to steady his quivering jaw. "Maybe later," he said slowly, quietly, "after…" And pocketing his hand, he headed down the hall.

Ginnan was with her when Connor returned, Liam in

his arms. She reminded him of the beautiful little angel his mother took out only at Christmastime, made of fragile, translucent china. Kirstie smiled when she saw Liam, held out her arms. "Hello, sweet boy." The words rasped from her like steel wool.

Connor tucked Liam in beside her, and he laid his little head on her shoulder. "Mmumm-mmumm," he whimpered, a thumb in his mouth.

"You're going to be just fine, baby, 'cause you'll have a mommy and a daddy who will always love you very much."

A daddy *and* a mommy? Well, if the idea gave her comfort, who was he to burst her bubble? Connor perched lightly on the edge of her bed and rested a hand on her knee.

Kirstie hugged Liam, kissed his baby lips. And eyes squeezed tight, she held him close for a long, long moment. Then, abruptly, she said, "Take him away. Take him now." Turning from him, she choked out, "I don't want him remembering…what's about to happen…for the rest of his life…."

Dr. Ginnan put a gentle hand on her shoulder. "You're quite a piece of work, Kirstie Buchanan," he said past a trembling smile. "I'm proud to know you." He picked Liam up and walked quickly, deliberately, from the room. To Connor, he added, "If you need me, I'll be right around the corner."

He nodded, and when Kirstie crooked her finger to summon him closer, he stood, placed a palm on either side of her head and leaned closer to her small, pale face. "What is it, sweetie?" he asked. "What can I get you? Do you want anything? Name it, and it's yours."

"Anything?"

"Anything."

Her heavy-lidded eyes opened wider, gleaming with

fierce intensity. "Marry Jaina," she said in a sure, strong voice. "That's what I want. That's *all* I want."

His heart thundered. Connor would have moved heaven and earth to grant her last wish. But *this?* He couldn't do—

She gripped his wrists with a strength that belied her condition. "Oh, Uncle Connor…it hurts…hurts so bad."

"I know, sweetie," he said, although he didn't know. How could he, when he'd never suffered like this? "Just let go, sweetie. I'll be with you all the way."

She groaned. "I can't…I won't go. Not until you promise…."

Connor could see that she was in excruciating agony. Pain shimmered in her eyes like diamonds and dotted her brow and upper lip with perspiration. He couldn't stand to see her this way. *Give* me *her pain, Lord,* he prayed. *Let* me *take on this confounded disease instead of*—

"I want to go, want to go so badly. But I can't. Liam needs you. He needs you *both*."

He didn't think he could stand to watch her torment a moment longer. Much as he detested dishonesty, he would have told her anything she wanted to hear right then to calm her, to comfort her, to ease her mind. And it wasn't really a lie, he reflected, since he had already proposed to Jaina. The problem might be getting her to accept. "All right, Kirstie."

She squeezed his wrists tighter still, lifting her head from the pillow. "You mean it? You'll marry Jaina? You'll *both* be there for Liam?"

His pounding heart thudded against his rib cage, reverberated in his ears. "Yes."

Her eyes never left his as she dropped back onto the pillow, spent. "Promise?"

She was not teasing now, as she had been when she suggested Jaina might fall in love with someone else. She was racked with misery from the pain. He wished she hadn't been so all-fired stubborn about taking the painkiller. It would have eased her suffering and—

"Promise?" Kirstie's burning gaze bore deeply into him, reading him, assessing him. If he lied now, she'd know it.

Later, he could deal with the consequences, with the details. Right now, this child deserved to be set free from her anguish. "I promise, sweetie. I promise."

The moment the words were out of his mouth, she closed her eyes and exhaled a long, relieved sigh. The furrows disappeared from her youthful brow as though the gripping, deadly pain had been vanquished by the utterance of those two simple words. "Thank you," she murmured. "Oh… thank you…."

Her grip on his wrists loosened, her jaw slackened. It was happening right before his very eyes, and Connor was powerless to prevent it. What had he ever done in his miserable, self-absorbed life, he wondered, to earn him the privilege of being the one to spend these last moments with this dear, sweet girl?

He was still leaning there, one hand on either side of her head, staring into her face. He hadn't noticed before— the light hurt her eyes, and so the staff kept the lights low—but she had freckles, dozens of them, sprinkled across the bridge of her upturned nose. *Freckles,* he said to himself, *like a little girl.*

And that's exactly what she was.

She was an eighteen-year-old *girl,* he fumed inwardly. This shouldn't have been happening…not to a *child!* Jaw clenched, he held his breath, helpless frustration prompting him to grip her pillowcase tight in his fists. He wanted to warm her, protect her, *save* her. But he couldn't, and he knew it.

And so Connor did the next best thing.

"Oh, Kirstie," he groaned, lifting her into his arms.

Holding her gently, tenderly, he kissed her temples, her cheeks and chin, and that adorable freckled nose. "I love you, sweet girl. I love you...."

Her lashes fluttered, and she met his eyes. Laying a cool, dry palm against his cheek, she smiled sweetly. "I love you, too, Uncle Connor." A weak little giggle popped from her dry, graying lips. "You'll think I'm as silly as silly can be."

"Shhh," he said, biting back a sob as he rocked her. He smoothed the hair back from her forehead. "I won't think you're silly. Honest."

She tilted her head back, looked long and deep into his eyes, then smiled serenely. "It was truly a pleasure, you know, meeting you."

And just as the world darkens gradually at sunset, the light in her bright eyes dimmed by slow degrees until there was nothing, not a spark or a glimmer of life left in them at all.

He remembered bits and snatches of a verse from First Corinthians. "And lo, I will tell you a mystery: In the twinkling of an eye, the trumpet will sound, and the dead will be raised imperishable, and we shall be changed."

She was with her sweet Jesus now, free of all her pain and worry.

With a trembling hand, Connor closed her long-lashed eyelids, then buried his face in the crook of her neck. He didn't know how long he held her, rocked her, wept into her hair—ten minutes? thirty?—he only knew that he felt like bellowing at the top of his lungs. *Someone should have held her this way while she was alive!* But his embrace wasn't warming or consoling or comforting her, wasn't doing her any good now.

And so Connor eased her back against the pillow, lovingly arranged her shimmering hair around her face, tucked the covers up under her chin. When he stood to kiss her forehead, one shining tear landed on her cheek. It slid down, disappeared, quickly absorbed by the crisp white pillowcase. The way it was swallowed up by the cotton reminded him how it felt to stand alone, barefoot on a beach at low tide, watching the soft sands drink up gently ebbing waves.

"The pleasure was all mine," he whispered. "All mine."

Kirstie hadn't been gone an hour when he called Jaina. "Liam and I will be coming in on the one o'clock flight."

"I'll pick you up," she'd said.

"I'm bringing Kirstie home. I want her buried in Baltimore, to be near her family."

"Of course you do. Don't give it another thought. I'll take care of whatever needs to be done."

And she had.

The wake, the funeral service, the cemetery plot, even the marker…she'd thought of everything.

The other mourners—Pearl, Ray, Rita, the Chili Pot staff—had taken Liam back to the diner, leaving Connor and Jaina alone in the graveyard.

He slipped an arm around her waist. "I like what you had them put on her marker." He read softly, "'Kirstie Ann Buchanan. She was loved, and she will be missed.'"

Jaina leaned her head on his shoulder. "I'm glad you were with her, and I'm glad you brought her home."

"I want to thank you, kiddo. I don't know how I could've gotten through this without you."

"You'd have managed it like you manage everything else…with quiet efficiency."

He inclined his head and winced. "If this had been business as usual, maybe. But I would have cracked if I'd had to make all the arrangements after…after…"

She turned to face him. "You've had a couple of pretty rough days, haven't you?" she sympathized, absently smoothing the black lapels of his suit coat, straightening his tie, rearranging the silk hankie in his pocket.

Someday, he'd tell her all about it.

Someday…but not today. "There at the end, Kirstie asked me to make her a promise."

Jaina's brows rose. "Oh? What kind of promise?"

He rested his hands on her shoulders. Such delicate shoulders, he thought, yet so strong and capable. *And it's a good thing, because…* "It seemed so important to her. I don't know if I'll be able to live with myself if I go back on my word."

"I can't imagine why you'd have to."

Connor's mustache tilted in a sad, half smile. "You might feel differently when I tell you *what* I promised."

She shrugged, cuffing the sleeves of her maroon blazer. "Why?"

"Because it involves you."

"Me?" Jaina undid the top button of her white silk blouse.

"Kirstie thought the world of you…"

Jaina sighed. She glanced at Kirstie's coffin. "I thought a lot of her, too."

"…thought *so* much of you, in fact, that she made me promise to marry you."

"Stop teasing, Connor," Jaina said, shaking a maternal finger under his nose. "We're in a cemetery, after all."

He tilted his head slightly, waiting for her to realize it wasn't a joke. He watched her dark eyes widen, her mouth drop open, heard her quick intake of air.

"But…but *why?*"

"Because, as she put it, Liam needs us both."

She seemed to hesitate for a moment. "And you agreed?"

He nodded. "Didn't have any choice." He hesitated. "I

asked you once. You didn't say 'yes,' but you didn't say 'no,'" he reminded her.

Jaina sighed. "Well, we've been batting the idea around for a while…"

"So…you promise to marry me, then?"

When Jaina met his eyes and nodded, Connor's heart thudded with relief. Smiling, he said, "You could do worse, you know."

She gave him a puzzled look. "What are you going on about?"

He shrugged a shoulder. "I mean, you could be marrying somebody else…someone like *Skip*."

All eight fingertips covered her mouth. "Skip is a dear, but I don't think there was ever a real chance of that happening, even for Liam."

Connor chuckled softly. "Glad to hear it," he said. After a long, silent moment, Connor added, "I'll understand if you don't want to go through with it. It was *my* promise after all, not yours."

She clasped her hands at her waist, chewing her lower lip. "The thing is…I think she's right," she said quietly, staring at the coffin. "Liam does need us both." She stiffened her back and, looking up at him through thick, dark lashes, said, "Maybe you were right when you said you should get the adoption papers finalized first. That way, my background won't hurt your chances."

"Nonsense. Judge Thompson has already put his John Hancock on the petition. Liam is as good as mine…ours," he quickly corrected.

She bit a corner of her upper lip. "Well, if you're sure…"

"We can't let Kirstie down, now can we?"

He didn't know how to define the expression that flitted across her face just then. Disappointment? Hurt? Regret?

"No. I suppose we can't."

He took her hand in his and led her toward his car. "The sooner the better, I say. What do you think?"

"Why put off till tomorrow what you can do today?" she answered, reciting the age-old adage.

"How's August 5 sound to you?"

"Sounds fine."

He unlocked the passenger-side door of his car. "Good," he said as she slid into the bucket seat. "Then it's all settled."

There was a spring in his step as he walked around to his side of the sports car. As he unlocked his door, he gave one last glance at the graveyard. Sunlight, bouncing from one of the brass handles on Kirstie's casket, flashed like a beacon—on, off, on, off…

Was it a signal? he wondered. Some sort of sign? God's blessing on the deal he and Jaina had just struck?

A robin began to trill in a nearby tree, and a soft, warm breeze rustled the leaves. The sky seemed bluer, the clouds whiter as Connor remembered the way the pastor had concluded the burial service.

"'The righteous are taken from calamity,'" he'd quoted Isaiah, "'and he enters into peace, he rests in his bed who walks in uprightness.' Kirstie walked in uprightness on the earth," the pastor had said, "and she will walk with God her Father all the days of eternity."

It seemed to Connor that it had all happened so fast. One minute, they were shopping for wedding bands. Then they were booking the church. And now, here he was, at the front of her church, waiting for her.

Jaina seemed to float rather than walk toward him down the long, carpeted aisle, a vision in white. The satiny sheen of her gown reflected the sunlight, muted by the rainbow of stained glass. He blinked and rubbed his eyes, hoping she was real and not a figment of his imagination.

Oh, she was real all right. More real than any woman he'd known. And soon, she would be his *wife*.

The wedding procession finally ended, and Ray left her there alone beside him. Connor took a deep, shuddering breath as the pastor read from the Good Book and led the congregation in a prayer, then said a blessing on the couple who stood at the altar of God.

But he barely heard any of it.

He'd heard women described as dazzling, pretty, even handsome, on their wedding day. But the only word Connor could come up with to describe her had been worn thin by overuse. Still, it was the only word that would do: beautiful.

He didn't recall feeling this way when he'd married Miriam. Didn't remember his heart beating this hard and fast, his palms sweating, or—

"Connor Liam Buchanan…" The pastor's voice penetrated his fog. "Do you take this woman, Jaina Clarisse Chandelle, to be your lawfully wedded wife?"

He glanced at her, smiled slightly and raised a brow, then mouthed "Clarisse?" Behind the gauzy veil, he saw her eyes crinkle in a mischievous grin. She pressed her lips together to stanch a giggle before sending him a comical "Behave yourself!" expression.

"I do," Connor said.

"And do you, Jaina Clarisse Chandelle, take this man, Connor Liam Buchanan, to be your lawfully wedded husband?"

He saw her long, dark lashes flutter, saw her bite her lower lip, heard her whisper, "I do."

She had hesitated for at most a fraction of a second, but that infinitesimal space of time was long enough to cut him to the quick. Miriam had done the same thing, he recalled.

"I now pronounce you man and wife. You may kiss the bride."

Connor lifted the filmy white fabric and laid it gently atop her head. She seemed so small, so vulnerable, standing there blinking up at him. Setting aside his own dashed hopes, male instinct made him want to wrap her in a protective embrace and shield her from all harm, from all pain, for a lifetime. All right, so she didn't love him now. But maybe someday, he prayed. Someday...

Gently, he pressed his palms to her cheeks and let his thumbs tilt her face up to receive his kiss. He'd intended a light brush of the lips, nothing more. But the moment his mouth met hers, Connor's spirit soared, and the gloom that had enveloped him since Kirstie's death lifted. *Once I was lost, but now I'm found,* flitted through his head, *and Jaina will lead me home.*

"Atta boy, Connor!" a male voice called out from the back of the church as the congregation applauded, shattering the moment. He ended the kiss and stood back, hands still cupping her lovely face. Slowly, her eyes fluttered open and met his. For a moment, he thought he saw love, real love, sparkling there among the green and gold flecks in her brown eyes, and his heart lurched.

She'd only agreed to this charade of a marriage because he'd told her about the promise he'd made to Kirstie on her deathbed. He remembered the day he'd slipped the engagement ring onto Jaina's finger, when she'd insisted he make a promise to *her.* He was never to tell anyone why they'd decided to get married. She claimed it was because she didn't want people thinking he'd married her out of pity. But he knew better.

His jaw tensed and his brow furrowed with determination. He'd have to harden his heart to her.

Either that, or learn to live with a breaking one....

She thought about it as they walked down the aisle arm in arm, smiling for the cameras, and as they stood on the steps of the church, accepting the congratulations and good wishes of friends and neighbors. It was on her mind as they sat side by side at the reception, eating their first meal as man and wife, and as they bade their guests good-night. But try as she might, Jaina didn't think she'd ever forget the cold, detached expression he'd aimed at her immediately after their kiss at the altar.

Ever since she was a little girl, she'd stuttered when nervous or tense. Jaina had learned that taking a deep breath and repeating the last thing a person said could prevent it. She certainly hadn't wanted to do a Porky Pig impersonation on her wedding day. *Do you take this man...?* she'd repeated mentally before saying in a sure, clear voice, "I do."

And then he'd given her that *look.*

You little fool, she scolded herself. *How can you believe he's really in love with you? Those longing looks, those sweet words...they're part of an act...a very well-orchestrated plan that's helping him fulfill Kirstie's dying wish.*

Well, she'd said yes, after all. And because she'd gotten swept up in the moment, in the hurly-burly rush of wedding plans, there hadn't seemed to be time to change her mind.

She was married now.

To a man who didn't love her.

And you have no one to blame but yourself.

Well, at least one good thing had come of the wedding. She was guaranteed a lifetime with Liam.

Jaina had made Connor swear that he'd never tell another living soul that their phony courtship, their so-called engagement, the marriage itself, had taken place for no reason other than to bring peace of mind to his dying niece. And she had to give him credit; Connor had done a dandy job of making it look good—for her parents, for her employees, for *everyone....*

He'd been the perfect gentleman…opening doors, pulling out chairs, offering her his arm as they moved around town. It was *because* he was a gentleman that she could trust that no one would ever discover the humiliating truth—that he wouldn't have married her if not for that promise to Kirstie. All that talk on the Fourth of July was, well, that's all it had been…talk. The proof? That *look*.

It was going to be next to impossible, she believed, pretending she didn't love him.

Jaina squared her shoulders and told herself that if she could so quickly fall *in* love with Connor, she could fall *out* of love just as easily…provided she put her mind to it. They'd been married exactly twenty-four hours, and already she'd had it up to here with his cool, detached demeanor.

To keep up appearances, he'd booked a room at a quaint inn in Pennsylvania. No one knew them there; no need for pretense in this charming little town. So why had he brought her breakfast in bed? Why was he standing there in the doorway with that gaudy silver tray in his hands, smiling like an innocent, wide-eyed boy who'd just picked his best girl a fistful of posies?

Connor put the tray on the table near the patio doors and selected one red rose from the three in the crystal bud vase. Bowing low, smiling, he held it out to her. "For my beautiful bride."

Her insides trembled. Jaina prayed it wasn't visible. "Thank you." Their fingers touched as she accepted his gift, sending a burst of fiery currents straight to her already pounding heart. Instinctively, she held the flower near her cheek. "It's lovely," she admitted, closing her eyes to inhale the delicate aroma of its velvety petals.

"Not nearly as lovely as you."

She opened her eyes and met his. Something burned in those icy blue orbs. *Fire and ice,* she warned herself. *He'll burn with his passion...or he'll freeze you out.* There would be no in-between, she believed.

"We should eat before it gets cold..."

His brows drew together as if she'd hurt his feelings. She certainly hadn't intended *that.*

"...since you went to so much trouble to bring the food up here and all, I mean."

He sat at the table, and Jaina poured coffee into the two snow-white china cups on the tray and steeled herself to his hard expression. *You'll be a kind and dutiful wife,* she told herself, *but you will* stop *loving him. You will stop, no matter how difficult it is!*

No...that was too much to ask. The most she could hope for was to be able to hide her heart away. Only with Liam could she ever wear it on her sleeve.

He lifted his fork, then speared a slice of bacon. He couldn't seem to meet her eyes, which reminded her again of that young boy, this time caught red-handed with his fingers in the cookie jar. For the life of her, Jaina didn't understand why her "let's eat" comment should have hurt him since he so obviously didn't love her. But he did appear to be pouting....

She glanced up at Connor, who continued to eat in somber silence. She had discovered, during their brief courtship, that as well as losing his beloved sister, Susan, he'd buried his grandparents and parents, lost a child and divorced the wife whose betrayal had caused its miscarriage. And now he'd been forced to marry a woman he didn't love—would likely never love—because his big-heartedness wouldn't allow him to refuse his niece's last request. *Oh, Lord,* Jaina prayed, *make me a good wife for him. He's suffered enough!*

Without even thinking about it, she impulsively reached

across the table and placed her hand atop his. "This is a nice beginning to our...to our partnership," she said, choosing her words carefully.

His expression softened slightly.

Surely Connor had dreams. As time went by, she would coax him into sharing them with her. Then she'd stand beside him, through good times and bad—just as she had promised at the altar—and help him turn his dreams into realities. Because they were married now, for better or for worse, and she had never done anything halfway. *Why start now?* Jaina asked herself.

Would he notice the little things she'd do to make his life more comfortable? And if he did, would he treat them as gifts or as duties? She smiled to herself, for while there was much about Connor that Jaina didn't understand, she believed she knew the answer to that question. He was, among other things, a good and decent man with a warm and giving heart. He would never take her caring and devotion for granted, not even if their marriage lasted as long as his friend, Judge Thompson's.

Jaina had no desire to burden him with the feeling that he must protect her from her own silly schoolgirlish wishes. And surely that's what a man like him would do...a man who'd go to such lengths to grant a dying girl her final wish.

"You were right," she said.

His left brow rose. "Really. About what?"

"I could have done worse." She smiled affectionately. "Much worse."

They'd been married all of two weeks when Connor had come home from work and announced they'd been invited to a posh charity ball. Black tie, tux, evening gown...the works. "I don't particularly want to go to this shindig," he'd said distractedly, putting the tickets in the sideboard drawer, "but I don't have much choice. Everybody who's anybody is going to be there."

"Maybe you ought to go alone."

"What?"

"I don't want to embarrass you."

He tore off his tie. "Embarrass me? What are you talking about?"

He watched her puttering around in the kitchen, drying blue-stemmed goblets with a terry tea towel, stirring the spaghetti sauce that was bubbling on the back burner. He'd always loved this house—especially the kitchen— but never more than now, with his beautiful bride in it. She'd insisted on handing the reins of The Chili Pot over to Ray, claiming he'd been the one who'd run the place all along anyway. So every day, when he came in from the office, she had a kettle of soup bubbling, a pot of stew simmering, or a roast in the oven. He'd never weighed more than 185 pounds, and in the weeks since they'd been married, the scale soared all the way up to 190.

"Well, you know…someone might remember about me and…"

"And *what?*"

She faced him, aiming that dark-eyed gaze his way, and set his heart to thumping like a parade drum.

"And…they might make life difficult for you."

The only one making life difficult for me is you, he told her silently, *standing there and looking at me with those eyes of yours, when I can't touch you….*

"People have plenty of dirt to dish up these days. They've got Hollywood and New York and London. And if they're really bored, they've got Washington, D.C., to gossip about. They don't need to dredge up stuff from your past."

Connor wished he knew what she was thinking because those closed-off expressions that flitted across her face from time to time drove him *nuts.*

"And then there's the matter of my limp. You don't want to be seen—"

"Hold it. Hold it right there," Connor had interrupted. "Your limp is barely noticeable…except to you." He tossed his tie on the antique buffet she'd found at a shop on Main Street. "If you don't want to go, just say so. I'm not about to force you to do something you don't want to do." And the proof of *that,* Connor fumed, could be found at the top of the stairs…in two separate bedrooms.

She stopped putting dishes away. "I never said…I didn't say…of course I want to go. I was only trying to give you an out…in case you wanted one."

The way she was standing there, blinking those sad brown eyes at him, made him want to hug her. Kiss the daylights out of her. Take her upstairs and…. "Jaina, sweetie," he said, softening his tone, "if I didn't want to bring you, why would I have brought the tickets home?"

She'd sighed heavily. "I guess that would have been the thing to do. Or not do, rather. If you didn't want to bring me, I mean."

He had fumbled around in his briefcase, not knowing what else to say.

And here it was, two weeks later, and he was standing in the master bathroom, this time fumbling with his bow tie.

Almighty God, he prayed.

It wasn't much of a prayer. Wasn't a prayer at all, really. Still, the power of those two simple words seemed enough to distract him from the feelings that simmered inside him. Feelings that, if he allowed himself, might one day make him forget that he'd promised to give Jaina the time and space she'd said she needed.

"Are you almost ready?" she called from the hallway.

"I don't think it would violate any rules if you came in," he said dryly. "I mean, you make up the bed every day, put my laundry away. We haven't needed a chaperon…so far."

"You're usually not here when I do those things."

And then she stepped into the room, a glass of water in one hand, a black beaded purse in the other. "Jaina!" he gasped. "You're…you're *beautiful.*"

She blushed like a schoolgirl at his compliment, and that only made her all the more beautiful to him. Her black gown accented her ivory complexion. Accented her feminine figure, too. The satiny material clung to her shoulders and arms and tiny waist before skimming over her hips and ending above matching shoes. As she moved, it shimmered with the silvery glow of reflected light, reminding him of what the pastor had said to him on their wedding day: "You married the prettiest girl in Maryland, Connor. She'll be a beacon in your life."

"You look pretty good yourself," she said, her voice cracking slightly.

He wanted to crush her against him. Wanted to welcome her into the room with a warm kiss. Wanted…

Get a grip, pal….

For weeks, he'd put on a show for her parents, for the men and women who worked at The Chili Pot, for Pearl, telling himself that the marriage—though nothing but a matter of convenience—must always appear as real and genuine as the diamond she wore on her left hand. He owed her that much—to protect her from the gossipmongers—didn't he?

He watched, his breath caught in his throat, as she raised the glass to her parted lips and drank.

She put the glass and the purse on his dresser. "Come here," she said, pulling him closer by tugging the ends of his tie. "Let me do that for you."

He stood there, arms hanging limply at his sides, and watched her tilt her head, studied her adorable little frown as she concentrated on the task. She smelled heavenly, looked lovely, and—

"There! That's got it," she said, smiling finally as her fingertips tapped the tips of the bow. Jaina turned him around to face the dresser. "See?"

He met her eyes in the mirror. "Perfect. Thanks."

She grabbed the glass and the purse, her pretty dress swishing softly as she moved toward the door. "I'll wait for you downstairs," she said. "There's no real hurry. We have about fifteen minutes before it's time to leave."

"Right. No hurry," he echoed. "I'll be down in a bit." When she was gone, he slumped onto the edge of his bed, held his head in his hands, then extended his arms and stared at his palms. "How are you gonna spend a lifetime under the same roof with a woman like *that*…and keep your mitts to yourself?"

Connor thought he heard music, then went to stand at the top of the stairs. Yes, definitely music, he realized. A tune he'd heard before…

He took the stairs two at a time, stopping in the foyer when he spotted her. She was in the living room, sitting at the piano, singing. "She has the voice of a songbird," Ray had told him just the day before yesterday. As if Connor didn't know it by then. He'd caught her humming as she dusted, as she fed Liam. Once, he'd come home for lunch and heard her singing Liam into his afternoon nap. She could croon every word from here on out and he'd never tire of the sound.

If he'd never met her, he might never have discovered the difference between a boy's love for a girl and the love a man feels for his woman. He might have gone right on believing that what he'd once felt for Miriam had been *it*.

But he had met Jaina, and now that he knew how deep and all-encompassing love could be, he wanted more than to share this house with her. Wanted more than to sleep across the hall from her. For weeks now, he'd kept his word, never crossing that boundary line. The dilemma… how to tell Jaina he wanted to forget their agreement.

He looked at her, innocent and pure and so alive! He was a man, full-grown and with a man's needs and desires. The solution to his problem scared the daylights out of him. He'd have to admit he loved her. Somehow, tonight, he was going to let her know how he really felt…how he'd felt almost from the first moment they met.

Almighty God, he began to pray. If the Good Lord felt any mercy, any compassion for him at all, He'd see to it that Jaina felt the same way.

"Connor, how long have you been standing there?"

He shrugged. "A while," he said, grinning.

She stood, smiling, and smoothed the skirt of her dress. "We'd better get Liam, head over to Mom and Dad's, or we'll be late. I hate to make an entrance." Jaina draped a deep maroon satin shawl over her shoulders. "I've already packed his diaper bag and his toys," she said, bending to lift him from the playpen, "so if you'll…"

She pressed a palm to the baby's forehead.

He read the look of alarm that widened her dark, glittering eyes. "What? What's wrong?"

"He's burning up with fever, Connor."

They stood hand in hand under the glaring emergency-room lights, watching their boy sleep. She had saved his life, and if he didn't already love her like crazy, *that* certainly would have clinched it.

The resident on duty hadn't seemed overly concerned when they brought the red-cheeked baby into the hospital. "It's the start of the flu season," he'd said offhandedly. "No big deal. Just give him baby acetaminophen and see that he gets plenty of liquids."

Jaina wasn't having any of that! Hands on her black-satined hips, she stood on tiptoe and said into the young doctor's face, "My father nearly died of something like this a few years ago, so I know what I'm talking about. Liam has the same symptoms. This is *not* the flu. It's meningitis, and if you don't do something soon, it could—"

"Mrs. Buchanan," he said soothingly, trying to calm her, "I've seen dozens of kids the past couple of days with the very same symptoms your son has. Trust me, this is a simple case of the flu."

She rattled off a list of medications and treatments the hospital should begin to administer immediately. When he protested, Jaina planted both feet on the floor and, though she couldn't have been more than five years older than him, wagged a maternal digit under his nose.

She'd been cutting articles out of newspapers and magazines since the day Liam had come into her life. The shoe box she kept clippings in to start with had soon overflowed with ideas and tidbits about baby care and child rearing, and Jaina had had to move her collection to a larger box. If she believed Liam had meningitis, Connor thought, then the boy had meningitis!

Connor stepped up and, crossing both arms defiantly over his chest, threatened to use the doctor's stethoscope in a way he'd never believed possible. The commotion alerted the resident's superior, who examined Liam herself and ordered a battery of tests that, in the end, proved Jaina correct.

If they had listened to that resident, Liam might be seriously ill right now, instead of sleeping contentedly as they awaited his release forms. Connor's relief was so great and so heartfelt, it nearly drove him to tears. Jaina might be stubborn and opinionated, but she was kindhearted, loving and bound and determined to do the right thing.

Almighty God, help me, please, he prayed.

A moment of silence passed before she cut him a sidelong glance. "What did you say?" she whispered.

Well, you said *you were going to tell her how you felt, and that you would do it tonight.* He turned her to face him, then drew her near. "I said, 'I love you.'"

Wide-eyed and breathless, Jaina licked her lips, swallowed, blinked.

He tucked a wayward curl behind her ear. "Well...?"

"Well what?" she asked, the beginnings of a smile tugging at the corners of her mouth.

He made a "come on" rolling gesture with his right hand. "This is where you're supposed to reciprocate."

Tilting her head, Jaina studied his face for a long, silent moment. Then she wrapped her arms around his chest and snuggled close. "Reciprocate." She sighed. "Such a romantic word!"

Connor grinned, then kissed the top of her head.

"I love you, too," Jaina said. She took a step back and looked deep into his eyes. "I think I've loved you from the moment we met."

He remembered the conversation he'd had with Kirstie about the girl of his dreams. "I can top that," he said tenderly.

"Oh, yeah?"

"Yeah. I've loved you all my life."

She nodded as though she understood. And then she said, "We made quite a team tonight, didn't we?"

Laughing, he shook his head. "I'll say. That resident won't forget *us* any time soon."

"I imagine we were quite a sight...you in your tuxedo and me in my evening gown...threatening to do bodily harm if our son wasn't given the proper care."

"Our son," he echoed. "I like the sound of that."

"Kirstie was right," Jaina said. "Together, we'll be good for Liam."

"Together... I like the sound of that, too."

"So do I." She snuggled close again. "When we get home, I'd like to do some rearranging."

He'd lived with her long enough to know that she could pick some odd times to move furniture, knickknacks, pictures... "Couldn't it wait until tomorrow, sweetie? Because I'm—"

"No," she said, bracketing his face with her hands, "it can't wait."

He took a deep breath. She had just saved Liam's life. How could he refuse her anything? "Okay," he agreed, smiling. "Soon as I change out of my tux. What do you want to move?"

"Me."

"You?"

"What's the matter...you don't want a roommate?"

A roommate?

She drew his face near, then kissed him, hard and full on the lips.

Epilogue

❧

Six years later

"Mommy, Susan is in my room again."

Jaina trudged up the stairs and stood in Liam's doorway, one fist on her hip. "Susan…"

The four-year-old stuck out her tongue at her brother. "He called me a geek!"

"Liam, what have I told you about calling your sister names?"

The seven-year-old hung his head. "That it isn't nice?"

"No, it isn't." To Susan, she said, "And neither is sticking out your tongue." The little girl looked at the floor, too. Their mother knelt on the floor and held out her arms. Both children flew into them. "Now, what do you say we go down into the kitchen and whip up a batch of chocolate chip cookies? If we're very, very quiet," she added in a whisper, "maybe we can finish before your little sister wakes up."

Liam rolled his big blue eyes. "Not a chance. Kirstie will smell the dough and she'll—"

"Don't pick on her, Liam," Susan said. "She's just a baby."

"Not *baby*. My teacher said when you're two, you're a toddler."

The brown-eyed girl looked to Jaina for confirmation, and when her mother nodded and pointed at herself, she said, "Oh, I get it. A *baby* lives in *here*." Grinning, she patted Jaina's well-rounded tummy.

"Right you are, Suzie-Q," Connor said from the doorway. "Did I hear something about chocolate chip cookies?"

"Daddy!" the children chorused, snuggling into his outstretched arms.

"Can I measure the flour, Mommy?" Susan asked, clapping her hands.

"And can I break the eggs?" Liam wanted to know.

Connor helped Jaina to her feet. "I'll tell you what," she suggested, giving her husband a sideways hug. "If you go outside and play quietly while Mommy and Daddy talk, the two of you can do *all* the work all by yourselves!"

They scrambled from the room and thundered down the stairs, squealing with glee, reminding her what a happy six years this had been. The children had both learned to ride the horses Connor bought from a farmer on Marriottsville Road, she'd sold The Chili Pot to Eliot, and her parents had retired to Florida. Skip had married a coworker and now had two children. The Buchanan peace was nearly constant.

She had even returned to singing, at weddings and funerals and in the church choir.

Once they were alone, Connor pulled her into a bear hug. "C'mere, you," he growled lovingly, "it's been a long, hard day and I need a kiss."

"But…it's not even lunchtime yet."

He grinned. "So whatcha gonna do…sue me?"

She took his hand, led him into their room and closed the door. "Maybe we can settle this out of court," she suggested.

Connor took off his tie and smiled as Jaina picked up her guitar. He sprawled across the neatly made bed and tucked his hands under his head.

He could be patient because experience had taught him that when her song ended, the *real* music would begin....

* * * * *

Dear Reader,

Years ago I read a newspaper article about a young woman who had abandoned her baby. She'd wrapped him in a receiving blanket, the report said, tucked him into a cardboard box and left him at the emergency-room doors of a local hospital.

On that same day, at that very hospital, I gave birth to my first child. I couldn't stand to be apart from her, not even for the few minutes it took me to bathe! Needless to say, I had a lot of trouble identifying with that young woman....

TV newscasts kept audiences updated on the baby's condition. And, oh, what a beautiful little being he was! I came up with a dozen scenarios about why this could have happened. Had his mother been too young? Too poor to take care of a helpless infant? What dreadful trauma had driven her to such desperate measures?

The answer, two decades later: *Suddenly Mommy.*

All my best,

Loree Lough

P.S. They never found that baby's mother. He was placed in foster care until a loving couple made him part of their family. But now and then, as my own children grew and thrived, I wondered whatever became of his birth mother. And when I do wonder, I say a prayer for her, because surely, wherever she is, her heart aches every time she thinks of that day....

Fan Favorite

Janet Tronstad

brings readers a heartwarming story
of love and hope with

Dr. Right

Treasure Creek, Alaska, has only one pediatrician:
the very handsome, very eligible Dr. Alex Haven.
With his contract coming to an end, he plans
to return home to Los Angeles. But Nurse
Maryann Jenner is determined to keep Alex
in Alaska, and when a little boy's life—and
Maryann's hope—is jeopardized, Alex may
find a reason to stay forever.

ALASKAN *Bride* RUSH

Available September wherever books are sold.

Steeple
Hill®

LI87620

LARGER-PRINT BOOKS!

**GET 2 FREE
LARGER-PRINT NOVELS
PLUS 2 FREE
MYSTERY GIFTS**

Larger-print novels are now available...

LILP10R

HARLEQUIN®

A Romance

FOR EVERY MOOD™

Spotlight on
Heart & Home

Heartwarming romances
where love can happen
right when you least expect it.

See the next page to enjoy a sneak peek
from Harlequin Superromance®,
a Heart and Home series.

Enjoy a sneak peek at fan favorite Molly O'Keefe's
Harlequin Superromance miniseries,
THE NOTORIOUS O'NEILLS, *with*
TYLER O'NEILL'S REDEMPTION,
available September 2010
only from Harlequin Superromance.

Police chief Juliette Tremblant recognized the shape of the man strolling down the street—in as calm and leisurely fashion as if it were the middle of the day rather than midnight. She slowed her car, convinced her eyes were playing tricks on her. It had been a long time since Tyler O'Neill had been seen in this town.

As she pulled to a stop at the curb, he turned toward her, and her heart about stopped.

"What the hell are you doing here, Tyler?"

"Well, if it isn't Juliette Tremblant." He made his way over to her, then leaned down so he could look her in the eye. He was close enough to touch.

Juliette was not, repeat, *not* going to touch Tyler O'Neill. Not with her fingers. Not with a ten-foot pole. There would be no touching. Which was too bad, since it was the only way she was ever going to convince herself the man standing in front of her—as rumpled and heart-stoppingly handsome now as he'd been at sixteen—was real.

And not a figment of all her furious revenge dreams.

"What are you doing back in Bonne Terre?" she asked.

"The manor is sitting empty," Tyler said and shrugged, as though his arriving out of the blue after ten years was casual. "Seems like someone should be watching over the family home."

"You?" She laughed at the very notion of him being here for any unselfish reason. "Please."

He stared at her for a second, then smiled. Her heart fluttered against her chest—a small mechanical bird powered by that smile.

"You're right." But that cryptic comment was all he offered.

Juliette bit her lip against the other questions.

Why did you go?

Why didn't you write? Call?

What did I do?

But what would be the point? Ten years of silence were all the answer she really needed.

She had sworn off feeling anything for this man long ago. Yet one look at him and all the old hurt and rage resurfaced as though they'd been waiting for the chance. That made her mad.

She put the car in gear, determined not to waste another minute thinking about Tyler O'Neill. "Have a good night, Tyler," she said, liking all the cool "go screw yourself" she managed to fit into those words.

It seems Juliette has an old score to settle with Tyler.
Pick up TYLER O'NEILL'S REDEMPTION
to see how he makes it up to her.
Available September 2010,
only from Harlequin Superromance.

CLASSICS

Enjoy these four heartwarming stories
from your favorite Love Inspired® authors!

Irene Hannon
ONE SPECIAL CHRISTMAS
and
HOME FOR THE HOLIDAYS

Janet Tronstad
SUGAR PLUMS FOR DRY CREEK
and
AT HOME IN DRY CREEK

Available in December 2010
wherever books are sold.

Steeple
Hill®

www.SteepleHill.com

LIC1210